TWISTER
REBELLION

LOGAN CAPESIUS

Manufactured in the United States, through amazon.com.

ISBN: 9798367655209
ISBN: 9798379068080 (pbk)

To the friends who have been there with steadfast support, for more than just the completion of this manuscript: Joel, Jackson, Adam, Ty, Andrew, Krissy, Parker, Makenzie, Abby, Chase, Michael, Camden, Chandler, Evan, Donovan, Ian, Moriah, Amy, Matt, Peyton, Anthony, Addison, & many more.

To Mindy Lichter, who has created and conceptualized the cover art for each of these novels. Your talents are exceptional, and I'm so grateful for your unequaled efforts.

Thanks to Alpha Readers: Vaughn Irlbeck & Alex Chekal

To my family. I write for you.

To Mom, whose strength has given me the courage to fight.

To the memory of Tom Capesius. We love you, Grandpa. Skol.

Love is hard to find in this world, even harder to lose.

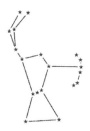

I

The day they took him is the day Orian felt the course of his life alter invariably, enacting a chain of events that could never be undone.

Two bald eagles soared high above the lush green landscape, where cypress and pine trees tapered over the rolling hills in wave-like cover. Thickets of vine and brush crawled along the jungle floor until they found a large, circular basin that swallowed the island.

Here, far above the lone city, the majestic creatures veered off in opposite directions. One flew southwest. The other fluttered its wings, landing softly upon a large flagpole that extended far into the sky.

"Orian," Professor Yjn snapped calmly into his ear. Her voice was soft but struck his nervous system like venom.

Orian sunk slightly into his seat. "Won't happen again."

"No, it won't."

As she turned her back to him to address the class, Orian stole one more glance. He hadn't looked away for more than a second, and the eagle was gone. He silently cursed to himself.

This wasn't the first time he'd been caught fetching his gaze out the five-inch-thick glass overlooking the Southern end of the island, an action in direct violation of the most important rule. *Face forward at all times.* He couldn't help it. Orian was far more drawn to the world outside, and he always had been.

The professor's sturdy, but short frame stalked toward the front of the room. This, the elevated 102nd floor, was Yjn's, and she would have their attention.

Twenty-four young faces received her admonishment with slight exasperation. For the actions of one, the collective is guilty.

"How am I to aid in your prosperity? How are you to fill your roles if you cannot abide by the simple, rudimentary rules? Your day has only begun, and the rules are not a request. Clear?"

"Ma'am," Orian only mouthed the confirmation while his classmates responded with strength.

Yjn nodded, pleased. She then directed all eyes to the large screen behind her. As it popped to life with vibrant colors, she found her desk chair. This is how every day started.

"Good morning, Ardosia." Donning a neon green suit and tie, the nameless woman's eyes turned to slits as her grin widened, accentuating the roundness of her face. Everything from her torso up filled the center of the screen. "Today is bright, and the stars will surely shine over us all…"

Orian feigned focus on the woman as her words floated past him. *Where did the eagle fly?* he wondered. It had been the first time he'd seen one within the limits of Ardosia. He wondered if it had even been there at all. Orian so desperately longed to look out the window once more, to see if the powerful bird would return, but Vardus would soon fill the screen. It took courage to disobey the rules in the presence of Professor Yjn; arrogance to do so when Ardosia's leader spoke.

There was a small click as the screen switched feeds to find a strongly-aged face with a few slight wrinkles at his forehead. President Vardus offered his bearded smile after being introduced by the nameless woman. As he spoke, Orian kept his judgments to himself.

Vardus had a distinct appearance. Wardrobe black–and only black–with his curly black but graying hair tied in a bun. Orian had never actually seen him in person, but the rumors have swirled a number of times. "Vardus is so tall!" "He's skinny, too." "Don't forget to mention *handsome*." And finally there was the issue of the buttons. It seemed unnecessary, maybe unprofessional to Orian. Vardus persistently undid his top three buttons, as if to convey his normalcy and the casual manner with which he approached life. And though he was widely respected as the island's founder, Orian often wondered whether the interior of Vardus's house of charm was constructed of brick or straw.

The room had already been silent, but an extended air of disquiet fell upon them as his morning greeting commenced.

"Hello, future doctors, teachers, and warriors. Students of Ardosia, we'll begin as we always do…" He raised his hand to his forehead, and the class followed suit. "In the name of the Father, and of the Son, and of the Holy One. Our Father who reigns above, holy is your name. May your will be done in Ardosia, and lead us not down the unforgiving path of disobedience. Amen."

It was the morning prayer, a daily routine firmly engrained in the Schedule–a list of mandatory events individually assigned to all students. Religion was a topic seldom addressed on the island of Ardosia, never directly anyway. Critical conversations of God, what He looks like, and where He spends most of his time were nil. His existence, as well as the existence of Heaven and Hell, were widely accepted, yet often acknowledged indirectly. If Vardus said there was a God watching over humanity, paying close attention to all that is done on Earth, it must have been true. Like all other information given on the island, it had never been questioned.

Orian believed in God. In his soul, he felt as though a Creator had to exist. Every time he peered out the window to view the trees in the distance, the lapping shores of Ardosia's lake, or great soaring birds, he felt confident in opposing the proposition of mere coincidence. Orian didn't know for sure that God was real, but the God he chose to believe in may not have been the same one preached by Vardus. The President's God was a freak, hellbent on utter control.

Vardus concluded his morning speech with a few words of wisdom and encouragement. Then the screen went black. Professor Yjn wasted no time.

"Begin with exercise 263 today."

The class shuffled quickly in their seats, activating the holographic panel that shot vertically out of their white podiums. Upon activation, the panel showed distant swirling colors of red and blue, outlining their reflections.

Orian looked at his own reflection, uninterested. Exercise 263 was among his least favorite. Granted, Orian harbored a particular distaste for them all, outside of the few coding exercises they completed. The young dark man in the mirror wished he'd been coding or doing something physical, but he knew by now that you rarely got what you wanted in life.

Rising from her desk, Yjn waltzed through the aisles of student podiums, examining each of her pupils with apparent interest. Her head floated high, her shoes thudding against the black marble flooring.

"I'm not hearing enough chatter," she complained.

Orian groaned. *Chatter, how rich.* Regardless, he took part in the mind-numbing routine. He didn't have a choice.

His eyes followed as the red and blue colors formed lines that eventually morphed into a squiggly silhouette. That's when the prompt flew to the top of the screen.

TAKE CARE OF YOURSELF

To complete the task, Orian cocked his head to the left so that his reflection fit perfectly into the lines, and he choked the words, "Take care of yourself."

The next prompt appeared: *LOVE WHO YOU ARE.* With the new mantra, the lines formed themselves into a different shape. Orian was forced to sit up straighter and puff out his chest to fit his reflection into this one.

"Love who you are."

"Louder, Orian." Yjn cast down her glare at him as she passed his aisle. His gut instinct was to relay the instruction directly to her, as Yjn could certainly use some love, but he resisted the urge, knowing he shouldn't prod.

Orian was already on Yjn's Watch List, and he preferred not to be transferred to another floor.

Orian enjoyed floor 102. His best friend, who doubled as his roommate, was stationed near the front, on the opposite end of the room. His name was Ladis. And at Orian's side was Dawn.

"The seat you're assigned just *happens* to be by the *hottest* girl in class. I'd give all my fingernails to have your spot." Since Ladis was short and scrawny and Orian was less so, the stars would be more likely to pair Dawn and Orian, something with which he did not concern himself. It would have been irrelevant information if Ladis hadn't frequented it too often to ignore. Ladis never shied away from reminding Orian of his so-called "never-ending luck".

Risking a moment's glance, Orian peered out the corner of his eye. He could see Dawn's curly brown locks falling to her side as she spoke to her reflection. He didn't share the same obsession, if you might refer to it as such, that Ladis had for the girl, though he would admit she was a fetching one. A few times beforehand, Orian had caught glimpses of her eyes: a captivating ocean blue.

"Off to a slow start." Yjn's voice in his left ear brought Orian back to the exercise. He hated how sneaky his professor was.

"Ma'am."

To appease her, he followed the panel's orders, fitting his face in the lines and carefully articulating the words: *THIS IS PERFECTION.*

"Good." Yjn's mouth curled as she sauntered toward the front. Now she would rest on her chair, content with her students' success. From her perspective, there were twenty-four two-way mirrors facing her. She would be able to track her students' progress while all they could see was themselves.

Regretfully, Orian continued 263. He followed the guide, recited the lines, and moved forward. Orian acknowledged his own proficiency in the mundane exercises that Yjn put forth. It's not that he considered himself to be better than his classmates. He simply knew shortcuts, remembered patterns. This is what propelled him to the top of his class. He usually finished all exercises in half the time of the next fastest, that is if he didn't feel like hacking past the mainframe and swindling his podium into accepting perfect results. In that case, he'd finish in minutes.

Instructions when completing exercises before the time limit were as such: "go back" and "work on things you missed the first time." After all, the tasks wouldn't have a need for completion if they weren't vitally important. A second go-around could only improve one's outlook.

Orian swung his eyes rapidly around the room immediately upon finishing 263. Good. No one was looking. Subtly, he tapped the gray-white prism before him. A keyboard popped out of the podium just below chest height, and his panel no longer held his reflection. Now he could see through to the other side. Even better. As she frequently did, Professor Yjn had let her confidence overshadow her judgment. She wasn't even looking at her class, much less Orian.

A natural rule-breaker though he was, Orian made a conscientious effort to appear as though he followed instruction at least half the time. Rapping the keys at lightning speed, he conjured a page of endless information, as he had done countless times before. Yjn would never know. To her, Orian appeared to be mid-way through Exercise 263, and that was sufficient.

With his middle finger, Orian keyed the up and down arrows to scroll through an immense supply of articles written centuries ago. One hundred years was a length of time too difficult for Orian to grasp, having only lived through a fifth of that.

Accessing an article titled, "The Art of Military Tactics", Orian's eyebrows shot up with interest as he dove through new, enticing information. Yjn liked to refer to her exercises as "learning", but no. *This* is where the real learning took place.

"You know she'll catch you one of these days."

Enamored by the article, Orian hadn't heard the voice, not until the words were spoken a second time. Had anyone else vied for his attention, they wouldn't have proven successful. But the violet richness of her words made Orian freeze.

He wouldn't dare risk averting his stare from the translucent panel before him. *Face forward at all times.* Beyond the floating words of the article, Orian confirmed that Yjn hadn't moved from her desk. She was as unsuspecting as ever, wonderfully examining a rose that she plucked from the vase before her. That's when the voice spoke again.

"You're not quite as invincible as you think you are … Mr. Orian." The words were convicting, but they had been uttered playfully. Without looking, he knew the source.

Orian could sense her smile. He kept his head down and spoke feebly. "Dawn, if you're not careful, you'll get us both transferred off of 102."

"My health is my mind, and my heart is my health."

Orian's eyebrows furrowed for a second, until he realized Dawn had still been working through 263, simultaneously reading her lines while venturing for conversation. If she spoke too many words outside of those that were prompted to her, Yjn would be alerted, and Orian's cover would be blown.

His heart raced, and his eyes never left Yjn who sat absently at the front. The beating in his chest waxed in an almost circular motion, like that of a train as it pushes itself forward. This hadn't been Orian's first conversation with Dawn. Amid a few prior exercises, Dawn had sparingly made comments to him and vice versa. Still, the rush was the same every time. Breaking rules was Orian's mantra, and the thrill never ceased.

She must have been near the end of her exercise because Dawn didn't say anything for another couple minutes that she wasn't supposed to say. When she finally did break away from her prompts, she said, "That brain of yours must be full by now."

From his peripheral vision, Orian noticed Dawn had maintained a forward posture, cocking her head to the side as she pretended to complete another prompt.

"I don't know what you're talking about."

Dawn huffed.

Orian didn't look away from the article. "It's better than 263."

"Sounds like blasphemy, you know … disobedience even."

Orian gulped, and his body experienced momentary paralysis.

"I'm kidding."

Orian thanked God that she hadn't been seriously considering the d-word, reporting him for "disobedience", the consequences of which could ruin his life.

Dawn tried once more. "You don't like 263."

"I like the coding exercises better."

"You're good at those from what I've seen."

"You've been watching me? How?"

"Not watching, no. I've just seen."

Orian's head rose. He noticed Yjn. Their eyes locked for a half-second before his darted. To her, it would be a coincidence. She believed him to be working diligently, but after the short exchange her suspicions might now be raised. It was a slip-up on Orian's part.

"We should get back to the exercise," he suggested faintly.

"I don't like 263, either."

Orian didn't say anything, but he was listening.

"Seems, I don't know … unnatural."

Orian pondered. The truth was he had never really paid attention to the reasons for his disdain. He thought in simple terms. He didn't like that which made him feel off or awkward. Oppositely, that in which he found purpose or fulfillment worked much to his penchant. But *unnatural* was an apt way to regard 263 and many of Yjn's exercises in general.

"Yeah," Orian summarized. "Unnatural."

Absent in the moment, Orian stared blankly through his screen. Not only was he unable to place a finger on what he was learning through Yjn's exercises, but, even more concerning, he couldn't discern what he was *supposed* to be learning. *Unnatural.* Dawn was right. 263 could be lumped with the rest of them and described as an unnatural void in which willing participants could escape reality. Orian was not a willing participant, which made his classroom success something peculiar, to say the least.

Equally as peculiar was Dawn's sudden aversion to him. She hadn't spoken a word outside of her prompts in a minute or so. By the time Orian figured out why, it was almost too late.

The clicking footsteps of professor Yjn had been previously drowned out by the volume of his thoughts. Now they were like approaching earthquakes recurring one after the other, making Orian fall off kilter as he fumbled to stow the keyboard into his podium. He needed to tap that little spot on the side, but he couldn't find it for the life of him. On top of that, he needed to make the article disappear. There just wasn't enough time.

Like a deathly church bell signaling Orian's demise, Yjn's footsteps worked in collaboration with his heart to produce a clanging sound that rung his ears. This was it. He'd teetered on the balance beam of fate, tempting it for far too long. It was only right that he'd fall off eventually.

Just before accepting his doom, Orian had a crazy thought–one that just might work. With a jab-like motion, he swiped upward at the screen. The article followed the motion and disappeared the next moment. Orian wasn't sure where he'd sent it, but it was gone nonetheless. Next was the keyboard.

Yjn was no more than two steps away from catching Orian red-handed when, through a stroke of massive luck, he found the spot. The podium had received the keyboard silently right as professor Yjn poked her head into their aisle.

"Are we having issues, Orian?"

"*To love oneself is to find the purpose of life.*" Orian cleared his throat, face forward, displaying a façade of ignorance. That's when he pretended to finally acknowledge Yjn. "Hmm?"

His screen returned to the two-way mirror it had previously been. Orian feigned ignorance as he tilted his head to the side and tucked a shoulder to his chin, continuing 263.

Yjn tutted as she watched him but held her suspicions close and said nothing. Her accusatory eyes were held on Orian for an uncomfortable moment, as if she thought her stare alone could break him.

Orian gave no sign of guilt, though his insides were boiling with it. No, maybe guilt wasn't the right word. He *was* guilty, but he didn't feel wrong for it, just on the brink of nervousness.

Yjn left his side, turning to the young man who sat directly in front of Orian. Spiky blonde-green hair complemented his pale white skin. Zak was his name, and in this moment his face displayed an innocent, utter confusion as he regarded the panel before him.

Once her eyes fell upon Zak's screen, Yjn froze. Her awful gasp silenced the room.

Suddenly, 263 was placed on hold. All eyes were on the professor.

"Zak, I–I … how did you find this?" She spoke in a hushed tone, so as to conceal the truth of her sudden horror.

His mouth had been hanging agape. "Professor Yjn, I-I'm just as puzzled as you. I swear one moment I was completing the exercise, and the next, this popped up. I don't even know what *this* is!"

Professor Yjn's eyes scanned both Zak and the panel with arrant intent. Despite having just tensed to the point of combustion, she suddenly switched her demeanor to one of ease and sensibility as she straightened, sighing. Yjn said softly, disappointedly, "Follow me."

"Wha– but I–"

"That's an order."

Zak hesitated, but he knew better than to deny a direct order. As Zak swiveled out of his chair, Orian peeked through his now-transparent panel to view the contents of Zak's screen. His heart skipped a beat when he saw the headline: "The Art of Military Tactics".

Orian's eyes bolted up and met Zak's with an overwhelming sense of guilt. The young man's face went from pale as a ghost's to scarlet red as he placed the undeniable pieces of the puzzle together. Of course, it was *Orian* who was responsible for this.

"Ms. Yjn," Zak competed for her attention as she dragged him toward the front of the classroom.

She silenced him immediately. "Nothing shall be said on your behalf from here on out." The ice picks she stared into Zak's soul froze his mouth, in addition to his pride.

It had been Zak's intention to inform her of the true culprit of the crime. To Orian's fortune, Yjn wasn't having it. Now the level of guilt weighing on Orian elicited a desire to stand and shout the truth to the world, that it had been *him* who procured the article, not Zak. But he couldn't. And he wouldn't.

Heart pounding, throat constricting, Orian almost vomited at what he feared would come next.

Zak had been held hostage at the front for no more than a minute when two guards dressed in white-gray miliary uniforms barged through the entryway. One had fair skin and the other splotchy, but both faces were stoic. They were simply following orders.

Zak had his eyes bulging out of his skull. Just now was he putting it all together, and he could not stand the thought of being transferred from 102, especially for an act in which he was not the perpetrator. He resisted when they clutched both his arms.

"No, wait!" he protested. "It wasn't me, I swear! I've never–"

A fist to the gut silenced him.

It didn't take long for Zak to accept that he could never overpower two of Ardosia's warriors.

His feet dragged against the floor as they carried him by the arms. The double doors opened, and they slammed shut. It was too quiet after that.

As though the entire experience had been nothing but a brief and irrelevant mirage, 263 was back in motion not a moment after Zak had been escorted from the classroom. Heads affixed themselves into red and blue outlines. Meaningless words shot forth from their mouths.

Orian couldn't believe his classmates' complacency, as though what had taken place was a daily occurrence. Only once before had someone been transferred to a different floor since Orian could remember.

Two realizations struck him then. One, he had never heard of the floors to which transfers were moved. Two, military men were the ones called to move the transfers themselves. Why?

They took him. They took Zak, and Orian felt an undeniable foreboding that it was the first domino to fall.

Orian shrunk in his seat as he felt a pair of peripherals boring into his side.

"It wasn't your fault."

He appreciated Dawn's effort at comforting him, but they both knew the truth.

Toward the front, Yjn had been seated and cleaning the bottoms of her nails with a pencil, expression as peaceful as a sleeping child. Orian watched her for a moment, assessing that Yjn's lack of remorse was a positive indicator that Zak had been transferred to a floor equally as respectable as 102. Or so he hoped.

Hands shaking, Orian brought 263 back to his panel. He swallowed, hoping to compose himself. He closed his eyes and breathed in slowly. Only after the shaking subsided did he open them. Then he told his reflection, "*You're free from the tragic bounds of the Earth.*"

A slight breeze buffeted the waters surrounding Ardosia. From his bedside window far above, Orian could see tiny white castles glittering the lake's surface while leaves turned in the distance. Safe and stowed in his air-conditioned unit, Orian couldn't feel the slightest movement in the air. He wished he could right *now*, not just when the Schedule called for it.

Gently, he rubbed the glass as though it was a barrier to his soul's entry into freedom.

Tomorrow, he would be able to feel that wind stroke his hair while he basked in the sun. It was on the Schedule for Orian and Ladis to visit the Ardosia Arena after class, otherwise known as the Coliseum. Built outdoors near the other side of the island, the Coliseum rose high into the sky like an oval that captured gasps of entertainment.

Orian couldn't recall which event they'd be attending, but to him it didn't matter. As long as he was out of the confining indoors, he'd be content. Orian prayed it wouldn't rain and that the sun would be bright and hot as it appeared to be now.

A bright spark in the distance drew Orian's attention. On the other side of the lake, the newly constructed Wall was in the process of being finished. Fifty-foot masses of steel and carbon-fiber siding stretched as high as the distant cypress trees, wrapping all the way around the island. The spark Orian had seen was a welder working to mend the final hundred-foot stretch of open land together.

Shortly after Vardus's daily prayer about a month ago, he addressed the construction of a new wall, citing it as a safety measure since he cared deeply for the well-being of his students.

Every time the welder took a break, he became nothing more than a tiny speck. But as he melted metal into metal, Orian marveled at how the intensity of the spark compared with that of the sun. It reminded him of the timeless battle between man and nature.

Regarding the Wall and noting its monumental size, Orian wondered at the creatures Vardus must be trying to keep out of Ardosia, or even the ones he was keeping *in*.

"Shower's open." Ladis's light voice snapped Orian out of his trance.

Behind Orian, Ladis loped out of the bathroom, violently scrubbing a towel through his dripping shoulder-length hair. He stumbled over to the dresser between their beds to retrieve a pair of sweat pants and a t-shirt.

Waving a hand, Orian said, "Thanks, took one this morning before class."

There was nothing intimate about a shower, but Orian treasured them nonetheless. This was one of the few activities in which the Schedule allowed for deviation of any kind. Class started at the same time for everyone. It finished likewise. Events were scheduled, and you were to attend them promptly. It was up to the operator, however, to decide how they would fit a shower into that Schedule. Although mundane, Orian felt a relieving sense of freedom in that decision.

"Besides," Orian continued, "it's almost 5:30. Green pepper and broccoli arugula salad on the menu tonight, I believe."

"Wouldn't want to miss that."

Peering out his window, Orian watched the beginnings of a fiery red sunset fill the Western sky. It filled him with hope, as it did most every other night: a hope that on the horizon was the life-sustaining freedom he sought. Examining a small fingerprint on the glass, Orian thought of Zak. He wasn't sure if the guilt would ever leave him, and perhaps it wouldn't. From here on out, he'd have no choice but to live with the terrible knowledge of his mistake.

"I'm starting to think you need a prospective role change." Ladis plopped backwards onto his bed, nestling his head into the pillows.

"What role is that?" Orian inquired, his sunset stare ever still.

"Window maker."

"Window maker?"

"You've been looking at them a lot lately … got caught in class today."

"I have no idea how to make windows."

"You could read about it, right? Through that Inter-whatcha-ma-callit."

Whipping around, Orian hushed his roommate with an ice-cold stare.

Ladis was referring to the place where Orian found his articles. One day, many years ago, he had stumbled upon a hidden universe while hacking past his podium's mainframe. What he found was the Internet. Orian hadn't had any specific goals in mind that day, but he knew that by digging long enough into the technological sphere, he'd come up with more than dirt. Indeed, he had. Before he knew it, scrolling through articles had become a daily occurrence, as he became infatuated with soaking up as much knowledge as possible. Of course, Orian did all this under the guise of obediently completing his exercises. Earlier today, he discovered just what *could* happen if he were caught.

Orian shuddered internally at the image of Zak being hauled away like a prisoner. He would have to be more careful if he didn't want to find himself in the same predicament.

Subtly eyeing the small black knob hung in the ceiling corner, he grumbled under his breath. "It's called the thing we don't talk about."

Ladis nodded. "Right, my bad."

Orian returned his attention to the orange glow of the sky, its final rays penetrating clouds like holy lasers. "I'm not much one for windows, anyway. Everything beyond them, though…"

"I know." Something in Ladis's voice was reminiscent of a dejected sigh. "How about coding?" he tried.

"That's my role, I suppose. And I'll fill it." Finally Orian turned to Ladis, who was now resting his head on hand. He appeared to be watching the sky outside, just as Orian had. They met one another's eyes. "There has to be more."

"More than what? Coding?"

"Coding, my role, all of it."

The roommates had maneuvered carefully through this conversation many a time before. Orian held no secrets, and neither did Ladis. It was why the two of them were so close, not just because they were required to be in the physical sense. Yet their desires could not have been more opposing. If they could be compared to animals, Orian was like the hawk who needed to soar high, while Ladis was a groundhog, content in his burrow where the shadows are home.

On many occasions, Ladis had wasted his breath, coercing Orian into an accepting mentality: accepting of this life and of the splendors they've been afforded. He believed Orian not to be pessimistic, but rather willfully ignorant of the gifts on display before him. Ambitious beyond repair could summarize it.

This time, he held his silence and listened to Orian.

"It's like I know a destiny worth much more than a *role*."

"Which is?"

"I'm not sure … I'm even less certain how to get there."

"Sounds like a problem."

Orian huffed.

Sitting up, Ladis inhaled. Orian knew what was to come, and he wasn't sure he was ready for it. Ladis lived his life with strong and solid conviction, like he knew every move was the right one. Out of this conviction came words of wisdom, often ones that Orian didn't care to hear.

"You're uncertain. We're already upon our final round of classes before entering our roles, and you're not sure yours is right. Yeah?"

Orian cocked his head, as if to say *more or less*.

"Your role is important, Orian. You need it equally as much as it needs you. That's not something to be taken lightly." Ladis's eyes swung around the room, falling upon each individual item: the beds resting against the wall side-by-side, the screen mounted on the opposite wall, their small square window and its leather brown curtain, the dressers, mirrors, and the attached bathroom. "All of this has been handed to us, and it's nothing short of a gift." He strolled over to the window. "What lies out there is unknown, Orian. It may be beautiful, and it contains the appeal of something foreign. But ultimately, it *is* unknown. While in here–" falling back onto his bed, Ladis rubbed his hands over the covers, "–we are guaranteed safety and comfort … what more could you ask?"

Orian listened first, thought next, and spoke after. "I don't know. I just know that what I want is not here." Orian scratched at his chin. "Ladis, have you ever thought about God?"

His brow crinkled. "What do you mean? Of course I've thought about God. We're all believers on the island. President Vardus is sure there's a God above, and so am I."

"Isn't it funny that we don't have a place to worship this god?"

"We worship here. In the Tower."

"No, but I mean …" Orian approached Ladis, lowering his voice. "I looked God up on the you-know-what. Everywhere you find Him, there are these steeple-shaped buildings called churches, with stained-glass windows and altars and crucifixes, and all of that. We don't have that here. I don't like it."

"I know what a church is. It unsettles you that we don't have one?"

"Yes! It doesn't feel strange to you that we pray at the beginning of every day and then seemingly shut off our minds and hearts to God thereafter?"

"I don't know. Maybe you're overthinking it."

Orian's mouth hung agape. He wanted to argue, but he went instead with, "Maybe."

The space between them grew quiet. No more words had to be said.

Orian's lips pursed as he looked off into space. Ladis was a sensible man, of this there was no doubt. But Orian would always disagree. He felt something more calling to him. No, he *knew* there was something more out there, past the lake that choked Ardosia, over the Wall, and maybe even past the endless trees beyond. Somewhere near the horizon was where Orian could find what he was looking for, but it would reach him only in his dreams.

A *ding* interrupted their silence, twisting Ladis's head to the front door. Through a small silver notch, two small boxes of cardboard had been delivered.

Ladis turned back to Orian. His mouth twisted into a smile. "Dinner."

II

In the pitch-black shadowy realm, she tied her night hair behind her head. Naught but a single candle provided the enclosed space with light. Here Talia was alone, as was the case for most of her life, both in part due to natural circumstance and personal preference. She wiped the drowsiness from her eyes as the closet door was jarred open by her free hand.

Beyond her collection of cotton-stitched shirts and hanging jeans, the black corset was stiffly arranged on a hanger in the corner. Talia snatched it, quickly nestling her petite frame into the uncomfortable outfit. Even before tightening the strings, the corset was snug against her torso. It would constrict her breathing at first, but as always, she would get used to it.

"Neal," was all she said to summon the only man in the world whom she trusted.

There was a feeble knock on the door before he entered, as if to double-check that his presence had been requested. A shorter man with glasses, a frail frame, and an awkward smile poked his head around the door respectfully, to ensure that the young woman had indeed put jeans on before calling on him. She had.

"Come in," Talia said. "Here."

She turned her back to him. Neal knew the drill.

She felt his hands tighten the strings. "B-breathe in."

Talia did. Pulling with his skinny arms, it took all Neal's might to adjust the corset to the proper tension. He tied it as tight as he could. Ideally, it would need to be readjusted in fifteen minutes, but there was no time. This would have to do. "Ar-are you ready?"

Draping a thin leather jacket over her shoulders that was also tight and black, Talia laid comforting eyes upon her assistant as the zipper rose close to her neck. "I'll be alright, Neal. Thanks for being here. Now go back to bed."

"I cou-could come."

"You don't need to prove your bravery to me."

"As you always say, the r-risks can be averted w-when–"

"–you have a numbers advantage. Yes, I know. You're greatly appreciated, Neal. Now …" she fixed a stern gaze upon him. "Go back to bed."

A silent huff of disappointment that belied his relief escaped as he nodded to her. "Y-y-yes, Tal. Be safe."

She hugged Neal closely, and he left. While Talia internally respected Neal's offer to join their militaristic efforts, she contained him to his realm of expertise, which was not so much physical as it was technological.

After strapping boots to her feet, Talia rose from her bedside. She patted herself down to ensure she had everything she needed. It was an unnecessary gesture. This mission necessitated only her wit and strong leadership, and the rest would be up to fate.

Talia blew out the candle so that a wall of darkness would envelop and protect her office while she was gone. She gave one final look into nothingness before shutting the door. Entering the outside world, a brisk wave of air surprised her. Cool nights were looming as Summer slowly yielded to Fall. A dazzling full moon watched over her camp.

Talia knew she had more than enough time. She'd always inclined herself toward punctuality, even excessively at times. That's what it took to be a leader, she believed. You must be ready before the enemy.

Scattered torches lit up the camp, lightly illuminating a path for Talia. Her boots slid noiselessly over the grass, blending in with the taciturn dead of night. Not even the slight breeze was strong enough to issue the sounds of quaking leaves.

Rubbing tightly against her skin, the corset proved unfathomably discomforting. Talia reached through her jacket and twisted, hoping she might gain some breathing room. As she passed a building with torches at each corner, she reflected how women many years ago wore corsets beneath their dresses. Back then, they had been even more constricting, created by men to alter the appearance of women. Skinnier, with larger breasts. That's all men preferred. Character mattered not.

Talia never submitted herself to the desires of man. Her corset had been created specifically for battle. It hadn't been sown of malleable plastics like conventional corsets, but rather a metal similar to chain mail, the primary difference being the microscopic holes found in Talia's armor, as opposed to the large holes of medieval armor. This specific item had been created for her own protection, and it had proven to be the most effective armor. If not for its repeated ability to deflect arrows and swords, Talia wouldn't think twice about tossing it.

After traveling halfway across camp, Talia approached the correct building. A long, narrow, arching structure stretched for a hundred feet. One side was cloaked in shadow, while the other soaked up the moon's face. When she approached the building, there had been a large bird with talons that gripped one of the arching poles. Its massive wings flapped as it danced into the night, a white head looking almost blue beneath the moon.

The building had been locked when Talia arrived. She fished the key out of her pocket.

As she opened the door, LED lights flickered on as she flipped the switch, providing ample light within. For an armory, the place could be described as claustrophobic. Weapons of all types glittered the walls: swords, knives, spears, and bows. A wooden island in the middle of the building took up most of the space. Talia recalled when the massive island had been built and placed within the armory. She helped staple the leather cover to its flat top. Back then, the cover had been smooth and dark, almost like that of a polished cherry wood. Now the leather covering the island was rough and pale. Time took its toll on most everything sooner or later.

On top of the cover was a lengthy, multi-layered bag with straps that contained the heart of their mission, the device that would grant their success. Also on the island were a few crossbows that would be handed out only to the most skilled warriors.

Talia grabbed her own crossbow, the metal cold to the touch as she moved to the head of the island. From here, she would wait for her men to filter inside.

Fifteen minutes passed in solitude. She used this time to check the functionality of her crossbow. She knew it would work just as expected, but it never hurt to check twice. Pretending to nock an arrow, she aimed down the sight, pulled the trigger, and did not flinch when the string snapped forward with a rapid click. Pleased, she placed the weapon behind her.

Then one-by-one, men in uniform stumbled weary-eyed into the building, surrounding the island table as if in preparation for a meeting, which in some sense they were. Talia had prepared few words since most of the mission had been covered the previous evening. They simply gathered now to consolidate weaponry and depart with every unit present. Nearly at full head-count, the men dressed in defensive garb–subtle chest plates, cargo pants, and boots–shifted back and forth on their feet as they shimmied into their armor. A glittery black adorned their chests, streaked by gold beneath their arms, a gold that hugged their ribs as if to remind them that breaths are numbered. Throughout the course of life, it's important not to waste any of them.

The men were all suited in their armor, standing erect. Only one spot hadn't been filled yet, and it was on the opposite end.

As Talia waited impatiently for the last man to arrive, she observed the pale and haggard faces of her men. You'd have thought they had just returned from battle and were not imminently heading into one. *What is it about men that makes them incapable of rising before the sun?* Talia hoped they didn't feel half as tired as they looked.

At last, a tall and burly man with a complexion not quite as tan as Talia's entered the armory with a smirk on his face. Planting his feet, his frame swayed lazily, like a canoe on calm waters. Then he paused.

Nice of you to join, Byron, Talia thought to herself. She elected not to address the tardy officer since she knew he was looking for attention. Instead, she spoke to her men as though Byron wasn't there at all.

"Stand tall. Wake the fuck up. People's lives are counting on us today." Her tone zapped the air like static and electrified her soldiers, just as she had hoped.

When Talia had first taken control, she struggled with men who refused to take orders from her. Now, after having clearly demonstrated her superiority in the world of hectic violence, her voice, her words, and her demeanor tended to resonate with her men. She knew that, as unfortunate as the truth may be, respect was better demanded than it was earned. She continued briefly, her hands splayed over the island.

"As discussed last night, this is a simple extraction. Many of you have been part of previous missions in some way or another. For others, this will be your first." She scanned each and every one of them, stealing all eyes in the room. "Stay close to each other. Act as a team. Communicate. This is how we'll win." Talia searched her men, who numbered about forty, waiting for someone to interject. Evidently, no one had the urge. Good. "You know your positions. Let's move."

With that, all men shuffled to their weapons, extracting only the necessary tools for the job. The room had gone from silent to a cacophony of bustling men and metal.

Four soldiers worked in unison to haul the cumbersome bag at the end of the island onto their shoulders. Talia watched them carefully, as if her eyes could provide them with extra support. What they held would be key to their success. A device far ahead of its time, manufactured by the IT department, was zipped-up within. Without delay, the men toting the bag strolled out the door, and the rest followed. Well, everyone but one.

The man who had arrived late held his head high and shoulders back as he approached Talia with feigned sorrow. "Look, Chief. I was–"

"You're guarding flank today."

Byron looked perplexed. His sorrowful veneer vanished, and his true emotions roamed free. "Flank? You said last night Frank was guarding flank. It fits perfectly. Flank Frank."

Talia brushed past him as she stole a length of golden fabric from an elevated podium in the corner. "I'll inform him that the two of you have switched."

"Talia–"

"That's General to you, not Chief."

"… come on. I'm not the first person who's been late."

"You won't be the last."

"But flank? That means–"

"Back of the line." Talia was losing patience, as was often the case with men. "Grab what you need. No need to delay your comrades any further."

"Hey." Byron switched to a deeper tone, one that he apparently thought was more convincing.

A woman with less of a backbone might have fallen for Byron's so-called charm, his objective good looks, or his brains. Talia would not. In fact, if not for the fact that Byron was far and away one of the most skilled and brilliant soldiers Talia had worked with, the troublemaker would have been stationed nowhere near her.

Talia played with the golden fabric as she said, "That's an order."

Byron questioned no further, face twisting with anguish as he left the warmth and light of the armory.

Talia was alone now, and she dropped the minor conflict in an instant. Her mind, instead, was delicately interacting with the possibility that she may not return to camp. She did this before every mission, and she encouraged her soldiers to do so as well. It was important to remind yourself that you had something to lose, something to return to, so that heart, mind, and soul all worked together on the battlefield to protect everything you treasured.

Once Talia was satisfied, she terminated the armory LED's and cloaked herself in darkness. She released one breath, then two, and closed her eyes. She imagined the success of the mission. She saw her unit returning with greater number than that with which it had departed. Her heart had yet to start racing, and at these thoughts she felt an even deeper layer of ease wash over her.

Talia released one final breath, wrapping the golden fabric around her face so that an angular slit revealed only her green eyes, obscuring all else from her neck up. Her crossbow felt no heavier than a feather, as its weight was evenly distributed by the strap over her shoulder.

She was ready.

Closing the door behind her, Talia moved to the front of her crew, who had been standing face-forward in line as they anticipated her guidance. She stopped in front of them.

"I almost forgot. Byron!"

"Ma'am," came his voice from the back.

"Find a strong partner. We're gonna need the boat."

His response came after a long pause. "Ma'am."

When he and another soldier returned with a white canoe hoisted onto their shoulders, Byron awaited Talia's command.

The General scanned her men. In their erect posture, she knew they were ready. Each had been trained through the extensive program she created, and their instincts would be sharp, as would their swords.

Together, they moved as a unit past the opening gates and into the jungle filled with trees that appeared to be zombified soldiers in the night, their limbs reaching for she and her men. They weaved their way through the forest and were touched only by their collective determination. By the following morning, they would reach the outer limits of a place Talia and many other members of her crew used to call home: the forlorn island of Ardosia.

III

Rain plastered the sheet of glass to Orian's left. He couldn't watch the storm, of course. *Face forward at all times.* That was the rule. But Orian sure could hear it.

Just his luck, too. On the day where the Schedule not only allowed but *necessitated* that he delve into the outdoors for an evening at the Coliseum, it was only fitting that the gates of Heaven should open and flood Ardosia with an armada of angelic river arrows. The water droplets sounded more like pebbles being cast at the five-inch-thick window, distracting Orian from the ever-enthralling exercise 78.

For this particular exercise, Orian was beholden to a genuine completion. This was one of the few he couldn't simply hack past. His podium would not accept any form of dissemblance, so he would have to work through 78 the old-fashioned way.

Vacantly watching his panel light up with the flashing words: *TRAGEDY LOSS DESPAIR*, Orian couldn't escape his mind. This was nothing new.

Between yesterday's occurrence with Zak–how he'd been stolen from 102 by two large men–the current ceaseless torrent smacking the window, and the imminent thoughts of an evening outdoors, Orian could not find it within himself to cancel out the competing noises.

He was suddenly startled by none other than the sneaky Professor Yjn.

"Orian, you're behind."

Normally, Yjn would have inserted invective or sarcasm in her speech so that she could mock the troublesome Orian. However, the softness with which she spoke was alarming. It even sounded like she cared.

Orian's eyes fell slightly. "Ma'am," was all he said.

Yjn cast down an imposing glare, or a sea of empathy. Orian wasn't sure. His gaze hadn't left the bottom of his panel, even as Yjn said before leaving him, "Please try your best to finish the exercise. It's so important that you do."

For whatever reason, Orian did as she had requested. Perhaps he was still too shaken up after yesterday to operate in his usual defiance. He probably wouldn't even open the Internet today. Instead, he perused the words: *TRAGEDY LOSS DESPAIR*.

78 required that Orian mimic an emotion fitting of the prompt. If his panel glowed green, it meant success, and he could move on to the next. If it buzzed red, it meant try again. Orian contorted his face to match an expression of, well, tragedy, loss, and despair. It didn't require much

effort because his panel went green instantly. Evidently his face had already displayed just as much unease as was necessary.

VICTORY JUSTICE PRAISE was the next prompt. Orian found this one to be trickier. Trying for a smile, he conjured emotions of satisfaction, but they weren't good enough for the program. He would have to dig deeper. While working for the right expression, Orian wondered at the purpose of an exercise like 78. Apparently, those who had created the curriculum valued the proper conveyance of emotion, disregarding its legitimacy. From what Orian gathered, Ardosia and its professors wished that its student population could lie both to themselves and to others, and do it well.

"102, I need you all to face forward. Head up, panels down." Yjn broke Orian's concentration. All panels in the classroom slid into their podiums with a collective hiss. "This doesn't happen often, but today we have a *very* special guest visiting." The double doors on the other end of the room were opened, but all eyes were directed toward the front, as they had been instructed. Nobody saw the tall man who had entered with the accompaniment of two bodyguards until he was standing at the front of the class. "Give it up for the leader and brilliant founder of Ardosia himself ... President Vardus!"

The students weren't sure whether they were supposed to erupt with cheery applause or offer a reverent silence. It seemed as though half the class opted for one option while the other half did the opposite, resulting in an awkward mix of the two. President Vardus strode in with an air of such confidence, you'd have thought his demeanor would be infectious, but the students weren't sure what to make of him.

Vardus, in his perpetual suit of black, was clearly disturbed by their lack of enthusiasm, but he hid it well. He sure was tall, just as the rumors had said. "Thank you, thank you. I'm so glad to be here on floor 105."

From the corner, Yjn corrected him with a whisper, "102."

Vardus didn't flinch. "It's a privilege of mine to visit with you all …"

As he spoke, Orian once again could not avert his eyes from that god-forsaken peeking chest. It wasn't enough that Vardus's graying black hair was parted all over the place, despite his efforts to contain it in a bun. Nor could he have simply gone for a normal color scheme outside of the all-black variety. But to top it all off–or not, rather–Vardus refused to lace the top three buttons of his collared shirt, exposing coiled, unsightly hairs. It was as though everything about him demanded attention while seeking the guise of humility–unsuccessfully, Orian might add.

While he should have been paying close attention to President Vardus's address to their class, Orian retained little of what had been uttered by the so-called tall, lanky, handsome leader. Talk of bureaucratic bullshit and kumbaya bored him to death. He felt it a waste of brain cells to soak up jargon of the kind. None of it was genuine, and it had all been fabricated. Whoever invented political speech had done just that: *invented.* Orian believed that if a method of spoken word had a need to be created, there was nothing natural about it, and it was therefore moot to his existence.

One thing did capture Orian's eye, however. It seemed that, for the majority of time that Vardus stood like a sentry before the students, the President had been drilling a persistent–should he say desirable?–stare into Orian, like he wished to know the thoughts occurring to him. It was unnerving.

The young man Orian could admit to Vardus's intelligence. Of course, the guy was smart. You can't found your own society on an island without even the faintest semblance of wit and cunning. But one might even say Ardosia's President was omnipresent in that moment, almost like he could exist in more areas than one. While Vardus made his announcement without stuttering or skipping a beat, he was also penetrating Orian's skull, extracting the golden ire of foreign conceptions. There was an ambivalence to him. Orian sensed something carnal, timeless, and arcane. His complexity made him dangerous, and it could be seen in those eyes.

On second thought, maybe the President hadn't been watching Orian at all. In fact, no he surely was not. His eyes, rather, had been keen on the person situated to Orian's right. Dawn. To Vardus, it must have been as if she were the only being, outside himself, present in the room.

A chilling shudder ran down his spine as Orian watched the way in which Vardus's eyes subtly feasted on the young girl's appearance. He wondered if he was the only person in the room who could see it. Or was he visualizing something that wasn't really there at all?

Being cooped up within the same area for too long tended to impart insanity. Twenty years within the Tower, spent almost entirely on floor 102, could have made Orian insane.

Shutting his eyes entirely might rid his head of any further deception. Orian rubbed his temple as he longed for the hour later in the day when he would finally relish in the outdoors, whether he should be soaked in rain or dried by sun.

Vardus concluded his speech and was out the room not a moment later, as if he had received what he came for and needed no longer to subject himself to the presence of a spiritless contingent of young men and women. His departure would have been offered the same lack of enthusiasm as his arrival, had Yjn not forcefully reminded her students that their applause was not just an obvious courtesy to their leader, but that it was required. President Vardus had been here and gone in an instant, making Orian wonder if he had ever really been with them at all.

Orian and Ladis seated themselves in section 23, right beside the arena's perimeter. Their seats were impeccable. The two of them had placed rain jackets over their shoulders, but there was hardly a need. By the time they made it to the Coliseum, the storm had dissipated into an easy mist that formed beads on their sleeves. Orian couldn't contain his joy.

"That smile hasn't left your face since we stepped outside," Ladis observed, his greasy long hair dripping with moisture.

Orian had been too involved in his surroundings to listen. Although he preferred it bright blue, with clouds and a sun casting light down upon them, he was hard-pressed to issue complaints over the gray weeping sky above. Right now, he could see it in all its glory. Some might consider the outdoor scene unflattering on a day like today. Not Orian. This is where he felt as free as ever.

Adorning the Coliseum were rows and rows of seating situated in a massive elevated oval around a flat surface below. The entire site was made of stone, concrete, and clay. He could see the way in which the light rain clung to the material, bringing out its darker tan color. Orian saw pairs of individuals seated all throughout the stands, similar in appearance to Ladis and himself. There were boys and girls, both young and old, all donning the same rain jacket provided to them. But he could not see the massive Wall that was under construction at the island's perimeter, almost like the Coliseum had transported him to a new realm. It made Orian feel as though he could finally escape, maybe even that he already had.

Lastly Orian took in a row of glass placed high on the right side of the Coliseum. A rectangular prism of gold folded its edges around the glass, and it sat above all else. If anything could contribute to feelings of unease, it would be that box, where Orian assumed high-ranking officials– and possibly Vardus–hid behind the tinted glass.

But as it was, Orian would allow nothing to ruin his ecstasy. The smell of the outdoors and the damp fresh air ushered relief into Orian's system. He was floating, until Ladis's resolution-seeking mind brought him back down to Earth. He must've been thinking about their conversation the previous evening.

"Have you ever thought of becoming a soldier?"

"Soldier?" Orian almost laughed.

"Yeah. They get to be outdoors at least five times as often as we do. I can see how much you love it out here. Once you find your role as a coder, you may never get to be outside."

"I know … but a soldier? Even if that was a viable option, I couldn't."

"Why not?"

"I'm certain you cannot just switch roles, and secondly … take a look at me. Do I look like soldier material to you?"

Ladis looked at Orian as if that were a stupid question. "Yes, you do! You have unbelievable genetics. I mean, look at you. For someone who's twenty, you have long arms, wide shoulders, and you're pretty tall."

"I'm much too skinny, though. And I've never done any training."

In some sense, it was a lie. Preparing to be a soldier was every bit as much about the psychological as it was the physical, if not more so. In that department, Orian was proficient. He'd studiously read and studied deeply on the art of war and team-member tactics. In fact, most articles he had found on the Internet pertained to this subject. It was the type of information of which he couldn't get enough.

"Exactly! Just think about what you could be if you did train. Lots of potential there. Anyway, I don't want to get off the rails. I just wanted to plant a potential seed is all."

That's precisely what Ladis had done. The truth was that Orian *could* see himself as a soldier. It's not that he wasn't interested in coding, which was his current prospective role within Ardosia's society, but he found his desires laid in more than one area of interest. He knew it would be impossible to fill more than one role. It was a rule that, along with the island itself, constricted Orian. He just wondered what it would be like to have the ability to chase all his desires at once.

A sudden voice boomed over the loud speakers.

"Ladies and gentlemen, welcome to the main event. We ask that you remain seated for the duration of the experience, and as always, do not leave until the Schedule calls for it. Enjoy!"

There was a rumbling below, its only purpose to fabricate suspense. Some of the local crowd cheered, but the effort was feeble. Orian didn't feel the need to stress his vocals and instead opted to relax and observe contentedly.

The rumbling lasted a while. Orian began to wonder if the suspense was alluding to anything at all. Suddenly the doors on the far side of the sandy oval burst open to reveal a massive beast with horns. Neither Orian nor Ladis were required to look over at the enormous jumbotron to take in the size of the bull. Even from so far away, they knew the muscular animal was built like a tank.

"Welcome youuuurrrr CHALLENGER!"

Before the matador in a black and red suit and sombrero had been revealed on their side, Orian had already deducted the game that was about to be played. He'd read about it online.

Being up this close, Orian and Ladis witnessed the fine details of the man by peering slightly over the arena's perimeter wall. He was only a few feet below and to the right of them. At the moment, Orian saw the side of his face glowing with sweat. Oddly, the matador did not appear to be nervous at all. It was almost like he had reserved all anxiety to the past, abolishing it the moment he entered the sandy arena. His face was still and robotic. His movements operated in a similar fashion.

Step by step, the man in his glittery outfit approached the center, closing the gap between himself and the bull. In one hand he carried a square length of red fabric, which Orian knew to be properly called a muleta. In the other was a long, thin blade. Orian's heartbeat increased as the bull pawed the soft and wet earth below, signaling its impending charge.

The bull's massive hooves pounded the arena floor, leaving in its wake eruptions of sand and gravel. Now stationed precisely in the middle of the oval, the matador appeared as still as ever. Both arms hung at his side. He showed no concern, even as death barreled toward him. Orian strained to watch. He wanted to scream at the man to turn and run, that he needed to get out of the way. The gap was closing, closing. At once there was a flash of red.

The crowd gasped, only to discover that the matador had not only duped the bull, but also everyone in attendance. A deafening cheer resulted, and both Orian and Ladis joined in the fun.

"Did you see that!"

"Incredible!" Orian agreed.

A loud huff escaped the bull. It was equally as rattled as it was angered. Turning toward sombrero man, the animal shook off its failure. With a new sense of determination, the beast aimed its deadly horns at him. It would not be denied.

The scenario was the same as it had been before. Mr. Matador lay in wait for the tumbling aura of monstrous proportions. He appeared as calm as he had upon entry. Surely, the matador could not successfully fool the single ton tank of muscle targeting his sternum another time. But he did.

Again and again, the bull was fleeced.

"Wow!" was the collective response. The entire Coliseum had erupted in constant applause. They were rooting for the matador, but Orian wasn't sure if they knew what was to come. Hanging at the sombrero man's side was that deadly blade, made for killing beasts. Orian had the feeling he wouldn't play with his food for much longer.

He was right.

Swiftly the bull barreled at the black and red man in an effort that it may have believed to be its last, so it didn't hold back. The man rose his blade once the beast was no more than twenty feet away. Shined flawlessly, the sword glimmered, even in the dull light of a gloomy evening. He would thrust it through the bull's shoulder and into its heart to end the event abruptly.

But the man's demeanor shifted suddenly. There came a wild gasp of horror from the crowd, as if they were just as loath to witness the death of the animal as they would be to man. They were fortunate to experience neither occurrence.

Just as the bull was coaxed into the final move, known as the Estocada, the matador froze with his blade stuck in the air, allowing the bull to escape the clutches of death that it wished to impose on its opponent.

Orian watched the man in the center of the arena closely. Bizarre was a descriptor that only scratched the surface. The sense of ease that encapsulated the man had apparently fled him. His robotic movements ceased, and at once, he fell on his backside.

Confusion spread through the crowd, quelling cheers and replacing them with worried whisperings.

With an awful terror, the matador's eyes darted around the arena, as if he were just now understanding the parameters of his circumstance. A high-pitched scream derived from the deepest reaches of his soul filled the sky, alerting everyone on site that something was clearly wrong. The possibility occurred to Orian that something had been wrong all along.

All eyes had been fixed firmly on the man, to the extent that the bull had become invisible. However, as the beast pawed once more at the sandy surface, the Coliseum's supports were burdened with the added weight of a thousand sinking stomachs.

Shouts of "Run!", "Look out!", and "Oh my God!" were directed at the arena. The matador's eyes grew wide once he registered the two horns that were hunting him down. It looked as though his death was imminent, but in a fortuitous leap, he escaped the bull's path.

No longer was he taking his chances. He threw his sombrero off to the side. For whatever reason, the hat had attracted the bull's attention as it promptly stomped on the article of clothing as a precursor to its intentions.

From the center of the arena, the matador twirled in a panic until he made direct eye contact with Orian, chilling his internals. Orian could see more than a struggle for life in the matador, some internal war, but he could not infer the other battle he was fighting.

The poor soul in black and red broke into an arm-flailing sprint, bee-lining at Orian and Ladis.

"Help!" he shrieked, his dark brows raised nearly to the sweaty mussed hair atop his head.

"What's he doing?" Ladis panicked. He latched onto Orian's arm. "Come, come we should go before he brings that thing *our* way!"

Orian shook off his hand. "No, wait. I think he wants us to pull him out."

"Pull him out! You must be insane."

"Ladis, we have to save–"

His breath was stolen as the bull started on the matador's trail. Even with his head-start, the man might not make it in time.

Still, Orian thought, *we have to try.*

"Please! Please help!" pled the man.

"Ladis," Orian jabbed at his shoulder. "Lower your arms over the wall with me."

Although a fierce protest was evident within him, Ladis slowly bobbed his head. He must've understood that if he were to switch places, he'd also want someone to save him.

The voice that came through the speakers this time was that of another man, and his purpose was surely not to entertain. "Do not make any attempt to rescue this man. I repeat, do NOT pull him to safety!"

At this, Ladis backed off again. "Orian, we have to do what they say. You know the rules."

"*Fuck* the rules, Ladis. Someone's *life* is at stake!"

"He chose to enter that arena."

Orian reached over the edge on his own. "Maybe he didn't."

Now it appeared that the matador had a fighting chance at survival. In his struggle for life, he had found an extra gear and ran harder. But the bull was closing the gap.

"Help, please God. Help me!" he yelled as he was ten yards away.

"Reach for my hand! Jump!"

The matador scrambled closer, and he leapt. On his first attempt, he came up short. But with a second leap, he caught Orian's hands. Orian strained to support the struggling man's weight, but he refused to give up with a life hanging literally before him.

The sound of the beast's rumbling hooves came closer.

"Pull me up, please!"

"Orian," came Ladis's scrambling voice from behind. "Soldiers are on their way! You have to let him go!"

I can't. I won't. Orian groaned as he placed all his effort in hauling the man over the edge. But he didn't have the strength. As he geared up to offer one final effort, the most horrible sound, the most awful thud pierced not only the man's soul, but Orian's as well.

Orian looked into the matador's eyes, welling with only a tear in each as his own vision began to blur. The sight was too awful, like nothing Orian had ever seen. Red oozed out of the man's sternum as the bull pinned his body to the wall with a single horn through his heart.

No, no. Oh my God. Orian desired to speak, to comfort the man in what would no doubt be his final moments. All that escaped him was a pathetic crack in his throat. Orian knew that soldiers were on their way, that the consequences for disobedience could be dire. He didn't care. He didn't give one single flying fuck. A man was dying.

A peep came, and a deference to his own mortality seemed to take over. Once more Orian looked into his eyes. At once, desperate words formed at the dying man's trembling lips.

"Th-th-they wanted, th-they took m-m-my head."

Brow furrowed, Orian attempted to understand him. What was he trying to say? He shook his head so that he might communicate his confusion. Who were *they*? How did *they* get his head? What did he mean? There wasn't enough time to inquire.

Before the man's life left him, he said two words that would forever shake the foundation of Orian's being.

"Yours, too."

At that, the man's eyes rolled back, his body fell hard to the ground as the bull retreated slightly. The beast considered the corpse with contempt and then plodded around the arena in apparent self-satisfaction.

Orian had gone deaf, his stare vacant. It was a moment from which he might never recover. Instantly he knew this.

Ladis was still at Orian's side. By the time they met one another's gaze, they were strangers to each other. Ladis paused, as if to assess the immediate damage done to his dearest friend. He warned, "Orian, what're you going to do?"

His question was in reference to the soldiers who were advancing on their position. There was no physical escape. A flurry of worst-case scenarios bombarded Orian's brain, but he was able to focus. Drowning out the noise and conjuring solutions was his greatest asset. So he shut his eyes.

The soldiers would be on him at any moment. His disobedience could have him transferred off of 102, at the very least. The same fate that had taken Zak could take him.

He decided not to wonder about any adverse possibilities. He thought of fighting his way out of the situation, but he shut that down instantly. He was outmatched in both number and size.

Think, Orian. Suddenly, he sighed, understanding that this could be his last moment with Ladis. With the same resignation shown by the man whose life was in the balance moments ago, Orian accepted his ill fate. He placed his hands in the pockets of his jacket, where he felt two small and soft objects. A light flicked on in his head.

IV

"I was following instructions," Orian explained, holding up two neon green pieces of foam. He rolled them between his index finger and thumb to further indicate the effectiveness of the noise-cancelling objects. "You see? I put them in tightly, you know. Safety first."

Orian let his hands fall to his side. Before entering the Coliseum, a nice lady had insisted that he and Ladis snag some hearing protection to ward off loud noises that might occur. Of course, Orian took the gifts gratefully and then stuffed them in his pockets. He didn't think they'd ever come in handy. Suddenly, the desperate tiny objects were his only way out.

Standing like stone walls before them, two guards must've offered expressions full of skepticism. Orian couldn't tell, however, because the sun had fallen. In its disappearance, the sky issued a malignant darkness to reflect the macabre event from which they had just departed. A pair of LEDs hanging from a column on the outer wall of the Coliseum shone directly at the backs of the soldiers, casting shadows across their faces. Orian and Ladis had been pulled aside to be questioned, and they both looked up to the silhouettes before them. Although Orian held little confidence that they could escape the situation, he knew an outward appearance of poise was imperative.

"When my friend Ladis here informed me that we were prohibited from offering assistance to the man in the arena, I didn't hear a peep."

"Mhmm," Ladis chimed in weakly.

The soldier who spoke had a deep, powerful, and thrumming voice. His accusation was fierce. "Messages were displayed clearly across the video board. You ignored them."

"I had my sights set on the arena and the frightening, large bull," Orian spoke plainly. He found that the more you attempted to explain yourself, the more evident the lie became. In this case, he was dancing carefully around the lies. "The video board was behind us."

Glancing between themselves, the men in gray-white armored uniforms outwardly pondered the validity of Orian's story. They weren't sold.

"Hand me the plugs."

Orian did, and the man on the left squeezed them, rolled them between his fingers as Orian had, and even put them in his own ears.

"Speak," the officer demanded.

Caught off guard, Orian frowned.

"Speak!" the other said.

"Uh–yeah. Sir, what are you doing?"

No response.

Orian felt Ladis's unease, and he feared it wouldn't be long before the jig was up.

"Did I tell you to stop speaking?"

Orian huffed. "You must love the sound of my voice."

Ladis nearly yelped at the testy quip. Orian knew compliance was his best bet at escaping the soldiers, but it just wasn't in his DNA to bow down to authority, no matter the circumstance. He also knew that his story was phantastic at best, so if he were to go down, he would go down swinging.

To their fortune, the soldier seemed unfazed as he removed the plugs from his ears. He held them in a fist at his side.

"Explain to me why I had no trouble hearing every word you said."

Any remaining optimism had been wiped clean from Orian's face. They were implying either that the hearing protection was suddenly faulty, or that they had never blocked out *all* noises in the first place. Orian gulped.

The soldier pressed him. "You want to know what I think? I think you're lying to me."

Orian's silence was practically his admission of guilt. A flurry of emotions racked his brain. Many times he had crossed the line in class, accessing the Internet, just barely escaping the accusations and punishments of Professor Yjn. He knew that eventually his luck might run out, but every close call had accumulated to produce a solid guise of immortality. Sometimes, Orian felt untouchable. How foolish he was to ignore the reality that it could all come crashing down in merely a day.

The darkness seemed to penetrate his soul, but Orian did not panic. Instead, he looked past the soldiers before him, up at the star-filled globe above. *Stars are gorgeous*, Orian thought peacefully.

A firm grip was established on Orian's arm, Ladis's too. He wasn't sure where the soldier would take him, and he didn't care. But Orian would surely exonerate his innocent roommate before he found out. As he prepared to spill all truths, a voice shouted from behind them. A young woman.

"Hey! Can you hear me now?"

Orian turned. Curly brunette hair bounced as the girl approached. She wasn't alone, either. The two faces passed through bright beams and were easily recognizable to Orian as Dawn and her roommate Trixie. Their sudden appearance must have flustered the soldiers equally as much as Orian.

The tension in the soldiers' grips released. All four men stood still as they anticipated Dawn's next words.

She slowed her jog, looking clearly upset as she stood face-to-face with Orian. "I spent the entire event clamoring for your attention. We were–what would you say, Trixie–ten rows behind these hooligans? And they didn't have the decency to look us in the eye. You could have waved, said hi, *something*. What chopped liver we are, huh?"

"Uh…" Orian and Ladis's disquiet had been replaced by respective confusion and red-faced embarrassment.

Dawn wasn't eager to spell it out for them, but her subtle wink clued Orian in on her intentions.

"Listen, ladies–" a soldier began.

"If you shove those ear plugs any farther into that canal," Dawn interjected, offering the solider not even a glance, "they're gonna get stuck and morph into your already-foamy brain."

Orian swung his gaze subtly back at the soldiers who exchanged stone-cold exasperation. They objected as Dawn and Trixie pulled the two young men toward them.

"Now, wait," one of them said.

"Ms. Yjn is not going to happy with you two when she hears about this."

Dawn and Trixie pulled them further along, and the Ardosian guards submitted to their confusion and remained still. It was as if the officers purported that the punishment administered by the young, fetching ladies would be far worse than anything they had in mind. Additionally, Dawn's clear frustration with Orian's deafness seemed to corroborate his story.

In a fortuitous change of events, Orian and Ladis had been freed. Apparently, enough chaos had been spurred by the awful event that the soldiers had much more pressing matters to deal with. Dawn tugged Orian along, Trixie doing the same with Ladis, until the guards were out of sight far behind them.

Finally, when Orian was sure nobody was near them, he whispered to Dawn. "Thank you."

They had made it to the other side of the Coliseum and were approaching a winding path that would lead all the way back to the Tower, and more specifically, floor 102. Orian was unable to process this reality. He'd already accepted his fate of despair. Yet, just like that, he was free, and the open path seemed to hint at it. He'd escaped the formidable clutches of Ardosia's finest, albeit with a bit of assistance. Once again, his luck was on full display.

Dawn let go of Orian's arm, though she was reluctant to do so. Maybe she feared the soldiers might find them again. "You're trouble."

"You can say that again," Ladis added.

Orian waived their negativity. "I didn't see you behind us, in the Coliseum, I mean."

"That's because we were on the other side of the 'Seum," Trixie said with a positive inflection of sass.

"Yep," Dawn confirmed.

Orian's brow furrowed. Suddenly nothing made sense. If they had been on the other end of the stadium, how could they have known about Orian's predicament? Countless more conundrums floated through his head, but all he could muster was, "How?"

"Please," Trixie rolled her eyes. "Everyone in the 'Seum was locked in on the stupid boy reaching over the wall. Not just us."

"When I saw you violating direct orders–as I do most every other day–I knew you'd weave yourself into an inescapable web of trouble. You. Are. Trouble."

"So why'd you save us?"

Ladis shot a weak glare in Orian's direction, prompting him to correct the statement.

"Me," Orian said. "Why'd you save me?"

Dawn shrugged, and though Orian continued to pester her, she offered a very weak explanation. "Because."

The concrete path was wide enough for the four of them to walk side-by-side as it bent near the water's edge. Still in the early evening, the lake surrounding Ardosia began to reflect stars overhead. Once they had made it halfway across the island, the moon peaked subtly through the gray clouds, illuminating the night. The rain had ceased earlier, favorably shifting the outdoor environment seemingly for Orian's pleasure. He would soak in the last outdoor minutes that the Schedule allowed before it required his return to floor 102.

Arranged in a line with Dawn and Trixie on the outside, while Ladis and Orian took up the inside, the quartet moved ponderously along the path. There was not a sound to break the night until a sharp cry emanated from Dawn.

"What's the matter?" Ladis was quick to offer aid.

"Look! There!" Dawn pointed at the glossy surface, drawing all eyes tentatively toward the lake.

Orian squinted. All that could be seen or heard was the lapping water as it inched ever-so-slowly toward him. He knew the waves would not be strong enough on a calm night to reach them. So what had Dawn seen?

"There it is again!"

Each of them followed Dawn's finger as it accused the shallow depths once more. A sliver of gray broke the surface before returning to its reclusive home where the light could not reach. Orian's shoulders slumped.

"It's just a dolphin," he said.

"Since when have dolphins lived in Ardosia's Lake?" Dawn wondered aloud.

"You haven't seen them?" Surprise filled Ladis's voice.

Orian was equally perplexed. "They break the surface *all* the time."

"I'll be fair with her," Trixie offered. "The dolphins are new. Last week, I think. Must have come with the Wall. Y'all been acting like they were here forever."

A week is basically the same as forever on this island, Orian reflected.

"Exactly. I can't remember the last time the Schedule sent me outside. No way I could have seen them until now." Dawn added, "I don't spend all my time looking out windows."

The jab was overshadowed by Trixie's postulation. "Pretty sure those things were trained to eat people on the off chance that some suicidal fool feels compelled to climb over that Wall. Should keep intruders out."

No skeptic replies were presented, though their thoughts were filled with questioning. Orian understood the importance of self-understanding. Even he could admit that he believed in a few outlandish conspiracies, in part due to the considerable time he'd allotted to the Internet. That place was full of as much wicked information as there was useful knowledge. But to believe that dolphins could somehow have been uncharacteristically altered with the instilled craving for human flesh … it was an ambitious claim. *Should keep intruders out.* If the prior assumption were true, it would certainly pose a theory. *Or maybe they're meant to keep* us *in.*

Like an ever-looming shadow of incomparable size, the Tower blotted out the sky as the four students returned to the lakeside building. This skyscraper was the home of all student learning on Ardosia. Orian knew there were other floors as well, dedicated to purposes unknown to him. He was determined to discover the hidden secrets of the Tower someday.

They were just in time, in spite of the hold-up with the two soldiers after the event. As the Schedule had dictated, they would take the elevator up to 102 and rest for the night. Orian and Ladis dropped the women off at their door, like the gentlemanly scholars they were.

Dawn and Trixie rested their backs on either side of the doorway, hesitant to gift the boys with their eyes. First to speak was Orian, who directed his solemn tone toward the both of them. "Thanks again. I mean it."

"You'll have to return the favor whenever I need saving." Dawn's eyes glinted in the shallow hallway lights. Orian could admit that Ladis had a point. Dawn was cute.

Before he said goodnight, Orian uttered something that he typically would have kept to himself. You never knew who was listening, but he felt the need to say it anyway. "You know I'm going to get out of here someday," he said. "I'll go past the Wall, and I'll pick both of you ladies the prettiest wildflowers you've ever seen."

At that, Dawn chuckled, fixing her blue eyes upon him. "*Benediximus et deus benedicat.*"

Orian looked to Ladis, hoping he could explain. He was just as lost.

"Huh?" Orian scratched his head.

"It means 'Good luck and God bless' in Latin."

Pondering that for a moment, Orian liked how it sounded, repeating the words in his head. *Benediximus et deus benedicat.* He smiled. "Goodnight, ladies."

Stricken with their presence, Ladis was loath to leave. Orian could tell by the way his gaze had been rigidly affixed to the floor. Ever the prude, following rules to the T, brown- nosing when necessary, the short man with shoulder-length hair seemed to contradict himself in this moment, like his innermost desires rendered him immobile. If only Ladis were presented with more time, more time to spend with Dawn specifically, he'd willfully abandon the rules and hold tight in proximity.

Their room was calling. Orian tugged at Ladis's shirt, pulling him away from the girls.

"Bye!" Trixie giggled as she ushered her roommate through the door.

At the far end of the hall was Orian's living quarters. His roommate stalled at the door, apparently possessed by the script of a cheesy film, ready to turn around and call for Dawn's heart in a romantic display of his pure affection. Orian pressed the flat of his hand up against Ladis's back, goading him all the way to his bed in direct denial of his lover-boy mood.

Ladis fell onto the mattress with a hearty sigh. "Man, she's beautiful." Orian remained mute as he undid the covers to his own bed. Ladis didn't mind talking to himself. "I almost wish she wasn't on our floor. It's like the story of Adam and Eve, but not quite. *Dawn* is my forbidden fruit."

Orian winced to himself at Ladis's analogy.

"She likes you, though, dude."

The words swept through Orian's ears like the space between them had been concave and hollow, incapable of retaining anything. He was focused on his bed, though Orian knew he wouldn't get a lick of sleep.

"Hey," Ladis ventured. "You listening?"

"Hm?"

"Dawn. I'm telling you, man. She's into you." It sounded like something painfully hard to admit. "And the way she said that line? *Benedictus* ... uh, whatever it was. That was hot."

Benediximus et deus benedicat.

"Nah," Orian said as he fell into his bed. "All yours, partner."

"You think she'd say yes? To me? Gosh, I wonder what it would be like to hold her. I wouldn't even try to kiss her. Unless she tried to kiss me first, of course. Then I'd let her, but I'd never make the first move. First moves are an archaic gesture, anyway. Rude, really."

"Go to bed, Ladis. Maybe she'll find you in your dreams."

That thought hadn't yet occurred to Ladis, and an optimistic squeak left him as he turned sharply onto his side and inserted his head into a pile of cotton.

Orian turned to the window to view a couple specks of light in the big dark sky. He found it amusing that his roommate at all times held a stoic demeanor, solid conviction, and a maturity beyond his years. However, his nature could be fickle when it came to girls, transforming him into a hopeless romantic schoolboy. It was this innocence that Orian admired. Ladis was his best friend, and he hoped they never parted. Lured into slumber by aspirations of lucid dreams, Ladis emitted a trumpeting snore within minutes.

Meanwhile, Orian found himself facing the blank ceiling, kept awake not by Ladis's occasional boom that contradicted his size, but rather by noises of the mind that would be repressed only in their yield to time. He fell in and out of hallucinations, his passage into the world of dreams prohibited. In the past couple of days, Orian had drawn near the line of "too close to call" far too many times. First, with Zak, where the consequences of Orian's own actions were absorbed by another student–an innocent student–resulting in his transfer off floor 102. His steely eyes would haunt Orian. Then today, acting in direct violation of orders … what was he thinking? The voice *Do not make any attempt to rescue this man* reverberated ceaselessly through Orian's brain, giving way only to the nightmarish, *They took my head* and *Yours, too*, which had been uttered by the dying man in his last breaths.

As ghoulish as the sight may have been, Orian's perspective shifted immediately from negative to positive upon its recollection. *I know exactly what I was thinking. Another man, a human–innocent or not–was on the brink of death. He deserved to be saved.* He scolded himself for questioning objective right from wrong. Orian understood that orders from Ardosia's elite did not dictate morality, though it would be suicidal to mention this belief to anyone but himself. No matter the pushback from the powers that be, Orian would follow that little voice in his head, also known as a conscience. His conscience, without any hesitation in that fateful moment, screamed that it was his duty to provide a helpless matador with a fighting chance at survival.

Yet a surfeit of luck had been depleted from Orian's stockpile already, and he wasn't a cat with nine lives. Even if he was, there would be few lives left. Future actions would warrant in-depth examination on his part if he wanted to stay on 102. The truth was such that Orian desired to be anywhere but the island of Ardosia. But since he was stuck here for the time being, he'd prefer to remain with his best friend and roommate.

Restlessly, Orian turned his body on his side, then the other side, shifting to his back, then stomach. *Agh! Curse the damned voices.* They instilled fear in him, something Orian was not accustomed to. A combination of courage and naïve tendencies prohibited fear from entering Orian's soul. To be ridden only with fear made one a coward. To have none made him a fool. It was this foreign emotion that, lying in bed, enacted a response known as *Fight or Flight.*

Noiselessly, Orian rose from his bed. The small black circle was planted in the ceiling corner like The Great Eye.

Orian rounded his mattress, avoiding an upward glance. Intuition informed him that intentions could be most effectively revealed through his eyes, so he ought to keep them on the floor.

The bathroom door closed quietly as he secluded himself within one of the few areas Orian knew to be private–at least he hoped. For a moment, he examined his reflection in the mirror, noting a somewhat pale complexion. Obviously, his skin would never look as ghostly as many of the white students from 102. Even Ladis, whose skin contained a hue of tan and brown that warded off all acne, was not as dark as Orian. It did not bother him that he looked different from most. In fact, Orian seldom interacted with this knowledge, for it was irrelevant to him. Offering the man in the mirror one final nod, Orian swept a hand across his fuzzy, buzz-cut temple, then itched the white fabric on his chest, before taking a seat on the john.

From his pajama pants pocket, Orian fished out a small tablet that he had surreptitiously snuck past The Great Eye in his ceiling. Electronics were to be shut down and stowed away during the night, but Orian had made an exception. After all, his natural instinct had told him to *Fight.*

Fight, to Orian, did not imply violence. It simply demanded action. He had to move, as if to exorcise the demonic fear that might possess him, should he allow it to dwell within his soul any longer.

Orian tapped on his screen casually. With the stealth of the tech ninja that he was, Orian breached the silly firewalls of their building like a mouse scurrying beneath a bedroom door. Nobody would ever know that he had snuck into Ardosia's technological system, which he–quite frankly–regarded as outdated and overly simplistic. What Orian had learned from the Internet expanded his technical proficiencies in the grandest way. No class of Yjn's could have–or would have–ever taught him the many secrets that were concealed behind rudimentary screens of all sizes and varieties.

Outside the bathroom door, there was a faint click. In just eight seconds, Orian had achieved success.

The next part was the easiest. Orian would bolt out the bathroom without a sound and move through the main door. A poltergeist is how he would appear to the black circle in the ceiling. Should someone behind The Great Eye wish to check up on Orian, for the status of his well-being of course, they wouldn't think twice about the lump of blankets on his bed that they would assume to be his resting body. Over the years, Orian had perfected his craft of deception, so he knew how to arrange his sheets in *just* the right way. He had done all this in the split second that he had escaped his bed.

The main door led him to the hallway, where there were fortunately no guards strolling the long, tight space. Surely, Orian had enough luck stored in the tank to sneak by tonight.

He looked left, then right, darkness enshrouding the space. Even the bright orange door behind him reflected the faintest glow in the night. A magnetism toward the unknown was Orian's *Fight* response. He was drawn to the stairs tonight rather than the elevator, so he went left. Usually, when Orian snuck out of his room in the middle of the night, his tendencies were benign–walking the hallway, peeking into the classroom, and that was it. Nothing else, outside of a storage closet near the staircase, could be found on 102 anyway. Tonight was different.

Orian surmised that he had an addiction to walking a tight rope. Adrenaline ran through his veins and filled him with an energy that the Schedule simply could not. Although he had received a considerable amount of time on that proverbial rope in the past two days, and he knew his actions required more caution going forward, like many of Earth's temptations, you want more when you're given more.

With the simplicity of flipping a switch, Orian hacked and eased past the locked steel door guarding the stair case. It latched shut behind him. In the space, with no windows to let in moonlight, a red glare seemed to highlight the area. It gave the impression that something sinister was lurking. Orian noticed the glare coming from a screen above the steel frame, with large red numbers reading: 102.

Suddenly, Orian was free. Although still within the walls of the Tower, Orian felt an exhilaration comparable to the times when he was allowed outdoors. He recalled that there were 150 floors total, having ridden the elevator and examining the buttons on multiple occasions. The only question now was *Which floor should I choose?*

His *Fight* magnetism guided him down, not up. So Orian descended a flight of stairs, then another. Each floor contained the same red glow, emanating from a screen above a steel door frame not unlike the one on 102. In fact, every floor was identical. Down, down, it all felt the same, but he felt guided down nevertheless. It was all identical until 31, where Orian's heart pounded with a newfound intensity, not simply from the superfluous descent. This was where he was meant to be, the unknown to which he had been led.

There was nothing to suggest that 31 was different than other floors. The door was the same, and the numbers glowed the same. But Orian had a hunch, and his gut he trusted more than most people. Guarded by a more intricate technological system, it took Orian nearly sixty seconds to hack past the lock, instead of the mere eight-to-ten usually required. This confirmed Orian's suspicions.

As he shouldered past the entrance, Orian marveled at 31. Immediately upon entry, the floor held a unique quality to which Orian was heavily attracted. For one, the space was wide open–a massive cubicle room extending from one end of the building to the other with windows all around. At the far end of the floor is where Orian's eyes were naturally ordered. There were large pieces of equipment which Orian had only read about on the Internet: industrial-quality cameras the size of bazookas, fluffy boom microphones that hung from skinny black rods, massive monitors behind them, and a green screen gathered on the opposite wall. Spectral light flowed inside, illuminating the technological galleria with a hint of gray.

Awestruck, Orian floated past inconsequential collections of chairs and tables and wires running along the floor, until he found himself in the middle of the square area, observing one of the cameras up close. He then walked around the desk, up to the green screen, and rubbed a finger down it, retreating instantly with childlike infatuation. Something about the area was awfully familiar to Orian, but he couldn't place it in his memory. He thought some more until it came to him.

Ah, yes, he remembered. The nameless woman from the screen in class appeared here every morning with the daily address, issuing announcements and a couple inspirational quotes before introducing President Vardus.

Until now, Orian hadn't realized that the images behind the news woman had been fake all along. Each morning, images of the sky, the iconic buildings of Ardosia, as well as plants and trees and countless other images filled the background. This whole time, they had never been real. For twenty years now, Orian had been fooled by the smallest detail. That's what green screens were for: the production of fake images that looked authentic.

It begged the question: If the images in the background could be found right outside, all throughout Ardosia's limits, what was the purpose of reproducing them artificially indoors?

A gutting pang jolted Orian out of his blissful and inquisitive trance. He had felt the presence of another before the door had eased open. Call it luck or instinct, something told him to hide–*now*. A production desk would manage for cover, and he scrunched his body behind it as the steel door to 31 creaked open.

Nothing stirred for a weighted moment, until a heavy pair of boots thudded methodically toward him.

Tha-thump, tha-thump.

Scratch that–*two* pairs of boots. Orian did everything humanly possible to hush the sounds of his drumming heart and erratic breathing. For the third time in two days, he'd pitted himself up against a wall with no escape–this time literally.

Closed-eye prayer might save him, but Orian struggled to hear his own internal voice over the curious whispers of the two men who had entered.

"You seeing ghosts now, *A*?" one spoke to the other.

Orian presumed they were guards who must have stopped on the other side of the door, probably scouring the area carefully with just their eyes for now, but not too carefully, in case there really *were* ghosts on 31.

The one named *A* didn't say a word, exacting internal curses from Orian. He took the guard's silence as an indication of his position having been revealed. But when A said, "Must be seeing things. Let's go," Orian nearly leaped with joy. Of course, he did no such thing, imitating the immobility of a rock as he bent low and waited for the guards to depart.

An exhale did not escape Orian until the men were clear on the far end of the floor, and even this he kept quiet. Another close call, too close for comfort. Orian made an agreement with himself then that he would steer clear of that imaginary tight rope he'd been walking, at least for a few days. This time, he'd pursue that goal with unassailable resolve–or so he thought. Apparently, fate had other plans.

Still hunched behind the desk, a growl like that of a caged and upset lion rumbled in Orian's stomach. He winced, for the sound had surely given him up. Reflecting on dinner, Orian projected outward waves of anger: *Spinach and tomato salad, if I make it out of this alive, or if I don't, you're never again touching my intestines.*

Once more the two guards approached, thin flashlight beams–likely mounted beneath crossbows–working the room like the most dangerous game of laser tag in history. Orian had never played laser tag before, only read about it, so he would have no prior experience on which to rely. Instinct would again have to guide him.

Orian recognized the one called *A*'s voice advancing on him with every second. "Wherever you are, come out now. You will not be hurt."

"We'll get you back where you belong, ghostie," the other voice shook.

Tha-thump, tha-thump.

Orian did not give up his position. Instead, he sought endlessly for a way out, for a solution to his predicament. A plan of action would need to be enacted within seconds. He looked around the dark space for anything to help him. It was likely he'd need a makeshift weapon of his own. The cameras were the first objects to stick out to him. *Too heavy and awkward.* Next were the inactive monitors on the desk behind which he hid. Orian could snag one and use it as a projectile, but he wasn't sure of its efficacy.

A: "This is your last chance. We will use deadly force if we must."

"We do come in peace," the other said before whispering to his comrade, "I'm covering our asses."

A didn't acknowledge him. A few more steps, and they'd find Orian huddled in the fetal position, looking like a sad and lost puppy.

That was *not* how he was going down. *Think, you lost imbecile. Get yourself out of this one, too.* Finally, Orian's eye caught the boom microphone a few paces away. The gray bit of fluff would be useless, but the pole from which it hung might be his only mode of defense. Although slightly awkward and desperate, he might be able to use it as a stick. There was no more time for thought, only action.

In a flash, Orian lunged for the boom.

One guard, who must have been trigger-happy, fired an arrow that whizzed through the air nowhere close to Orian. Now only a single guard would have to be disarmed, for it would take too long for the other to re-rack his bow.

"Hey!" *A* shouted.

Orian was given too many seconds to react. As he observed the spry white face looking down the sights of a crossbow that threatened Orian, he saw not an ounce of fear, but rather a reluctance to pull the trigger. Orian made *A* pay for his indecision, bringing the boom down on him. The pole was flimsy. Either that, or *A*'s body was built like a brick wall, for the boom snapped in half over his back. He fell over nonetheless.

Despite the failure of Orian's weapon, the boom had provided him with the distraction he needed to skirt the guards, slip through the night, and zigzag toward 31's only exit.

With *A* down and his friend too startled to act properly, Orian would create separation between them.

Nearly tripping over wires and chairs, Orian rushed as fast as his legs would carry him. Halfway across the floor, he felt the whizz of another arrow flying beside him. This one had posed a much more promising threat than the one before.

"Get back here!"

Orian fled through the door as a final arrow struck the wall. The close encounter with death was deflected by Orian's continued luck.

He flew up the stairs, leaving the guards in the dust. Confidence could be killer, and Orian knew this. Not once did he convince himself of the success of his escape until he was sure of his safety. His feet pounded the stairs. He inferred that, by now, *A* would have radioed for backup. This would give Orian a couple of minutes maximum to reach 102.

Scrambling voices called from below. "Stop! We know who you are!"

Orian had to assume that the guards were fibbing, that they might be hoping to instill defeat in him. It only propelled him further and faster in his ascent. Orian produced his tablet, hacked past 102's door in four seconds–a new record–zipping through the hallway until his room number shone like the hopeful northern star to him. Another quick hack to unlock his door. Then he slipped into the bathroom to assume the position last observed by the black circle in the ceiling corner.

There, Orian waited. And he waited some more. His heart pounded with as much adrenaline as it had during his attempted rescue of the matador. It pumped with more speed and, admittedly, more passion than he'd ever felt. Was he invincible? Of course not.

Orian sat humbly on the john with dreadful anticipation for the moment that two angered guards would rap large fists on his front door. If they found him, they surely wouldn't offer the same grace they had before.

But their calls for one disobedient student never came.

In silence, Orian waited for an hour before finally exiting the bathroom. He slid cautiously into his bed, as though one more careless mistake, no matter how small, would be his last. The comforter was pulled over his chest, though no rest would be achieved in the few hours Orian had to spare before daylight.

A's face popped in Orian's memory. The soldier had held a stone-cold expression while aiming a deadly weapon at Orian's chest. With the flick of his index finger, he could have easily taken a life. But he hadn't.

Orian's stomach growled again, in unison with Ladis's nearby snore. Together, the noises produced an awful symphony, which for no known reason, reminded Orian once more of the dying matador.

- *They took my head.* Followed by: *Yours, too.*

Chills took Orian's spine, paralyzing him. He wondered at the horrible fate of the poor man and the fate of life in general. Orian subscribed to the idea that any good afforded to humans–men and women alike–was rarely a reflection of justice. In other words, one could not *earn* or *capture* good deeds from the world. Sometimes, fortune was a matter of, well, just that. In that same stroke, circumstances many might consider vile or wicked were also not to be perceived as the fulfillment of justice in the universe. Such circumstances are no more deserved than good fortune, although many times the recipients of atrocity are worthy of their punishment.

Still, the tip of a bull horn slicing a man in half seemed excessive. No matter the harm the man in the arena may have done in his brief crack at life, Orian believed his macabre death could not have been warranted. He might even have considered the matador innocent–as innocent as any man could be, at least.

Ladis snored, but it wasn't bothersome.

Before exhaustion sapped Orian's adrenaline, he speculated finally as to the fate that might befall the man. Would he be spared by God and reach the shining gates of Heaven? Or would he be forsaken to the fires below? Orian would not reach an answer before daylight, as the need for rest flooded his system.

V

Damp, rotten, and old. That's how Diamon–like diamond, but without the concluding *d*–might refer to the Underground. The stone-clay walls gathered moss and dripping water, while the absence of windows repelled all light. Cavernous and extensive, the Underground was an enclosed series of arches that wrapped around in an ovular way, just as the Coliseum did two stories above.

When Diamon was first assigned to his role, he had trouble navigating the Underground without gagging, retching, or vomiting. Scents of hellish decomposition and, well, more decomposition filled the area, retained in the world below by an impermeable layer of steel, then soil above. It took many years of acclimation to adjust. Acclimation, in Diamon's case, referenced the burning of all his mighty nose hairs over time and, as a result, the complete diminution of his sense of smell. Nevertheless, he had acclimated, and that was something to be proud of.

Currently, the heavyset and balding manager of the Underground was caught in a cycle of lift and place. Lift the lantern, move it several feet, place it on the floor. Hobble backward toward the body at the edge of the circle of light, lift, grunt to accommodate the struggle, and place the corpse a few feet further.

"Woof."

After setting the pathetic body with a massive gaping hole through its chest on the cracked and hard ground, Diamon determined himself worthy of a snack break. Chest heaving, he fished in his pocket for one of the two candy bars he stowed there for just such an occasion. His large torso and rounded belly presented difficulties when reaching the candy, but the man in his orange and green vest did prevail. Sweat rolled down his face. He swiped at it with the palm of his hand before unwrapping the bar and dabbling in delicious milk chocolate.

The blank-staring, ground-bound man in black and red did not object to the momentary pause of his transfer. Diamon had been working through this cycle for nearly fifteen minutes now. He was fatigued. The corpse likely understood this.

"You know where you're going, don't you?" he said to the matador in between bites. No response came, a testament to his fear, Diamon assumed. *What a coward.*

On the far end of the Underground is where Diamon was required to haul the body. With only one entrance stationed at the *other* end, this process took Diamon almost an hour from start to finish. But he was grateful. This was his role.

Diamon thought back to the moment when he was assigned manager of the Underground by President Vardus himself. Their conversation was brief, but it was legendary. Standing near the innocuous door right outside the stadium, Vardus, in his usual black garb looking down on Diamon, instructed, *No matter what, this door remains locked at all times. Nobody in. Nobody out.* Diamon had said, *Yes, sir,* but Vardus was so busy he'd already left to attend to other matters. Diamon was entrusted with the Underground, and it was yet another addition to his lifetime resume that confirmed his importance.

Upon the completion of the snack break, another five minutes were spent leaning against a nearby pillar to resurrect any lost energy. Again, the matador did not object.

The cycle of lift and place commenced. Lift the lantern. Lift the body. Such was the routine until the ultimate corner of the Underground arrived another fifteen minutes later.

The body fell to the floor, followed by a hefty sigh. Diamon patted his hairy, sweaty back as an acknowledgment of his effort, lastly dragging the body and setting it next to the collection of bones, maggot-ridden black flesh, and tattered clothing in the corner. All of these had been contained in the wrought-iron cage, where Diamon preferred to spend miniscule time. Even he, with his vanquished fifth sense of smell, felt the need to cover his nose in this horrendous area.

The lantern was assembled on the floor outside the cage, and a swinging door was shut to secure the area. The light within flickered, giving an even more ghostly aura to the Underground. As Diamon locked the swinging door in place, one large square section of the wall inside was sucked upward to let the tiger in. On occasion, he would watch the beautiful animal feast on its newest meal, but today Diamon wasn't interested. As the adolescent tiger enamored itself with cold flesh, Diamon collected the lantern and walked toward the only entrance and exit that was inconveniently placed on the other end. This returning journey would require a second candy bar.

VI

S oft beneath his boots, the floor of the Earth made no sound as he inched closer to his target. Even if his feet had produced the crunching of leaves or snapping of twigs, the mistake would have been masked by the sounds of nature that were abundant at this hour. Birds chirped high in the dense tree cover above as they floated from branch to branch. Somewhere in the distance a woodpecker was scouring old bark for breakfast. Families of cicadas sung their morning songs. All other creatures, predator and prey alike, were either asleep in dens or obscuring themselves in the brush, hiding or waiting for the right time to strike.

Hudson could not have been less concerned with the likes of tigers, jaguars, or panthers. He was focused on his mission, following the tracks left deep in the mud. A buck, one that he estimated to be well into its years by now, would have no idea that Hudson was on its trail. Today he would succeed because his experience and inhuman size made *him* the king of the jungle.

On morning and evening hunts alike, Hudson had all senses finely tuned for the moment. He was like a spirit living existentially in the world, a soul imbibing his surroundings so that he was present in all, and yet invisible. He swept through the brush and in between trees with a stealth that defied his stature.

For just over an hour, or maybe it had been two, Hudson had been following the hoofprints and scat. He sensed the presence of the animal getting closer and closer, as if he could feel its heartbeat magnetically linked with his. The longer he delved into the woods, the stronger the pulse.

Hudson had climbed the steep, tree-rooted hills, descended slopes with grace, and navigated through the natural valleys that had been yet undisturbed by man, all while breaking only the slightest hint of a sweat. Staying in shape through all his years attributed to his success. After all, the more you sweat, the larger the chance that your prey might smell you.

When Hudson finally approached the buck, it was as scenic of a moment as he'd ever seen. The antlered beast had been perched at the top of a slow and steady incline within the forest, where a clearing had allowed one persistent ray of sunshine to break through the tree cover and illuminate the golden brown, muscular body of one of nature's most majestic creations. The animal was beautiful. Perfect though the moment was, Hudson's heart did not skip a beat.

Hidden on the other side of a massive tree trunk, Hudson tacitly slung the bow off his shoulder and nocked one of the three arrows he had brought. He could have elected to use his crossbow, but the weapon functioned too perfectly. Look down the sight, aim, and pull the trigger. The minimal margin of error had taken the thrill out of the hunt for Hudson, hence why he fashioned his old wood bow instead.

Rotating his body around the base of the tree, Hudson assessed the distance and change in elevation between he and his target. As far as takedowns went, this would not be his most difficult, but it would also not be his simplest. He once again admired the size of the animal. Mentally he addressed the potential problems that could arise. Perhaps the skin and muscle guarding the buck's heart would be too thick and act as an impenetrable armor. The potential challenge would have excited Hudson if he was still capable of emotion.

Pulling back on the string, Hudson stood straight, arching his back as he raised the bow and arrow to shoulder height. He pointed the arrow just above his target, accounting for fall. *Breathe in … breathe out.* This was the advice he had been given by his father, and it was the same advice Hudson had passed along to his son. Though neither of them were present any longer, he heard the phrase in this moment nonetheless. *Your world must go dark. There is nothing beyond, nothing before. Breathe in … breathe out.*

Hudson made the outside world disappear, until the calling of the birds went silent and the rustling of the leaves paused. His vision seemed to zoom in on the buck. It stood practically still, sniffing the air as it chewed on

berries. His father's calm voice rang once more in his head.
Fire.

In a swift motion, Hudson released the string. The bow
thrummed, but he heard nothing. Time worked in slow
motion as the arrow floated seamlessly through the air,
over dewy brush, under weighted branch, and past
microscopic flying insects until it thudded directly into the
heart of his prey.

At first, the buck gave no hint of reaction, as though it
had no idea that its life had been hanging in the balance. It
twitched once, turned and ran in the opposite direction.

Hudson calmly released the breath he'd been holding.
Step-by-step he began stalking toward the injured deer.
There was no need to rush. Should the buck escape, it had
been nature's destiny for the animal to survive, and he
need not interfere with destiny.

Soon it had pranced over the brow of a distant hill, its
antlers disappearing a moment later. Hudson stumbled
past the brush, eventually reaching the spot where the
arrow had initially impacted. A large pool of blood
glistened on the mud below as the sun worked through the
clearing above. Hudson examined the life-sustaining
liquid, universal to all living and breathing things. The
animal had lost a significant amount. Now it was up to the
beast's will as to how far it would go before collapsing.
Hudson hoped it would go far.

Upon reaching the hill's apex, he looked down upon the
valley below, and he saw the buck no more than a few
hundred yards ahead. If the tree cover in this specific area
had been denser, he may not have seen the struggling
beast at all and would have resorted to its blood trail
instead.

By the looks of it, the animal didn't have much time left. It would soon fall due to blood loss. Hudson praised the beast internally for its valiant effort. It was an effort equally as great and genuine as any human had ever given in their final moments. But he could not bear to watch the buck falter any longer. It was nature's intent that the he be put out of his misery.

Hudson broke into a jog. Fifty yards separated him and the antlered beast. At this moment, resignation fell upon the animal. Sooner or later, this always struck. Its legs gave out, and it toppled over sideways, giving one last huff as though to concede to its captor.

Slowing his pace, Hudson hung the bow over his shoulder. He approached the animal slowly. Its breathing was heavily labored as the arrow protruded out of it skyward. Up close, the true extent of the buck's beauty was revealed to Hudson. He felt only the smallest tinge of remorse, knowing that God had willed the circle of life into His universe and that this animal was a gift, one for which the large man was beyond grateful.

Hudson bent closer, resting a gentle hand on its large muscular neck. A sudden calm reached the male as the two beings, who were bred of the wild and for the wild, made eye contact. Respect was exchanged between them before Hudson plucked the knife from his pocket. He gave the beast a comforting nod before he slashed its throat and ended its pain. Offering a moment of silence for the majestic creature, Hudson remained solemnly on his knees as blood flowed peacefully into the soil. He stayed there for a minute before rising.

He then removed the pack from his broad shoulders, fishing out a massive tarp. Hudson unfurled it on the jungle floor beside the deceased deer. Firmly he gripped the rack and hauled the limp body onto the center of the tarp. He then placed his bow carefully at the front of the tarp. Hudson heaved a sigh.

Craning his neck in a full circle, he assessed his position. The sun above was obscured by the tree cover, so it would not provide any meaningful direction to Hudson. Regardless, he needed no reference, for the compass internally constructed within him had been honed to perfection after a few decades within the forest. He knew precisely where he was and in which direction to go to find home.

Hudson wrapped a large strap around his left shoulder first and the other strap around his right. Connected to the tarp, these straps gave him leverage to move the animal. He leaned his wide frame forward. Taking one step, he felt the initial weight of the buck, and his enormous legs trembled. But the tarp began to glide over the jungle floor, and as Newton hypothesized, objects in motion tend to stay in motion. Hudson dragged the beast with relative ease from there on out, grunting only as he scaled inclines. Hudson determined that a mile's hike separated him from home, and it would likely exhaust most of his energy. He could have drained most of the buck's blood before the trip to preserve his strength, but he elected conversely to preserve the tender meat within. The meat alone would sustain him for the next few months, if not longer.

As the deer was drug over the damp forest floor, Hudson eventually felt the straps digging into his shoulders. The tattered shirt beneath his jacket was forming a deep rash from his traps to his pectoral muscles. Hudson projected that by the time he hauled the tarp to his homestead, he'd be bleeding. He didn't mind. Pain was constant, so it became easier to ignore in his ripe age. Plus, with every stride and every searing tug against his skin, Hudson's thoughts were less inclined to waver toward bruises much deeper than the surface.

Half the trek down, Hudson was drenched in sweat. He hadn't paid attention to the peaks and valleys of the homeward journey. Complaining when land rose and rejoicing when it fell were primeval actions. Hudson knew that in the long run, changes cancelled out to form a flat balance. They always did.

The stench of the corpse was only beginning to form. Wafted toward Hud's nose, it barely poked at the hairs inside his cavernous nostrils. Though nearly untraceable to him, the acrid rot would float through the jungle and find noses a thousand times more sensitive. It wasn't long before Hud's instincts were brought to fruition.

The large old man paused when he heard the brush to his right rustle. He had been standing no more than ten feet away from whatever was lurking toward him. The animal no doubt believed itself to be hidden, possessing the element of surprise. But Hudson was ready for whatever should come his way, whether it be a spooked jackrabbit or a bloodthirsty assailant.

Standing tall, Hudson undid the straps, letting them fall gracefully at his sides as his eyes swept over a lush growth of knee-high leafy plants before him. Again, the creature shifted through the plants like a shark swiftly bolting through a sea of green. That's when Hudson caught a glimpse of the animal's coat: orange with faint hints of black and white. Tiger. He'd been prepared for such a predator, but he hadn't anticipated that there'd be two.

The tiger at Hudson's front finally catapulted itself from the ground, launching directly at him. With a mighty swipe, Hud came down on the adolescent creature, drawing forth a mixed growl and whimper as its body struck the ground hard. The wild animal backed off and scampered into the brush from which it had come.

However, the tiger that attacked from behind had gone immediately after the carcass, successfully snagging a significant portion of its liver and intestines before Hudson shooed it away. As the two tigers retreated together, they left the human they had victoriously duped with boasting roars. Then they were gone.

Guerilla tactics. Hudson scolded himself for having fallen for the hit-and-run strategy. With time, the jungle had evolved. It was still evolving, every being within continually learning. He should not have overlooked the possibility that animals might work in conjunction with one another. Overconfidence was a large key that could single-handedly pry open the multifaceted box to one's own demise. Someone with his experience should have known better. It was evolution, after all, that had brought thousands of aboriginal species together into one jungled habitat–evolution and nuclear war. The strongest species survived. Many others fell.

Where Hudson now found himself, the effects of radiation had been minimalized. Hills and forested lands hadn't been conquered until after the war. The Old Nation and millions with it fell to nuclear bloodshed. In this massive expanse of jungle, where man's mightiest weapon never touched, Hudson dwelled. He stuck to its reclusive corners, while the rest of what remained of civilization congregated elsewhere, just as they should.

The rising stench of old blood and out-of-use organs did not bother Hudson. He had accustomed himself to all aspects of life in the wild over the past two decades. Still, the smell would attract new and more voracious predators.

Hudson knew he could fend off two, three, or even four tigers. His sheer size demanded respect from wild eyes, which gave him an immediate advantage. Yet he did not want to take his chances, should he find himself circled by many more than that. He would have to hurry home to avoid such an instance.

Now a fair amount of blood had been spilled across the tarp. The hind tiger must have used its claws to rip away at the beast's golden-brown flesh, altering its appearance to that of a pinkish-red. Using his arm, Hudson swiped at the pool of blood until most of it was off the tarp. He did this to avoid creating a trail on the latter half of the journey.

Before Hudson could strap up, the buck had to be re-centered on the tarp. It took a slight pull of the rack, then man and beast were ready.

By the time Hudson returned home, the sun had ventured to the other end of the sky. In a few hours it would set.

The location in which Hudson had chosen to erect his cabin many years ago was ideal. He'd managed to find a spot where the trees parted and bowed in allegiance to the land he now called home. A massive grassy peak dwarfed the small, thousand-square-foot lodge at its back. Hudson thought of the miniature mountain as a place where man meant to drill up, up, and up, but nature's surface had not yielded and instead maintained the pointy drill shape as a reminder to humankind that it had won the battle in this region. To add on to the peak's allure, the trees had been replaced with native flowers of purple, yellow, and blue. Hudson had never picked a single one, and they bloomed in colorful masses all season long.

A few hundred yards to the East, Hudson had discovered a natural spring where the purest water on

Earth could be found. To his knowledge, he was the only one who currently accessed it. Hudson had no neighbors. He had no friends. And family …

He shook the thought. Hudson hadn't been in contact with the outside world since he'd chopped down the trees that now made up the walls of his house. A few gentlemen, whom he considered colleagues at the time, installed the refrigerator and freezer, powered by solar panels they had generously bolted to the roof, in between the sod. Afterward, they said their goodbyes, and that was that. Since then, Hudson had seen nobody, which was alright. In isolation, he'd come to find peace at most hours of the day.

Dropping the tarp next to his fenced-in garden adjacent to the cabin, Hudson rolled out the notches in his neck. He was tired. If the sparse, but shoulder-length hair on his head hadn't gone white, he might have a quick recovery, but Hudson knew he would be sore for the coming days. His youth had vanished. Such was life, and he had accepted it.

Comprised of wooden posts that he had solely driven into the ground, Hudson's fence guarded a tennis-court's length of fruits and vegetables. The fence, at the time of construction, had demanded nearly as much wood as the cabin, built tall with barely any space between the posts, so as to keep out small and large animals alike.

On the opposite side of the house sat a similar enclosure, except only trimmed grass had been contained within the posts, and it was much smaller. Drilled into the external cabin wall there was a hook. This is where Hudson would hang and dress the deer.

Inside, the bow was hung near the door, and the pack previously containing the tarp had fallen to the floor. A knife slid out the block in the kitchen, and Hudson went outside to work on the buck. By now, he was nothing short of an expert when it came to preparing meat.

Nightfall came. Hudson's wrinkled and callused hands were bloody. Everything that could be eaten had been stowed away in the freezer.

Equally famished as he was exhausted, Hudson allowed the latter to prevail. Tomorrow he would eat, but for now he would rest, relishing in the fact that he had made it through the day without ever having to confront the ever-looming morbid thoughts of his wife and two children, who had been killed nearly two decades earlier by his compatriot James Vardus.

VII

Stained-glass windows are magnificent works of art, arranged in patterns that transform the powerful, but mundane sun into something gorgeous and gripping when its light passes through the colorful panes. Radiant beams of scarlet, orange, and yellow shone on Vardus that morning as his socks twiddled atop his desk. He reclined contentedly in his dark leather office chair after having successfully conducted another morning prayer. The President reflected upon the words, *Our Father who reigns above, holy is your name. May your will be done in Ardosia, and lead us not down the unforgiving path of disobedience. Amen.*

He remembered inscribing the words into their routine, finding dull inspiration, of course, in the old religion. As with every morning, the recording occurred in his office for convenience. Vardus was a busy man as the leader of an entire people, and time was precious. Having the ability to perform most all necessities within the comfort of his office saved him that much needed time.

The office was built with simplicity in mind. A bed folded seamlessly out of the wall to Vardus's left. A single large screen adorned the wall facing him, a personal bathroom secluded and hidden by one door was placed in the corner, and there was a double set of doors for those who filtered in and out. Vardus considered himself a creature of few desires. Peace, comfort, and joy were chief among them. Any additional wishes he might have were granted to him in a timely manner, but those were few and far between.

However, on this particular day, President Vardus felt the tempting fuel of desire burning within him upon a wick in his heart. Like a candle, Vardus would allow the fuse to burn for some time before his edges melted. Patience, after all, was a virtue embodied by virtuous men. First, he had business to resolve. He would get what he wanted eventually.

"Sit down, Yjn."

The short woman strolled in, adjusting her glasses as her heels tapped the hard wood. Her hair was tied back in a bun today, and Vardus observed that she had taken extra time in doing her makeup. A thin pair of khakis fell almost to her ankles, while a loose long-sleeve fitted her chest–not loose enough to reveal the dragon tattoo on her back. Yjn dressed to impress.

"Thank you. I'll stand ... if that's alright with you."

"Absolutely." Vardus smiled brightly. "You wished to discuss ..."

"My student. I was wrong about him. The one named Orian, I mean. When you alerted me to the possibility that somebody had been savvy enough to hack past our mainframe and access the Internet, I thought he was the only one capable. I hadn't realized it was my student named Zak all along."

Yjn confessed her misattributions lightly, as if she didn't understand the depths of Vardus's patience. He would not be angry with her. Besides, she was ...

"Wrong."

The teacher's body shook, and her face reddened as a result of shifting into a sliver of scarlet light projected by the stained glass. "Pardon?"

"You're wrong, Yjn. About the boy–both of them, really. I suppose due to a technicality, you were right the first time around, but you were wrong when it mattered." When she didn't say anything, Vardus offered his comfort. "It's alright."

"Please explain."

Taking his feet off the desk, Vardus slid his chair closer so that he might rest his elbows on top and place his hands in steeple formation. "Upon further examination, Zak was of no use to us. Innocent boy, but still useless. We put him with the rest."

"So ..."

"The boy called Orian was the culprit all along, yes. I knew this, and video evidence has been a constant source of corroboration, displayed even further in an ... incident this prior evening. Troublemaker, he is."

A dumbfounded scowl crossed Yjn's face. "It's not–"

"Possible? Sure is."

"But the Internet site was on *Zak's* screen. Not Orian's."

Vardus chuckled. The woman was smart. It was a necessity for all professors on Ardosia to exude a certain level of intelligence, but her oversight beleaguered him. "This boy is capable of much deception."

Yjn retreated within herself, wary that she had failed in her role as a professor. This was obviously not the case. Professor Yjn was one of Ardosia's best. Though this small slip-up was an inconvenience to Vardus, it would warrant no punishment. Her case had been aided by the natural resolution to the incident.

Outside the door, where two soldiers stood guard, there came a knock.

"Come i–"

"Just a minute!" Yjn called, interjecting. She then pierced the leader of Ardosia with her eyes. "Vardus, I'm afraid I don't understand. You insist that Orian, my student, has shown streaks of disobedience for, from what I gather, quite some time. You've known about this, yet no repercussions have been cast his way. Is Ardosia no longer concerned with O-rates? Do we not uphold our own laws?"

At the end of her tirade, Yjn squeaked with a hint of uncertainty. She should have known that Vardus had a plan, that testing his judgment was never wise. Nevertheless, she pressed him. Vardus didn't mind.

"Our O-rates," Vardus said calmly, addressing the term used to reference the levels of peace and good behavior observed in Ardosia's student population–AKA obedience-rates– "are intact. Dropping slightly, but intact. As for the boy, I want to see what he can do. Thus far, he's shown great promise. I believe he'll aid Ardosia in its continued rise if we give him more time to excel. Locking him up or killing him would be such a waste of talent. We're letting his talents flourish, keeping a close eye on his progression. That boy Zak, on the other hand, offered nothing of value outside of a positive attitude and a warm smile. Too obedient, if anything."

"Why hadn't you told me if you knew Orian to be guilty the whole time?"

Rising, Vardus slid into a pair of soft cotton slides near his desk. He stretched, took a few breaths, all while Yjn stood her ground. He moved behind her, placed his hands on her shoulders. She tensed slightly, but he meant her no harm.

Sensually Vardus spoke into her ear. "I believe you to be a bird of excellent color and potential, Yjn. Should a mother bird teach her chicks to fly by hoisting them on her back? Of course not. You are my wonderful bird, but you must learn to fly on your own."

At this, she relaxed. Yjn adjusted her glasses once more. "Yes, sir."

Releasing his grip on Yjn's shoulder, Vardus ambled to the foot of his bed, where an elaborate collection of synthetic green leaves were planted into Earth-like carpet cylinders to simulate trees. These were contained by massive sections of glass that rose from the floor to the ceiling. A rock fountain had been placed in the middle of the display, all of which had been built for Woody, Vardus's adorable and growing tiger.

"Hi, there," Vardus tapped on the glass that formed the wild animal's square enclosure. At the moment, Woody was balled up in the corner, resting in his den of synthetic brush. For now he could rest, but his composition of cuteness would be needed soon.

A strand of hair must have escaped the bun. Vardus slid it behind his ear, and while staring at his precious pet, he said to Yjn, "You have what I want?"

Another knock came through the door. The guards were becoming impatient. "Yes," Yjn managed. "She's right   outside."

"Thank you. Return to your class on 102. I'm sure they're expecting you. Bring her in as you leave."

Just as they had when she entered, Yjn's heels tapped the hard wood upon her departure, replaced by the timid shuffling of another.

In the glass Vardus saw the young lady's reflection, and his desire burned with more ferocity, but he gave no such impression. He had been a leader for over two decades. At this point, he'd mastered the art of concealing emotion.

The young lady cleared her throat to signal her presence. Measuring her frame in the crystal-clear reflection, Vardus made a quick comparison between them. Although he towered over her, as he did with most people, this beautiful young lady shared his lanky build. He might even go as far as saying that her curves were more attractive than his. His hair had once been the same shade of brunette as hers, but now his held streaks of gray, and what hadn't yet grayed turned black.

Something he could never hope to emulate were those eyes, he would soon discover. Bright blue and commanding attention. Vardus turned to her in feigned surprise, lighting his face up with a squinty grin.

"Ah! There you are, Miss …"

"Dawn. From 102, sir."

"Dawn! Enchanted to have your company. Please," Vardus motioned to the chair beside his desk. "Sit."

She did.

"'Each time dawn appears, the mystery is there in its entirety.'" Vardus said this as he made his way to the chair behind his desk. "Rene Daumal."

The girl's face remained blank. Vardus had forgotten of Ardosia's students and their habit to *face forward at all times*. Dawn was offering her attention as though Vardus was her professor. He felt the need to demand that she relax and treat this as a meeting of intellectuals.

Clearing his throat, Vardus flicked an itch off his nose.

"Can I get you anything? Water, a snack?"

"No, thank you."

The President nodded, the air between them still. "I'm glad you're here."

Understanding she didn't have a choice in the matter, Dawn's face remained expressionless.

Vardus then lowered his tone. "Tell me of your role."

"I have yet to be assigned one ... sir."

"You're supposed to be graduating toward a role at the end of this season, are you not?"

"I am."

"Hmm. So tell me what you're interested in, Miss Dawn."

"Dawn is fine."

Vardus was surprised at the natural defiance that arose within the girl. In his many years of life, Vardus had been forced to take a stand on several occasions. When the Nation fell, by his doing, he stood against many who called him an extremist. Hundreds, maybe thousands of strong-willed men and women had been slain either by his hand or by his order. He was no stranger to opposition, but he found himself quite attracted to that quality as he identified it in the girl before him. She was strong, fierce, and feisty. He had to adjust himself.

"Dawn," he said. "Forgive me. Please, what is it you would like to do … in your role, I mean?"

The girl waved a hand through her curly hair, and a quiet breath escaped Vardus. His desire had accelerated from a burning flame to a massive conflagration. He wondered how long he could contain himself.

"For the longest time, my role was to become a professor. That's what I was interested in, and it's what I wanted to be. I guess I didn't pass the evaluation last year, due to 'improper philosophical conduct', whatever that means." She shrugged. "Haven't been assigned a new role since."

All of this, Vardus knew in great detail. During his most recent visit to 102, he had fixated on her and determined that he would study her profile extensively. He found that her teaching evaluation had indeed indicated improper philosophy. This woman's values didn't align precisely with that of Ardosia and its people. It was a wonder, really, that her O-rate had been pleasantly high throughout her schooling. But Vardus knew her type. Dawn was a ticking time bomb, a fickle presence waiting to spur on revolution, no matter how trivial it may be. Women of her type could never be allowed to teach, for they may cause more harm than good.

"I'm sorry to hear that."

"Mhmm."

"Is there anything else to which you might gravitate, in terms of potential roles?"

Dawn thought. "Um, I guess I'm not sure. There are a few subjects and exercises I've enjoyed that…"

With his hands laced together, Vardus presented faux interest in her innocent jargon as she spoke. The girl's role had evaporated, and with its disappearance, so had her purpose in life. She did not appear to be bothered by it, comforted by the naïve assuredness that God might have a plan for her. In some sense, she was not wrong. In her presence, Vardus understood that, yes. God did have a plan for her. As one role falls through the floor, another appears in its wake. Vardus stumbled rather easily upon the conclusion. Imminently Dawn's new role would be both assigned and fulfilled.

As she continued to speak, Vardus, the patient man, couldn't keep his eyes from bouncing down to the girl's supple breasts. She was young and, no doubt, inexperienced, her innocence eliciting a carnal response.

"You're an attractive young lady, Dawn. I find myself inclined to you."

Being direct was not always the best mode of action, but it was the only one he knew. Vardus hadn't realized she was still speaking when he told her this, and it brought forth from her a newfound silence. Whatever enthusiasm she might have held moments before was gone.

"Oh," was all she said.

The reluctance to violate Ardosia's first rule was evident, but Dawn did so anyway. She no longer faced forward and instead allowed her eyes to roam the room. Vardus watched as she admired the stained-glass window behind him, noted the subtle gleam bouncing off the dark wood of the floor. Finally, her eyes rested on the folding bed to her right, where the sheets sat in a messy formation on top.

There it is, Vardus observed. *The fear, the discomfort.* It was in her eyes, and it was the miracle mead that had sustained his youthful appearance through all these years.

"I should get going," Dawn said, refusing to meet Vardus's primal gaze. What she hadn't realized is, by this action, she had sealed her fate.

"You should take a look at my tiger. His name is Woody." Vardus rose from his seat and began rounding the desk.

Dawn glanced toward the glass cage where the tiger had awoken and was seated curiously in the light. An inflection of desperation escaped her. "I'll be late for class on 102. Don't want to upset Professor Yjn ... or the Schedule."

"Don't you want to see him?" Vardus stood tall behind her as the girl was seated and still.

"I see him now."

"Ah, but up close. Surely, you wish to see Woody up close."

It took her a moment to respond, and her answer upset him. "No, I don't. I'm going to leave."

As she attempted to rise, Vardus placed his hands firmly on her shoulders, forcing her back into a seated position. A yelp escaped her, but she covered her mouth. By now the tears would be streaming. Vardus was unaffected. She had a new role now.

Bending low to whisper in her ear, Vardus told more than asked, "How about you pet my tiger, Dawn?"

VIII

O rian knew not which day it was. Ardosia never taught them how to differentiate between Monday and Thursday or Wednesday and Sunday. On the island, days didn't exist. There was only daylight and night and a Schedule to be followed. Months didn't exist, either. No February, no June, no November. Years were real and were observed as such by Ardosia, but students only knew one year's passing into another when they were informed of it. There was no spirit in the air, no collective excitement, and no fruitless resolutions to alert them to another go around the sun. One day passed into the next, like the rest. Then they were in a new year. That's how it worked.

Although today Orian knew not which day it was, nor that it would alter his life forever, he sensed early that there was something ... different about it.

To start, morning message with the nameless woman commenced on screen, working into morning prayer with Vardus. Professor Yjn wasn't present ... nor, even more evident to Orian, was Dawn. Orian assumed everyone would be shuffling or stirring like him, free at last from the watchful gaze of their professor and perhaps curious as to her whereabouts. But they were still. Even Ladis faced forward *at all times*, as though he and the rest of them had inferred a secret test being observed. For now, Yjn was gone, so Orian risked a glance out the window.

His eyes captured a load of information in that split second, and the wave of untamed excitement that fled his system was almost enough to squelch his suspicions of a "something ain't right" kind of day.

The sun shone on the tumbling waves of Ardosia's lake and on the swaying tree limbs in the distance. A flock of black birds shadowed a small portion of the cloudless sky as they fluttered their wings. Orian wondered at the jungle beyond the Wall, supposing he might fare better in the wild than on this island prison everyone refers to as Ardosia.

And in the last millisecond of his glance, Orian thought he saw something foreign, long and narrow, and white at the lake's surface. Was it the mouth of an albino whale surfacing for air? No, it couldn't be. Whales lived in the ocean, and Ardosia's salty "lake" was a man-made structure no more than twenty-five feet deep ubiquitously. But what had Orian seen? Just then, Professor Yjn pounced into the classroom.

As if assuming a normal routine and ignoring her own tardiness, she postured herself at the head of the room and said, "46. Exercise, um … 46, yes."

All students worked diligently. But not Orian. His brow furrowed. Yjn's demeanor was … off, somehow. And was she seemingly out of breath? As the panel from his podium rose, Orian feigned intent on Exercise 46 as he eyed his professor. She turned her back to him to face the board for a split second, so he took advantage.

Risking another darting glimpse to the outside world, Orian fixated on whatever was floating on the lake's surface. Due to its distance, his eyes needed a moment to adjust. He squinted. *Is that … a boat?*

He'd never seen one, not in person. Yet undeniably, there it was–a small white boat, or a canoe, pitching with the waves with only one passenger. Orian faced forward again as a precaution, but his mind focused on the golden spec he saw protruding from the boat. If anyone were to be sailing Ardosia's waters, Orian would have assumed it to be a soldier, but soldiers didn't wear gold. Who, then, could he have seen? Was there anyone there at all, or had it been a mirage? He wanted to peer out the window again, but Yjn faced the class, apparently just to ensure the successful completion of 46. That's when their eyes locked, and Orian saw something cold, maybe even sinister, in her glare.

Orian's eyes shot down to his panel, but the forceful tapping of heels against the floor told him Yjn was already on her way over. His charade of teacher-fooling would prove to be unsuccessful this time around.

"46 is simple for you, I take it."

Like a wicked witch hungry for twenty-year-old hearts, Yjn planted one hand on hip and bore voracious eyes into

Orian. When he met her gaze, he could've sworn she summoned an indoor tempest to darken her angry features and blow at the strands of hair escaping her ponytail. It was as if she were alluding, in the most grandiose fashion possible, that her power over him was undeniable and should not be tested. To Orian, she might as well have been asking for it.

"I was actually hoping for your help. Thank *God* you're here." An invisible wristwatch drew Orian's eye. "You're late, but you're here."

A huff similar to that of a bull duped by a matador blew out her nose. Yjn chewed on her cheek, presumably biting down the fury of insults she was ready to hurl upon him in a cascading array of trash talk. She may have believed herself to be above triviality, but Orian was not.

"Why, Professor, must simpletons like us abide ruthlessly by the Schedule when not even our superiors display such commitment?" Without realizing it, Orian had risen his voice so that everyone had been made privy to the current feud on 102. Silence struck the floor like an inverse crack of lightning and thunder. Progress on Exercise 46 halted unanimously. All eyes–or ears, rather– were drawn to the back left corner of the classroom, where Yjn straightened herself, aware that she now had an audience and that Orian had a point.

"You're nearing the edge of a cliff, Orian," she grumbled under her breath, in between teeth clenched tightly as a vice grip. "I suggest you stop backing yourself closer to it, lest you fall." The way she emphasized *fall* indicated a proper threat had been issued.

Images of Zak being hauled out of 102 flashed through Orian's mind. The guards had fiercely gripped his arms, like he was a prisoner. Orian knew that the same fate could befall him if he were to pry further beneath Yjn's thick skin. Time upon time he'd told himself to be more careful in his affairs, but Orian sensed something out of the ordinary here. Now, more than ever, he felt untouchable. He needed to continue.

"Not to worry, Ms. Yjn," Orian sneered. "I've been assured repeatedly that my safety is the number-one priority of Ardosia's leaders ... such as yourself." The red in her face should have told him to stop. Orian wasn't about that. "I'm sure you'd never let me fall off a cliff. Would you?"

With the intent interest of all her students, Yjn had now been backed into the corner she had reserved for Orian. Critical thinking was rare on this forsaken island, but Orian had confidence that its prevalence was enough that there might be a few eavesdroppers pondering the same inquiries he had put forth. At this point, Yjn had no choice but to provide them all with an answer.

"Of course not. Never would you fall." Her smile seemed to bare a grizzly-like set of canines before she whispered in Orian's ear: "You're walking a thin line." As if Orian didn't already know it.

Professor Yjn, fuming, acted as though she were heading to her desk at the front. Yet Orian's incessantly prodding nature took hold of his mouth, freezing her in place.

"And Dawn?" he nodded to the empty seat to his right. If he hadn't already crossed the line, he knew this would take him there. His entire existence on this island had been full of deceit and control. He may have been digging his own grave, but at least it would be done autonomously, of *his* accord–no one else's. Finally, he said, "Where is she?"

"Hm?"

He had a feeling Yjn knew. "The girl who has sat in *that* chair for the past twenty odd years. Where is she?"

Steely cool eyes worked Orian's nervous system. She appeared to contemplate her answer, but only for the slightest tickle of time. Yjn leaned over at the waist, where her khakis met a black top, and in a mix between a whisper and an announcement, she pronounced a statement just loud enough for everyone to hear, one that Orian deemed irrefutably chilling.

"What girl?" is all she said before waltzing confidently away from him.

Orian's jaw dropped. *What girl?* Had Professor Yjn really shrugged off the existence of one of her *own* students? This prompted Orian to speculate that whatever the circumstances surrounding Dawn's current existence, they couldn't be pleasant. Little did Orian know, this was only the beginning of the absurd wave of events that would overtake him.

Yjn had taken no more than five steps before being hit by an invisible wall. Orian's eyes were keen on her. She stopped, looking almost as though she desired an explanation from herself for having shown such carelessness regarding a student. Her face contorted with confusion, but Orian would come to realize her confoundment was due to a sudden fixation on a clear-glass window. Maybe there was a set of sticky fingerprints somebody had left behind. But then Orian remembered the boat. Yjn wasn't looking at the window; she was looking through it.

"What the …" Yjn muttered. Her eyes folded into a squint as she was drawn to the sun-reflecting pane.

This is when Ardosia submitted to chaos, beginning with the abandonment of its first rule: *Face forward at all times.* Not one head had refrained from whipping to view whatever had grasped the unsettled attention of their professor. Shockingly, Orian was one of the last to strike a glance out the window–he'd been too enthralled by the collective defiance that the students of 102 abruptly decided to elicit. A shot of pride had stolen him.

"Oh, *shhh*–" Yjn stumbled backward, falling on her behind when a spider-web pattern cracked, but did not penetrate, the five-inch-thick glass precisely where Yjn's face had been–the crack issued by a singular arrow.

The next five minutes happened too fast for reality to be registered properly. It began with what Orian could distinctly remember as the second arrow. It arrived unwonted moments after the first had been lodged into the glass. This one drew an interweaving spider-web pattern with the former. Orian had a feeling a third would be coming.

"Everyone get back!" Frantic eyes of a terrified woman extended the same baleful plea as her voice. Yjn said, "Away from the windows!"

Unsure whether Ardosia was really under attack or if this was some devilish drill initiated by Vardus, Orian went deaf to the calls aimed at him. He could not hear the booming cries of those terrified students. He stood, called instead like an acquiescent zombie to the glaring sun. No doubt, Yjn would be rifling outrage at his gall–all immaterial to him.

Time warped into a series of slow motion, where distant leaves and needles were shaken from their rooted branches to fall like blissful snowflakes to a violent ground. The high-pitched songs of birds, Orian supposed, were probably stolen by a black hole currently shattering the space-time continuum. He wasn't sure what was happening, but he was going to find out.

As he gazed fearlessly beyond the battered glass, a calm washed over him, contradicting the gravity of the moment. What may have been a blinking instant felt like a revitalizing slumber behind closed eyes.

"Orian!" came from behind. Not Yjn. Ladis. Yet even his pleas weren't manageable.

He at first caught sight of limp, unmoving bodies of Ardosia's soldiers–presumably the ones who had been guarding the Wall, as they were slumped at the edges of the unfinished portion of the site. Before the third arrow came crashing into the glass, Orian had perceived the truth with wide eyes. His heart leapt.

Where the only unfinished section of the Wall remained, there in the opening, a squad of ten, fifteen, maybe thirty men gathered, having already overcome their opposition. Their reflective garb of black and gold shone like stars in the distance, forming constellations of freedom and battle that instilled glorious hope.

They encircled a pointy and shiny silver object that Orian couldn't make out, even when squinting. Still, it drew his attention for a long second. It was clear that these rebels clad with armor, spears, and arrows were not friends of the island. Perhaps they were proponents of chaos, here to impart terror and squall any lives that should challenge their agenda–including those of students like Orian. He didn't have time to ponder the imminence of his fate as the final arrow–fired from the golden figure in the boat–turned the so-called impenetrable barrier to 102 into a sheet of falling glass. Ardosia was undergoing an invasion.

Hands up to shield his eyes, tiny pricks stabbed Orian's palms. Life-sustaining outside air infiltrated the classroom and filled his lungs with refreshment. Finally, Yjn's demands were audible to Orian again.

"Retreat! Everyone, retreat!" She'd been too involved with all her students to notice Orian any longer, beckoning them away from the glass. "Single file, back to your rooms. The soldiers of Ardosia will protect you! They'll keep you safe. Retreat!"

Mad waves of panic and intrigue sent indecision across the floor. Half the class complaisantly followed Yjn's orders as they made a mad dash for the double doors leading to safety, some whimpering, others sobbing. The other half seemed to be locked in on the curious display outside. For all they knew, more arrows could rain down on all of them, ending each of their lives, but intuition told Orian this wouldn't be the case. He second-guessed himself, however, when he did a double take, zeroing in on the pointy, shiny silver thingy as it rotated on a tripod and aimed seemingly straight at him. Then it fired.

He ducked out of the way as a much larger arrow shot through the opening in the window with blinding speed, impaling itself into the concrete wall on the far end of the classroom. Sprawled on the floor, Orian quickly realized that the weapon hadn't been an arrow all along, but rather a grappling unit of immense length, attached by a half-mile long line of sturdy black string. Then, from the arrow-thingy, whatever it was, at least five hanger-looking attachments assembled themselves in a Transformer-esque way. Orian had the Internet to thank again for his familiarity with such a machine. It was a zipline.

To Orian's surprise, Ladis had been one of those who was evidently disquieted by the decision forced upon him–whether to flee or stay. He stood on the other side of the suspended line, having not yet obeyed Yjn's orders to retreat. Their eyes met. Orian's bounced to the string and back, insinuation written all over them. Furiously shaking his head, Ladis mouthed *Don't*. Then, *You could get hurt,* which Orian interpreted as a sudden change of heart, discerning from his lips the words: *Go for it!*

He needed no encouragement. Orian looked out the window once more, noting that the zipline had actually fired nine more lines into the building, a few below and some above. Where the circle of invaders stood, some were beckoning, others aiding students who had already fled via their gracious zipline. It was clear to Orian that these black and gold rebels weren't here to kill, unless their hands were forced. They were here, rather, on a rescue mission.

Orian saw Ladis again, who appeared to be working on an opposite train of thought, leaning more toward the safety Yjn was offering. Yet Orian could tell nevertheless that his roommate's heart was split. *Come with me,* Orian begged through cerebral connection. His silent pleas were interrupted by the more vocal Professor Yjn.

"Orian, don't you dare."

The two of them were suddenly locked in a visual embrace, Yjn by the double doors, Orian near the broken window. Orian swept the room, eyeing Ladis, then the line, then Yjn. He understood that by going with his gut, he might never see Ladis again. It pained him, but he knew what he had to do.

"Orian, *no!*" Yjn threatened as Orian bolted into action.

Just then, two of Ardosia's soldiers burst through the set of double doors. For a reason completely unjust in Orian's eyes, Yjn sent both guards after him—and only him. Despite the select few who took their ticket to freedom by hopping on the zipline, and the others who might make an attempt, Orian was evidently the most important target.

He paused for a moment, joy welling in his heart at those who had bolted at their chance to escape–Dawn's roommate Trixie being one of them.

For so long, Orian thought he was the only one. A lone, lost soul amongst content, and possibly confused colleagues. But no. One, two, three students had already fled the coffin of 102 and ultimately the constricting satanic cathedral of Ardosia. At least two more of 102's students were lining up for an escape, which meant time was running short. Two hangers remained, only one of which Orian could use to soar down the line and into the hands of safety and freedom. And the guards would be upon him in literal seconds.

He shot a quick glance at them, and his shoulders slumped in amusement. *Hello,* A *and friend.* The two soldiers Orian had encountered the other night while viewing the news room on 31 were back, and by the looks of it, thirsty for revenge. He had swindled them both in an ascending fashion once already by zooming up a staircase. Orian wasn't sure if he could do it twice–this time utilizing gravity with a zipline.

Another student grappled down to safety, leaving one open hanger for those who were still trapped in indecision. Meanwhile, Yjn was collecting as many students as possible, ensuring that nobody would hurt them, should they submit to the double doors and lock themselves in their rooms.

Ladis was one who, after much consideration, denied his ticket to freedom and instead chose his life on 102. Despair always seemed to strike at the worst time, and it clutched Orian's heart then as Ladis walked out. Inadvertently, he'd given the guards more time to approach their target. Together, they stood side-by-side in athletic stances, waiting to tackle Orian.

"*A*, it's that damn ghostie!" the one on the left pointed. He inflated his chest in an apparent attempt to intimidate.

A watched intently, focused solely on his mission, which was to detain a disobedient student. Orian scanned his surroundings like a zebra staring into the faces of two voracious lions. While the men may have had size on him, Orian knew from the other night that he was quicker and perhaps more cunning. His eyes settled on the five rows of podiums. They could be used as obstacles.

Orian knew the likelihood of outmaneuvering two guards was slim, and once Yjn abandoned her post at the door and coordinated with them, the prospect of escape became even dimmer. The three of them–two guards and a professor–approached warily in a semi-circle, the distance between them closing.

In the face of immeasurable odds is when Orian seemed to find his comfort. His breathing slowed. So did time. With celerity, he came to a decision.

A row of podiums separated Yjn from the middle guard. She was clearly angered, and her anger would provide strength, simultaneously marring her reflexes. Orian bolted toward her. Barreling at your teacher, who stood arms wide ready to knock the wind out of you with a tackle, was an experience Orian never though he'd cross off his bucket list. A spin-move, as he'd discovered through the Internet, can be implemented to evade tackles. Yet he must not have displayed the right form, instead colliding with Yjn who took him to the ground with ease. In another moment, the guards would be on top of him. He'd be dead, for all he knew.

Luckily, Yjn was light. He pushed her off, grunting. By the time he rose, the guard who insisted Orian was a ghost was on him, dismayed and embarrassed when Orian elbowed him in the nose, springing forth a geyser of blood.

"*Ahhhh*, I can't breathe. *A*, I can't breathe!" His words were labored, and Orian paused to lament his actions. He'd never meant to hurt anyone. Soon he would learn that the pursuit of happiness required pain, mostly one's own and occasionally others' as well.

A stood no more than a couple of feet away, anticipating Orian's next move. The previous evening, *A* had been shaded by darkness. In the light Orian was given a better look at the young man. He was tall with light skin and blue eyes, a face that portrayed innocence, of all things. If Orian had the time or the persuasive skills of a salesmen, he might scurry out of the situation and ask *A* to a nice dinner. Orian was interested in his story, for he knew there was much to unpack. Alas, he had neither the time nor the skills to wriggle his way out of this one. Yjn was on the ground. The other guard howled in pain. Yet *A* was emotionally unaffected. He didn't know why, but Orian thought he could reason with *A*.

"I think you get it," he said, hands up on either side. "You know why I have to leave."

A gave no sign of validation, other than a quick peek at the ground.

"You know what it's like to feel trapped with no escape, I can tell." This seemed to strike a chord, drawing even more curiosity. It provided the distraction he needed.

Though Orian felt remorse when he barreled through *A*'s shoulder, as he could tell there was a shared experience they could have bonded over, it was necessary for him to find the last hanger.

A stumbled, losing his balance.

Flying past rows of podiums, Orian beamed for the zipline. He trusted that fortune would be on his side, but reason should have told him that the law of large numbers would come into effect sooner or later. Time after time, Orian had waltzed carelessly through the minefield of life, spared by God. It seemed now that God could no longer prevent Orian from being ensnared by his own foolishness.

"Where's it gone?" Orian asked himself, referring to the final method of escape. Upon the glimmering black line, there hung not a single hanger. That's when he saw a small man gliding on the line to safety. All optimism was extracted with a needle-tipped syringe. The last hanger had been taken. There was no way out.

Yjn and *A* had lifted themselves off the floor and would detain Orian at any moment. He could have given up, but such was not his way. So he ran toward the open window, stopping near its edge. 102 floors below, the ground, although moist from the previous rain, would accept Orian's body like asphalt if he were to jump.

His eyes widened when he put a hand on his hip. Today Orian was wearing a belt. Quickly, he unlatched it from his waist and threw it overtop the zipline.

"Orian, wait!" came Yjn's voice, maybe ten feet behind him. It seemed odd that she might wait until now to try to reason with him. "You don't know what you're getting yourself into. Those people are savages, they'll tear you apart. Stay here, where you're safe." Her mouth quivered into a smile.

Orian looked longingly into the distance where the rebels had already collected a number of students. Swarms of soldiers were approaching them, via bridges attached to the Wall. In no more than a couple of minutes, the rebels would either be forced to battle to the death or head back in the direction from which they came. Even if Orian made it to them, he found it likely that he'd die trying. And what if Yjn was right? Was he being lured into a mortal trap? *Hell, everyone dies eventually.*

With that comforting thought, Orian jumped, having wrapped the belt twice around each hand and once overtop the line. He jumped.

At first, his eyes were shut, fearing the worst might happen. He could slip, hands sweaty and unable to support his weight. He could fall to the ground a hundred stories below and turn into a pancake. To his fortune and surprise, neither of these outcomes occurred.

Gliding through the air, he smiled and projected a victorious laugh so that the world could hear. The wind blew gloriously past his face. It buffeted his hair and spirits alike. He was finally going to do it. Orian was escaping Ardosia, but his bliss was quickly interrupted.

As he zipped down the rope, he noticed the leather from his belt being worn away at an irredeemable rate. There's no way he'd make it to the other side. Orian gaged the distance between him and safety, and he thought there was a slight chance. Then his line started shaking, swinging this way and that. Since wind was not a factor, Orian struggled to ascertain the cause of his plight. Although not the smartest maneuver, he turned his head to look behind him. Standing beside the line all the way up in 102 were *A,* who held an ax in hand, and Yjn, who appeared to be barking orders at him. Orian didn't have to be a mathematician to put two and two together. He'd have slumped if he could have.

In one swoop, the ax came down on the line, causing Orian to tumble and flail through the air.

The time he spent falling felt like an eternity. His heart raced as the watery face of death loomed before him. At this point, he'd zipped past land and was over the lake, so there was a speck of hope to be found. However, even after having descended several stories, Orian estimated the distance between him and the lake below to be over fifty feet–a potentially lethal height. His entry into the water would have to be precise.

Abandoning his makeshift hanger, Orian tossed the belt and pulled his arms in close, emulating the shape of a pencil. Thanks once again to the Internet, Orian had a bit of an idea as to the proper form. He gained velocity, the water's still surface approaching like a flat wet coffin. It occurred to Orian that these could be his last moments. If he were to break bones upon entry, swimming to safety would be impossible. He would drown.

Orian splashed into the lake. Twenty feet below the surface in no time at all, he found himself disoriented by the way the depths sucked him underneath like a vortex. Dark blue enshrouded him. Orian couldn't tell up from down, left from right, or if he'd even lived. Holding his breath for as long as he could muster, Orian patted himself, thankful that he hadn't seemed to break any bones. Then the surface appeared to him, the sun's rays penetrating just deep enough for him to catch sight of Heaven. He swam to them, remembering the techniques he'd been taught on this very island many years ago. Swim training was one of the first days Orian had been outdoors, and even through a beginner's struggle, he'd felt the outside world's gravitational pull ever since.

With a heightened sense of ebullience, he kicked and swatted until he rose to the surface.

Gasping for air, Orian's arms shot high into the sky in an attempt to beckon the person in the boat. They'd been wearing gold, he remembered. He had no idea where they were, only praying they were close. Small waves lapped into his face, seemingly aiming for his mouth and lungs. It was as if Ardosia didn't want him to leave, couldn't allow him to. If the island couldn't have him, nobody could.

"Over here!" he yelled, wiping the water out of his eyes. Orian twisted this way and that. The golden boat-savior was nowhere to be found. Orian bobbed up and down for nearly half a minute when he finally saw his path to safety … mooring at the shoreline. "Wait! Please help!" The water pulled him under again. Exhaustion from treading water was setting in. He applied all the air he had left in his lungs once he broke the surface. "Over here!"

Not one rebel in black and gold shot him so much as a glance. They were packing up to leave, and the boat was left to float without a captain.

Ardosia's soldiers trod over the bridges, narrowing the distance between them and the rebels. Though Orian wished the invaders would stay for another minute, he understood they had to leave if they wanted to avoid a blood bath.

Once more, hope had been ripped from Orian's grasp.

A lone figure bobbing at the surface, Orian felt trapped. His one and only exit at the opening in the Wall would soon be occupied by Ardosia's best. He could swim to them, only to be captured. The only other direction he might be able to turn was back … and Lord knew he'd rather pour torrents of lake-water down his own lungs than return to the wretched island. The longer he treaded, the more Orian believed drowning to be his best option.

Then a sudden flash of blinding light drew Orian's eye to the left. No more than seventy feet from the unfinished opening in the Wall, there appeared to be a tunnel of sorts. Without a clue whether it jutted through to the other side, Orian wasted no time. He poured every ounce of energy and adrenaline into swimming toward the tunnel.

By now, many Ardosian soldiers, easily identifiable in their gray and white, would be in pursuit of the invaders. Should one curious soldier peer into the waters from above, he might find a target in the shape of a twenty-year old boy. Orian would have to avoid splashing, lest he find himself pegged by a shower of imperial arrows. So he implemented a swim technique known as the frog, submarining for as long as he could manage.

Orian knew this was a fight for his life, so he sparsely came up for air. His lungs screamed at him as he swam underwater, and the lake must not have been as clean as advertised. Orian's eyes were beginning to sting from having them open as he swam, due equally to muddy contamination and salt, he surmised. He didn't care. Discomfort would soon become a constant in his life. Orian assumed it best to adjust now.

Keeping pace for what seemed like enough time to reach the tunnel, Orian found himself still swimming. Sooner or later, he would have to catch his breath. Stealthily he rose to the surface, and his heart dropped to the bottom of the lake. Not only had Orian veered off-line, but he estimated that he would have to swim for another hundred yards before reaching his destination. Just when he thought his problems had peaked, he squinted to his left. In the distance, he saw three skinny ducks swiftly floating toward him. Orian wiped the water from his eyes, and upon second glance, he almost laughed. They weren't ducks at all. Rather, three fins were effortlessly sliding through waves like saw blades.

"Dolphins," Orian told himself. Though they were far away, he remembered what Trixie said about them. *Pretty sure those things were trained to eat people on the off chance that some suicidal fool feels compelled to climb over that Wall.* Orian laughed at the conspiracy then, but now, as the fins approached fast, he allowed his mind to wonder, determining rather quickly that he wouldn't take any chances. Those dolphins were moving at a speed indicative of ten-day-empty-stomach hunger.

Adrenaline coursed through Orian. He had to be running close to empty by now, but his mind didn't dwell on the possibility. Doing his best to imitate the speed of a dolphin, Orian found an extra gear. After continuing for another minute, something pierced the water beside him. It happened again, on his other side this time. His eyes, ignoring the salty sting, darted underwater. Whatever had penetrated the surface was skinny, about two feet long, and it came to a point. Great, they knew where he was.

Arrows started raining down, so he dove deeper. Lungs need air, and Orian was running out. Fires ignited within his chest, set to consume him. Blazing silver tips rained down on him. Orian was close to giving up.

Then he saw the tunnel ten feet away. In one final push, Orian lunged and muscled himself to safety.

Light came in at an angle but didn't make it far. The tunnel was dark, so Orian hid in the shadows, coughing up water. He fell flat against the steel cylinder, where he found temporary solace. Though its jagged design was rough on his back, he closed his eyes for a moment, as if preparing for bed. He spent thirty seconds in a state of calm before hoisting his torso up so that he could look back at the deathly waters he'd escaped.

Outside he could hear soldiers jeering at him, but their cries fell upon deaf ears. Orian's chest tightened at the three deathly animals circling the waters just below the edge of the tunnel. Their fins might as well have assembled into a pentagram, the hell-spawned dolphins evidently flustered at his escape. Orian was not yet convinced at Trixie's conspiracy of flesh-eating porpoises, but her case acquired more merit by the second, as their movements appeared to be more robotic than natural.

A blinding flash illuminated the tunnel at Orian's back. He jumped, startled. Orian recalled that this must have been what attracted him to the tunnel in the first place. Originally, he assumed God had been on his side, inspiring physics to alter itself in a flash of bright light, to appear as a beacon of hope for Orian. In a sense, God *had* provided him with an escape, but the flash hadn't been issued by divine forces. It had derived from something man-made.

Slowly, Orian turned. Further along, he saw nothing but darkness. Intuition told him someone was there. That's when another weld was applied to the tunnel, resulting in one more blinding display. Somehow, the welder–a few feet away–hadn't been privy to Orian's presence until now. He jumped.

"What the!"

"Hold up, calm down." Orian's instincts were to placate the man. At the moment, they were both technically unarmed, but a weld could do serious damage. Therefore, the constructor in darkness would have the upper hand. Violence was not an option. Orian would have to rely on subterfuge to escape this jam. His eyes moved left and right. He'd have to come up with something quick. He managed a fib. "I've come to inspect your work."

The welder, still invisible to Orian, cleared his throat. "Why you all wet?"

Orian looked behind him. In between breaths, he said, "I was enjoying a swim."

A scoff came from the darkness. "Wish 'Enjoyin' a Swim' was on *my* Schedule. Say, what's your role then, young man?"

"Um ..." *Think, damnit.* "I'm an ... inspector. Here to ensure the best work is done on Ardosia's mighty Wall." Orian stood tall and rubbed his hands on the outer edges of the steel cylinder, nodding his head convincingly. "Might I say, your handiwork is exceptional, Mister ..."

"Dredt."

"Dredt, yes I really love your craft." Orian inched further into the tunnel, afraid more arrows might suddenly be fired through the opening. He hoped the soldiers wouldn't chase him here. He kept rubbing the ceiling. "It's special what you do, I–"

"My welds are up to par where you're standin'?"

Orian gulped. "I would most certainly say so. Absolutely. While I've forgotten my night vision goggles, I can tell, just by the way your welds ... *feel*, that they've been completed with expert-level precision."

"I appreciate your kind words, Mister ..."

He couldn't procure a fake name on the spot, so he blurted, "Orian," regretting it immediately.

Shuffling sounds came closer to Orian. He assumed the welder named Dredt was approaching, confirmed only as half of his mask slid into a sliver of light. Dredt lifted it to reveal that he was a one-eyed man, stealing an offensive jolt from Orian's torso. Dredt chuckled. "Didn't mean to scare you."

"Not at all, my apologies for ..."

"This?" the welder pointed to a gruesome slit where at least a glass eye should have been, but instead there was only a permanent scarred slash. "No offense taken. You want to know how it happened?"

Truthfully, Orian didn't care. It took all his might to hold solid eye-contact–or slit contact, whatever you'd call it. He just wanted out of this tunnel, no matter where it led. Orian glanced down at the welding tool in Dredt's hand. "Accident?"

"No," he smiled. "It was no accident." Out of instinct, Orian recoiled again. He went to apologize, but the welder named Dredt went on before he could interject. Offering a smile that was only half-visible to Orian, he said, "You should have seen the other guy."

Orian was officially as unsettled as humanly possible. He said nothing.

"I became a welder many years ago." Dredt started rubbing the walls, exactly where Orian had been a moment ago. "I'll admit, it took me a while to get the hang of it. Really didn't care for my role at first. But the years gon' on, I've inclined myself toward the ... craft, as you put it." He stopped rubbing the outer edges of the tunnel, paused, and then flicked the tops twice, producing a hollow noise. "I *am* an expert, but it don't take no expert to understand that these? They ain't welds." Orian cursed to himself. "So I'm 'a give you one chance to tell me who the fuck you really are or ..." he double-tapped his welding tool, allowing the sparks to speak for him.

Orian's heart began racing. He could only see half of the man who called himself Dredt, but the welder probably doubled him in size. He was the same height, very heavyset. A wrestling match in close quarters would surely end in Orian's death, or whatever might happen to him after two taps from the welding tool.

Just beyond the tunnel, the dolphins kept spinning in a mad circle. Orian's mind raced, but he was stuck. Then the darkness obscuring Dredt gave Orian an idea, one he was loath to commit. He had to remind himself that he had no choice.

"You hard o' hearin'? I said–"

Orian jammed his thumb with as much force as he could muster into Dredt's other eye.

Dredt howled in pain, doubling over. This gave Orian enough time to steal the welding tool and press it into the man's face. It was a horrific act, of which Orian would not have thought himself capable weeks ago. He discovered that when you're fighting for your life, no matter how immoral the prospect, yours tends to be the only life that matters.

Pervasive odors of burnt hairs and flesh masked all else.

Being a skinny man, Orian hurdled over Dredt, having just enough space to sneak past him. He could have run through the tunnels, but a primal rage overtook him. There was a job to finish. Rearing back, Orian used both legs to kick the man, who was still screaming with rage. He was surprised when Dredt rolled nearly to the edge of the tunnel.

Without blinking, Orian slid over to him. Dredt made a swing, missing completely and scraping his knuckles on the wall instead. It was time for him to be put out of his misery. A kick with finality was placed on Dredt's chest, who then tumbled backward into the lake, where he thrashed violently.

Orian wanted to look away, to avert his eyes from the horror he caused, but he couldn't help but watch as the man's rage transformed into terror-filled pleas for help. His cries escalated in pitch as three dolphins tore bit-by-bit at his flesh, over and over again. First, they attacked his arms, so he couldn't swim. Then his legs. Then his face, until, after blurting a desire and a need to see a family again, his screams ceased.

Orian covered his mouth. Tears welled in his eyes. "Oh my God," was all he could utter before turning back to the darkness, welding tool in hand. He couldn't believe what he just saw—what he'd *done*. He moved slowly into the tunnel, placing as much distance between him and atrocity as possible. He had to remind himself that he had no choice. Only one could have survived the encounter. It was either him or Dredt.

Orian wasn't sure where the tunnel would take him, but the welding tool would act as his lantern. He gripped it tight. All he knew was the necessity of action. So he ran and never stopped, occasionally double-tapping a brilliant flame for guidance.

IX

An inflection of fear mottled the young professor's voice. He stood, hands crossed before him as he said, "Three, sir. We lost three."

Vardus's body took the rigid form of his chair, but his face refrained from disappointment. Neutrality and balance were emotional keys for leaders like himself. He merely nodded. "And Professor Yjn?"

She cleared her throat, pulling a loose strand of hair behind her ear. "Six ... sir." It was all she dared to utter.

The noble President's internals were on fire. He thought this woman to be competent, but *six?* Her O-rates weren't any lower than the rest of Ardosia's professors. Nobody could have predicted such a catastrophic failure. It could be attributed only to her ineptitude. Still, Vardus took a deep breath. "You're all dismissed," he said.

A modicum of tension seemed to evaporate from his professors. Vardus saw it as they had worked their way in, single-file. It hadn't left their faces for the duration of the meeting, until now. He didn't understand why they were tense in the first place. The President of Ardosia had shown no indication of reprisal in recompense for their pathetic, sorry uselessness. Nothing about his demeanor could have given the impression that he would enact justice by offering his flesh-hungry dolphins an unintelligent meal. This time, he had exuded tranquility and would let them all off with a warning.

As all ten of them proceeded to leave his office, Vardus said, "Yjn, you will stay."

She nearly flinched. Yjn paused, then waited for her colleagues to withdraw from the captain's quarters. The double doors were shut with finality. Vardus motioned for the guards keeping watch to remain outside. Eventually, he was alone in his office with Yjn and his friendly tiger Woody.

His eyes swayed to the adolescent feline, who arrested him with attention-seeking whimpers. He pawed the glass, imploring one of the humans to aid him in an exit. Vardus would answer those pleas after he handled business.

"Come," Vardus said.

Yjn tip-toed into the light of the stained-glass window. Red was cast across her face.

Forming his hands in steeple formation, Vardus pressed his lips together. He heaved a dramatic sigh to illustrate his disappointment. Afterward, he clicked his tongue on the top of his mouth. "My esteemed professor. How are you?"

Unsure of herself, she answered, "Sir, I-I'm so sorry."

"That is no reply." Vardus rubbed at the wood of his desk, following the etching put in place by Mother Nature. "I'll ask again. How are you?"

She sighed. "I've been better."

He feigned a smile. "As have I."

Vardus measured his professor, who resisted eye contact and instead stared down. Her hair disheveled, her black top ripped at the V, Yjn was of desperate appearance. His hand wandered to his pants to placate his brewing interest.

"Six," he finally addressed the elephant in the room. "That's as many as we've lost. Granted, 102 has never before been a victim of raid … but six." Vardus rose from his seat, sliding into his slippers that had been waiting for him at the edge of his desk. He paced back and forth while his hands worked the stubble that had appeared on his jaw. In the past, he had been a clean-shaven man. No longer. "Six," he said the word once more to grasp its true extent. "It pains me to have lost six of them to the Savages. I love my students. You're well aware of this, Yjn. They have lives, comfort, roles–everything they could ever want–right here on Ardosia." He shook his head. "Just to be *stolen*. It breaks my heart."

Professor Yjn maintained silence as he continued.

"We can acquire six more, no problem, and at least our troublemaker was not of the six who fled. A disaster that would have been. He shows so much promise, that Orian fellow." Vardus nailed his cold dark eyes into the tender woman. "He rests humbly in his dormitory now, I presume?"

Yjn said nothing, her frame shaking subtly.

Vardus bellowed. "Oh, don't joke with me now. I've shown enough resolve already." He wiped at his nose and stepped closer to her. "Orian. He is resting in his dormitory, yes?"

Yjn blurted her response like it pained her. "No. Orian's gone."

Neutrality is key. The words spun through Vardus's brain as his blank stare penetrated Yjn. Her eyes closed, the tangy scent of fear emanating from her. She might as well have begged.

Vardus turned away, the professor's sight both arousing and upsetting to him. If he continued to gaze upon her petite body, he might have succumbed to the desires of his vein-popping fists that wished for nothing more than to elicit both pain and pleasure, from her and from him. But Vardus didn't want to make any rash decisions.

Slowly, he ambled to Woody's enclosure. The tiger gazed up at him with glossy eyes. He must have been hungry.

"Me, too," Vardus whispered.

Hunger for a time of peace and prosperity, the vision he'd promised to himself, to his followers, and to the people he loved, had been just over the horizon. The boy named Orian had been the last crucial piece to the puzzle, with his unique gifts that elevated him far above his peers. The President's patience had already been worn thin by the trials of life. Vardus was unsure whether he could handle more.

He felt the rage welling up within him, starting just below his waist, working its way up to his chest. Should infectious fury wander to his head, he might do something drastic, like pounding his fists through glass. If it weren't for Yjn's sudden squeak, he may have done just that.

"There is good news," she offered. With Vardus patiently awaiting her announcement, she said, "Orian was not taken by the Savages."

This interested the President. "Go on."

"We detained him on 102 for as long as possible, but he managed to escape via … unconventional methods. We were able to knock him down short of the Savages, where he fell into the water and swam to a support tunnel. We believe he escaped to the forest beyond from there."

Vardus's brow furrowed as he faced the glass. "This is good news?"

Yjn swallowed. "We believe it's possible to send a tactical unit after the boy. He couldn't have made it far by now, and–" she was interrupted by an aggressive cracking noise.

A balled-up fist shook and remained in contact with the glass that did not break, but cracked in a spider web around Vardus's knuckle. His breathing was fierce, demonic. Woody reacted with terror, retreating to his den in the corner. Exorcising the impatience that overtook him, Vardus lowered his fist. He unfurled it at his side as blood began to spill on his wood floor. It might as well have been water.

"If he has made it to that jungle … alone, the Orian boy is already as good as dead."

"But, sir–"

"There will be no tactical unit sent after him." *Another one gone,* he thought to himself. Vardus rotated so that he faced the woman. She no longer provided him with the same attraction, so he kept his distance. "His escape will be seen as *your* failure." Yjn nodded. Few moments were spent wondering at a just punishment for her. Vardus, the forgiving leader he knew himself to be, dismissed her at once. "Leave."

"Hm?" Yjn was confounded.

"Leave," he said calmly again.

"James–"

"LEAVE!" His impatience, in combination with the reference to his former name, left him tense and volatile. If she hadn't departed at his raised voice, he may not have demonstrated such grace.

Behind him, the double doors opened and closed. She was gone. He abandoned the glass enclosure without apologizing to Woody for his outburst. The tiger would have to grow up eventually.

Entering his personal bathroom, Vardus washed the blood from his hand, red turning to pink as it was diluted by water. He rinsed off, snatching a white towel from the rack to stop the bleeding.

Vardus gazed at his reflection just above the sink. He'd seen this side of himself on many previous occasions. Prolonged stress was no stranger. Vardus recalled what it was like to found his own nation on an island. Loyalty, he remembered distinctly, had been both his greatest asset and gravest issue.

Life on Ardosia had once taken a turn for the worst long ago when many had been lost in their own dangerous individual identities and ideologies. Questions arose regarding the fate of Ardosia, its future, and even the sanity of their President. Vardus had even lost his original Right Hand due to these harmful wonderings.

Revolutions are frightening. Vardus understood this more than his ex-Right Hand could know, but only a coward wavers when taking the leap into new order. Images of that man's family panged lightly on Vardus's heart. Contrition tumbled through his stomach at what he had to do, but he shook the regret, knowing they were much better off now than they were with him. What a shame Hudson had to succumb to cold feet.

Eyes red, bags beneath, Vardus splashed water across his face. He cocked his head in an exasperated fashion when a thin streak of maroon red drew his attention in the mirror. From his cheek to his jugular, a scratch that drew blood had crystalized into a scab. He struggled to obtain the cause of his wound, but then he remembered the bitch, and more specifically, the way she struggled in his arms. What was her name? Horizon? Dusk? While the scratch annoyed him, he enjoyed the ones who struggled. Overcoming their resistance served as proof to him, proof that he was destined to be a leader of men, proof of his dominance.

His plan, however, faced too many frequent interruptions from those damned Savages. They had taken one of his most talented, most promising students in Orian. Well, they may not have taken him, but they had presented him with the opportunity to escape.

There had once been a student many years ago, referred to as the Creator. Vardus only recalled Creator's character, for he was an odd one. Yet he'd been the most promising student Vardus had ever encountered, hence the nickname. But he, too, had been abducted by the Savages. Taken years ago from Ardosia, Creator's disappearance had stalled the creation and implementation of the Twister Program. The Orian boy had given Vardus recent hope, but now he was gone, too. Twister would have to wait for another prodigy.

Vardus would create it on his own if he could, and he's tried a hundred times over. But his expertise did not lie among the realm of technology. A humble man, he could admit when he needed the assistance of someone more naturally gifted. The Twister Program's most recent failure had been observed in the Coliseum, where the matador showed initial signs of success. Then, for whatever reason, Twister had faltered, resulting in another irrelevant death.

Vardus had watched this unfold from the comfort of the President's Suite. He remembered his anger, but there had been room for optimism. Twister had worked in subtle ways. Still, he needed someone like Orian, or the Creator, to turn the Program into a convincing success. The woman he had working on the code currently was as inept as an intern, but there was no one more skilled to guide her.

Leaving the bathroom once the bleeding stopped, Vardus sauntered across his office to Woody's glass enclosure. The poor animal had secluded itself in fear, nestling in its den. Carefully, Vardus rounded the corner. He touched the glass, placing little pressure on his thumb and index finger. Possibly, he could send waves of pacification to the tiger.

"It was never my intent to scare you, little guy." He opened a small door attached to the side of the enclosure. "Come on out, Woody."

Mistrust racked the tiger's body, as he stepped forward, noncommittal. Then he crawled back into his den.

"Come on, my friend."

After pondering his master's tone, Woody padded slowly to Vardus.

"That's it. Yeah, good boy."

Vardus lifted the tiger into his arms. The room was quiet, save for Woody's whimpering. He examined its eyes, where the fear had eroded–most of it, at least. Patting its fur, he said, "It's okay, your time is near."

Before placing Woody back in his cage, Vardus eyed the crack he had issued in the glass. It was another testament to his strength, simultaneously a demonstration of his restraint. Had his mind succumbed to the anger that had been steadily rising within him, he might have done something much worse than break glass or draw blood from his palm, something like killing or raping Professor Yjn. Perhaps Vardus, after many years, was turning a new leaf.

They had been running for nearly an hour, sweat dripping from their faces, clinging to both shirts and armor. Pure adrenaline had sustained their will thus far, bolstering their chances of a clean hit and run.

They stopped for breath after traversing nearly seven miles of forested land. Talia surveyed her crew, who formed a bending human wall at their rear. Late afternoon sun gleamed off their black and gold armor, formed by malleable, microscopic chain mail. Meanwhile, thirty or more refugees were bent over, hands on knees, subduing gasps for air. In the past hour, their lungs had been stressed to a greater extent than they ever had on Ardosia. Talia internally praised these students for both the courage in their souls and the fight in their hearts.

They stood amongst a thicket of trees that reached high toward the sun, where their dense leaves obscured the rebellion from Ardosia's drones, should their military launch an aerial search for Talia and her team. Talia leaned against the wide base of an old hickory, silencing her crew with a closed fist. Majestically, she unwrapped the golden fabric from her face, and her night-colored hair fell past her shoulders. Birds called in erratic waves, grasshoppers chirped, grass rustled. For a minute she listened.

By now, she and her crew, according to her estimation, would have traveled at least two miles from the island. Talia suspected that they had already escaped the clutches of the Empire. She stood for another minute to be sure. No soldiers approached. Only the sounds of buzzing cicadas, chirping cardinals, and creaking wood infiltrated Talia's ears.

At last, when the coast was surely clear, Talia directed her attention to a soldier groaning in immense pain. The two men who had carried him on a cumbersome stretcher had set him atop a layer of brush. Now they stood beside the wounded man. Coughing and aching, they leaned upon one another to regain their stamina. She went to them first.

"Good work," she said before shouting to the rest of her men. "I need two fresh bodies, stallions to replace these men."

Instantly, a competition broke out. Men scrambled over one another to prove their courage. It was the young, spry soldiers who made it to her first. Indiscriminately, she chose two of them.

"Do you have enough left in the tank to carry George back to base?"

"Yes, General," they said in unison.

"Good. Go. Take him to medical ASAP, and I mean fucking ASAP."

They bent over, hoisting George's stretcher on their shoulders. Now at eye level with Talia, George leaned over to receive Talia's praise, grimacing from the laceration imposed on his left leg.

She said gently, with a low voice that implied satisfaction, "You're a brave man, George. Let's get you back to your family, huh?"

"Y-yes, General," he said, shivering. He left her with a smile as he was carted back to base.

It seemed that all eyes were locked on Talia, the leader of this rebellion. The escaped students appeared equally awestruck and afraid. Surely, they had no idea what they had gotten themselves into, so Talia felt the need to assuage their concern.

"Hi," she tried to smile at them.

Their collective reply was an awkward stare. One brave student in the middle of them spoke up: a darker girl with braids in her hair. "Who're you?"

Talia searched for the source of the inquiry. "I'm General Talia. Who might you be?"

The girl appeared to ponder the invitation. Her manner was not one of fear. Likely, there was not the slightest hint of it in this girl's system. She nodded back and spoke with a slight twang, "I'm Trixie, and you can call me that." Trixie walked forward and extended a hand.

"Trixie," she said. "The honor is mine." She walked over and shook the girl's hand, understanding that Trixie would be the spokesperson for the contingent of bewildered students. Resting watchful eyes upon them all, the General said, "Walk with me."

They did.

Leading the new rebellion with Trixie at her side, Talia guided the horde of wet, scared escapees. Her men were assembled at their sides and backs to ease their worries. She remembered what it was like to be in the position of a refugee, afraid and unsure. It was important that she gain their trust quickly.

Together Talia, her men, and the students swept through the brush, moving as one unit. Talia inferred exhaustion with a few backward glances. She knew the students would submit to their weariness if they thought it was *okay* to do so. As was always the case, shifting mentalities was the first order of business. "Stand straight," she ordered without raising her voice. They did as she asked.

Now that they would focus more on maintaining robust posture than appealing to their restful desires, Talia was determined to answer the queries swirling through their minds and quell any misgivings. She did not stop trudging forward as she spoke.

"I applaud every one of you for taking a leap of faith with us. The courage required to abandon your life of seamless comfort and assurance is not lost on us. You'd be interested to discover that the men at your side have *all* taken the same path as yourselves. They, too, latched onto the opportunity to escape Ardosia. It's an act requiring immense bravery, so laud yourselves accordingly."

Talia led them further, allowing her words to settle in before she continued. "What you've done could have been the most foolish endeavor of your lives, for all you knew. My men and I could have been hell-bent cannibals looking to harvest your internals for sustenance, or we may have simply tortured you for the pleasure of it. Obviously, this is not the case, but surely, these thoughts and considerations raced through your minds in the fateful moment you decided to escape Ardosia. It was the largest risk you've thus far taken, one that I *promise* will pay off.

"Why, then, have you elected to follow in the footsteps of so many before you? Why did you bounce at the same opportunity to escape? Think for a minute. And if after a minute, you don't already have your answer bursting with excitement through the walls of your being, I encourage you to turn around and head back. Keep walking until you find yourself at the gates of Ardosia, where you should arrest yourself for being as vacuous as they hoped to make you. Your answer has no need to be spoken. No reason to convince anyone else. You alone should know."

Trixie interjected with steely sass. "I left cuz Vardus is a creep. I heard he eats women's placentas after they give birth. Gets some sick pleasure out of it, or somethin'."

A silence of intrigue captured the rebellion. Talia observed, "Your conviction is stronger than the God-awful wall they built around you. Kudos." At this, she took an opportunity to walk backward and face them since the ground they were working was relatively flat. "Your conviction, perhaps not your reasoning, should mirror hers." Talia swept her gaze over them. Many faces peered downward in thought while others faced forward. She twisted her body around.

"Where are we going?" a voice from the back of the pack wondered. "And how much further until we get there?"

Advancing on a slight incline, the group held close as they navigated through the forest. As they delved deeper, the muggy conditions waxed, the stillness of the air offering no reprieve. All the while, gentle bird calls echoed.

"Our trek is almost over," Talia assured them succinctly. Woven vine hung from low-lying limbs. "Watch your heads."

Five minutes passed before Trixie spoke on the students' behalf. Her eyes crossed Talia and her men. "Who … what are you?"

"That depends," said Talia.

"Depends? On what?"

"What type of answer you're searching for."

"A straight one," Trixie said strongly. "Had enough o' the politics on that island. Tell me straight."

Talia was beginning to like this Trixie girl. "Fair enough." Before she began, she gestured toward her soldiers, "We're a family of sorts. Misfits, orphans, refugees, all working in conjunction."

"Orphans?" Trixie was stuck on the word.

"People without parents," Talia said placidly. She'd given this explanation on several previous extractions. "It's what we are. Each and every one of you beautiful souls were created in the joining of a man and woman, but they were taken from us. Or rather … we were taken from them."

"I'm as confused as a penguin who's just discovered it got wings but ain't no use for 'em." All students hummed in unison with Trixie's sentiments.

Talia chuckled. "We all have a mom and dad. But we were taken before we could know them. Vardus, as well as his professors, know that the quickest and surest route to power is through the next generation. Steal the children, obtain the future." She shook her head. "All we ever were to them was a LEGO piece upon which they could erect their empire."

Trixie appeared to be stuck in a nodding cycle, until she cocked her head. "LEGO?"

Talia huffed in amusement. "Right, I forgot how much they suppressed your knowledge. Not to worry. My people will get you up to speed. Anything and everything your unlimited minds wish to know."

"What do you do?" Trixie blurted.

"We do a lot."

"Like?"

"It'd be better for me to show you."

They scaled another incline, this one rising higher and higher in a seemingly endless fashion. Dusk was setting upon them as the tree cover attenuated. More open land brought lush grasses, wild flowers, and prairie rodents. Students marveled at a brave mouse that dashed between them. Curiosity piqued, they paused behind Talia, who mounted a crest. They could not yet see what awaited them.

Talia found the crest, where at its edge the land fell into a concave valley far below. Favoring the students with a stern nod, Talia anticipated her favorite part of the extraction. "Everyone made it okay? Yeah? Good." She angled her body to the side, "Welcome to your new home." Talia beamed with pride. "We call it Merciadel."

A tentative shuffling overtook the new members of their society, until one soldier ushered Trixie to the crest with an inviting hand.

Unveiled before their eyes was the pride of Talia's life, the home she'd helped build as a young adult. It was always prettiest in the evening, when the sun leaned on the horizon.

Merciadel was a vast expanse of flat ground, where the buildings gave way to twice as much open space. The entire estate took up at least three times the amount of land that covered Ardosia's island. As the sun set, light slapped against the Western edges of structures and trees, casting elongated shadows over the hard red ground. It was as if an unoccupied desert had been preserved in the middle of the jungle since the dawn of time, fashioned by the hand of God specifically to accommodate for those who would find themselves at odds with evil in the world. Made of heavy red sand over silt, the ground here distinguished itself from the rich darkness of the forested land stretching in all directions. It should have been barren, but their harvests were rich, and the trees were healthy and strong.

To an elite, Merciadel was nothing special, perhaps a land of poverty. But to those who inhabited it, Merciadel was home. Everything from brick-and-mortar factories, to miniature neighborhoods of wood-built houses, to fields for training and for play adorned the grounds where two tenets of fulfillment remained their priority: freedom and safety. There were scattered trees, both outside and in, rising in the beautiful arbitrary fashion nature had selected. The massive property was guarded by surrounding wooden posts to ward off intruders of both creature and human likeness. Flags protruded every twenty yards to pridefully display that this was their land: the land of the free. Protected both by men and the will of God, Merciadel had survived onslaught after onslaught– presented by man and nature alike. Talia had to believe that a higher power was on Merciadel's side. It was the only way they'd survived this long.

Trixie's face lit up. "Holy Shannon, y'all gotta see this!" She started jogging recklessly down the steep face of the hill, her braids bouncing up and down as she went down into the valley where the simple man's paradise awaited her.

"Go on," Talia urged, gesturing. She was received with a few excited, but wary glances. With more precaution than Trixie, the remaining students descended into the valley.

Talia remained where she was at the top of the hill while her soldiers escorted the students to the site. From here, the view was unmatched in her eyes, as beautiful today as it had been when she watched the town rise before her.

"This is the only time I see you smile," a voice came unnervingly close to her ear.

Talia backed off. "Byron."

"Always Ms. Tough Girl, hardened by her past. I get it. You have a nice smile. I'd show it off if I were you."

A silence fell between them, filled with Talia's anger.

Byron's head wandered. Then he fixed her with a look of forced satisfaction. "I deserved that, guarding flank. You were absolutely right to place me there. You're a good leader who knows when men need punishment. I needed punishment, but I'll say flank wasn't so bad. Frank really ought to stop bitching."

Her gaze hung over the valley. "You're a terrible liar, Byron."

"No lies in this smile."

Not amused, Talia said, "You will not be promoted." She knew this was what he had been working toward.

For months now the position of Colonel had technically been vacant. The case could be made for several soldiers to fill the spot, but it remained empty to encourage nobility and stronger bonds through competition amongst her men. Every one of her soldiers saw themselves filling the Colonel position, including some who least deserved it.

"Oh, come on!" Byron pestered. "I've learned my lesson. Guarding flank taught me *so* much. My leadership skills are really honed in now, I swear."

"A leader is never late. You want that position? Punctuality might be a good place to start."

Byron heaved a dramatic sigh, sweeping his eyes across the valley below: the place they called home. "Contrition. That little tug of remorse. You feel it right?"

Talia squinted at him. "Attempting to guilt trip me into making you Colonel isn't just imprudent, soldier. It's suicidal. I've beheaded men for committing less grievances against me."

"No, no, no." Byron nodded at the students who flooded the front entrance. "I mean them." Like a bunch of ebullient puppy dogs, they scurried inside, encouraged by Talia's men to take a look around at their new home. "Your insides must corrode with all the lies you tell. It's a classic trope for men to become the monsters they swore to destroy, but seeing it from a woman somehow makes it seem worse."

Wide, unbelieving eyes poked at Byron. *"Lies?"*

"Oh, please. Stick it to the man in your inspirational introductory speeches to these guppies. Criticize Vardus for his vice of tyranny. Excoriate his system of 'roles'. Pretend that Merciadel isn't the same."

Talia's voice turned cold. "Merciadel is *nothing* like Ardosia. How dare you?"

"Sure it is," Byron offered. "I mean, Ardosia has nice buildings, a massive lake, and a coliseum. Meanwhile, we have … well, we have each other, I guess."

If she were a lesser woman, Talia might have struck him across the face for his outlandish jargon. She might have castrated him and pinned his balls to a tree. Byron embodied her problem with men to a *T*. Overconfident and dissatisfied, no matter the gifts before him. Blind to the true beauties of the world, men swarm to short-term pleasures of lust, wealth, and esteem. Talia hardly had the patience to interact with such a buffoon. "So go back to the island," she said.

Hands up, Byron said, "Whoah, whoah. Don't get ahead of yourself, honey. Merciadel is home, I agree. But look at them." Many of the new members of their society were afflicted with immense jubilation, exhilarated by the freedom they had just acquired. "They believe they're free from restrictions, loose from the bonds of government, no longer required to fill a role. Simply put, darling, it's a lie."

Talia ignored the fact that he had called her both *honey* and *darling*. Those words elicited the urge to vomit. "If you're suggesting that our protection of freedom is a guise because we follow the path of law and order, I suggest you keep your troubles to yourself. Do you not believe in the principles we've set forth? Are you not satisfied with the life you have here? These students, although inexperienced, are not stupid. They're smart enough to make their own decisions. What they see in Merciadel is a way out, a path to freedom–exactly what it's meant to be. And yes, they'll all find a role within our walls. But at least they will *choose* how to provide a benefit to our society. If you believe that not to be a gift, but rather a chain to be worn around your ankles, you don't belong in our ranks at all."

Byron lowered his head. "I believe you're misconstruing my words, Tal."

"You do *not* call me Tal. Understood, Private?"

Byron said nothing. To their right, the sun had merged with the sea of tree cover, threatening darkness. He sauntered over to the unmoving General, placing a hand on her shoulder. "Look, I haven't intended to offend you. Sometimes you can be unrealistic … and just a bit uptight is all."

Talia felt her face burning. The man was his own worst enemy. She started to believe he was hers, too. "You're dismissed."

Still for a moment, Byron nodded then left for the front gate of Merciadel.

Talia composed herself before following. She was the last one in the gate as the sun fell beneath the curving hills. Torches lit the camp as Talia motioned to a guard, prompting the gate to be closed. This would seal Merciadel for the night

"Hold up," a student stumbled over, worried. "You're not just locking us in here like they did on the island, right?"

Talia had been intent on the process of locking the gate. She turned to the girl with a smile. "Trixie, hi! No, no. Here, you're free to do as you please."

"So I can leave right now if I want."

She shrugged. "You have full, unfettered autonomy over yourself now."

"Alright, just makin' sure. I don't really wanna leave. It's nice here, but I can't be a prisoner no more."

Talia favored Trixie with another smile. "I would have highly recommended that you wait until morning, anyway." She nodded to the gate. "What lies on the other side, during the night especially, is a death trap. Not to insult your outdoorsmanship, Trixie, but I think you can understand that in the battle between man–or woman–and nature, it often doesn't turn out well for man out here."

"Or woman," Trixie added, pensive.

A slight breeze picked up. Branches swayed and leaves rustled, giving the illusion that creatures may already be lurking, in the trees and elsewhere, as they waited for a free meal in human form.

Leading the young woman more toward the camp center, Talia said, "I'm glad you want to stay. Let's get you and the others to your bunks, shall we?"

"Bunks? You mean we share beds and rooms?"

"For now, yes." The ladies strolled side-by-side. "I'll admit that we may not have the lavish amenities offered by Ardosia, but we will soon. Safety has to be ensured first."

The students were gathered, their collective jubilance declining as night took over. They were exhausted and would sleep well. Escorting them to dorms reserved for newcomers, Talia showed them the hall where they would rest. She stood outside the building as they moved in past her. Many shared thanks and took their sleeping arrangements graciously. Others said nothing, perhaps digesting the stark contrast in their new lives. Trixie was last among them, standing at Talia's side. She was full of questions.

"You keepin' us safe from what's out there?" Trixie looked past the wooden wall upon which flags billowed. "What *is* out there?"

Happily, Talia reported, "Nothing we can't stop. Merciadel has trained some of the best fighters in the world. I'm sure you noticed how we fared against Ardosians."

"Hmm," Trixie pondered, allowing her curiosity to roam. "Night like tonight … think your fighters could survive out there? Maybe even alone?"

Stars poked brilliantly through the layer of night. Talia admired them, wondering at just that. The wild contained some of the fiercest creatures known and unknown to man. Their primal instincts guided them to hunt and kill, occasionally just for sport. Her men were strong, but out there, survival depended equally as much on luck as it did strength. Before proposing a good night's rest, Talia said to Trixie, stern, "No man, regardless of skill, is going to survive out there alone."

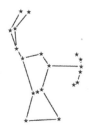

XI

Persistence and optimism. Surviving twenty years inside the physical and psychological encampment of Ardosia would not have been possible without them. Orian couldn't count the nights he spent either praying to God or venting to Ladis about the bitter taste the island, the Schedule, and President Vardus had, day-in and day-out, left in his mouth. Trudging through the exercises, overcoming Yjn, and finding the courage to rest when he was restless. Those were examples of his persistence. Believing that one day, something in the horizon might possess the world to behave differently, to open a portal for Orian so that he might escape his miserable life. Though desperate, that was his optimism. Orian took a moment to thank God for making these as inseparable from his bones as the DNA strands that composed them. Now his legs wobbled with each step, sweat infiltrated his eyes, and the dreadful disease called doubt threatened Orian's will as night fell upon the jungle. He would have to rely on persistence and optimism yet again.

Breathing hard, Orian shouldered himself against a tree. Above, an ethereal wind cast its brilliance through the swaying branches as it issued peaceful tunes of nature. The young man did not fight to suppress his cheery grin. It was surreal to Orian, all of it. The escape, the drop, the swim … the death.

He skirted the clutches of Yjn and two guards. He was no longer constricted to a classroom. At long last, he felt the rush he'd always craved, as abundant as ever when he busted through an arched tunnel beneath the Wall. Everything Orian had ever known as "normal" was now moot, and he couldn't strap the resulting elation. But his grin eventually faded.

Orian had also left his closest–and perhaps only–friend Ladis behind. He watched a man's life vanish at the carnivorous desires of air-breathing fish, their jaws snapping contentedly at human flesh. And his escape had come with the pressing resistance of a small fleet of soldiers who chased him through the jungle for several hundred yards before they were lost or chose to give up. He encountered these soldiers after exiting the tunnel. It was almost as if they had been chasing someone else and had accidentally stumbled upon a little lost boy with a welding tool. Nevertheless, Orian evaded their tail.

Could Orian's escape have gone better? A million times over, yes. The universe could have reserved one more hanger for Orian so that he wouldn't have had to resort to a leather belt as his lifeline. He could have jumped earlier and left under the protection of the rebels. Maybe then he wouldn't have been forced to kill an innocent man. Ladis could have gone with him...

Orian shook the thought. The only cards worth pondering are the ones life has dealt, not the ones you wish you had. It's up to you to make the best of each hand. Orian admittedly hadn't understood this analogy until he familiarized himself with a game called Texas Hold 'Em–or poker, for short–via the Internet. The idea of the game intrigued him greatly. There was also the prospect of gambling, which was something he felt he did quite often in life, to this point without chip or paper currency. Someday, Orian would learn to play. But first, he had to outlast another challenge life had presented him.

As the night rolled in, it swallowed the hills and cloaked the trees, the light of the crescent moon competing unsuccessfully with the impregnable shade. In the vast jungle, Orian was naught but a speck. Darkness fell upon him, too. Fear of the dark Orian had been aware of, just not subject to it. He embraced the natural quality of the cycle between day and night and what they implied for humanity. The day was meant for seizing–Carpe Diem. Moonlight was meant for rest.

Leaning against the rough bark of a tree, Orian felt the aching of his joints, the soreness of his limbs, and the weariness of his mind. After what seemed like several miles of delving into the unknown, Orian felt sure that he had shed the Ardosian tail following him. He was less certain about the watchful eyes of lurking predators. Although inexperienced in the wild, Orian was not oblivious to its accompanied dangers. Aware of most potential predators, he fell circumspect primarily to his imagination. Yet of all the weight that now stacked Orian's brain, he was loath to remind himself of his need for food. His stomach growled on cue.

"Shush," Orian commanded his trim belly. For all he knew, a lion, tiger, or sasquatch could have interpreted the involuntary growl as a challenge and just then decide to launch itself from the shadows at him. He shuddered. *None of that.* Orian had almost forgotten about optimism. God would not have allowed him to escape with his life just to die at the hands of a wild beast in the middle of a vast, seemingly endless jungle where nobody–absolutely nobody–would ever find his remains, whereupon his existence would be coterminous with a nearby pile of scat starting to clog Orian's nasal cavity, which is to say utterly meaningless. *It's good I'm an optimist,* he reminded himself.

Weaponless, technology-less, and without a bed, Orian was alone. Inexplicably, he didn't feel alone, almost like a spirit was hanging at his side for protection. He watched as low-swinging vine and skyward-growing brush danced in the night. He was mindless to the potential eyes they concealed, eyes that could be waiting. They didn't matter. He had made it this far. Ardosia was behind him. As far as Orian was concerned, he was in paradise.

His eyes peeked through a small hole in the canopy above, where a spectral pane of gray-blue light broke through the cover. Moonlight was meant for rest. While Orian believed himself to be vulnerable if he were to recline on the jungle floor and snooze like a carcass for a few hours, he was even more disconcerted about the thought of moving on through the night. Moving equaled noise. He felt the less noise he made the better. The tree he was leaning against was hospitable, a welcome place to stay for a night. So Orian allowed his knees to buckle. He sat on the ground, exhaling madly. Rest was unfavorable when he wanted to run, while bogging humidity clung to his shirt, but he had to shut his eyes for just a few minutes

...

XII

Chunks of wood crackled and smoked as embers rose toward the elevated slab of maroon sustenance. Venison cooked quickly in comparison to beef and pork, and Hudson preferred his meat rare. His makeshift rack, which was an old spear that he sliced through the meat, was bolstered by two wooden supports—one on either side of the pit. This allowed Hudson to spin the meat a foot and a half above the flames. Slow-cooking his meat stole his attention for a longer period so that he might not be drug through the muddy past in the absence of distraction.

Rocks formed the circumference of the pit. They had been gathered many years ago and placed several hundred yards from Hudson's cabin, where the prevailing winds were allowed to swoop down through one of the few openings in the jungle and reduce the humidity in the area. He didn't mind walking so far just to prepare his meals. There wasn't much else to do with his days, anyway.

Hudson flipped the meat twice before it was suited to his liking. His father had taught him the right way to cook meat when he was a child. Those days, though long gone and never to return, were of fond memory to Hudson in his ripe age.

After removing the venison from the spear, he placed it in a hand-woven bag, as he would carry it back to the cabin. Then the fire was vanquished by casting a tarp over the pit, snatching the oxygen that those tongues of flame needed to survive.

His twenty-four-ounce portion weighed like a feather in his hands as his boots trundled through the dense jungle floor. It was a humid and sticky day that slapped sweat on Hudson's wide neck, his joints aching due to age, but he hardly noticed. Pain and discomfort were the tenets of life. The more you tried to avoid them, the less living you did.

A couple hundred yards from the cabin is where Hudson first heard the peculiar noise. It seemed to stem from his home–a mix between a painful screeching and a desperate bray. Hudson hurried his pace from a saunter to a stroll. Through the air, the noise carried with strength, like a cry for help. As Hudson topped the final hill, he peered down to his property and noticed nothing out of the ordinary, until the cry shot forth once more, giving up the fawn's position.

Back in the day, Hudson might have belted contagious laughter. Today, he managed a smirk.

In between a couple of fence posts, a small fawn had lodged its head, perhaps in search of garden vegetables.

The little one had managed to insert himself through one of the miniscule cracks, but he would not be able to escape on his own. It seemed the more he struggled, the worse his situation became.

Hudson approached the animal with curiosity, but his proximity only drove panic through the fawn. It screeched and brayed and did everything in its power to escape, wearing the pelt on its neck to the point of bleeding.

Through the front door, Hudson entered his sod-roofed and solar-paneled hut. He set the venison onto a cutting board near the sink, then exited through the side door where he would find the garden. The fawn made eye contact with him, and yet again its valiant efforts only worsened its situation. The large man instilled an unhealthy amount of fear as he approached, evident in the way that the fawn gave its final attempt before submitting to its fate of an early death.

Kneeling next to the hurt animal, Hudson laid a massive hand on its head, to which it recoiled, sapping its remaining energy. Its body started to fall limp, but the sight of a few peppers in Hudson's other hand gave the animal hope. Although a smile would be a gesture that it may not understand, Hudson offered one to the fawn anyway, to wash ease over him.

Warily, the baby doe eyed Hudson, then sniffed the peppers, then eyed Hudson again. Reaching forward, it took one cautious bite of the vegetables. It took another. And another, until it was unaware that Hudson was gripping the animal just above the neck, on top of its head. Swiftly, he dropped the peppers, angled the fawn's neck, and pushed it through the fence. In a split second, the fawn darted off into the trees, freed from its deathly bonds after all.

Hudson couldn't help but chuckle at the precious little girl as she blended into the distance, but when he heard himself laugh, he was startled. It was a noise that had become foreign to him, to the point that he hadn't been sure he was capable of laughter any longer. This ability, along with the release of the fawn, intrigued him. He may have even felt a sliver of hope, for what reason he was unsure.

Returning inside, Hud prepared a plate of chopped venison and vegetables for dinner. He set it on the table, placed a towel over his lap, and folded his hands into each other. Gently, he offered a prayer of thanks to the one God above.

Reverence and prayer were uncomfortable to Hudson, and they had been for some time. After a considerable amount of time absent from faith, Hudson wondered what it would be like to rekindle the flame. It wasn't as simple as riding a bike. It was strange, and it hurt knowing that his faith would never be the same as it was before … well, before. Maybe it wasn't supposed to be the same. Regardless, Hudson had made a concerted effort to sneak back into his prayerful ways, one inch at a time. Praying before meals had been a rediscovered ritual of his for just over a year now, and he wondered if God had really accepted him like the Prodigal son or if his prolonged lack of faith had already damned him.

After praying, Hudson ate his meal gratefully. There was a time when he viewed the world and everything in it with a bitter attitude. In many ways, he still did. But there comes a point when moving on is less painful than hanging on. At the same time that Hudson's soul rejoined the spiritual realm, his body fell back into his habits of exercise.

He was glad there was no one for which he might offer advice. If they were to ask for inspiration, he'd be compelled to lie to them and say that working out and praying fulfilled him in every way imaginable and that they would find such actions fulfilling as well. The truth was that Hudson, no matter his routine, felt the same, devoid of most emotions. The truth also was that he was unsure why he exercised and prayed. It didn't fulfill him any more than if he didn't partake in the actions at all. He found the older he became, the less answers he had, but he was okay with that.

After finishing his meal, Hudson washed his plate and stuck it in the cupboard with the rest. There really was no need for him to have more than one or two plates, for he would never have company. Yet there was an excess in his cupboard–just because.

He ambled into the living room, where a circular wooden lamp desk sat beside a recliner that faced a fireplace. In the modicum of open space is where Hudson performed his pushups. Once he finished these, he would have an hour until bedtime.

In this final hour of the day, he allowed his walls to fall as recompense for warding off the demons over the previous fifteen. He would have to fall into his recliner, for he had not the strength to stand during the cerebral exercise. First, the fire was lit to offset the chill that would soon result.

Inhaling sharply, the huge man closed his eyes, leaning back into his creaking chair. He did not have to work hard to summon the flashes. After all, they had been fighting all day to get in.

Their cries strummed chords of horror, aiding the orchestra of the Devil. A man entered the black and white frame. Hair in a bun, freckles peeking out of the top buttons on his chest. He looked sadistically pleased with himself.

"You did this on your own, Hud."

The image panned to a beautiful woman–middle-aged, fearfully and wonderfully created. Her hair held a natural perm with streaks of both darkness and light tied behind her ears. Breaths floating in the crisp air before her, she appeared to detest the dress she wore, as if she'd been forced to slip into it. Beside her was a young boy, six years old at the time, the red in his eyes evident even through the colorless frame. He held his arms close as he shivered beside the pit, donning a onesie with fish dotting the cloth. Finally, there was a girl, age four and three-quarters, who held her doll close. Of the three, she appeared to be the least afraid, her faith in God and his plan admirably unwavering. Still, fearful tears escaped her, no matter how she worked to hide them. Their names were Esmer, Adger, and Loren Steehl: Hudson's wife, his son, and his daughter.

Mercilessly, the soldiers stood ten feet away–six of them with guns aimed pointedly at their screaming targets. The man in black came back into frame, with a faux tear filling his right eye.

"It really does hurt me to do this, pal. No choice. No choices in the matter, because you made yours. YOU did."

"James, please. Why are you doing this?" The camera panned to Esmer. Her pleas, to the absolute knowledge of Vardus, would drive knives through Hudson's heart, should he be forced to hear them. "Spare my babies. Take me, but spare my babies."

Again, James came into view. He pursed his lips in feigned regret. Sighing, he said, "In my new country, the

magnificent country of Ardosia, laws will *be upheld." He
shook his head. "No exceptions."*

"James, no! James!"

*Heavy and long barrels weighted the soldiers' hands.
They'd been on display for too long. It was time.*

*"I won't make you watch this, Hud. And for the record,
I am sorry."*

*In a final motion, the camera panned down. The screen
went black. Hopeful pleas continued until they were
silenced by the bone-shaking, earth-shattering, gut-
wrenching, and utterly deafening barrel cracks that sent
rounds into the hearts of the Steehl family, whereupon the
feed was cut.*

Hudson opened his eyes. A single tear fell. The flames
held behind the sheet of glass near him roared with
newfound intensity. For the past twenty years, he hadn't
surpassed this memory. He knew that until his death, it
would haunt him, and maybe even beyond the grave it
would, too.

Hudson would never be able to wash the traumatic
video from his mind.

Interacting with these thoughts worked undoubtedly to
Hudson's detriment, but his family was intertwined with
his DNA. Every memory of them swirled in a reclusive
corner of his brain, but the recollection of their final
moments seemed to escape more often than the others.

A tight chest and gritted teeth were his symptoms.
Profuse sweat and heavy, erratic breathing. Paralysis, too.
Hudson could have saved his family, but he saved the girl
instead. It was a memory he would not dwell on now. In
the face of his wrongdoings, he could not move.

The big man surmised that his mistake had never been
rooted in his actions. No, his mistake was loving too

fiercely, allowing mortal humans, whether they be derived from him or not, to grip his heart strings so closely that they should mold into the fiber of his being. It was a mistake that Hudson vowed, from that point onward, never to make again.

He thought of the girl he saved again and remembered, *The magazine.* Lying face-down on his stand were a collection of irrelevant colorful pages. Hudson swiped through them until he found the only page that mattered. The paragraphs were gibberish, but in them he found the coded message. It was one that eased the sharp stabs plaguing his heart, at least until they would return in the morning.

XIII

Erie formations of gray and black blotted out the sun, engineering a day so dark and sullen it could have been mistaken for night. Mist fell sideways as it floated spiritually through the air before finding a surface to cling on: native grasses, skyscraper buildings, a coliseum, an umbrella.

Lightning cracked at six that morning, followed by booming thunder. James Vardus, President of Ardosia, didn't so much as blink when the stained-glass window had shaken intensely. *Another escaped,* he had been thinking. At what point would his trials end? Could he not live in the peaceful world he was attempting to assemble? The anxiety angered him. It depleted the reserves that fed his carnal desires. They would need refilled.

Vardus had already been lying awake in his bed for hours when the storm rattled his window. Usually, the President relished in his rest, waking only for morning prayer at eight and occasionally returning to bed after. Sloth was one of the seven deadly sins, but the weight of an entire people rode persistently on his shoulders. And now he was reaching sixty-some odd years old. He stopped counting years ago. His body, although in pristine shape for his age, was growing languid. He didn't mind giving in to his need for shut-eye.

Today, however, Vardus had showered, dressed, and passed through the bottom door of his grand Tower by six-thirty. In pursuit of the fulfillment of his needs, he found himself stranded in the middle of Ardosia on a tortuous concrete path. He was visually arrested by the perfect water droplets cascading down onto his island. The umbrella he held over his head was black. It went well with the jacket and leather gloves he donned. Those were also black. Nobody really cared to inquire about the symbolism of his attire, which was alright. Vardus was a humble leader who needed no recognition. He didn't hesitate to remember what black did. It absorbed. Heat, light, and sin were carried by this, the darkest color. Vardus did not need recognition because his mission was clear, and he carried his cross with pride.

He must've been the only creature stirring at this early hour. Lonesome in the outdoors, he perceived no existence of other life, feeling like a man strolling through purgatory alone. For many minutes now, Vardus found himself captivated and stilled by the ethereal mist. It was silent. So, so quiet for a storm. It was a sign, to Vardus, that strength, power, and noise had no correlation.

Winding down the path, the first birdsongs traveled through the rain, delighting Vardus's ears. He held such passion for the wildlife around his island, and he loved to hear those birds sing.

Approaching the far West end of Ardosia, where no students and only select staff were allowed to roam, a dense tree cover remained. At the time of the island's construction, just after the fall of the Nation, a nursery had been installed there. Right Hand Hudson planted them, and Vardus requested that they remain, even after that poor old bastard left. He knew he would need a secluded area that provided respite and relief, somewhere where he was sure to find peace and quiet. Treacherous weeks like these necessitated an escape to his happy place.

Amidst the trees there was a trampled path that wove naturally through the old nursery. It veered off from the concrete path and snaked into the high wall of overgrowth. It had taken Vardus some time to get here. A considerable distance had been placed between the island center and Vardus's holy place so that no simple fool could stumble upon it.

Folding his umbrella and stowing it beneath an armpit, the President was swallowed by nature. He ducked beneath overhanging branches, swiped at pine needles reaching for his eyes, and limbered through tight spaces until he came out upon an opening secluded by surrounding thickets. There were two buildings here, the only two that God had ever required: a church and a house.

The cathedral clung barely to life at the South side of the opening. Built near the trees, moss overgrew the stone, and the wood inside was slowly rotting. Its use was rare, but Vardus treasured the archaic majesty of it nonetheless.

And at the North end of this reclusive hideout was the house. Humble though it was, Vardus considered it to be a generous mansion he had bestowed upon those who inhabited it. The house stood two stories tall in the middle of the stretch of open land, resting on an elevated stone slab. Its exterior was a shade of ugly green, not unlike the color of the jungle. It drew Vardus's eye from the crest upon which it rested. This is what he had come for.

In reverence, Vardus reminisced on the early days of Ardosia, when he and his side of history had defeated those who stood perilously with the Old Nation. Those days, despite their banality with tragedy, seemed so much simpler to Vardus. His path had been clearer, his conviction more robust, and his prostate in better condition. Leading a nation was riddled with difficulty, and it had aged him mentally, if not physically.

Yet here was his most sacred house, the one that he and his Right Hand had built together. Sedulously, Vardus and Hudson labored to erect this stronghold of peace. In just over two months, it was finished. With a little help, they poured the concrete foundation. Walls went up first, and seemingly in the blink of an eye, four bedrooms, two bathrooms, and a shingled roof had come together. Since Hudson preferred to avoid the politics and people of the island, the house had originally been built for he and his family–a place of solitary seclusion. Here, he would have found the peace and distance from mayhem for which he'd been searching. He could have been the under-the-radar leader he was meant to be. A true shame Vardus and the big man came at odds with one another.

The umbrella unfurled in the President's hands as the mist escalated into a light rain. It provided the man in black with cover as he started toward the domestic green structure. Weekly were Vardus's visits to this lonesome hideout guarded by three or four men at all times. Generally, he viewed these visits as a courtesy he provided to those living within, but this week he needed them nearly as much as they needed him.

A deep breath escaped him as all four window panes at the house's façade came into view. Ridiculously, Vardus felt his heart rate rise. Was he nervous? Couldn't be. Perhaps he was subconsciously lamenting his previous struggles with the girls beyond that door. He held various types of intimate relationships with all three of them, though they weren't always receptive to him. There was a time when Vardus had put forth valiant efforts to prove his worth so that they might engage with him. But he had neither the time nor energy to entertain consensual romance.

Each relationship contained something unique and special. The older woman, whom he called May, had become more complacent with time. Gray streaked through her luxurious brown hair, and she'd kept a supple frame through her years. Vardus loved many of the dresses she wore, whether they be spotted with polka-dots or flowers or nothing at all. Somehow, he didn't even mind when she wore black, though that was *his* color. Vardus reasoned that May could don nightshade because she was owned by him and would be seen only by Vardus and the mute guards outside the house.

Vardus loved that May didn't fight near as much as her spitting-image daughter, whom he labeled Miss. Miss was a rebel. He'd expended his fair share of patience with her, but the challenge she presented was all the more entertaining to him.

And then there was the third, just a girl.

Water splashed around his boots as Vardus ambled through a puddle he'd overseen. His hands started to shake, and his body stiffened. Adrenaline was working its way through him. Over the years, James had been with many women, but none ever instilled the thrill he received from May and Miss. His pants required adjustment before he continued.

"Sir." One of the guards greeted him as he climbed the doorstep, folding the umbrella. Vardus forgot to acknowledge his soldier.

He knocked three times at the door. There was a pause. Then a few clicks came from the other end.

Patting a nervous hand on the bun atop his head, Vardus swallowed. The door opened to reveal the youngest of the house, a girl of twelve years.

Vardus nodded at her with a redeeming smile. Her shoulders were wide for her age, stretching the pink shirt James had given her in a prior visit. Her gorgeous blue eyes would pierce the souls of Ardosia's men someday. Worn on her face was the same expression as always: stoic to the point of zombification. Vardus assumed this trait to be a debilitating wisdom beyond the possibility of her age. The girl was only twelve, after all.

Yet there she stood. Inside, there were two women whom he held in his heart, but they meant nothing when stacked against the little girl before him. Here she was: the blood of his blood, the strength of his lore, the poise of his structure. This girl was the third of the house. Her name was Morro, and she was Vardus's daughter.

"Hi there," Vardus offered feebly.

Morro's frame held still before she ushered her father through the door.

XIV

Ladis's stomach grumbled as he sat at the edge of his bed, waiting for dinner to slide through that little hole in the door. The room was dark. No lights were on. The television display didn't even dare. Only the occasional crack of lightning illuminated the space. A brooding stare captured Ladis.

There it is, he thought, unable to comprehend the empty bed beside him. Atop it were the perfectly-made sheets that repudiated the fact that anyone had ever lived with him. In the bathroom, just one towel hung on the rack. Now Ladis was alone, and he abhorred it.

Earlier that day is when the cohort of soldiers barged through his door and confiscated all possessions that Orian had left behind. The men were intimidating, Ladis reflected. Never once had they made eye contact with him as he observed docilely from his bed. It was as though he was just as invisible to them as the person from whom they were stealing. He remembered how sorely he desired to berate the soldiers for their dishonorable conduct, but then he thought, *No. None of this was ever Orian's, anyway. Not the pants, shirts, ties, tablets, or pillows.* Ladis's fingers rubbed against the rough white-cloth T-shirt against his own skin. *And this isn't mine, either.* Everything that he and Orian had ever "owned" was truly the property of Ardosia. The way the soldiers so carefully folded every shirt that Orian used to wear, ensured every sock was a pair, and carefully stole all electronics … it all made Ladis wonder whether he was worth as much to Ardosia's leaders as the possessions he temporarily called his own.

Slowly Ladis rose to find himself at the window. From here, there was a perfect view of the unfinished opening in the Wall, obstructed slightly by the falling rain. This was precisely where the invaders had pulled off their heist, taking several of Ardosia's students. Regretfully, Ladis recalled that Trixie, Dawn's ex-roommate, had been one of those who fled. He had seen the whole thing transpire–half from the classroom and half from this very spot beside his window. He was loath to relive the memory.

Orian's anxiously excited face popped into his mind. They had been standing on opposite ends of the classroom, a taut line having just been fired through the broken glass window. It seemed to have separated him from his roommate almost immediately. Ladis remembered the way he had internally begged Orian not to leave. But the moment that the opportunity for escape had presented itself, Ladis knew. He knew that Orian would jump–literally–at his chance.

A thousand times in the past twenty-four hours, that moment replayed through Ladis's head. He saw it over and over, the way Orian's soul returned to him then. In some ways, Ladis couldn't blame him. Orian had chased something he always longed for, and Ladis might have done the same in his shoes. Hell, for some disturbing reason, Ladis had almost done the same in his *own* shoes!

Ladis recalled the voice in his head that had nailed his feet to the floor. *Go with him,* it had urged. *Leave Ardosia behind.* He remembered considering the zipline and one of the remaining hangers, like it offered a paradise greater than this one. Never before had Ladis procured thoughts of such extreme and ludicrous nature. Yet he had not only heard the voice, but he felt strongly compelled to abide by its calling. He was unable to ward off the tinge of hope that he felt then, and he struggled to deny the same flurry of emotions lingering even now. Ladis wasn't sure how to reconcile it.

What if Orian was right all along? he wondered.

Ladis shook the thought. In Orian's absence, he was beginning to think and sound like his conspiratorial ex-roommate, whom he both missed and hated at the same time. The two of them had been through so much together–literally their entire lives up to this point. And Orian had left, for what? The horrendously dangerous jungle beyond?

The storm swept over the distant hills, unrelenting winds and torrential downpour battering the trees. Protected by the small glass pane and only window in his room, Ladis felt grateful that he had made the decision to stay within the Tower on floor 102, that he had a roof over his head. He wasn't sure if the same could be said for Orian. *God, I hope he's okay.*

There it was again. The longing to defy himself and partake in something outrageous and rebellious–to do something Orian would. Ladis scoffed at the virus taking over his mind. It was completely antithetical to his credence. Still, as he gazed out into the inclement world beyond, he couldn't explain how some part of him wished to be there with Orian.

Ultimately, Ladis attributed this wave of uncharacteristic desire to shock. Yesterday's surreal turn of events had left him dazed and emotionally concussed. Luckily, a distraction came just then.

Behind him at the door, there was a subtle double-tap. Ladis turned just in time to view a small cardboard box slipping through the delivery port. Without flipping a light switch, he sauntered over to it. He wanted to remain in the dark for now. Rubbing the cardboard, Ladis silently thanked whoever it was that dropped off his meal, and then he opened it. Sunflower seeds over cabbage. Ladis's eyes mulled over the food. Tragically, he wondered whether his dinner would fulfill the type of hunger he now felt.

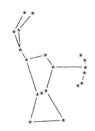

XV

Orian woke to the sound of dripping water going *crunch, crunch, crunch* against the leaves of the forest floor. With one hand, he wiped the crust from his eyes to find that his skin permeated with sweat. He had not a clue how long he'd been asleep, but it must have been a while. Orian batted his eyes. He found the courage to climb to his feet, and in doing so, he began to wonder why his entire body had been drenched in perspiration. His face curled as he pulled at the soaked T-shirt, while he leaned against the hospitable tree that accompanied him through the night. Perhaps it watched him as he had encountered intense overnight dreams.

Orian looked up, the canopy above revealing little of the sky, but enough for Orian to piece together that he hadn't been a sweaty mess after all. It was raining.

Stretching his arms above his head, Orian felt the joints of his back crackle and pop. Then he released a yawn that indicated a waking comfort one might receive, knowing they're in line for a four-course, five-star breakfast in luxury. Orian's stomach chewed itself at the thought. He was still as hungry as he had been when he fell asleep, and the sounds of dripping water alerted him to a horrible case of cottonmouth. This, admittedly, had been the part he hadn't really given prior thought to–things like the fundamental human needs of food, shelter, water. At some point today, he would have to do some hunting for edible plants. He just hoped he could find a couple.

Crunch, crunch. Water fell on leaves on the other side of the tree. Orian thought nothing of it at first, but then he looked around. His brow furrowed at the mist flowing through the air. It was raining, but it wasn't raining hard. And although water would collect atop the trees and eventually fall in drops, would they be so condensed as to *crunch* against leaves? Peeping his head around the base of the tree, Orian investigated and nearly yelped in doing so. He hid swiftly behind the trunk.

His eyes were shut tight. Breathing became erratic. Orian's mind could hardly comprehend the sheer size of the creature he'd seen no more than ten feet away. Curiosity, likely about to kill the cat, tugged at Orian's chest. Slowly, and without making a sound, Orian peeked once more. This time, he watched in awe as the beast prowled with its head bent low to the ground. For reasons unknown to him, Orian felt surprisingly calm in the presence of a quarter-ton, claw-wielding spectacled black bear. He shouldn't have.

Just then, the bear had been alerted to his presence. Orian scolded nature for being radically unfair. He hadn't even made a sound. What could have possibly betrayed him? At that moment, his own stench flooded his nostrils. *That'll do it.*

At once the massive bear moved at Orian, but it did so with elegance and poise ... perhaps the same curiosity Orian had paid in return. Heart lunging to escape his body, Orian took a few scattered breaths, remaining as still as Daniel in a lion's den. Meanwhile, the bear approached him slowly, its large and grotesque nose sniffing madly at the air. Orian hoped to God that he smelled like anything but a meal to the animal.

The bear came closer with each plodding step. Orian could now see into its eyes, which appeared oddly innocent to him. He wouldn't allow looks to deceive him. His troubled mind told him to bolt in the other direction, run for his life, and escape certain death for the umpteenth time in the past three days, but he thankfully had recalled an article from the Internet that guided hikers either to be still or crawl into the fetal position in the presence of bears. There was simply no way to outrun one. Orian chose the first option: be still.

However, as the spectacled bear was now face-to-face with him, he pondered his choice—all of his life choices, really. Leaned up against the tree, Orian felt his hands gripping the bark as tightly as humanly possible. He flinched as the bear reared up onto its hind legs, but it did not swipe its claws against his face, knock him down, or feast on his flesh. Seemingly interested in Orian's position against the tree, the bear had instead mimicked him, reaching its front paws around its circumference. *So that's why they call it a bear hug,* Orian observed. Feebly, he peered up. If he thought the size of the bear on all fours had been frightening, Orian realized that it could get worse, much worse. This massive creature, huddled up against the same tree, towered high above him. It would have been a true sight to behold if not for the fact that the taut string of Orian's life could be cut with one downward clawing swipe.

As majestically as the bear had risen, it began its descent, shuffling down the edge of the tree. It stopped halfway down, acknowledged the face of the adjacent human with curious sniffs, and tested him with a lick just above Orian's brow. It was slimy, terrifying, gross, and touching all at once. The lick must have also confirmed that Orian was not, in fact, prey worth eating.

Like a neighbor visiting for morning tea, the bear growled his goodbyes and carried on. Orian watched as its snout prowled the earth's floor for something more appetizing than himself.

Orian didn't make a single move until he was sure the bear was gone. While he was fortunate to escape alive due to his stillness, Orian realized that he might need a more practical defense strategy in the future. He would need a weapon.

After scouring the earthen floor for a measly five minutes, Orian stumbled upon a fallen branch that was long and straight. It was thick enough to suffice as a weapon, yet nimble to be wielded comfortably as such. He found a rock that had been chipped to form a dull edge, but it would do the trick in sharpening a spear.

Once it was finished, Orian weighed his new defense mechanism in his hands, tilting it to the left and right, noting how well-balanced it was. It was as if nature, or God, were aiding him on this treacherous but exciting journey. He kept the rock in his pocket for future use.

Pleased with himself, Orian determined to set forth for another day's travel. Today he would have to find shelter, and if not that, at minimum he would need food.

That morning, Orian felt a sense of urgency with no desire to dwell on lost sleep and discomfort. He began his journey, poring through the damp hanging vines that obstructed his view as he moved through them. The less he saw, the more anxious he felt, but beneath that anxiety, Orian had felt an even greater sense of belonging. This foreign world was daunting, yet destiny would have him here, nonetheless. Always deferring to the power of choice, Orian was beginning to believe equally in fate.

After traveling for an hour, he turned around. Having delved too deep into the wooded wild to estimate the direction from which he had come or the direction he was going, Orian could have, for all he knew, been returning to the vengeful hands of Ardosia's Wall, where he would be apprehended and treated as the vilest prisoner. He had to remind himself that instinct–not fear–guided him. It told him that he was getting further and further from that wretched place and that he would soon encroach upon his destination, wherever that may be. Orian trusted his instincts, so he moved forward.

A peaceful rain fell upon the mountainous hills, showing no indication of letting up. Orian's shirt was stuck to him like a second layer of skin. It both accentuated his muscular build and kept him cool. Navigating the jungle was a laborious task made even more exasperating by the wet, sticky mud. Yet Orian looked up and grinned as rain dripped onto his face. What a blessing it was to *feel* nature instead of watch it from the wrong side of a glass pane. He smiled and continued onward.

Orian traveled for miles. Gray conditions obscured the shifting from morning into day and day into night. His legs ached quickly after climbing, weaving, and descending through heavily-vegetated hills, but he persisted, led by the compass in his gut. At some point during the day, Orian had encountered a veil of lush growth cut into a steep incline–what he determined to be a large, yawning cave. Briskly he passed by, fearing the potential eyes of bloodthirsty creatures obscured in darkness.

Soon Orian would need to find a cave of his own, or shelter of some sort. And food. His stomach had been eating itself all day, and although much of the vegetation sprouting from the ground appealed to Orian's starving hunger, he could not differentiate between sustenance and poison out here. His approach to life had always been that of a fervent risk-taker, but there was no room for chance-taking in such a foreign environment.

In the jungle, Orian had found a natural path where naught but flowers, roots, and mud rose from the ground, so he followed it on the off chance that it was man-made, leading to shelter. Falling rain had dissipated into a mist, clouds giving way to penetrating starlight that shone on the edges of trees.

Ducking beneath a branch as night fell, Orian did a three-sixty. Had he been walking in a massive circle? He swore he'd come upon this exact space before, noting the way the land rose and fell to his right, how there was nothing beyond the dense, endless thicket before him, and the way in which the path snaked up ahead. It all looked the same. Perhaps he'd been traveling for too long. Orian pondered where or when he might stumble upon civilization. He knew that the invaders had both arrived and retreated through the trees, so life had to be nearer than it seemed. Right?

Suddenly there was a shift in the brush to Orian's left. It happened too quickly for him to adjust. Later he would have to re-wire his survival instinct of icy stillness. What jumped out in front of him could have been a dangerous predator that would seek to end his life and live off his innards, but when he heard the creature squeal and honk, Orian's paralysis ended. The animal popped out from under the leaves of a nearby plant. Squirrelling through the path before him was a wild boar, small tusks jutting out from its mouth and a fat, wide frame hustling across the mud. Orian paused, watching the tusks bounce up and down as the dark, mud-spattered pig scurried onward. Had the animal jumped out and attacked him, one of those tusks could have skewered a limb right then and there. Ignoring the potential danger, Orian felt a compulsion to follow. So he did.

Swiftly Orian chased the pig. He leapt over a large, rotting log that the animal had passed underneath. The path wound this way and that, requiring dexterity, the likes of which Orian hadn't known to be in him. Somehow, he kept pace with the boar, closing the gap. At first, Orian had not a clue why he was chasing the animal, working only on a wild impulse. Running, he eyed the moist makeshift spear in his hands, and his stomach growled madly. It was as if primal instinct had taken over because Orian's conscience recoiled in shock at what he was about to do.

Nevertheless, he followed the boar with impregnable resolve. Adrenaline washed the achiness from his joints and the exhaustion from his lungs. He was filled with newfound hope and energy but quickly began to wonder how long he'd be able to keep up. The boar dodged Orian's first attempt at a stab. It should have disappeared into the brush, but for some reason it held true to the muddy path that sharply rounded a tree, then another. Orian almost lost the boar, but he dug deeper, requiring greater speed from himself.

Squealing and honking, the boar issued its warnings with intensity before it stopped in its tracks and whirled around to face him. It had allowed Orian to catch up, but why? He slowed, taking a closer look. It was meaty with a dirty black fur coat, soaked and smelly, and its tusks were pointed triangles that insinuated danger. The animal was still.

What Orian had deemed to be surrender was just the opposite. Lightning quick, the boar jumped at him with malicious intent. Orian was lucky to dodge the first attack by rolling sideways into the brush. His back screamed after rolling across an old root, and he grunted with pain. Still, he rose to his feet to see the boar charging at him once again. This time it was determined to wipe out the human threat, leaping at Orian's chest. Abandoning all thought, Orian allowed his instinct to take over. With a mighty lash, he drove the wooden spear forward, where it sliced through the boar's sternum, just below its head. With a grotesque crunching noise, the wild animal had been stabbed in the heart.

"*Gahhh!!*" Letting out a guttural, otherworldly cry, Orian drove the spear deeper into the animal's chest, pinning it against the ground as its strong legs flailed and attempted to drag Orian, but he held on. Even with the animal's life surely gone, Orian admired the way it fought. Though its squeals were horrifying as it struggled to come to terms with life-ending scattered breaths and a bloody tongue, Orian did not allow himself to grasp the true horror of what he'd done until the deed was finished. After a while, the squeals gave way to diminutive snorts, snorts to labored breaths, breaths to mortal stillness.

Chest heaving madly, shaking without end, Orian slowly took his weight off the spear, keeping only his hands attached. The boar did not move. Orian was hesitant to take a hand off the weapon, eyes wide and glued to the creature he had come to overpower. It was only after a minute that Orian could be sure enough to release his grip.

He fell to his knees, beside its front and back hooves that were stained in warring mud. The spear protruded from its body at a deathly angle, creeping starlight reflecting tragically across the upward half. Shakily, Orian placed a hand on the boar's belly, having never touched another animal before. Already it was turning cold. Orian shuddered at what he had done, also not forgoing the necessity of his actions. The boar had been healthy, sturdy, strong. Lean meat would be gleaned from it. There was just one problem. Orian had never cooked nor eaten meat before.

Orian knew from the Internet that the animal's meat could be cut from its bones, placed over a fire, and consumed. Whether he had the ability to carry out the process, he was unsure. Before any incisions could be made, a fire would be needed. But it was still wet. Orian would have to wait for the storm to pass. In other words, he would have to wait until morning, which was alright with him. His body begged him for rest.

The boar was drug by its hind legs to the closest tree, where it would sit for the night. Orian stared down at it. Fur greased with misty rain, scarlet blood lay in a wavelike pattern along its side. The beast had given a mighty last stand, but in the end, man was victorious.

Orian plucked the spear from its limp body. He would sleep with the weapon overnight, should he cross paths with another pig or bear–one not so friendly as the first.

Cutting a few elephant-ear leaves from a growing plant, Orian laid them out on the ground to cushion him through the night. This way, he might not wake covered in mud. As he laid the last one down, Orian stuck a hand into the soil out of curiosity. He pulled up a solid chunk of mud and examined it. Twice over, he rolled it through each hand before lying on his back against his leaf-cushion. Twirling the chunk of earth in the starlight, Orian pondered the way his skin was almost seamless in color. To him, it confirmed yet again that he was right where he belonged. Through bleak, unknowing circumstances, Orian would persist in nature because nature was, and always would be, his home. He was one with it, as it was one with him. At this, Orian turned on the leaves, rose, removed them all, and laid down on the earth's sodden floor, where he found comfort, sinking and forming his own mark on the world.

XVI

"**D**amnit," he murmured. Another body in the arena gone. Another attempt failed. Vardus had grown accustomed to the shrill cries of his students as they dashed out of the Coliseum in horror. He remained unaffected as they stormed for the exits in a mad rush of bodies. Those that had the outdoor event in their Schedule today had born witness to one more prisoner down and dead. What they believed to be a tragedy was truly another sack of bones to be thrown on the extensive pile.

Vardus rubbed fingers painfully across his temple, sighing. The Twister Program, despite his deepest wishes, would need more time and someone more qualified to complete it.

Today a prisoner from outside Ardosia's Wall, another Savage in the jungle, served his role as an experiment. His name Vardus could not remember, only that he had never wielded a bow and arrow in his measly little life, having been a gleaner of produce since birth.

Yet today, they had thrust the thrumming weapon in his hands and sent his compliant body into the fray. Here in the momentous oval, tall and wide wooden obstacles protruded from the sandy ground. Evenly spaced and shaped like ladders, poles, or ramps, the obstacles presented a difficulty where there had been none before. The peasant's mission: eliminate all enemy presence, which in this case, was a collection of nine mad and hungry chimps stolen from the jungle. Per usual, Twister had demonstrated success in the beginning … only to falter and result in the termination of another subject.

Vardus's dispassionate eyes had watched it all from high up in the golden President's Suite. There was ample room within. A self-serving bar, high-top chairs and tables, and a granite counter beside the massive window made the Suite a getaway of sorts, a place where Vardus could relax.

Not once had his pulse risen or fallen during the course of the event. Even at the start, when the prisoner had emerged from the tunnel, his face cold as a corpse, Vardus awaited the inevitable. Promisingly, the prisoner began by thrumming arrows that impaled two chimps as they were dancing madly around the obstacles. The prisoner started with robotic confidence, his actions precise and emotionless. Obstacles designed to challenge were used to his advantage as he hid behind them, obtained high ground on ramps, and baited the chimps into the ladders. With the help of the Twister Program, he had successfully eliminated over half of his targets. Then there were three.

In an instant, the effects of Twister had worn off. Once it did, the prisoner searched the arena in a panic, unable to comprehend his position. He favored the bow with contemptuous eyes as his inner frailty rose to the surface. Stunned, he dropped the bow and pled for help. A few of Vardus's colleagues, who had accompanied him in the Suite, cringed as the three chimps pranced after the running man, eventually pinning him to the ground, ripping off an arm and the skin of his face before mercilessly beating his broken corpse.

Vardus only huffed. One of the many benefits of sand, Vardus thought as blood spilled from the body, was that it imbibed the remnants of disaster.

"It was a new record, Mr. President," a voice from behind came. "Five minutes, thirty-eight seconds."

Vardus felt the tension in their voice. Acknowledging his own impatience, he exuded a calm manner, knowing that progress was still progress, even if it harried his ambitious tendencies. "Tell Analee of my gratitude."

"Yes, sir."

Analee had been the most qualified technician in Ardosia, though that wasn't saying much. She was smart, Vardus could admit, but she did not possess the necessary knowledge of the in's and out's of programming. For two years now, Analee had been working tirelessly on Twister's creation, making small leaps on occasion. Vardus began to wonder if he would ever see it to its end. He needed someone like the Orian boy … or the Creator.

"Sir," someone to his right spoke up. His voice was deeper, inflected with much more conviction than most. It was one of the many reasons Vardus had chosen him as his interim Right Hand so long ago. With confidence and loyalty, he'd managed to keep that position for nearly two decades.

"Matthew, what do we have?"

Matthew was a shorter man of stocky build. His skin was pale, and his hairless head shone brightly in the sun that popped through the viewing window. Today, as he did most days, he wore a gray suit and tie, a respectable man. He had a round face, and he'd aged arguably more than Vardus had in the last two decades, even though he was younger by nearly fifteen years. His dark brow crinkled perpetually while he sat blank-faced, having just observed the event at Vardus's side.

Matthew's gut rose and fell with his steep sigh. "I'll get right to it, no time to waste, of course." He gave Vardus a wary glance before continuing. "Numbers are low, Vardus. Across the board. Not just in vegetables, nor spices, not only herbs, plants, wood, nor metals. Vardus ... *all* of our yields are low."

The news was a jab to the President's core. Stoic, Vardus replied, "Have you not heard?"

"Heard what?"

"Of the exodus, Matthew."

"Um," he stuttered. "Moses freed the Israelites from the cruel Egyptian order, of course, and then–"

"I mean *our* exodus," Vardus snapped. "No more than forty-eight hours ago, we lost nearly two scores of students ..." Vardus nodded to himself, unable to fathom such a ridiculous number. He made his point curtly. "Less students, less mouths to feed. Lower yields are no problem. Besides, you know better than to bring me problems. Find me solutions."

"Of course, sir. Here." Matthew procured a tablet. "If you look, we've tracked weather patterns within a twenty-mile radius, which accounts for nearly all our production sites. This year, Mother Nature has been a tempest. Look … see right there? Increased rainfall and extreme weather, the likes of which we haven't seen in fourteen years."

Vardus eyed the tablet curiously. "Do we have the data from the previous spell of inclemency?"

"We have it all, Mr. President."

"Show me."

Swiping at the screen, Matthew created two separate windows, split down the middle. "If you see here, the stretches of tempestuous weather, for all intents and purposes, mirror each other. Sure, there was more rainfall then, but there have been more severe storms this season."

The President was losing patience. "Matthew."

He looked Vardus in the eye. "Right." Matthew pinched at the screen to create two more windows. Now there were four boxes showing "We did a yield comparison …" his voice trailed off.

"Let me see." Stealing the tablet, Vardus inspected the numbers closely. He cocked his head to the side, surely inspecting an error. His mouth hung agape. "Down twenty and a half percent? No, not possible. Run the numbers through again. There was a mistake in calculation."

Matthew shook his head slowly. "I wish that were the case. I've cross-examined the data several times over, of course. I've run tests to ensure our metrics are accurate." Scratching at his bald head, he hesitated to continue. "Our yields are lower, beyond the calculation of statistically significant." He paused. "Sir, these numbers are astronomical."

Incredulous, Vardus handed Matthew the tablet. The two of them operated in silence as he stared mindlessly out over the arena.

Down below, soldiers were taking care of the remaining chimps before kindly aiding the fat vested man in dragging the loose corpse to the dungeon. Not much remained of the prisoner. The sight was grotesque, even for Vardus.

His eyes worked back and forth. At last, Vardus's concentration folded into a careless shrug. "The weather was much worse this year. I think it only fair to give the farmer peasants the benefit of the doubt."

In the vast forested land beyond Ardosia, there were farms scattered variously in the trees. Some were propped on hillsides, some in valleys, and others on flatter lands. Families who had not been a part of Vardus's rebellion, who had somehow survived the nuclear war that ended the Old Nation, worked these faraway grounds where the radiation did not toil. Year after year, they tilled the soil, upending the shodden and stale roots of the previous harvest. They planted seeds. They watched as sustenance sprouted from the ground. Then, when they harvested, Ardosia's brave men were there to barter with the farmers. Crossbows and heavy gray-white armor made Vardus's men particularly good negotiators. In exchange for a great percentage of their yield, Ardosia would provide protection. All farms agreed.

A thought occurred to the President then. "What if they're stealing from us? Are they concealing a portion of their yields to sustain themselves?"

Matthew's gaze was dim. "The same thought crossed my mind, too, but soldiers have reported the status of farmers' health ... they're all skinny as camp prisoners. Our soldiers searched recklessly through houses, at my order. Not even the farmers have food. The only remaining explanation ..." Matthew rubbed his chin contemplatively. "... is sabotage. But if they were sabotaging yields, they'd be starving themselves."

Throughout history, sacrifice in the name of defiance was no stranger. Vardus had seen plenty of it in the final battles of the Old Nation. Those who stood with that doomed country weren't afraid of death, and if not for the atomic measures taken to win the ideological battle, Vardus may have fallen to those fools. In that terrible choice he was forced to make, he had sacrificed many of his own rebellion to ensure its ultimate success.

In a new day and age, however, Vardus struggled to imagine that farmers may possess a similar level of courage and dismal foresight as defenders of the Old Nation. Surely, they wouldn't be willing to sacrifice their own well-being in the name of obstinance. Besides, the trade Ardosia had offered the agriculturalists was more than fair.

"No." Vardus waved a hand. "I'll take this matter up with Mother Nature and toss accusations her way. Give these farmers grace. That said, it wouldn't hurt to implement the techniques we've discussed, should grace run dry."

Again, Matthew shook his head. "Intimidation seems only to inspire ..." He stopped, unwilling to utter the possibility.

"What?" pressed the President. "Inspire what?"

"Rebellion," Matthew sighed.

"Is that what you're suggesting? Rebellion?" Vardus scoffed, laughing. "You think those peasants have either the courage or absence of mind to rebel against *us*? Ardosia's soldiers outnumber all enemy presence, two-to-one at minimum. Our men are ruthless trained fighters, and once Twister comes into effect ... the rumors of sabotage and rebellion will only further be quelled, Matthew."

One of Matthew's traits that Vardus respected, though it beleaguered him often, was his fearlessness. He spoke to Vardus plainly, whether he had good or awful news to report. The President reflected fondly on Matthew's fervent nature with regard to his position as Right Hand. Vardus wished all Ardosians were like Matthew, filled with passion and desire to fulfill a role to the absolute best of their ability. He thought of this as Matthew spoke.

"Have you seen the O-rates as of late, Mr. President?"

Vardus scrunched his face. "Please, we've known each other for twenty odd years. How many times have I asked you to call me by my name?" Vardus was the name he was referring to; almost nobody was given permission to use his first name James.

"Vardus, I'm afraid you're stalling, avoiding the conversation altogether. Our O-rates since the exodus are lower than we've seen before. As you're well aware, they'd already been declining. Now, though? Now they're irredeemable."

O-rates, the metric for which Vardus and Ardosia's professors monitored and recorded the levels of acceptable student behavior, had always been an accurate indicator. It measured favorable qualities–avid listening, participation, and patriotism. If these were truly in decline, the island's future was at stake. Twister was needed now more than ever before.

Rising from his chair, Vardus craned his neck to both sides.

Matthew also rose.

The President opened his mouth to decry the possibility of rebellion, on all fronts. The weather, not farmers' self-sabotage, was responsible for decreased yields. Shock, not rebellion, had attributed to O-rates taking a massive hit. Both yields and O-rates would climb again. Surely, they would. But Vardus shut his mouth. Even if all this proved to be true, Matthew's sword-like admonishments had a sliver of reason attached at the helm.

"I only warn, Mr. President, because it is my job. I trust in your judgement and leadership. It has yet to lead our new and wonderful nation astray. Yet I fear that things cannot get much worse before the effect on our island becomes detrimental."

"Your diligence is noted," Vardus addressed. "At the moment, rebellion does not concern me. Please continue to implement the methods we have previously discussed. Larger squadrons, more weapons. Staple a few glares to the faces of my men, if you must. The farmers will turn up. They will."

At that, the Right Hand nodded respectively, though Vardus knew there was fire within him. Then he left, and the two of them parted for the evening.

On his return to the Tower, where at the very top Vardus's office and living quarters located, he thought of what Matthew had told him. *Rebellion*. The word echoed in his head. It simply couldn't be possible. But the more he thought of it, the more fear crept into Vardus's soul, if he had a soul left to stain.

James Vardus entered his office in deep thought, nearly forgetting that Woody had been returned to his glass enclosure earlier in the day. The veterinarian had been instructed as such.

Vardus wandered over to a precious sight. As he lay curled up in his den, Woody's stomach rose and fell. Ardosia's President tapped the glass affectionately, but the tiger did not stir. "Hi, little thing," he said, although he knew Woody could not hear him.

Multiple colors came brilliantly through the stained-glass window, as day was perfectly upon Ardosia. However, despite the sun's appeal, Vardus had the urge to rest on his upcoming decisions.

Squeaking, his bed folded out from the wall. The cushion was plush, a pillow stuffed under his neck. Vardus stared at the ceiling, pondering those rebel Savages who had stolen his students. The final count had been upwards of thirty, maybe forty. Though arduous to admit, Vardus was profoundly upset at the prospect of an impending war in which the rebel cause would be decimated. He needed the Savages alive. They were invaluable to his cause. That truth angered him.

Lifting his head to catch one last glimpse of the tiger before submitting to his dreaming mind, Vardus felt a sudden calm. He could rest peacefully, knowing that Woody's de-clawing procedure had passed without complication.

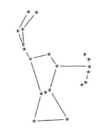

XVII

Sprinting through the wooded area, he surpassed trees like they were rainbow colors in a telescope that came at him threateningly, only to disappear beyond the lens. His feet did not make sounds through the brush. They were like lily pads floating above murky waters; he hopped from one plant to the next as they propelled him furiously onward.

There was a profound tumbling to his left. "We must go," a deep, strong voice urged.

Orian looked to see his bear friend striding ferociously across the flooded swamp, electing not to use the lily pad brush. His enormous paws brought small drops and sent petite waves spiraling, though the sound they made was like that of a heartbeat drum. *Ba-dum. Ba-dum.* Orian wondered where the voice had come from, until the bear spoke again, running alongside him. "We're running out of time." Orian's brow furrowed, incredulous. Then he remembered that he ought to stay focused on the path ahead to avoid running headlong into a tree. "Where are we going?" he asked, to which the bear responded in a huff, increasing his pace, angry. It said, "To help. We must help." Orian didn't appreciate the vague guidance, posing his asperity. "Care to elaborate?" But the bear said nothing. Orian shook his head. In a sudden flash, the Wall was erected at the horizon, Ardosia's Tower filling the sky beyond. Attempting to retreat but having no control over his body, Orian's eyes widened with terror. *No, I'm not ready to go back. I can't go back.* "Why'd you take me here? We can't go here! I'll never go back! Never!" At last, the bear favored him with a peculiar smirk. As it opened its frightening jaw, Orian's world faded, and he woke from the dream.

An unnerving stench poked needles through Orian's nose before he could even wipe the sleep from his eyes. Hoisting his torso with both hands as supports against the ground, a damp mugginess was next in line to berate his senses. The sun shone brightly above. It sent slivers of light through the canopy and evaporated much of the previous night's rain. By imbibing the moisture, the jungle air had become so dense it was tough to breathe. Orian didn't mind. The air he was breathing was incomparably better than the polluted oxygen found on the island.

Looking down, Orian surveyed himself. Shirt, pants, arms, and face were caked with mud. He did tend to roll around in his sleep. Figuring the soil skin layer might detract the risk of predators, Orian shrugged the discomfort.

Speaking of predators …

Orian's eyes didn't have to search long for the boar carcass. Neither did his nose, which he plugged as he approached his next meal. Flies swarmed the open wound where Orian's spear had impaled the pig. Its flesh had already begun the process of decomposition. Orian would have to make a fire over which he could roast the meat, and soon. He just hoped he'd be able to find dry wood somewhere in this damp ecosystem.

Carefully Orian examined the pig. What a barbaric lifestyle he'd chosen for himself. It occurred to him that he might be reduced to hunting and gathering for the remainder of his days, which in all likelihood, were numbered. Yet not even the slightest hint of regret had been triggered. His new life would simply take some adjustment, even if there wasn't much life left to live.

As for the boar, Orian was able to sling it over his shoulders with relative ease. His shoulders were broad, but this pig must have been in its adolescent stages, making the weight bearable. Immediately, Orian made haste in his search for firewood.

He traveled along the path, as he had the day before, and to his great fortune allotted to him by God above, he discovered he hadn't been wending in a wide circle after all.

The boar was hardly a feather on his shoulder when he stumbled upon a dreamlike sight. Grateful eyes rested upon a circular pit, its outer edges constructed with stone. It was too good to be true, Orian thought.

His first inclination was not that he had stumbled upon a perfect firepit, one suited with a rack for spinning meat, but rather that he had finally run into civilization. After dropping the boar to the ground, Orian ambled in a wide circle beyond the pit, frantic and unable to locate any sign of nearby life–human or otherwise. There were no buildings, no spaces of absent trees … nothing but the monotonous continuation of the jungle landscape. Perhaps the firepit had been created long ago by nomads. No matter the case, Orian wasted no time.

Next to a close tree, there was a pile of firewood. Orian stole a few dry pieces from the bottom of the pile. It should have dawned on him then that fresh firewood *was* an indicator of civilization, not a natural phenomenon. It *had* to have implied an owner who lived within a reasonable radius, but Orian's stomach had gone without food for two days, his lips touching only the rainwater that had dripped from leaves high in the sweltering sky. Needless to say, perfunctory conclusions weren't so easy to come by in his current cerebral state.

Beside the pit, there was a small wooden box, unlocked. Orian rummaged through it and was able to procure both flint, steel, and wood chips–the perfect fire starters. After assembling three pieces of firewood in a steepled triangle, Orian struck the steel several times over with no luck. Hadn't this been the tactic used on the Internet? He aimed flint and steel in the direction of the firewood, more closely this time. Then he paused. *This is someone else's lifeline. This is* their *firewood.* His eyes searched once more for any sign of life and did not prevail. At last, he shrugged.

A gust of wind rustled bushes at Orian's back, triggering a lucky spark. One wood chip had caught fire, kindling upward. Before the chip could disappear at the hands of tangerine flame, a steel pole rearranged it beneath the firewood. Orian wasn't sure it would catch. He could be here all day. *Please, God,* he closed his eyes, praying. Using the same process, he lit another chip, to no avail. He tried again. A secondary gale blew the brush behind him, and simultaneously the fire began.

"Ah! Aha! I did it!"

A final satisfactory glance was laid upon the burgeoning flame before Orian rounded the pit, heaved the boar that smelled like beets and mushrooms, or like rotting flesh, onto his shoulders and levied the turning spear off its rack.

Once more, a gust of wind blew at the brush that was now facing Orian. It caught his attention for a brief moment before its allure enthralled him. There must have been a wind tunnel forcing its way through the jungle in an oddly specific manner. Large sprouting leaves waved to the left and right in a line. Orian realized too late that the rustling, which was now moving at him in alarming fashion, had been no gust at all.

"Oh, *sh*–"

The boar went flying from his grasp as a sparkling black ball of fur pounced at Orian's chest. Backward he tumbled, falling luckily not into the fire, but onto the concrete dirt beside it. He fell to his back, a panther on top of him.

Once, the beast's jaws snapped beside Orian's ear. Its claws dug into his shoulders. Orian winced and cried out from the pain. "*GAAAAAHH!*"

But he remembered … when odds were stacked most against him, there was no use for panic. *Embrace the challenge*, he told himself, as he lay squirming beneath the deathly grasp of black fur. With colossal effort, Orian planted his palms at the panther's chest, throwing it off like it was merely a kitten.

He scrambled to his hands and knees, survival eyes watching the panther intently as its tail swatted the air in front of him. His mouth folded into a frown, however, when the large black cat forwarded no interest in Orian and instead dashed a few feet beyond him … where the boar carcass lay at the edge of brush. It had been no wonder that Orian was able to overpower the predator so easily. The boar, not the human, had been the panther's primary target the entire time.

Helplessly, Orian watched as the feline dug its fangs into *his* hard-fought meal. Orian's hunger had escalated to the point that it no longer tugged at his insides. Now it hurt, badly. Yet even more relevant was the rage that shook him. Teeth clenched, Orian bared them in a muffled scream of unfettered hatred. Contrition had bitten him, although in a slight manner, when he had ended the boar's life. Orian would feel nothing, not even a speck of mar on his conscience, when he–not curiosity–killed the cat.

Leaping from his crouched position, Orian stole the poker he had used to move the burning wood chip. Accidentally he had left its tip reddening in the flames, but this accident would feel alright, like justice. He approached unknowingly to the panther, thinking, *A stab through the heart is too good a fate for this mongrel. Hit him where it hurts.*

The panther had time to back away from the carcass only a few inches before it was struck in the nose with a burning tip. Orian had meant to end its life right then and there in a performance of justice, stabbing the animal in the same schnoz that had traced his location. But he hadn't anticipated that the panther would reel back from the boar for even a second. The poker glanced instead off its nose. Smoke and the scent of burnt flesh rose from the animal as the reddened steel bounced off of it, diving straight into the dirt. The panther screamed and roared a snarled sound before shaking off the pain in an instant. Orian had no time to remove the poker still lodged in the ground before the panther was on him. Suddenly, this was no war over a pig ... this was a war for the right to life.

The panther came at him with blinding speed, pouncing at his chest like it had before. Orian was unable to divert his path, frozen. Its weight forced his back to the tree, where it trapped him. Fiercely it dug its claws into his shoulders again, this time with the intent to kill. Burning hot blood rolled down Orian's chest, beneath his shirt. He let out a remarkable cry. Jaws snapped perilously to his left as he choked the cat with all his might, not believing for a second that he might be able to cut off its airway, but rather hopelessly keeping its teeth at a distance–teeth that were closing in with each ticking second.

Orian knew the claws were too deep to remove them on his own. He removed one hand from its neck, thrusting his thumb in one yellow-green eye that might have been mesmerizing if not for its mal intent. Even this did not affect the cat. *I'm done*, Orian thought with a fair deal of resignation. *My luck has run out.* But he did not give up. His last moments wouldn't be spent quitting.

The panther snarled, seemingly in victorious fashion. Orian screamed again to let the black cat know that he was not finished. Even in the clutches of death, Orian felt the compulsion to taunt authority. Orian lost strength, and the panther took advantage, striking at his face. Dodging to the right, Orian lived to see another moment as the beast crunched bark. Like a man spitting a bullet, it hawked up the wood, aiming for one final blow.

The sharp pain in his shoulders was too much to bear. Finally, Orian flinched. He couldn't acknowledge the baring fangs that would end him. This would be it. Although his time on Earth would come to an abrupt ending, he couldn't ask for more than what he'd been allotted in his final moments. In the persistent pursuit of happiness, Orian would perish. He accepted this as the panther reared one final time, its yellowing canines flashing his life before him.

Thump.

As sudden as death, time stood still, as did the big black cat. Orian opened his eyes to see that the panther's were wide and frozen. Its grip on him weakened, and its claws retracted, springing a torrent of hot blood from his shoulders. He was too numb to feel it. Suddenly, another sickening noise flooded Orian's ears.

Thump.

This time he saw it. What he had originally assumed to be the sound of the conclusion of life was truly the tip of an arrow. Seemingly out of nowhere, it had gone all the way through the cat's stomach. Not one, but two. Nearly impaling Orian, they had both fortunately taken only the cat. The black panther's coat dripped with blood. In a state of shock, it backed off, stumbling and barely maintaining a four-point stance. The cat eyed Orian. It bared its teeth feebly. Then its eyes shot to its sockets before it tottered over and fell hard to the brush. It was dead.

Scattered breaths hit the air. Tips of his fingers shaking, Orian felt the cold chill of death leave his body. It had come so close this time, but yet again he had prevailed. Orian looked up but saw no one, only the same lush landscape as before.

Surely someone had saved him. While God was on Orian's side, celestial arrows did not rain down from Heaven to save him, he was sure. There had to have been a human someone who was responsible. Orian's voice left him in a squeak.

"Thank you," he said but was met with silence. "Thank you!" he said again, his voice carrying into the wooded area, echoing off the trees. He wondered if anyone was really there.

Silence. The crackling of the fire was all Orian heard. "Hello?" he offered, his voice alluding to the pain that weakened him. "Please, I-I need help."

In a horrifying flash, a loud crack struck the tree behind him. Orian flinched and froze. His shaking did not cease. Above him, thrumming like a door stop, was yet another arrow, its tip lodged deep into bark. The fatal blow had missed him by no more than a foot. At this Orian understood … he was in enemy territory.

Before another arrow could be fired his way, he dashed. Hanging low in the bushes, Orian kept himself hidden by vegetation until there was enough tree cover to seclude him from the man or force or ghost who had previously been his savior, now a rogue assailant.

Another arrow struck the base of a nearby tree. Orian turned, thinking that if he could just see the man or woman or *thing* attempting to kill him, he might be better suited to avoid the attack altogether. He'd be able to place obstacles between himself and the bow-and-arrow specialist. But there was no one who entered his view.

So he ran, and he kept running, forgoing the tragedy of a lost meal, ignoring the ever-present thirst that ailed him. Orian ran for his life, something he'd gotten used to lately.

"Help!" he screamed at the sky, realizing his mistake only after he'd done it. If he had already evaded his attacker, this would have given up his position.

So he turned another gear, peddling his feet as fast as they would carry him. He wove in and out of trees, following no path. He had to make his moves unpredictable. Orian verified his success when he heard no more arrows, but that didn't stop him. He ran hard, as hard as he ever had.

For what seemed like miles on end, Orian kept pace, fighting the fatigue that threatened to shut him down. Over hills, through streams, past endless trees, he went.

Eventually, he deferred to his body, which had no more energy to give, no more calories to burn, and likely … no more blood to lose. Vision and legs faltering, Orian retched and puked beside the base of a tree at the top of an incline. What left his mouth was not vomit, but more blood.

He fell to the ground, back flat against the mud. His head banged a tree root and stayed there.

Eyes blinking, Orian peered up pleasantly to view his friend Ladis overlooking him.

"Hi, buddy," Orian said with a smile. "Sorry I left."

But his best friend said nothing, offering concern and maybe some disdain.

"I'm sorry, Ladis. I just … I just–" Orian closed his eyes, and when he opened them, Ladis was gone. "No! No, come back! I need help! Please, buddy. I'm sorry I left! HEEELP!"

His voice reverberated through the jungle before his eyes gave way to utter exhaustion, and his body fell into that long-feared deep sleep, otherwise known as the gate to the underground.

XVIII

Once an arena designed for respite, jubilation, and a time-filler for the Schedule, the Coliseum's reputation was shifting drastically to a house of horror. Twice now, Ladis had entered the stone and clay arches and found a front-row seat to see yet another victim fall to the barbaric challenges sent forth from within the oval's walls.

First was the matador. Now it was a shirtless man, his chest and face painted in a green and gray camouflage. Acting like a warrior for a short duration, the man could only ward off the onslaught of orange and black stripes outfitted with dagger-like claws for so long. Just as with the matador, his confidence faded like the flame on a smoldering match. The tigers ripped him to shreds. Awful screams filled the air immediately.

But the soldiers ... the soldiers didn't blink. Unexcitedly, they ushered students out of the Coliseum, mundanely instructing them all to return to the Tower, as if their routine shouldn't be disturbed by the death of an entertainer–a man ... a human being. Ladis trusted the security presence on the island of Ardosia. Maybe their training had turned them into robotic, emotionless machines on purpose, since emotions tended to cloud judgment. Still, he shuddered. He wondered what they must have had to endure to abandon the components of human nature–things like caring for human life. Perhaps they'd seen death before, many times, and they were no longer strangers to it.

Ladis began to wonder if the matador and the painted-camo man weren't the only ones to fall in the Coliseum recently.

The sun hung lowly in the sky, casting a thin shadow across the winding path home. Ladis clutched himself, shivering. Whether he shook due to the brisk evening air or something else, he could not determine.

Small waves lapped on the lake while the sun's reflection stretched in a thin streak from one side to the other. Fins popped out of the water, and Ladis looked away sharply.

He thought of Orian's escape, having already blotted out the morose events of that day. From his bedroom window he had seen it all. He had watched as Orian swam to safety within the confines of a support tunnel in the Wall.

Ladis's shivering intensified then, and his eyes shut tightly. *The man, that poor man.* When a potent mix of emotions swims through the brain, it's hard to remember what was felt in the past. There was empathetic elation, selfish disdain. Most of all, Ladis remembered the terror as a large man fell from the tunnel, not long after Orian had entered. His body had been mutilated by the dolphins, and Ladis wondered then whether that man had fallen of his own accord ... or if he had been pushed, kicked, murdered. Ladis thought he knew Orian like a brother, but perhaps his rebel-like tendencies knew no bounds. He could hardly stomach the thought of Orian as a remorseless killer.

Anger toward his lifetime roommate persisted, but equally as persistent was a knocking understanding, a knocking to which Ladis had kept the door closed. He felt it easier not to interact with chaotic thoughts. Nothing could justify what Orian had done. He left without courtesy, stuck to selfishness, and maybe even snatched the life of an innocent man. No, absolutely nothing could justify those actions ... right?

The challenging voice hadn't gone away, a quiet prod that made Ladis wonder if Orian had righteous cause to do what he'd done. Hugging himself, Ladis shook his head madly while he traversed the wavy path home. What's wrong is wrong. Sometimes, the world is black and white, with no gray.

His shoes scraped lightly at the concrete beneath his feet, as he grew inadvertently weak in the knees. In the past week, Schedules had been modified to something more extreme and intense than ever before. Class time had increased, requirements for passing exercise scores sky-rocketed, and Yjn had been a little more on edge as of late. In fact just the other day, Boris, who sat two seats behind and two to the left of Ladis, let out a powerful sneeze in class. After a violent flinch, Yjn had accused Boris of disturbing the peace. Yesterday, a girl named Zayda who sat in the back raised her hand with a question. She was then lectured about being alone in a role someday, with nobody to answer questions for you. Zayda cried.

Ardosia was home, and Ladis lived in luxury here. But even he couldn't ignore the possibility that something potentially sinister was brewing within the confines of the island. Its probability was low, Ladis thought, but it was a possibility nonetheless.

No, that had to have been Orian's voice talking to him again.

Eventually the sun fell even with the broad array of trees at the horizon. A deep, dark shadow reached across half the island and would soon envelope Ladis, where he currently stood sentinel at a break in the path. For reasons inexplicable, the path that cut through the center of the island and disappeared over the crowned hill called to him. This path was prohibited for students, but that did not matter to Ladis. The pull was still the same.

He didn't have Orian here to clarify, but Ladis was certain this is what his roommate had meant by that undeniable *tugging* force he used to talk about. Many nights lying in bed had been dedicated to thoughtful conversations. They'd often been one-sided, favoring Orian, where dreams of ultimate defiance were relayed. Although he had begun to listen with feigned interest after having the same conversation for years on end, Ladis explicitly recalled that *tugging* force Orian talked about so frequently. He stared at the cut in the path. Though unsure, Ladis felt confident that he was feeling it now. But why?

Ladis measured the path home, then the one to his right. For at least a minute, his eyes bounced between the two. He couldn't believe he was spending so much time in contemplation. What was there to contemplate? Ladis had seen what happened to those who disobeyed direct orders. If he took this uncertain path to God-knows-where based entirely on an uncharacteristic, rebellious hunch, he might be caught and removed from 102, the floor where life was good but increasingly lonely with Orian's disappearance. His other option was the sane one: abide by the Schedule, return to his room at a decent time, finish the short distance between himself and the Tower at once, and rest peacefully in safety. Finally, Ladis made his decision.

He forged onward down the curving concrete, denying the questionable appeal of the other, less secure path. Ladis held his chest high, pleased that he was still capable of critical thinking.

He rode the elevator all the way up to 102, smirking. He held the same prideful smile to his bed that night where he laid awake in hopes that his mind would overcome the *tugging* the next time it inevitably returned and coursed addictively through his veins.

XIX

Steam rose off his body and clung to the steel ceiling in a row of steady droplets. Hair darker than night but streaking with lightning gray had fallen from the bun down to his shoulders as he smoothed an organic orange-scented shampoo through his kingly locks. Boiling hot, the shower relaxed the tension that pulled his shoulders taut, wrenched his fingers in closed fists, and erected his manhood. Times had been increasingly arduous as of late. Vardus would have to revisit his happy place, lest his sanity go by the wayside.

Gently, he lifted a towel from the rack and stepped out of the shower. Vardus wiped himself dry, twice over before completing his ritual. Most folks, he had learned, shut their shower curtain after use, as if to conceal the draught that captures filth, like a corner of unnatural collection. Not

James. Ardosia's President was particular in many ways. Strict organization was a necessity in life, and he organized his shower curtain similarly. He strung it out seven inches from the edge, measured by eye and not by ruler, because it looked and felt right to him. The rest of the shower was without concealment, how it should be, Vardus thought.

With considerable celerity, James dressed in black, applied cologne, dressed his hair in a bun held together by a thick pointed nail, and descended the elevator in his prized Ardosian Tower. In a world where there was only time to waste, Vardus felt like he had none. He zoomed in a speed-walk across the island, over its crest, and eventually to the Northwest corner. There he found a protective grove of trees. His needle-like body cut through the natural winding path quickly.

Vardus's fingers began to shake when he knocked on the door of the old green house at the crest. He adjusted his buttons, questioning whether he should undo another. Leaving the top three undone gave him room to breathe, so he allowed them to remain as such.

The creaking cathedral rested at the bottom of the hill. Taking a brief glance in that direction, James nearly considered something ridiculous, like praying. Vardus couldn't explain his nervous tendencies. They may have simply been failed attempts at masking his desire for the tender women he called Miss and May. They would be waiting inside, just as they had been on his most recent visit.

Suddenly, the latch was undone. Vardus straightened.

Wordlessly, Morro opened the door, offering the same unsatisfied gaze, as to be expected from a twelve-year-old. She had tied her hair back in a low bun, which made

Vardus smile. Though his bun was typically high, they shared their hair style nevertheless.

"Hi, dear. May I come in?"

Morro, his daughter, turned her back to him and walked into the kitchen, but she had left the door open. That meant *Yes, come in*, Vardus assumed. She was wearing tight khaki jeans that rolled over her skinny legs, in addition to a tight-fit red shirt. It was exactly how he preferred her to appear. She rode to the counter, where she began dicing vegetables with precision. The knife hit the cutting board with repetitive dull thuds.

Heavy, ankle-high boots–black–hit the hard wood. Vardus shook them off at the door. Inside, the house was built with modesty in mind, just as the original intended owner had prescribed. A marvelous light fixture with multi-colored glass panes hung over the bright wood kitchen table, set for four. Between the table and the tight counter with a little square window above the sink, there was not much room. Even the girls had to slide carefully around chairs when setting food dishes down.

Hard wood transitioned to an old, stinky carpet at the living room, where a couch faced a small television, and that was it. All that was left to the house were bedrooms and bathrooms, located upstairs. Somehow Miss and May enjoyed residing here in this shithole. They never complained.

"Something smells tremendous," Vardus said, to which the girls did not reply. It was okay. They were supposed to be quiet, unless otherwise instructed. "Is that a roast I smell?"

"You picked it out." May, the oldest of the women, spoke. When questioned, they were to answer, so she had done well.

Vardus was pleased. The pleasantries did not end there, either. Vardus noticed that May had donned the blue sundress with yellow and white flowers that he so enjoyed. It concealed the skin that was beginning to sag, though she didn't have much of it.

Oh! And Miss, too! She was wearing that nice low-cut V-neck that he *loved*, since it showed off those wonderful, supple, and youthful breasts. Mother and daughter presented themselves in a lovely, courteous manner, seated at both ends of the table with their hands stowed away below. Dinner had been made and set, and the aromas filling the air delighted Vardus's palatable nose.

When he saw juice pooling against the plate upon which the roast sat, a two-pronged long fork sticking out of the meat, Vardus said, "Roast is my favorite." What the women perhaps did not realize is that the meat had been entirely plant-based, but it cooked and tasted the same as beef. *Incredible!* Vardus had thought the first time he was introduced to the concept of plant-based alternatives. He loved them, and they soothed his conscience.

Once Vardus slung his jacket over a chair and seated himself, Morro finished cutting her vegetables and followed suit. Simultaneously, they slid into the table. *My, how well things are going*, Vardus reflected. Typically, he was met with more resistance by the three girls. How brilliant that one night may go according to Schedule.

Their glances were cast timidly in Vardus's direction, all three of them. They were waiting for the President to serve himself first.

"No, please. I may be many things to you women, but I am still a gentleman. Go ahead." He motioned to the roast and pot of vegetables in the center. When nobody moved, he said, "Morro, honey. Why don't you go first? And maybe you could cut Dad a slice while you're at it?"

The girl eyed him with a faceless expression. Her mouth pouted almost, but such was her appearance. Gradually, she rose from her seat, plucked the large steel meat knife and began slicing portions for everyone at the table. "Here," Morro said as she served Miss, May, herself, and finally James. They all responded, "Thank you, Morro," as they reached their plates out.

"Prayer," May commanded, and her closed-eye grace commenced. Her voice was low and patched with wisdom, monotonous and soothing. "Dear Lord, we thank you for these gifts, of the many you bestow upon us. Shine your light graciously toward these sinners, if you may. It is only in Thy name that we pray. Amen."

James laid a curious eye on May, but she did not budge. The wise woman was stoic, per usual, as she wrapped her delicate fingers around fork and knife. It was an interesting prayer she had offered, fastened with subtle defiance. He was both angered and intrigued.

No one stirred as they began digging into their food. Vardus watched the girls eat, laying stealthy glances upon each of the women throughout the course of the meal. They were all so unique in their own ways, easily observed in almost every situation, even while dining.

Miss picked at her food, as she always had. It implied the reservoir of distaste she harbored not only for most meals, but for life in general. She was feisty, indeed. And oh, was she pretty … just like her mother May. Her mom was delicate in the way she ate, proper and petite. Those were the most apt descriptors for her. Golden-brown locks ran in the family. May's casual appearance was that of a tied bun with two curly strands falling at each end, while Miss wore hers straight.

Vardus remembered one of his first encounters with the girl he called Miss. "Come," he had offered his hand. "Through these woods is where you'll find home." She was just a four-year old girl at the time. Miss had taken his hand and walked at his side without a peep, under branches, all the way up to the green house. When Miss was young, she was complacent, perhaps out of fear. As she had grown into a young woman, however, her fear had transformed into courage and resistance. Her womanly strength was cute.

As for May, her progress had worked in much the opposite way. Oh, how she used to fight Vardus's desires, citing them as "immoral" and "corrupt" while he bent her over the table. Her age had silenced her, in addition to the dissolving of her conscience–if not her conscience, then her will. She embraced food as she ate, no matter how difficult to swallow.

And born the fruit of Vardus's loom was Morro. From birth, she had been a stallion, DNA laced with agency. Morro had always been strong, walking at nine months old. She matured quickly over the years. Now, at age twelve, she looked much more like a young woman than a little girl. Her appearance drew a swelling pride from Vardus, even as she tore at the roast with her jaw. Her table manners would need adjustment.

With elegance in mind, Vardus sawed a chunk from his roast and placed the tender meat in his mouth. He nearly spat it out when the voice of May broke his silence. His eyes darted toward her. She had spoken out of turn.

"How are proceedings for the President of Ardosia?" She did not look directly at him, poised rather like a princess as she slid her knife into roast.

For reasons unknown, James did not mind the temporary disobedience. He even backed off lightly, impressed. He thought for a second. "It's been a struggle if we're bringing honesty and some evident *courage* to the table." The woman did not flinch. Vardus waited for it, but she was steady. So he continued, "But few matters are too difficult to surpass."

"Mmm."

His eyes were drilling holes into the woman, but she was a wall that absorbed them.

"More roast, President Vardus?" At the other end of the table, Miss's voice rose in seductive way. She must've noticed his apparent hunger after he demolished his first cut.

"That would be ... lovely, Miss," he said wistfully. *Had she called me President?* His gaze did not leave her as she plopped a thick slice of meat onto his plate. *She never calls me President.* Vardus's curiosity was piqued, but his hunger was stronger. So he ate. He ate until his plate was clean. Voracity squelched, James sat back humbly in his chair, a napkin dotting his chin.

Like clockwork, May gathered all the plates from the table and set them in the sink. Miss wiped the surface down. Morro collected the leftovers and put them in the cooling fridge. In no more than five minutes, the ladies had all returned to their seats attentively.

Vardus had been in the process of cleaning his nails, so pleasantly reflecting on the deference to Schedule on display. Miss was quiet and obedient. May appeared to have something on her mind, and it must have been a whole lot of something because she was a harder book to read than the Hebrew Bible, yet James could see the tiniest glaze of sweat across her forehead. They had all dressed nicely tonight, he thought. Why?

"You want something," he said. Suddenly the pleasantries–their positive attitudes, their attire, the entire dinner–came to the President as nothing more than an act, and he was no longer subject to their appeal.

Apprehensively, mother and daughter offered their eyes. Morro appeared careless to the situation. When Miss's head shot down, May maintained her fearless gaze– fearless until Vardus leaned forward, setting his elbows on the table. They didn't try to hide it.

"Enlighten me," he commanded.

May breathed in through her nose. "James …"

"You know better than to call me by that name, May."

May closed her eyes. "Vardus," she corrected. Suddenly there was a wavering to her persistently still voice. "We would love to offer a compromise."

His eyes bounced between Miss and May. This time Miss spoke up, the young woman whose V-neck was distracting. "Mr. President, we've been cooped up in this house for two decades. Not once have we been allowed to leave, even for a stroll through nature, even to visit the church at the bottom of the hill. I see that cathedral through my window at night, and I wonder what it would be like to pray in there." Her tone rung with girlish wonder. "I used to dream of picking the dandelions that litter the grass, climbing the pines that guard our flank, and now … well, now I still do." She paused, folding her face to exact empathy from Vardus.

The truth was that James wasn't all too concerned with her desires. She and her mother had entered Ardosia as welcomed guests, but they had become his prisoners through unfortunate circumstance, yet they were fortunate to be blessed with his grace. Vardus had allowed them to live in solitude within the little green house at the edge of his island instead of killing them. That was the deal he had struck, whether they had agreed to it or not.

Though James had an idea where this was going, he would entertain their pleas for the moment. He sighed. "You said there was a compromise, yeah? What might you be so bold to offer me, and for what am I bargaining?"

Miss and May exchanged glances, while Morro played with her thumbs. Sliding one strap a little closer to her freckle-spotted shoulder, May stole the man's attention. "Vardus, for one night, you may have us both, Miss and myself. We'll do it all, whatever you ask, for as long as you please." He was beginning to love the sound of this, but James feared what might come.

"And?"

"And in return, you set us free."

Vardus scoffed. Then he guffawed. "You can't be serious." His unbelieving stare worked its way past the two women as he rose from his seat. He laughed haughtily again. Placing both palms flat against the dining table, he stole a few more glances from Miss and May. *By God,* he thought. *They are serious.* This angered him. "How fucking foolish can you pretty little women be? You think there's a price on your bodies? You think your happiness concerns me? Ha! Both of you aren't worth the mud on my boots, the stain in my drawers, the bodies I've buried!" Vardus paused, thinking about what he had uttered. His intent had been to insult the mother and her daughter in the way they had insulted him, but did he really believe his own words? James didn't treat these women like the rest. They were special to him in a way that couldn't be put into words. Miss offered her thoughts that mirrored his own.

"So why not let us go?" she asked. "If we mean nothing to you, our disappearance from this island won't matter."

But it would matter, Vardus thought. These women weren't just his prisoners. They were his *trophies*. And among these trophies was his most prized possession in his daughter Morro. Giving them up would be like tossing away his life's work. He would not have that.

"No," he said placidly. Vardus stood straight, repeating, "No."

While averting his gaze, his peripherals picked up on slow, alluring movements to his left. Miss had risen from the table. She rounded the corner ponderously as she approached him. Though it was difficult, he kept his head down while Miss tossed her hair to the side and began to slip the V-neck over her shoulders.

May, the older and motherly woman she was, turned to little Morro. "Go upstairs, dear."

Vardus gulped. "No, no."

Morro didn't appear inclined toward either direction. She sat still and motionless.

"Yes, Morro. Please go upstairs."

As she slid her chair backward, Vardus piped, "No! I'll have her here."

Both Miss and May looked almost appalled, but after they shared a glance, they determined it was best to appeal to the President's desire.

"She will stay … and observe." Vardus looked to Miss, whose chest was more exposed than before. "You will continue."

Hesitantly, she slid the shirt even lower, then lower still. A weak breath escaped James as she exposed her breasts: an enticing offer.

But Vardus was an honorable man. He knew that, in a moment of passionate heat, he might release those words that he held tight. While fucking the petite young woman, he might promise her everything she had wished for, and being the man of honor he pledged himself to be, he would be sworn to those promises, regardless of the context in which they were made.

So no, he would not indulge. To escape her temptation, he threw his gaze off to the side, where May had already removed her sundress completely.

"I said no," Vardus squeaked. He cleared his throat and deepened it. "No, you will not leave my island."

"We know," May said, her angelic legs tracing over one another with each seductive step toward him. What amazed him most was how perky her breasts were, even in old age. Her physique hadn't changed a bit in the past two decades.

Miss said behind him, "We just want to give you *everything* you've ever wanted."

Now he felt her chest pressed against his back. He was throbbing with desire, struggling to restrain himself. So badly he wanted to whip around and grasp the young woman's frame. He wanted to dig his nails into her skin and draw blood, then lick it. Yet he did not waver, even as she began unbuttoning his shirt. He also didn't refuse her actions.

At last, once both bodies were pressed against him, Vardus gave into his carnal yearning. He stole a tongue-filled kiss with May, turning then to grab Miss between the legs.

"Lord Vardus will take what he wants," he said, low.

He pleased the young woman, and she moaned. Her moans were unlike any he'd heard from her before, addicting to his soul. So he kept at it, and her moans raised to a begging scream. The whole time, Morro had sat at the table, watching with disinterest. Vardus couldn't place his finger as to why, but he enjoyed that she saw him. He would show her how one of his soldiers might properly please her once she was of age. James's fingers worked Miss to his tune.

Finally, Vardus unhooked his belt. He pushed Miss over and thrust. She screamed again, and again. He was so good at it, she had said. She begged him not to stop. But it had been her last scream that alerted him.

One eyebrow arched suspiciously as he continued to fuck her. *She's selling it*, he observed.

So he stopped.

Just then it occurred to him that he hadn't touched or heard from May since their kiss. Vardus turned.

"*AHHHH!*" In a fast downward motion, May sliced at Vardus with the meat knife previously intended for the roast. If he had turned a moment later, he would be dead. But his instincts had prevailed yet again.

Vardus grabbed at May's wrist, stopping the attack in its tracks. "You bitch." He laid his fury-filled eyes on her, kicking her in the stomach. She backed off, grunting and clutching at her chest. The knife clattered on the hardwood below.

"*Raaaa!*" Miss jumped on Vardus's back, knocking him off balance before he could reach for the knife. "Mom, kill this son of a bitch!"

Vardus reached for her. He snagged her hair. "You're going to regret that, Miss." He issued his threat calmly and with conviction. "Guards!"

But they didn't come in at once. Vardus wondered why they hadn't stormed in at the sound of all the commotion, but then he remembered how rough he liked it. His men probably hadn't heard anything out of the ordinary thus far, so he warned them, "Guards, I'm being attacked!"

Ten men stormed through the door immediately, while Miss yelled, "That's not my name, you fucking lunatic! Miss is *not* my name. I'll kill you, I swear I'll kill you!"

The attack had been suppressed almost instantly. May had picked up the knife again, only to be restrained by two of his men. Miss was wrenched from Vardus's body, her screams echoing throughout the house. The women were both still naked, and his soldiers did not hide their watchful eyes.

Morro sat as still as ever, not having moved an inch from her seat. Her face showed no emotion. Not dread, no horror, not an ounce of empathy. Pulling his pants up to his waist and buttoning his black shirt, Vardus offered a smile to her, as if to assure his daughter that it would all be resolved soon. She didn't seem to care.

Miss was tossed to a corner, as her nails had clawed at one of the soldiers, producing a scratch down the side of his face. She huddled into herself, terror-filled eyes boring Vardus's skull. "You know my name," she said. Then, louder, "You know my fucking name!"

Paying her no attention, Vardus told his men to take her upstairs and escort Morro to her room.

"Leave May," he commanded, so they did.

As to be expected, Miss was not taken without a fight. It took three men to subdue the young woman and haul her up the stairs. At last, when her screams were muffled by the walls, two guards remained at May's sides, but Vardus instructed them to leave.

The door slammed once, and man and woman of similar age faced each other in their chamber of solitude.

May shivered. She must have been cold. Vardus didn't give one flying fuck. For all he cared, the old hag could freeze. His steely eyes examined the woman. *Conniving.* It was the only word he could think of, but he mustered another.

"Clever," he admitted to her. Vardus started to pace, while she stood still, not bothering to cover her extremities. "Attack when your enemy is least expecting … or most distracted."

She watched him with cool distaste.

"What you misunderstand, May, is that I am not your enemy. Look around you. Do you see the house I've made for you, the beds I've provided for you and your daughter for twenty-odd years, without cost?"

May huffed.

Vardus ignored her. His feet hit the hardwood methodically as he strolled back and forth. "Do you forget the daughter who is just as much yours as mine? Morro is beautiful, given to me as well as you. How crazy you must be to try taking a father away from a young girl!" At this, May was fuming. James could see it in the way her cheeks turned to roses, her body prickled like thorns. "My, I might have even considered your proposal if not for this … mishap." It was a lie. He would never have considered anything. Stopping to plaster a devious smirk onto his face, he said finally, "He would've been so upset with you."

May's eyes bored into his at the provocation. Brilliant flames threatened to burst from those pearls. "Get out of my house." Rage had passed through the filter of her voice. May's nails dug into her palms. "Get out," she said again.

Vardus tried not to look so pleased with himself, but he'd received the reaction for which he'd been yearning. As he approached the wise woman slowly, her eyes shut tight, and her jaw clenched. If she fought back, it would only make it more enjoyable to him. He was face-to-face with her now, though she refused to retract the lids covering her eyes.

"Get out of my house," she said, almost whimpering. May hadn't opened her eyes, but she felt Vardus next to her, no doubt. When he said nothing for far too long, she bore her sapphire pearls into him and stared directly into his soul. Perhaps she thought it would scare him.

His mouth curled. Plainly, he told her, "I own you," before thrusting his hand at her throat, pushing her up against the counter, and undoing his belt buckle. Her face would undoubtedly have bruises the next day, after Vardus pounded at her with his fists in outrageous pleasure. *Small matter*, he thought. The bruises would be gone by the time he came back next week.

On the wall, the clock ticked steadily. Late morning sun rolled in through the blinds. It hit Talia's back and warmed her as she stuffed her face in paperwork. Her office presented the stillness she desired and an ambiance that calmed, which she needed greatly. Walls, floor, and desk constructed of wood, she felt one with nature and at home here. A bookshelf to her right, antlers mounted at her back beside the window, and a cardboard circle at the final wall. Talia frequently used this target to hone in her knife-throwing skills, or blow off some steam.

As she had always instructed, the report she was given began with the bad news. George, who had been injured in the previous extraction, had succumbed to the wound in his left leg. In the throes of close-combat, he'd been struck by a sword. Infection that had caused his entire leg to swell into a purplish-green mess ended up taking his life. Before his leg could be amputated, the disease had entered his bloodstream and found the heart. At least that's the explanation forwarded by Mercian doctors.

Angrily, Talia placed a hand at her brow. Considering the difficulty of their heist, losing just one man was a success. To her, one was still too many. George had a family: a wife and two kids, who were no doubt mourning him already.

Numbers were as high as ever after Talia's most recent extraction. Saving an average of eleven students per mission, Talia and her men blew that average out of the water when thirty-four had returned with them just a few days prior. Many of these students were already finding roles that suited their liking. It had been a risk to attack during the day. Always, Talia stuck to the night during extractions, but this risk had paid off.

Production in the textile mill had reached new heights, which was no small note. Yarn and fabric, used to make clothing of all sorts, had been their greatest asset to bartering with nearby tribes who offered their food in return. Soldiers' numbers were rising, too, not only in terms of bodies, but also in terms of skill. Of these reports there was only optimism, which gave no reason to Talia's growing anxiety.

Darkness rarely strikes in the night, Talia's predecessor Andrew used to say. He'd taught her to always be on her toes. It was her job.

Talia thought favorably upon the group she had recently retrieved from Ardosia. They were a brave group, risking their lives to escape from the heights of Ardosia's Tower. Had it been absurdly dangerous to choose ten of the highest floors at which to launch their lines? Sure, but Talia needed the boldest and bravest in her ranks at Merciadel. By selecting floors where an escape required almost suicidal courage, Talia ensured strength in the numbers she would acquire.

She thought back to the moment her arrows struck glass. Standing straight as a balustrade in the small white boat, with bow in hand, she had fired seamlessly across ten floors. Glass shattered, ziplines slung inside by way of the silver tripod invented by her tech team. In the sand, it had been planted, each of the tripod's legs sending anchors deep into the soil for stability.

While students fled via those ziplines, Talia and her men fought valiantly, taking many an Ardosian soldier to his grave to preserve the freedoms that they had never known before. Despite the efforts of the island to force incumbent generations into a constricting mold that would keep them content and stupid for the rest of their lives, students of all personalities had rebelled and joined the Mercian cause. Silently, Talia grunted as she thought of Trixie. The girl was reminiscent of herself when she was twenty.

In Talia's twenties, she had been training to be a soldier under General Andrew. A tall, poised, and occasionally abrasive man, Andrew had held a soft spot for Talia since Merciadel's founding. He was a man of distinct and threatening appearance, with a thin buzz cut so short that he may as well have been bald, with arching black eyebrows, and a jaw line that insinuated Andrew was never more than a step away from marching to war, just for the hell of it. Appearances could be deceiving, however. Although a military man, Andrew was a pacifist who abhorred the pointless death of man. That's what made him so effective.

General Andrew was the one who had made the exception for Talia's entry into the military, having noted her innate skills and desire to enact justice. While he forded the male soldiers no excuses and oft harshness of tone, he had let up ever-so-slightly when he scolded Talia. In return, she admonished General Andrew, holding a knife pointedly at his genitals, "Treat me the same as the men, or you'll no longer be one." It must have been her fearlessness, in addition to the positive relationship she had formed with Andrew, that had warranted her succession as General upon his death, much to the dismay of her colleagues. Talia wondered if someone like Trixie might replace her someday and if she would be met with scorn at such a decision, as General Andrew had.

To this day, Talia thought upon Andrew's memory, mirroring her leadership styles after him. He was capable of making the tough decisions. Making friends was irrelevant to him, as long as he didn't make enemies. Lastly, General Andrew was a man of the people, not because he knew he should be, but because he desired true relationships with those who had risked life and limb to erect the first walls of Merciadel. He used to go out in the mornings, speak with the farmers and laborers far on the open end of Merciadel's walls as they tended cattle and sheep, plucked apples from trees, vegetables from stems. Talia did the same. They were always up early, so she woke before sunrise.

Her favorite morning visit was a farmer named Pake. He was old and old-style, the overall-wearing, straw-cowboy-hat type. And since he was in the far corner of Merciadel's walls, approximately two and a half miles from her office, he was always the last visit. Their conversation was typically the same every day, but it lifted Talia's spirits nonetheless to greet the sweet old man. She'd start with, "Are the cowpies or Kin's pies more appetizing today?" To which, Pake would grin, a few of his teeth missing. "Always my lady Kin's," he would say, their house resting in the background, near the barn at the end of the lot. Talia: "But Pake, you're out here with the cows!" He'd chuckle. "That's right, but you be sure to tell my wife what I said, you hear?" Talia once said, "I'll earn you some brownie points, Pake," and her favorite response was, "As long as they aren't pie points." Pake would hum something about "living the dream" whenever Talia left him to his work.

Today, however, Talia had not ventured to greet the farmers, not even Pake. Stress levels were high, and she had solutions to create.

Two subtle knocks came at the door, followed by the entry of a skinny young man with short, messy hair. He adjusted his glasses and asked if it was okay to come in after already having entered in a flurry.

"Yes, Neal," Talia offered a nod of concern. "What is it?"

Although standing in place, his movements were frantic, hands shaking, cheeks twitching. "Our men, th-they're out there w-with, um, w-w-with–"

"Neal, breathe."

Blinking twice, Neal took a sharp inhale and started over, speaking as quickly as a jackrabbit ran. "Byron and some soldiers found an Ar-Ar-Ardosian."

Talia stood in alarm. "*An* Ardosian? Just one?"

"Mhmm!" Neal nodded rapidly.

"Well, where did they find this Ardosian? I swear, the balls Vardus has … although shriveled and sterile without a doubt …" she shook her head. It made no sense. Why would Vardus send a single Ardosian?

"No! They heard s-s-something in the woods this morning, so Byron c-c-conducted a search team."

Without my permission, Talia noted. Contemplating, Talia worried when she heard the name *Byron,* particularly in unique circumstance. The man and his ego were ruthless, and his instinct had probably been to murder the Ardosian on site. That would not do; a breathing Ardosian with information was worth far more than a sack of bones. Talia had to know. "Is the Ardosian still alive?"

"B-b-barely."

Anger coursed through her. A headache was in the midst of forming. The wheels of her office chair crashed against the wall behind her as she kicked it. Shaking her head furiously, she said, "I swear to the one true God, Byron is done this time. That temper … that fucking temper of his …" As she imagined Byron sparing no mercy to the Ardosian, Talia continued with her tirade. "… could've been such an asset. The information we could have gotten out of–" Meanwhile, Neal observed her with curiosity and a hint of confusion.

"T-t-tal? Talia? Hey, *Tal!*"

Merciadel's leader looked at Neal as though she were realizing for the first time that someone else had accompanied her in the office. "Neal, what is it? We damn well better have the Ardosian in custody or in a God-damned medical bed … and they had better be breathing. Tell me they're breathing."

Raising his hands in a placative manner, Neal tried to smile. "The boy is breathing, but I-I think you misunderstand."

Talia tilted her head to the side, as if to offer an ear so that she might hear him better.

Neal shifted his feet. "The Ardosian is no soldier ... he's a student."

Neal and Talia bolted to the medical building, reducing their run to a brisk walk in the presence of onlookers, so as not to stir up a nervous panic. Leaders were to be composed, especially in the company of eyes. Yet Talia wondered if her face was flushed as it felt, likely betraying the rush she felt in her chest.

"Where is he?" Talia demanded as she and her right-hand man stormed into the Emergency Unit: a square section of the medical building where there were ten beds—five on each side. "Take me to the Ardosian."

Eyeing her clipboard, the nurse replied with, "Nobody allowed in the ER," but when she glanced closer and recognized who she was speaking to, her body shook. "Oh, uh, corner bed, behind the curtain."

"Thank you." Talia shouldered past the nurse, with Neal at her side.

Flickering overhead lights alerted Merciadel's General that future budgeting may have to be allocated to the ER. The white-washed walls were stained with patches of brown. She hadn't been in the confined building for nearly a year now, and it looked as though it had been through war since then. *It has*, Talia reflected. The war with Ardosia, while analogous to the Cold War between Russia and the U.S. where ideologies battled, had still involved the sacrifice of many men. The ER was a reflection of the wear Merciadel had endured. Yet they would hold strong. Persistence and numbers were key, and Talia knew that her goal was not yet to defeat Ardosia and "President" Vardus–though it had been before. No, her main desire now was to construct her own nation, able to support itself and its allies. Someday, they would be immune to Vardus's targeted attacks. Then she would make it her personal agenda to fix the ER.

Shadows bounced beyond the curtain frantically. Breaching typical protocol, Talia swiped at it. The doctors and nurses working on the unconscious specimen didn't seem to notice.

Doctor Shelly, her braided blonde hair resting calmly against her back, lasered her glasses on the stitches she worked into the boy's shoulder. Both left and right had been lacerated deeply. *Were those ... claw marks?*

"Shelly, run it down. What happened?"

Without averting her gaze, she said in a monotone, "Kid got lucky we found him. He'd be dead if not for Byron, here." Doctor Shelly nodded affectionately toward the soldier standing proudly beside the bed.

"Please," he winked, nodding at the wounded kid. "This boy needed help, and I offered it, as is my job."

Shelly laid her eyes on him. "You did great."

Another one bites the dust, Talia thought as she watched Shelly fall for the Womanizer. Forgoing the opportunity to remind Byron that he had disobeyed orders, Talia questioned him. "How and where?"

Byron placed hands on hips, working to hide the smirk creeping across his face. "I was out on my morning run around the property, you know, saying hi to Mrs. Jennings and her kids in the housing district, getting in shape, preparing for our next mission, as a soldier is meant to do, and–"

"*Byron.*" Talia glared, meaning *Spare me the details.*

He sighed. It ailed him to be brusque. Byron gave a shrug. "I heard yelling in the distance. I knew it had to have come beyond our outer wall. So I sent out a search team." When Talia cocked her head, he rolled his eyes. "Yes, I led the charge. My–*your* men were armored and prepared. We traveled in a seventy-five-foot swath until Othor stumbled upon a dead body. Except, as it turns out, he wasn't dead! Checked for a pulse, and carried him here." He held his hands at his side. "There, you're all caught up."

"What else do we know?"

"I wish I could say." Byron ambled over to an empty bed when Shelly brushed past him. Talia agreed it'd be best to be out of the medical professionals' way as they operated on the student. "The kid was unconscious, so he wasn't receiving questions."

"W-what about age, origin?" Neal chimed in. "H-how did we know h-he was a student?"

"Ah," Byron seemed to recall. "Frank did say something about seeing a late escapee during the extraction mission. He thinks he might have been from the same floor as a few of our recent additions."

"And he waited 'til now to say something about it?" Talia was skeptical.

"I guess. He remembered the boy falling from a broken line right as we withdrew to the trees. Frank watched Vardus's dolphins pursue the kid once he fell, figured there was no hope for him, thought he was as good as dead, hence why he never brought it up to anyone. But when we found this kid," Byron nodded to the boy,

"Frank said there was no doubt he was the same one flailing in the waters of Ardosia's lake that day. You should have seen Frank's face. He was staring at a ghost."

"But ..." Talia frowned, looking intently upon the student, noticing just how much he appeared like a man. His build was muscular. She could tell since his shirt had been thrown to either side after the nurses cut it down the middle. The cuts in his dark skin begged the question: "How? How did he survive out there?"

Byron had been wondering the same. "Your guess is good as mine."

Together they watched the medical team operate on him, forcing tubes in places tubes shouldn't go. In the jungle, predators avoided the sunlight like vampires. At nightfall, they emerged from the brush, slipping from their dens. Any man caught in the wild during the evening would be defying astronomical odds to endure darkness and see daylight. And by Talia's calculations, the extraction was two whole days ago. That meant the young man had done it *twice*.

Miraculous, Talia thought. Her eyes narrowed on the unconscious boy. Now the nurses had practically finished their work on him. His wounds were stitched up, IV in place, heart rate steadying.

In life, there were certain faces that, upon first glance, could be recognized as special, unique. Those of beautiful women, noble men, or burn victims, for instance. But this boy was none of those, not to her knowledge, and still his face possessed an innate quality that arrested Talia on the spot. Was it danger she sensed? It surely couldn't have been that Talia found this young man's face to be handsome. Always Talia had known better than to appeal to natural physical attraction. So what was it that she sensed in this boy?

Who are you? she wondered.

"Shelly," Talia commanded as she snaked by, "Before you go, what kind of condition is he in? Is he going to be fine?"

Consulting her spreadsheet, Shelly said, "Rough go at it for him, that's for sure. Lacerations as deep as half an inch in some spots, deeper in others. We're lucky Byron here caught the boy, or his life would be toast." Byron beamed with pride. "Anyway, he should make a full recovery by sunrise tomorrow."

"Be sure I'm the first to know when he's conscious."

"Sure thing, General." There was a sassiness to the way Shelly uttered the word *General* as she strolled from the ER–not before casting batting eyes in Byron's direction– but Talia's focus superseded such frail attacks at her character. She was in charge in Merciadel. Some people liked it, some didn't. Such is the divisive nature of politics. Talia hated politics.

Now just she, Neal, and Byron stood alone in the ER while the student's chest rose and fell at the opposite side of the room. Talia couldn't place what had intrigued her, besides the fact that the boy was one lucky son of a gun to have survived a couple of nights beyond the walls. Her first action when he woke would be to remind him to thank his lucky stars. She wondered at his story, but it could wait.

"So ... General." Byron's voice was laced with insinuation. He stood almost on his toes, eyebrows raised as he flicked his golden hair to the side.

"You're not getting Colonel."

He sighed. "Maybe tomorrow."

"Dismissed."

Byron exited the ER, pride intact.

Neal adjusted his glasses, inching toward the student's bed apprehensively, as though preparing to be suddenly attacked. "W-what will we do with him? Should we make him a p-prisoner? Don't know if we can t-trust him, you know. Could be a really big r-risk. He is Ardosian."

Talia responded without taking her eyes off the boy. "We'll determine his fate tomorrow, when he tells us just who he is. Frank could be wrong, and he might not be a student at all. Maybe he's a soldier who fled the ranks. That might explain his success in defeating the fatal darkness of the wild. Even then, I'm not sure *my* men could do so, let alone an Ardosian." She shook her head. "Whoever he is … he left that island for a reason. I'll bet my blade he poses no threat."

"Y-yes, General," Neal conceded before exiting the ER.

Standing over the bed, hands behind her back, Talia was alone. She hoped she was looking at the next loyal Mercian. Of course, she did not yet know the young man, but she suspected he had immense courage, of which there could never be too much. Yet something preternaturally tugged inside her, warning that if God would protect him through the jungle, He clearly didn't want the boy dead. Perhaps there was something special about him. Or he was just lucky. Whenever he woke, she would find out for herself whether a steel blade would suit his hand.

Before slipping away, Talia laid one last look upon the unconscious boy, not deigning to gaze upon his muscles. Perhaps with the help of young men like him, Merciadel would claim victory in their quest for national autonomy, sooner than later.

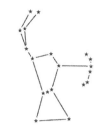

XXI

Golden, scarlet, and turquoise leaves shimmered in the intense rays that penetrated and highlighted their veins. In slow motion, they fell around him, delighting Orian's eyes. Gleefully, he let out a childish laugh as he twirled and twirled, eventually tumbling into a large pile of them. Crunching beside his ears, the leaves felt like soul-resting pillows against his head. He'd never found more comfort in his whole life … until the colors melted around him. Orian watched curiously at first, then with horror as he realized what was happening. Disintegrating, turning to dust and ash and mud, the leaves folded in around him until they were a sloppy mess dragging him into the earth. He let out a silent cry, which seemed to anger the mud, as it spat into his mouth, enough to drown him.

His body wriggled, or attempted to, as tree roots stretched and stretched across his chest and legs. Firmly, they wrapped themselves around him, sucking him into nature's belly–first his legs, then his torso. Orian's face was all that was exposed to the heavenly realm around him. It hurt, knowing that paradise was so close, but at the moment, he was trapped in a deathly circle, separated from the picturesque flowers, trees, and mountains. Slowly, mud crept into his ears and mouth. And there it was–the grim reaper, the summoner of death in the form of a large black cat. It prowled at the edge of the circle of mud, wondering if revenge was worth the taste. Neon green eyes seemed to reflect the tongue that licked its lips. The last Orian saw before resigning to mortality was the panther pouncing at him, claws first. He leapt right before his eyes were skewered.

"LADIS!"

The panther and the mud and the tree roots all disappeared, and so did his paradise. Orian's frame straddled the rails of the bed as he lifted himself upright. The room was white, light flickering above, and arched walls of splotchy appearance. After coming to, Orian observed that he was in some type of medical room. He rubbed sweat off his dark forehead as his brain inside ached. Last he remembered … what did he remember? It hurt forcing his mind to recall, but suddenly he did. *The black cat … it was real, not just a part of my dream.* Orian winced as he stroked his wounded shoulders. *And then … what happened next?* The truth was that he had not a clue how he'd managed to escape with his life. It seemed like his brain was vying for an escape of its own as it pounded at the outer edges of his skull. *That's right.* The memory dawned on him. *The arrows.* First, one arrow had been fired through the panther. Then another. That's how Orian had lived. Yet next he knew, there were more, each one aimed at him. Orian remembered running and running … but that was it. That was where his memory eluded him.

Orian scanned the room. Outside the subtle buzz emanating from the light in the ceiling and the steady drip of a leaking faucet, the medical room was completely silent. If this was Heaven, Orian thought, the glorious tales were in need of serious revision.

He wondered why it was so quiet. Surely, he couldn't be the only one here, right?

With a great deal of pain, Orian summoned the courage to roll out of bed. When his bare feet hit the linoleum, he could hardly stand, wavering weakly. His vision faltered as his body did, but he righted both. He ripped the IV from his hand and waited a second for nausea to subside. Edging beyond the curtain that partially enclosed his bedspace, Orian's suspicions were confirmed. He saw no one else. But he did see an exit sign, suspended above a small frame in the corner.

His jeans and white T had been discarded, replaced by the spotted white gown he now donned. It waved at his calves as he flew out the door into blinding bright light. Orian shielded his eyes. His toes wiggled when they hit a sandy-clay mixture. It was soft at the surface, yet firm below, and it extended in all directions, supporting unlit torches, weaving through buildings, and sprouting tremendous trees that dotted the skyline. Out here, still nobody appeared, but commotion in the distance struck Orian's ears, followed by deeply-uttered commands. He was going to find out where he was. If he had been presumably found in the jungle, someone must have saved him. Orian would find them, too.

In pursuit of answers, Orian rounded the square building, its edges reflective, white, and stained with sand. Was it a hospital of sorts? To his left was a various assortment of structures, some made of stone concrete that rose in L-shapes, others tent-like, and a few more appeared like wooden shacks. The architecture was diverse, but what about its people? Orian was determined to find out.

"Quicker!" someone shouted on the other side of the hospital. "You strike with as much lethargy as that, you may as well chop your own head off. Again!"

Orian ran toward the voice, where the dull clashing of wood and the grunts of men resounded. He wasn't sure what was going on, but he knew he'd find someone who might provide him with some answers. Whipping winds rippled the edges of his gown, tempting to expose him to the world. Small sand particles pestered his face, but he held a hand before his eyes to preserve them. When Orian reached the edge of the hospital, he found himself in awe of the sight before him.

"Good, Othor. Hone in that strike. Lighter on the toes, Sergei!"

In an open plot of land surrounded by scattered trees and a couple of long, arching tents, a short, skinny man with fare skin and dark hair was conducting a … what was it? A sparring session? The man was young, Orian could tell, even from a distance. Maybe thirty years old. And though he was short of stature, he exuded a poise in body language that demanded respect, and his commands were heeded dutifully.

"Men with knives, you afraid of a little bruising? Keep holding back on your strikes, and we'll abandon our wood for real steel. Strike harder!"

That seemed to work, as those in close combat worked to inflict pain on their opponent by jabbing short, slightly-pointed wooden sticks into gut, ribs, and back. Truly a barbaric sight, but simultaneously awesome.

"Swordsmen, how many times do I need to repeat the word *technique?* For God's sake, I'm not cleaning any of your wounds if you skewer each other on the battlefield. Y'all know how the General loves her numbers! Can't imagine she'd be thrilled to know we took one of our own out there."

The man yelling orders distinguished himself, donning dark blue clothing from head to toe, as opposed to the sand-colored camouflage adhering to the chests and legs of his sparring men and women.

Refreshing sunlight bent around the edge of the building and hit Orian's face. The heat felt great, but he was elated more so by the exhibition before him. These men were fighters of immense skill and technique. Orian had clicked on many links and seen old videos of sparring when searching the Internet at Ardosia. Each of these men would put any instructor Orian had ever seen to shame. They fought valiantly with each other, and they seemed to enjoy doing it, projecting haughty laughs into the sky, twirling with grace, and striking precisely, always. Orian had been so focused on their movements, the ways their hands folded and turned effortlessly, how their bodies were rooted like trees to the ground one second and then floated like feathers the next, that he hadn't noticed the ceasing of commotion.

Only when swords no longer clashed and grunts couldn't be heard did he realize that all the sparring men and women were staring curiously at him, as he had done in return. He hoped their eyes weren't longing for the murder they showed. Suddenly, their commander turned as well.

His eyebrows slanted. "What can I do for you, young man? Are you lost?"

"Frank! That's the kid you seen yesterday, nah?"

"Hell, it is!"

"Yeah, the Ardosian!"

That word seemed to unsettle many of them. *Oh no,* Orian thought. How could he have been so careless to wander out here, not knowing whether these men were friend or foe? The truth was Orian didn't have any foes … but clearly, *they* did. Some started to sneer at the sight of him, others growled. The commanding officer opened his mouth to speak, but Orian let instinct take over before he could do so.

Without a second thought, Orian turned and sprinted in the direction from which he had come. He had not a clue where to go, but he dashed anyway. He heard shouts behind him, and he knew the men were in pursuit, but for how long could he outrun them? *It's not about out-running; it's about out-smarting.* Yet how was Orian to accomplish that? This was their home soil, and he was outnumbered probably a hundred and fifty to one. Exceeding him in stature, the men and women on the sparring field were also much wider and more muscular than him. They had every possible advantage. But that wouldn't stop Orian.

He didn't make it far before he was toppled over by a wall of man, and for a moment his vision went white. Face down on the ground, Orian groaned. When he flipped himself upright, he was looking up into a circle of amused faces.

"What was this boy thinkin'?"

"Prolly what girls think when they see you, Frank. '*I gotta run!*'"

A deep wave of laughter was aimed at Orian before their commander cut a path between them. Orian got up on his elbows, terrified as a newborn deer surrounded by wolves. What were they going to do with him?

"What do you think, Cael?" one of the men spoke up.

"Yeah, Commander. Should we fry him?"

The man whom Orian presumed to be Commander Cael stood over him. His dark hair was cut short in a pointed V at his scalp. Commander Cael's face was skinny. Along with his V-shaped hairline was an analogous jawline. He didn't appear upset or angry or happy, for any matter. It was like he'd dealt with running boys in gowns a hundred times before. He was dressed in tactical gear, similar to that worn by his men, but they were all in tan or green while his garb was a lighter hue, in between royal and navy blue. Cael offered his hand.

"Let me help you up, young man."

Apprehensively, Orian took the offer.

Brushing off some of the sand and dust from his gown, the commander said, "What were you thinkin', runnin' like that? Could've hurt yourself."

Orian had no reply. He looked down shyly and saw the assortment of medals that adorned the man's chest. Wherever this place was, he was clearly of high rank here.

"Commanding Officer Cael." He stuck out his hand again. This time it was meant to be shook.

Embarrassed, Orian offered his own.

"Pleasure to meet you, young man."

Orian nodded.

Cael smiled. "Got yourself a name?"

"Oh, uh … yeah. Yeah, I do."

One of Cael's dark eyebrows arched. His eyes were sharp, like swords.

Giggling waves took over his men, but Cael shot them down pointedly. Then he looked back to Orian. "Mind telling me what it is?"

"Orian, sir."

"Interesting name, Orian. And if it so pleases you, I'd prefer you don't call me sir."

"Sorry, sir–uh … Cael?"

"Sure," he smiled. "You can call me Cael. Or Commander. Whichever you prefer."

"Commander," Orian said. He realized then that he was still shaking Commander Cael's hand. "Oh, uh … sorry." He rubbed his temple. "I'm not all there right now, I guess."

"Wouldn't expect ya to be! Heard you came all the way from Ardosia by yourself. Believe it or not, you, young man, are kind of the talk of the town right now. To make it out there on your own … you must be one lucky bastard."

"So I've been told," Orian intoned so that nobody heard him. "Were you the one who saved me? I mean I presume *somebody* saved me, right?"

"That would be me." A tall man who appeared to be the perfect soldier cut through the crowd. His voice was deep, his jaw cut to perfection, and his haircut … perhaps a little too preppy for Orian's taste, but it was clean. Flipping his golden hair to the side, the man laid a hand on Orian's shoulder. "Name's Byron."

Orian winced but nodded his respects. "I don't really know what to say. Thank you."

"Don't mention it." His hand slid off Orian's shoulder, and it stung against the wounds imparted by the panther. At his flinch, Byron said, "Whoops! Sorry, fella. Forgot you'd been attacked by a monkey."

Rubbing his wound, Orian returned, "Panther, actually."

This caused the men to stir.

Byron's brow furrowed. "Gotcha. I can tell by lookin' at you that you must be good at scaring pussy away."

The men behind him snickered.

Cael ignored the comment, fixing one more smile on Orian. "Welcome to Merciadel."

Merciadel. This place was one tumbleweed away from the Wild West by the looks of it, with more modern architecture. Merciadel didn't quite strike him as a fitting name, but he shrugged it off. As Orian started to utter his gratitude, he was interrupted.

"The fuck out of my way! Please, men." Orian hadn't expected to hear those words, let alone from someone with a lighter voice. It had emanated from a woman, no doubt. She sounded fierce. If Orian thought these mem respected Commander Cael, he guessed they would graciously fall to their knees if the woman were to demand it of them.

They parted to form a path right to Orian, and he was struck by her appearance. Like Commander Cael, she was also short, and her hair was even darker, falling just beyond her shoulders. Dressed in tight black cargo pants and an army camo long-sleeve, she was menacing. And then around her neck … where had Orian seen something like that before? A golden scarf trailed down her chest, flapping lightly in the wind. She stopped for a moment, as if to confirm that Orian was the one she'd been seeking. Then at last she approached, offering no hand.

"General Talia." She announced her name almost like she expected Orian to write it down. Was it spite he heard? But why? They'd only just met. "I hear you're from Ardosia."

His eyes wandered nervously. "That's right."

General Talia clenched her lips into a tight half-grin. "Right, well ... soldiers! Back to your training." The men shuffled, and before long they were gone. Commander Cael was the last to go, offering a thumbs up in encouragement. "So," the General continued. "I heard you were a student in the Tower, is that correct?"

"Yes, ma'am."

She frowned. "Do I look like a ma'am to you?"

Orian frowned back. "Um ..."

"Don't answer that." Apparently, she had no time to waste. "How did you make it all the way to Merciadel? That's quite the trek there, boy."

Orian huffed. "Do I look like a boy to you?"

Talia's eyebrows shot up. She gaped at him.

"Don't answer that."

A thin smile struck her face, but she banned it a moment after. "We had reports that you swung from one of our lines on your own. You elected not to use our gliders? Foolish."

"That's true," Orian confirmed. "That second part was not by choice. All gliders were gone when I got to the line. I was late, due to a few ... obstacles."

General Talia was intrigued by that. "You're from 102?"

Orian nodded. How did she know?

"By God," she whispered to herself. "I thought we had done well with five … but six?" Somehow, this news impressed her.

It dawned on Orian then that he must have made it to the land of the rebels, the same intruders who had stormed through Ardosia's Wall on the day when Orian had leapt from the Tower. Then Orian thought, if she knew about floor 102, maybe she knew some of those who had escaped.

"You have five from 102. Who are they?"

Her eyes were like shining diamonds, strong and almost difficult to look at when the sun hit them. "I'm only familiar with one."

"Who is it?"

"Her name is Trixie."

Trixie. She made it. One of the last encounters Orian had with Trixie, she had made an outrageous claim, or so he thought. It was something about the dolphins in Ardosia's lake being carnivorous with an alacrity for human flesh. At the time, he remembered scoffing internally at her conspiracy. If they were to meet again, he would have to let her know that she was right, somehow. Orian would also have to extract any other conspiracies she might have, for future reference.

"I know Trixie," he said.

The General's face revealed nothing, except some distaste perhaps. Her gaze couldn't be described as condescending, but it brimmed with bridled fire. "What were you doing in the trees?"

Orian looked behind him, beyond the fence. "You mean out there?" He shook his head and shrugged. "I was getting away. Tried to leave with the men you sent, but I didn't reach you in time."

Orian then told her about his swim in the lake and how he barely eluded the carnivorous porpoises. The General didn't even blink at that detail, so he continued, describing how he fled through the tunnel, was nearly caught by Ardosian soldiers, how he killed a boar, was attacked by a panther, and how he woke up in a medical bed. The only detail he missed was the death of the man working in the tunnel beneath Ardosia's Wall, and he had missed it on purpose. General Talia didn't need to know he was guilty of murder–or manslaughter, at least.

General Talia heard him, all of what he gave her before she opened her mouth. "For the record, I didn't just send men to Ardosia. I *led* them."

"You were there?" Orian frowned. He looked down at her golden scarf, and his eyebrows rose to new heights. "The boat! You were the one firing arrows from down below!" Orian knew the scarf had looked familiar.

"Walk with me," she demanded. The General started with seemingly little concern as to whether Orian followed or not. She was more interested in the training of her men as they strode by the sparring session. There were more grunts and sounds of metal crashing.

"Your soldiers are very skilled," Orian offered.

Her eyes flicked to him but for a second. Letting a puff escape her nose, General Talia did not slow her pace to speak, her boots crunching methodically against the ground. "And what could a student of Ardosia possibly know about soldiers in training?"

Not for a second did Orian consider the idea of concealing his use of the Internet at Ardosia. Discovering new faces presented an opportunity right from the start to hack the code of trust. He could tell the General was wary and guarded. Maybe she didn't trust anyone, and despite her rough-around-the-edges way she presented herself, Orian could tell General Talia was worthy of his honesty.

"I've read many articles over the art of combat. Watched a few videos as well, all online of course."

"How do you know about the Internet?" she sounded perplexed.

"I just found it, I guess."

"You *found* it? Nobody finds the Internet by happenstance, especially not within the Tower."

Orian shrugged. "Coding and hacking are a few of my specialties. We had these exercises to do in class. They were terrible. I hated them so much that one day, I decided I'd figure out how to 'pass' them without really passing them. Hacking through the mainframe, I'd trick the system into accepting perfect scores, and I'd read articles instead. Figured I'd make my days more interesting and learn about stuff I *wanted* to learn about."

As they turned the corner of a brick-and-mortar building, General Talia said to herself, "Impressive," which was as much respect as she'd paid Orian since they met five minutes prior.

For a while, they walked side-by-side in silence, the General keeping a pace ahead as she led him down the middle of a stone-paved roadway. It gave Orian the freedom to admire the humble nature of Merciadel. There were no Towers here, not a Coliseum, no lakes filled with sharks or dolphins or bodies, and though there was a surrounding fence, at least it wasn't a massive Wall comprised of bulletproof material. He felt safer, more at home here.

In between one-story houses and long stretching buildings, seemingly at random, massive bending trees rose high and spread their arms to provide large circles of shade. Swirling winds kicked dust and sand, which made the vegetation seem surreal to Orian. Who knew trees and weeds could survive in a place that looked like inhabited desert? Sparse grasses rose in uncompacted areas, and even a few dandelions poked through the stones beneath their feet.

Working down the straight and wide path, General Talia spoke to Orian. "How did you do it?"

"Hm?"

"You made it through two nights, alone in the jungle. I wouldn't send my finest men out there alone, especially not after that sun hits the horizon. How did you live?"

"Oh, um, I guess I'm not really sure. My roommate Ladis always did tell me how lucky I am."

Shaking her head, General Talia chortled. "It takes far more than luck to do what you did. So tell me the fine details. I know you managed to kill a boar–impulsive and elementary, but I get it. You were hungry. As for the panther, I imagine you were in the territory of a hostile tribe, which is why they attempted to shoot you. Nothing short of a miracle you got away from them."

"I don't know," Orian proposed. "If it was a tribe, it sure didn't seem like it. There weren't enough arrows fired to imply multiple assailants. I remember I was next to a pre-made firepit. I guess they could have had one of their tribe standing guard."

Just then, the General stopped in her tracks. The golden scarf waved at her chest while she frowned in thought. Summarily, she went, "Hmph," before continuing her walk forward. "Did you sleep?" she wondered aloud.

"Too well. I was going to sleep on leaves, but I don't know …" Orian was almost embarrassed to admit that he had elected to sleep in the mud instead. Maybe he hadn't been in the right frame of mind. For all he knew, he could have been on the verge of hallucinating–tired, dehydrated, and starving. Maybe that's why the mud had provided him with extra comfort. Regardless, he provided General Talia with this detail, without delving into the specifics.

"Of course," she mumbled. "Mud masks scent."

Orian chose not to dive into it any further, so they forged onward. On the way, those whom Orian assumed to be current citizens of Merciadel were sure to offer their warmest welcomes, after greeting General Talia, of course. She met most of them with twice as much warmth as she'd offered him. Eventually, they had walked far enough to skirt any more human interaction. It was beginning to give Orian a headache, hearing, "Glad you made it out of Ardosia!" or "Welcome to Merciadel!" or "Heard about your story, kid. Thank the Lord for your life!" It wasn't that Orian was unappreciative of their hospitality, but rather that his brain was in no working order to receive it. He would need time to recover. He wasn't sure all this walking helped, either.

Without warning, General Talia cut in front of Orian, sliding off the path toward a single door. She said, "Stay here," before disappearing. The door clicked shut, leaving Orian alone outside … still dressed in spotted white cotton.

The structure that General Talia had gone into was one of the few multi-level buildings Orian had seen. Its main layer had been formed with brick, but they must have run out of the thicker yellow bricks because red and brown stretched up the remaining two-thirds. Old grimy windows dotted its side, and Orian couldn't see through any of them, though he tried.

Orian's head swiveled. He guessed they were somewhere in the middle of Merciadel since he could no longer spot any exterior fencing. He began to wander when the General shot out of the door.

"Here. Change into these." In her hands were folded cargo pants, and on top of those was a gray muscle shirt, moderately stained. The clothes must have been used by somebody else before. Orian wondered if perhaps they had been a soldier's, who was now gone.

"Um," Orian stammered, looking around. "You want me to change here?"

General Talia pointed further down the path. "There. No, not the bigger one. You see the one with the black shingles?"

To Orian, it appeared like a luxurious outhouse, small and compact but relatively large for a changing room. He nodded. "Yeah, I see it."

She led him onward, all the way to the door, where she stopped. "You will change into these clothes. Inside, there is a bed you can lie on until I have Simone return for you. She'll give you a tour of Merciadel. That is, if you think you can manage." If Orian wasn't mistaken, a challenge had been issued. He'd run through the jungle for hours with claw marks in his shoulders. He'd lived through two nights amongst beasts, which he'd been assured was impossible. Although he was drained and could afford twenty-seven hours of rest, he wouldn't show any sign of weakness, and he would rise to the occasion.

"Easy," Orian shrugged.

General Talia paused as she pondered him. Her eyes flicked up and down, mulling over him before she turned and left without another word.

"Hm." Orian pressed his lips together as one eyebrow rose. He wasn't sure what he'd done, but General Talia had apparently been offended by his existence. No matter. Rather than taking offense in return, he regarded her with intrigue until she was lost beyond the way.

Flipping around, Orian was ready to shed the gown and slip into some real clothes. Above all, he was excited to do it in the privacy of this changing room. Smashed between extending rows of houses and yards, the building appeared to have been a tiny tan house squished for convenience.

The door did not creak, nor did it groan when he opened it, but that's where the pleasantries of the estate ended. Inside, Orian fumbled for a light switch on the wall, but he came up with only spider webs. It took him five minutes to realize that there was a touch lamp standing alone on a desk tucked in the right corner of the space. It was the only source of light he would have, other than the thin trails sliding through the one and only meal-box window in the side wall. There was also a cot stowed in the left corner. In between the desk and the stained sheets hanging over the edge of the low-lying bed was a thin aisle. That's where Orian changed.

His joints were tight. His body was battered. Luckily, the shirt and pants General Talia had handed him were made of a soft cotton fabric that caressed his wounds. They fit him snugly. Afterward, he folded the gown and sat it atop the desk, where a decade's worth of dust and grime had collected. Orian wondered how long it had been since someone had been inside this room.

Light poked out from the desk lamp in a weak half-circle, flickering against the wall. Now changed, Orian had successfully completed everything on his to-do list. So he stood, waiting. His eyes wandered inside the cramped space, but he determined quickly that there was nothing more to observe. A bed, a desk, and a weak-lit lamp could only be inspected for signs of the spectacular for so long. Eventually, Orian became bored as he waited for someone named Simone, who would be giving him a tour.

That, at least, had been the information General Talia had left him with. Since Orian's eyes could no longer wander, his brain assumed the exercise. Frowning, he wondered at the possibility that this small shack might possess infrared scanners that were presently searching his body for anything sinister—an irregular heartbeat, a life-ending infection, or foreign DNA that might be considered a contaminating substance within the walls of this nation.

He allowed the thought to hover but ultimately deemed it to be ridiculous. Though the cot appeared rigid and likely housed a bed bug or two, it drew Orian's eye all the same. Orian was exhausted, and if the woman named Simone wasn't coming for him anytime soon, he'd affectionately seize an opportunity to rest.

Leaving the light on as he crawled beneath the sheets of the cot, Orian blinked a few times at the ceiling. Here he was in this new world, alert that it might be just as corrupt as the island of Ardosia, wary that it may be a camp where intestines are harvested and child hearts are devoured by elites. However, equally as likely was the chance that Orian had stumbled upon a land governed by objective truths and morals. Or perhaps Merciadel was somewhere in between. In any case, he had no more energy to speculate.

Though the mattress was firm against his back, Orian's eyes rested immediately. If he dreamt, he didn't know it. Black darkness had swept over him.

Orian could have been out for an hour, maybe ten minutes, but it felt like a mere second had passed between the time he closed his eyes and the moment unwelcome sunlight streamed through the doorframe.

Orian shot up. Past the threshold, a silhouette stared at him menacingly. He thought to scream, but he quickly recognized the person before him.

"Up," General Talia commanded. "Simone is sick, so it appears I'll be showing you around."

Wiping the sleep from his eyes, Orian planted his feet and walked outside with her. The sun had fallen to the edge of the horizon. There, it shed its light over trees that imbibed its final warmth before damp coolness would overtake the area. Shadows stretched across the stone path that General Talia traversed in front of Orian. He wondered if she always walked fast or if she took pleasure in listening to the ailed grunts Orian issued as he struggled to keep up.

"I don't mean to be rude, but could we slow down a hair?"

"We have a lot of ground to cover, Orian."

It meant "no".

Orian wasn't sure how long they had circled the property. First, General Talia had led him by the brick building of two shades since it was right beside the changing room. She called it the textile mill, indicating its vital importance to Merciadel.

"That's why it's in the center," she said. "I like to say that cotton weighs more than gold."

She explained to him how yarns and fabrics were used to barter, primarily for food. While they did have farmers of their own, Merciadel was home to many, and self-sufficiency was implausible. For clothing and other uses that cotton provided, they were able to sustain a voracious military, in addition to growing families.

Next was the tech building–which looked like a giant square mirror, its body covered in bright silver panes upon which sunlight glinted into his eyes.

The General gestured with an extended arm. "We have some of the best tech experts in the world here at Merciadel. Innovative doesn't even come close to describing them." Orian watched how she stood straight and proud, noting the subtle way she seemed to light up. "That zipline you slid to safety on? My men created the blueprint for the machine. It worked flawlessly."

Almost, Orian thought.

They continued onward. General Talia directed Orian toward open fields for recreation, where a few children laughed and played in the last hours of dawn. A couple of them were kicking a small soccer ball between one another's legs, until one of them fell and started to sob. Beside Orian, General Talia was still, intently watching the kids.

"Is he yours?" Orian inquired.

Since the General hadn't heard him, he opened his mouth to ask again, but she said curtly, "No." By appearance, General Talia wasn't old at all, maybe a few years Orian's elder, a decade at most. He didn't think the implication that she may be a mother would be offensive. Still, there was a fire in her response that she immediately doused.

"No kids," she uttered solemnly. "Leaders don't have time for children, not if they're fully committed. And I am. Merciadel means more to me than any family ever could. Besides, men are boys who aren't interested, not for longer than one night." She cleared her throat. "Let's keep moving."

Orian was led to a target range, where the General promptly picked up a bow, firing an arrow directly into a toppled-over bale of hay. It thudded hard. She stared at the hay like it had done her a lifetime of wrong. "I train my men here, with the help of Commander Cael. It isn't just a goal of ours to be *better* and more prepared than our enemy. It is the requirement." General Talia set the bow down, and they kept moving.

She said, "Our military makes up nearly a quarter of Merciadel's population. My men and women are literally our lifeline."

Orian couldn't help but wonder, why the necessity for such a large military presence? He blurted, "Are you at war with Ardosia?"

The General slowed. As she did, Orian peered at the side of her face. Final rays of sunlight gleamed over her, highlighting the concealed scars held beneath the top layer of skin. There weren't a lot of them, but the scratches were noticeable in this light. She stroked her night hair back, blankly watching the approaching path. "Are we at war with Ardosia? No."

"If not Ardosia, then who?"

She sighed, explaining brusquely, "A large military presence doesn't imply anything other than potential strength, Orian. Your name was Orian?"

"Mhmm."

She started forward again, with Orian following closely behind. "At the moment, we need everyone we can get because although we aren't at war with Ardosia itself, we are at war with President Vardus."

"What's the difference? If fighting a nation's leader, are you not at war with his nation?"

"War is an inexplicable entity, and in this battle, we've willingly pitted brother against brother, lover against lover in some instances. Private Kaija has a brother in Ardosia's military whom she was forced against in a previous extraction mission. Agent Moss collected intel from his best friend's devices in a covert operation. Almost all our soldiers have friends or siblings they left behind on that island. Because we are at odds with their self-proclaimed President, our hand has been forced. My men *and* women have no choice, and so we find ourselves ailed by the priorities of a nation, over the priorities of a people."

Orian struggled to imagine what that would be like. What if he were forced to eliminate Ladis? For what? The cause of a nation? He wasn't sure his morals would allow such a thing. "What are you fighting for?"

General Talia let out a huff of amusement. "Same thing everyone fights for."

"Money?"

"Control."

"Control?" Orian appreciated the General's honesty, but it perturbed him.

"President Vardus battles for dominance over an entire people, maybe even the world if he were to have his way. In Merciadel, we fight for a different type of control: that of our freedom."

"Huh?" Orian didn't understand.

"For everything in this world, Orian, there is a price. A sack of peppers runs for one square of cotton. Remaining in good physical shape? That'll cost both sleep and comfort. The price of freedom is the blood of innocent men and women, millions of them over the course of history. I don't like it any more than you, but it is a timeless battle, one I fear will never end. But that won't stop us from trying." She summarized with this: "Even freedom requires that someone ensures it becomes impregnable. I've spent my life fighting for it. Pussies and politicians wouldn't ever speak the quiet part out loud and tell you that it requires control to obtain freedom, but that doesn't make it any less true. Freedom will never be free."

A queasiness punched Orian's gut then, whether from weariness or the disturbing nature of the world, he didn't know. He elected for silence as they kept on.

Finally the sun sank beneath the trees. In the pre-dusk dark they saw a church, and at long last they swerved through crop fields of corn, cotton, soybeans, and more before ending up right where they started. By the time Orian's tour had concluded, his gray muscle T had become even more sweat-stained than it had been before. He was out of breath and perhaps slightly triggered. In his mind, it had been an unnecessary venture to farmers' fields. Although he hadn't indicated that his knees, legs, arms, and shoulders felt as though they would fall off during their trek, his breathing had become more labored than it would have in the midst of a high-intensity workout session. His body was in no shape to walk several miles around a property, and he believed the General to be well aware of it. If not for Orian's affinity for Merciadel from the moment he'd seen the place, he might have been more vocal about his frustration.

Like the foundation of a skyscraper, first impressions were important. All proceeding knowledge of something– or in this case, *somewhere*–was stacked atop that foundation. What Orian had concluded was that he enjoyed Merciadel, a lot. In the air, there was a sense of passion for life and living. Courage and healthy pride came in abundance. All who had greeted him had done so with glimmering smiles and genuine care. So, despite the lingering frustrations buried beneath his swelling ebullience, Orian presented himself delicately. He didn't want to appear too eager.

General Talia stopped beside the changing room Orian had used earlier. Somehow, she seemed unfazed by the chill that had swept over Merciadel in the presence of darkness. Her hands were on her hips. "This is Merciadel. It is my home, and it will be forever." She cleared her throat. "You were quiet … outside of your breathing. Ardosia doesn't train students in the physical realm, not like we do." Spitting to the side, she eyed him.

Tentatively, Orian scratched behind his ear. "You have much to be proud of, General. Your citizens seem to have immense loads of respect for you. So do I. What you have here is something special. And um …" Orian stuttered. "Well, if it's alright with you, I'd like to stay."

For the second time tonight, General Talia smiled. Her first grin had come at the hands of Orian's physical exhaustion. Suddenly, she was full of surprises because she also stuck a hand out with no disrespect attached to it. "We were counting on it."

Orian was wary of her. He feared she might pull him over her shoulder and pile drive him into the ground, just for fun. But their interaction was cordial and tame. "Thank you."

"Your shift begins tomorrow," General Talia uttered succinctly. Her smile faded for a moment and then after examining him quickly, it returned. "On second thought, how about you rest up for a day? You've been through enough."

Eyeing her with an admirable curiosity, Orian's mouth curled into a smirk. Now he knew why they'd walked all the way out to the fields. The General had been testing his resolve, and she must've liked what she saw.

General Talia turned and began walking. Her exit seemed abrupt, almost rude, so Orian waited to speak until she showed no signs of returning to say goodbye.

"Um, General. General!"

Keeping stride, Talia peeked over her shoulder. She was beginning to meld into the night. "What is it?"

"Where will my shift be?" A giddy grin took him as he guessed. "The hall? The textile mill? No, wait …" It had to be the tech building.

"You'll find out soon enough. Now get some rest."

In front of Orian, there was the textile mill. Behind him was the changing shack. And to either side was the stone path that wove through Camp Merciadel. Although his special awareness exceeded that of a novice, Orian had no idea where he was to go.

Whirling about, Orian asked, "Where should I sleep?"

She laughed. "Where did you sleep earlier?"

Orian looked behind him. He realized then that it was no changing room at all. It was his living space. He gulped but would not be ungrateful for a bed. He'd spent the past couple of nights resting in mud.

"Thank you!" he raised his voice.

The General laughed again. "Don't mention it." As Orian measured the door before him and began to open it, General Talia spoke up once more with a friendliness to her tone that Orian had yet to hear. "I'm impressed by you, Orian. Brave guy. Maybe a little stupid, but we can fix that."

By now, she was almost invisible. Peering into darkness, Orian said, "Thanks ... I think."

Orian could hardly contain his excitement, to the point that he didn't feel like resting the next day. He wanted to dive right into his position at the tech building. Though it hadn't officially been granted to him, Orian guessed that the General had picked up on his technological talents, after they'd discussed his ability to hack into the Internet. Who would have thought that he'd be rewarded so highly! He just arrived, and already he was receiving more proper treatment than ever displayed in Ardosia. Yet he knew a night's rest would be greatly beneficial. As Orian leaned forward to enter the shack, he heard the General's call.

"Oh, and one more thing."

"Go ahead, General."

Orian no longer heard the scraping of boots against stone. Her distant silhouette had gone still. "Get plenty of rest. You'll need it."

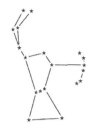

XXII

He hadn't been assigned to the tech building. Nor was he delighted with a spot at the mill. He could have slapped food onto plates at the hall, for all he cared. Crafting armor, trimming grass with scissors, or picking dandelions from the stone walkway until not a single weed remained. All might have been better options than the task he'd been given.

In the old creaking stable, the stench was a constant finger down Orian's throat. When the wind howled, the supports shifted, and Orian feared he might be buried in a pile of wood and rusty nails and ... something else–something horrendously acrid–at any moment. At least the old man Pake was nice.

"You stuff the fork *into* the hay and glub." *Glub* was Pake's word for poo. His wrinkly neck strained. His denim overalls were stained with either mud or glub. Orian couldn't tell. "*LIFT*!" He grunted as he hoisted the fecal matter and straw on a flatbed trailer, exhaling madly as he flipped the fork over. "And that's all there is to it, son. Gettin' to be too old to do it myself. Thank the Lord you came t' us! Now don' get me wrong. Just cuz this old fella wobbles don't mean you can't ask ole Pake for help." Slapping him on the back, Pake handed Orian the pitch fork. "You try."

Orian took the tool apprehensively.

"No judgin'!" Pake held his hands up at both sides.

Adjusting the fork in his hands, Orian stared into the face of his enemy–a twelve-foot-tall pile of straw and horse manure. "Here goes nothing." Eyes shut, as if afraid to fail, he jabbed the fork into the center of the pile. When he went to lift, he found that the load was too heavy. So he jabbed again, this time toward the top of the pile.

Pake offered a look of forced encouragement when he saw the miniscule load he'd conjured. "No big deal!" he told Orian. "You'll come 'round to likin' this, trust me. Just be sure there's nothin' leftover when you're finished, Ryan." It would take him a few more days to learn Orian's name. "Now if you'll excuse me, I should be getting back to my dear Kin. Cherry is the flavor of the day, my favorite. Once you're all done there, feel free to come on in and enjoy a slice of pie for yourself!" Before hobbling out the stable, Pake turned to Orian one more time with a wide toothy grin. "'Preciate the hard work you're puttin' in, son."

Orian's nod was only half convincing. Pake adjusted his straw hat before leaving Orian to his duty–lots and lots of duty.

It was his first day, and he couldn't have felt more nervous, or useless for that matter. On several occasions over the course of his first hour, Orian had overestimated his strength, stabbing too low. Manure weighed more than he realized, and it smelled worse and worse every time he tore a fresh stack from the pile. Other times, he was guilty of not loading enough. *Why did the General assign me to a farm, of all places?* Orian's talents would have been much better utilized in the tech room, where perhaps even he could have shared his expertise. Maybe he could have been a military man. He remembered Talia having mentioned something about *strength in numbers.* Why couldn't he contribute to that strength?

Just then, Orian's back tweaked. He winced. Grabbing for the cramp, he winced again. His shoulders still burned. The wounds would take a while to heal. Yesterday, he had taken advantage of a do-nothing day and rested until nearly lunchtime in hopes that he might wake feeling better. It had worked, although barely. When it had been time to eat, he left his small living quarters and was ushered to a dining hall where a meal was served. He poked at the main entrée after receiving a plate. "What is this?" Orian asked the chef wearing a hair net. He spat his response. "Protein, son. Looks like your skin and bones could use a little more." Orian had given a concerned look, so the chef clarified. "It's beef, boy. Eat up." After his first bite, Orian's taste buds soared with elation. Then he finished and went up for more. "Sorry, kid," the chef said. "You'll have to wait 'til tomorrow. We all gotta eat." He had gone back to rest after lunch and didn't wake until sunrise. In dire need of regeneration, Orian didn't argue with his body's desires.

Pain shot down Orian's back again. *Maybe this is why I wasn't assigned to the military.* No cripples could meet the standards of the esteemed General Talia. She was tough, Orian could tell. She had earned his respect, but judging by his assignment on the farm, he had not yet earned hers.

Loading another sheet of glub onto the truck bed, Orian became fatigued. His head fell when he remeasured the pile. If anything, it looked mightier than it had before, despite the base of the rear end of the truck that was now completely covered in dung. This was his job. Mundane, sure, but to his surprise, he felt a tinge of joy, maybe fulfillment in his contribution, no matter how finite or painful or useless it may have seemed to him at the moment. *Is this what a role would have been like on Ardosia?* he wondered. If so, his vision of the island had been drastically overdramatized.

Stuffing load after load onto the bed, Orian escaped through memory. His first thoughts were unpleasant, recalling Zak and his accident that had costed the pale guy his spot on floor 102 of Ardosia's Tower. Daily did that memory haunt Orian. Ladis came into his mind next. He chose to picture his best friend smiling, like the day he'd first met Dawn. "Oh, she's gorgeous, Orian. Don't you think she's gorgeous?" Chuckling to himself, Orian hoisted another fork full of a hungry horse's markings. He found the more time he spent in his head, the more oblivious he became to his circumstance. So he forged on with a recollection of his morning.

At the sound of hard knocks on his door, Orian had woken from slumber, jubilant and active. Even in his new home that was storage-shed sized, he couldn't squelch the rush in his chest or the thumping that rose to his head, telling him the world outside was wide with endless possibilities. After dressing in another pair of cargo pants identical to the ones he'd worn the day before, he slipped a dark green t-shirt over his head, tucking it in of course, and fled out the door into steamy rays of morning sun that hacked through fog. Orian's rush faded as quickly as the dense air when General Talia personally informed him where he'd be working.

Addressing his apparent disappointment, Talia said, "What? Farmer Pake has been asking for help for quite some time. I think you'll be perfect." Instead of retorting his internal protests and fervently vying for the tech job of which he believed himself worthy, Orian nodded humbly, thinking, *How bad could it be?*

Amongst the swarming flies and invasive reek, Orian realized just how bad. It took him until lunch to stack every last square inch of scat and straw atop the truck bed, and by then he had worked up the appetite necessary for the meal Pake's wife had cooked him.

When Orian had gone in to inform Pake that he would be taking lunch at the cafeteria, the farmer's wife Kin overheard, scolding him accordingly. "Where in the Nation's Falling do you think you're going? They don't have anything close to Mama Kin's cookin' at that rat-infested dining hall. Come, come." Kin had been donning a denim chef's apron, one with a pink flower sown into the chest. Her curled white hair seemed to bounce atop her head as she beckoned him to the kitchen, where Pake had already been seated at the head of a four-seater table.

Orian sat next to the old man. "My lady's cookin' is to die for. No way she was gonna let you eat anywhere else." Their course had contained something called a "casserole", according to Kin, in addition to grits and beans.

"Who will be joining us?" Orian asked when he saw the heaping portions bestowed upon the wooden table.

"Just us," Pake said, his eyes imagining the first bite. "Dig in, son! Don't let it get cold!"

"Go on now," Kin goaded.

Nervously, Orian loaded his plate with a serving similar to what he may have been given at Ardosia.

An eyebrow arched on the old man's face. "I hope you're not fool 'nough to disrespect my wife's cookin'. Come on, boy. I know you worked up a sweat out there. Gonna take more than a couple spoon-full o' my lady's casserole to stop that growlin' stomach o' yours. When I say dig in, I mean dig in!"

"Oh, uh … um, I wanted to be sure there was enough for you two as well."

Kin's smile was warm and rosy as her cheeks. "Please, take as much as you'd like, sweety. I know my dear boy Pake appreciates your work."

"That I do."

"You are very generous." Orian pressed his lips together. "Thank you." He doubled his serving. Both Pake and Kin weren't pleased until he tripled it.

"There you go, son. Ever had chicken casserole before? No? Hm, well if you had, I'd have told you it's nothin' like my wife's. What a lucky man you are. Your first taste will be the best."

Kin blushed. "Stop it, honey."

"Let's pray." Solemnly squeezing his eyelids shut, Pake grasped two hands–Kin's right and Orian's left. Orian looked across the table to Kin, who also closed her eyes. Uncertain, he mimicked them as Pake began. "God who provides the greens and the wealth of love, come be our guest as we welcome young Ryan to the family of Camp

Merciadel. I'd like to thank you for my beautiful wife, whose skill rises from the kitchen to the bedroom." Orian heard a playful huff and a slap, but he kept his eyes shut. "Lastly, we thank you for the gift of life, knowing we'll be eager to join you in your kingdom when the last day is upon us. Amen."

"Amen," said Kin.

"Amen."

Without further ado, they ate. Quickly Orian saw how important meals were to this wise couple. They ate and ate without speaking once, polishing their plates like the meal would be their last. They didn't talk of the weather, nor of the work to be done, and not once had they asked Orian about Ardosia. The silence was refreshing, and so was the food. In his life, Orian had never tasted anything so delectable as chicken casserole. There were cooked green beans, carrots, and a whole lot of foreign ingredients that excited his taste buds. Scarfing hist first portion down, he hungrily eyed what remained of the casserole, the grits, and the beans.

"Eat as much as you'd like, dear," Kin offered him the spoon to shovel more onto his plate. In an attempt at modesty, Orian took a helping similar to his first, though he could have stolen the entire dish.

"Be sure to leave room for dessert!"

Orian wiped at his mouth after chewing. "Dessert?" He'd never tasted a dessert on the island.

"Cherry pie," Pake said pridefully.

Though Orian hadn't heard of a cherry pie, he anticipated it to be special. If it were anything like a chicken casserole, he'd graciously accept a dessert.

Pake and Kin had waited patiently for Orian to finish before Kin stole the cherry pie from the oven. A minute break between entrée and dessert gave Orian the chance to inspect the house's interior. After leaving the stable earlier, he had noticed the outside of the house was stucco white, much of the paint having been stripped off the sides, ostensibly after years of wind-whipping erosion. The porch was creaky with a swing hanging at the far end. Clearly the exterior had absorbed all damage, because not a dent or scratch was to be found on the walls or floors of the interior. Light blue paint on the walls hadn't faded or stripped. Hanging beside the dining room table were a couple of framed photos. The sun glinted off the frame, so Orian was unable to steal a glance. He imagined they were photos of the old couple together.

"The first slice goes to our guest." Kin used a smaller plate to lay a steamy portion of cherry pie before Orian. "We're happy to have you, dear."

"You're really kind. Thank you."

"And to my husband … and to me!"

At first sight, cherry pie lacked appeal. The crust appeared to be a little soggy. Also, if Orian wasn't mistaken, weren't cherries red? These were almost brown. Even so, Orian would not cast judgment before getting a taste. A smile hit his face as he imagined the impending party in his mouth. Before taking his first bite, Orian thought he saw a wary glance coming from Pake. He offered no attention but to that of the heaping mound of pie resting upon his fork. Eagerly, he stuffed it into his mouth.

The dessert hit his tongue. Orian coughed, wincing.

Kin's eyes were wide with concern.

"Hot," Orian said as he forced the pie down his throat. It was a lie. The pie was only warm.

Kin gave a nervous, twitching smile. Pake simply examined Orian intently as he chewed slowly on his portion. Orian's first taste of the dessert was horrendous. Even the meals he'd been given at Ardosia were more tasteful. The cherries were bitter, the crust a swamp, and it stained his breath with reek. Yet, willed by a desire not to upset his hosts, Orian tried for another bite, this one equally as disturbing as the first. He set his fork down, unable to continue.

"Everything alright, son?" Pake wondered. His fork slid into the remaining end of his pie.

"Yes," Orian lied. "I'm ... I'm stuffed." He could tell they weren't convinced, considering the way he'd demolished the casserole just minutes prior. "We never had this much food at Ardosia. First time over-eating." Orian shrugged, hoping he'd sold his case.

Pake nodded slowly. Kin forced a smile. Slowly she slid Orian's plate toward herself. "Don't worry," she said. "I'll wrap this up and put it in the fridge for you to finish later ... when you're not so full."

The meal concluded. Pake rose, laid a loving kiss upon Kin's cheek, and said, "The work won't do itself, darlin'. Ryan and I best be going."

"Right, dear. Enjoy!"

On the way out, Pake wrapped an arm around Orian's shoulder. He asked, "How was it?"

The porch creaked as they stepped off, their boots landing softly on wavy grasses. "The entrée was excellent," Orian said, avoiding the topic of dessert. "Truly amazing."

"My wife is a special woman."

Pake led Orian away from the stable. Near the far end of the house, a large, winding tree towered high. Next to it were a collection of chopped logs and a sawed-off stump, inlaid with an ax.

"How about my lady's pie, huh?" Pake gave Orian a steely gaze. "Somethin', ain't it?"

Orian gulped. His smile was weak. "I've never had dessert before. I liked it."

With his arm still across Orian's shoulder, Pake gave a gentle squeeze that aggravated his wound. He shot a careful glance behind him before leaning close, whispering. "I know it's awful, son. Brutally awful."

Orian frowned. Was he being tested? "Huh? No, Pake. It was great. I, uh–"

"Cut the crap, Ryan." He took his arm away. "It's okay. I know my lady's pie is as appetizing as the dung you loaded this mornin'."

Maybe even less so, Orian thought to himself.

Head drooping, the old farmer sauntered close to the stump. "Been forcin' it down my gullet for fifty years now. More, even. Never gets better." Pake led Orian around the stump. He plucked the ax from it and tossed it aside.

A shallow breeze swept low and rose to Orian's neck. Leaves bristled. The grasses hummed. "Why not tell her? If it's so bad, why eat it?"

Balancing a log on the stump, Pake adjusted the fresh wood so that it didn't wobble. He then grabbed the ax. Pake weighed it in his hands. Its metal edge shone brightly, as if just sharpened. With one fell swipe, it came down on the wood with speed that contrasted Pake's age, splitting it in two, clean as butter. "You're young, kid. From what I hear, it's a miserable life on that island. Too much comfort for the blind. You, you're not blind, so I think you'll understand this when I tell ya. Don't 'magine you've been in love?"

Orian shook his head. "If I ever have, I was unaware."

Pake's laughter was grisly. "Good answer, kid." Another log exploded, splinters flying sideways. "Kin and I have been together through it all. She's my rock, son. I do love her more than life. When I go, I hope she goes with me, right at the same time. That's true love, you know." Orian understood what he said, but he couldn't connect the dots between love and pie. Pake wiped sweat off his brow, sending a dark streak across his overalls. "Loving a woman ain't just loving everything about her– smile, flaws … meals. How do I put this? Well, love is like dinner with my lady Kin. You with me? My dear's casserole. Amazing, no?"

Orian nodded. "I could have eaten the entire dish."

"The first course is always the best. It goes down smoothly, makes you feel all warm and giddy inside. Then you eat the sides. Those are also good! Sure to be dinner's staples–reliable and healthy for ya. Yeah, the green beans and the peas don't tickle my fancy, but they are good for the heart. And don't even get me started on the lima beans." Pake spat at the stump. "At last comes the dessert. By that time, the flavors have all been expunged. You can recall the tastes of the entrée and relish fondly in the way they made you feel, but that part is over. Once you get to my lady's pies, dinner becomes a mentality, a commitment."

Dinner … a commitment. Orian chuckled at the thought. "I don't get it. Kin makes a mean casserole, and I'm sure her other dishes are just as awesome. Can't she taste the difference?"

Pake's eyes drifted to his fields, swaying in the breeze. "A woman's love has no taste buds, son. Whether sweet or bitter, cool or warm, it is unconditional. An amazing thing

God has created for us in women. What I mean to say, son, is that in life, you're going to meet someone or find somethin' you love. Pursuing whatever that may be … it'll be easy at first, just like the entrée. Your sides are the middle o' the road, the part of your pursuit that has been firmly established. By the time you grow old, feelin's disappear. You can eat your dessert with a smile and choose to enjoy it. You can look upon that cherry pie with disdain and complain while you load it into your mouth, or you can push it to the side altogether, in search of somethin' beyond that rainbow.

"The point is that I love my wife, Ryan. I eat that pie, and I enjoy it because I *choose* to. At some point, when the feelings that accompany your love and passion disappear, you will have a choice to make." Pake took one more log off the sorted stack. Setting it upon the stump, he grabbed the ax in both hands, but he did not raise it above his head. Instead, he ambled to Orian, his face tightly grinning. Gently, he laid the ax in Orian's hands. "This world needs love, Orian. Lots of it. It's gonna beat you down, make you wanna throw up, maybe. But when it comes time to choose, *always* choose to love."

Handing Orian the ax, Pake declared that every last log was to be split in two, but it was alright if it wasn't finished by dusk. There was always tomorrow. "Till there isn't," Pake chuckled. "Oh, and be sure to unload my truck before sunset. Take 'er up by the entrance and find the cliff. Be careful now. You send only the straw over the edge and not yourself. Awright?"

Orian swallowed his unease. *A cliff?* It sounded dangerous, but he mustered a firm response. "Yes, sir."

Pake left him a grin before hobbling toward the house. Orian peered over to the stables and saw the rusty pale-green truck. "Wait!" The farmer turned at Orian's voice. "I don't know how to drive a truck."

So Pake showed him. It was surprisingly simple. Turn the key. Press the clutch. Give some gas. And you're off.

After completing his driver's ed quick-course, Orian carried himself back to the stump where he spent the next four hours loading logs and splitting them. He had only made it through half the stack before the sun glowed orange in the Western sky, nearly set. Muscles on fire, back one more swipe from cracking like wood, Orian almost unintentionally dismissed his final duty of the day. Fortunately for him and his previously-impaired sense of smell, the bed-stacked stench was carried by a breeze until it slapped Orian in the face, reminding him that there was still work to be done. After that, he could rest.

The cab door latched shut with Orian inside. As if the ax had become a part of him, Orian had accidentally lugged the tool to the truck, not realizing it was still in hand. He could have returned it to the stump, but he tossed it in the passenger's seat instead. Blade down, its hilt sat on the head rest. "You can sleep," Orian told the ax. "But I'll have to wait."

A few turns of the engine later, the "old rust bucket", as Pake referred to it, was "humming like a kitten." Orian struggled only briefly at first, as the old farmer indicated he might. Still, Orian thought that killing the engine twice wasn't bad for his first time. The gears didn't grind on him at all, either. They just made a few screeches when he shifted up and down.

Steering the large machine down the center of a dirt path, Orian followed its direction until he came upon base camp, where he had woken at the hospital. On the way, the window was rolled down, arm hanging out, Orian inhaling the fresh air. While the sun's final appearance for the day instilled him with ease, Orian worried that it might fall below the trees before he reached the cliff.

Tires crunched on gravel as Orian downshifted. The path he'd followed diverged to the left and the right. Since the one on the right led directly into the town square, Orian proceeded to the left, and sure as ever, he approached the cliff before long.

"Whoah," Orian said to himself, standing at the edge of a fifty-foot drop. The truck was parked sideways at his rear, with the break pulled tightly up. A shuddering tingle rose through his body as the cliff engendered worst-case scenarios in his mind. He would have to implement arrant caution when dumping that pile of glub.

To Orian's surprise, backing the truck to the edge of the cliff was the easy part. The tires came almost frighteningly close to the edge but were secure on land. There was only one problem. Pake had never taught Orian how to tip the bed upright.

Sweat fused to his brow, in the driver's seat, Orian considered all possibilities, mulling over the impractical ones, like hopping in the truck bed and pushing every last bit over the edge with his bare hands. In the end, he came up with nothing. Orian would have to find someone, anyone to assist him. He could drive back to the town square, but he'd already positioned the truck perfectly and didn't want to risk sending Pake's prized rust bucket to damnation. The sun's aid was minutes away from leaving him, too. So Orian ran.

It took him no more than five minutes to reach the open town square, where there didn't appear to be a single soul. In a frantic rush Orian searched, his feet kicking up dust as he prayed to stumble upon anyone that might be able to help him. Spinning around to watch the sun, Orian estimated his time was short. *Pake wanted this done by nightfall.* Even though the farmer was a generous man, Orian took him for a hard, strict one as well. Disappointing his newly-appointed boss on day one was not on the bucket list.

At last, he noticed a tall wooden stand, stationed fifty yards from the closed-gate entrance, adjacent to the fence. Rising from the ground beside the stand, there was a torch lit dangerously close to the rickety wood. On the stand, there was a guard.

"Hey!" Orian shouted. He rushed to the stand. "Hey, sir!"

A scruffy, bearded man peered down, eyes red. He flinched, speaking in a rush. "What's going on? You seen an Ardosian?"

"My name's Orian. I'm working for Pake. Is there any chance you know how to raise a truck bed?"

The man had a freckled face and a stocking cap pulled below his ears. Orian received no response, other than a long, blank stare that conceded to an aggravated eye roll.

"I'm serious. Hey! Please, I need your help."

"Move along, kid. Supposed to be watching for Ardosian scum. Never know when an unprompted attack might show, and I'm the only one on watch. You're gonna have to find someone else."

Orian's boot kicked at the mud. What was he going to do? Any minute the sun would go down, and Pake would be anticipating his return. Again, his head revolved in a 360-degree fashion. There was no one here to help him—no one except the guard.

Narrowing his eyes, Orian aimed his sights closely on the man perched high above. As if for show, the guard's head was moving on a swivel. Left and right, left and right, he scanned beyond the fence. There were only trees to be spotted.

In the last bit of light the day offered, Orian caught another glimpse of the man's eyes. *Why so red?* "Alright!" He threw his hands up. "I'll be gone. General Talia might help me. Know where I can find her?"

"In her office," the guard grumbled caustically.

"Of course, her office." Without a clue as to where that was, Orian began to prod. "General Talia is so nice and understanding. She'll be happy to help me." With index and thumb, Orian scratched at his chin. "Mmm, doubtless she won't be pleased to hear that her watchman was sleeping on the job."

Biting eyes swept over the edge of the stand, down to Orian. "What?"

Orian was strolling back and forth. "I like to deal with controversy peacefully, but I'd understand the General's frustration. What if Ardosians were to attack, and the only man who could've warned everyone was hailing a snooze?" Orian shook his head and tsked theatrically. "Her soul is emblazoned with retribution, I can tell. Can't help but wonder what the punishment might be for negligence."

The watchman scoffed. "Get lost, kid. It's a lie she won't believe."

"I've seen sleepy eyes many times before," Orian called up to him. The man might never have dozed off. Still, Orian pressed him further, pretending to know otherwise. "Besides, the General won't think to mistrust an innocent newcomer who doesn't yet know to shut his mouth, especially if the perpetrator has been accused of taking on-the-clock naps before."

Gripping the armrest firmly, the man's pale knuckles went even whiter. "Listen, kid. I don't know who you think you are, but–"

Orian seized his opportunity. Turning his back to the guard, he strode toward center camp, hoping General Talia's office was somewhere in that direction. "Thanks for your help!" He waved.

Marching on, Orian's nerves shook him ever so slightly. He tried to still himself as he walked on and on. Orian was beginning to think his plan had failed when the watchman finally called from behind.

"Wait," he uttered in a low, guttural tone that rasped into the evening air. The man looked both ways before ushering Orian over.

Feigning no rush, Orian ambled to the watchman's side, looking up with an innocuous grin.

"What do you know about the soldier's life?"

Blank eyes met the watchman.

"Nothing. Exactly. 6 a.m. training every day. Having General and Commander breathing down your neck the whole time." A strong hand stroked his beard. "I've been in battle. I've watched brothers fall, and I have to live with it. Then we get put on guard duty four times a month. Try sitting up here with abso-fucking-lutely nothing to look at but mud, this fence, and the wind against a few goddamned trees. You just try, and we'll see if you can keep the weight off your eyelids."

During the length of the man's tirade, Orian nodded steadily. He certainly heard the watchman's plea. It was compelling, but Orian had a task to complete. "So you're not going to help me?"

"Hold it right there." Two hands rose in a peace offering. Although it pained him, the man's lips twitched into a smile. "Show me where the truck is."

Flipping the bed upright proved to be much simpler than Orian could have anticipated. It took the watchman, whose name Orian learned to be Guerdo, naught but a second to find the switch. Orian felt a rush of embarrassment to discover his solution had been a small controller mounted on the inside of the door with two buttons: one that tilted the bed up and the other to return it to rest. Guerdo might have become disgruntled at Orian's oversight had it not been for the pact of common ground the two of them had organically come to on the way to the truck.

"You were on floor 89?" Orian asked in shock as they walked briskly toward the cliff, where the truck rested at its edge. Guerdo had a shift to return to, and so did Orian. They hurried. "I was 102. Strange coincidence."

"Hated every second of my life in the Tower." Guerdo spat passionately. In his passion, an accent escaped him. "Aye, and tuh hell with that fucker Vardus. Creepy bastard."

The truck had been a ten-minute walk from the watchman's post. It amazed Orian to discover how quickly hatchets could be crafted and buried. No more than ten minutes were required for the men to dispel enmity and move forward as colleagues, if not comrades. Their shared experience at Ardosia hadn't been the only bridge between them, either. As they had walked from base camp to the cliff, Orian became infatuated with Guerdo's life as a soldier. It turned out that, from the watchman's perspective, the soldier's life was grueling, emotionally taxing beyond anything Orian could have imagined, and in the end, worth every bruise, groan, and loss that had ever come along the way.

"There's something to be said about stepping up to a certain wall of death in battle, burying the poisonous fear within and drowning it with courage, all for love of nation and neighbor. There's nothing more rewarding in this life than sacrifice, not for oneself, but for others." Guerdo went on to say that if he'd have had it his way when he first arrived at Merciadel, he'd have fashioned a life as a stick-to-the-shadows citizen who goes to work, eats his meals, and goes to sleep, every day until death. Somehow, the General had convinced him to join military training one afternoon. "I hated it," Guerdo laughed. "Vowed after day one I'd never go back. I was bruised, sore, and pissed. But lying in bed that night, I found something I wasn't even searching for."

"What was it?" Orian asked.

"Truth. Turned out that in all that toil and sweat and pain I found a mirror to the soul, and I didn't like what I saw. Before the military, I was a self-serving man, one whose only interests were laid in what *I* could do for *me*. In a life of pleasure, seeking only *my* benefit, I found nothing but pain, imparted not only on myself but to anyone around me. It's why all my friends came and went so quickly, the good ones anyway. It wasn't until I began to understand the concept of sacrifice that I truly understood what it was to love my life. We're not meant to serve ourselves, kid. Remember that."

Once they approached the truck, Guerdo did the honors of dumping the large pile of scat over the edge. In a collective mound, it floated and floated until it smacked felled trees, old cars, and all other trash below, just as the sky flipped to dusk.

Looking at Guerdo's thin smile, Orian felt grateful for his help. "I'd have never thrown you under the bus to General Talia, by the way," Orian told him. "I know you must be exhausted. I was just desperate not to let boss man down on day one. If it means anything to you, I have large respect for the life a soldier lives. Sometimes I envy you." A sidelong glance left him.

A sarcastic hoot fled from Guerdo's gullet, as if he'd heard it before. "A man can envy glory, but in jealousy he forgets the blood in its shadow."

The breeze whispered its concurring thoughts. Empathy pressed its cold hands against Orian's chest. He could only imagine what Guerdo had endured. The way his eyes were cast longingly out over the edge, where there was naught but a deathly drop, followed by a lush sea of swaying leaves, and a thin stripe of orange across the sky … it made Orian wonder.

Suddenly, Orian felt a stab of contrition. He hadn't meant to imply that Guerdo's life had been sheathed in glorious moments, worn in the pride of wearing a chest plate, or emboldened by freedom's colors on his back. Sometimes it was easy to forget the tragedy that preempted victory.

"The farmer's life isn't too bad, I'm learning." He tried to supplant his previous comments with humor. "Ole Pake has taught me more than my brain can handle in a day. Have you ever been that way, to the farm? Kin's pies–"

"Hold that thought." A stiff, furry hand stopped Orian. He thought he'd angered the watchman, but an intense focus had crossed Guerdo's face, indicating something else was afoot. Orian looked down to the dirt at his feet, where

Guerdo's stare had led him. There was nothing. Then he realized the sense he should have used wasn't sight. It was sound.

Guerdo held up an index finger as Orian motioned forward. He shushed the young man. Orian froze. "Wha–"

"*Shh!*"

Breath cut short, mind intent on listening, Orian couldn't hear whatever Guerdo could ... until a deafening noise cracked across the sky, followed by the deep cries of grown men. They were coming from base camp.

"Shit!" Guerdo sprang into action. "Shit, shit, shit!"

"What, what is it?"

Guerdo shoved Orian out of the way, hopping in the driver's seat of the truck. The engine roiled and screeched, but finally it turned. Guerdo slammed the driver's door shut. It left Orian in an ambiguous frenzy. What was he to do? The watchman uttered the answer with force.

"Don't just stand there, get in!"

Orian rounded the hood, jumping in the passenger's side, where the ax had been resting as peacefully as ever. That sharpened blade had no idea what was happening, and neither did Orian. He tossed the ax behind his seat.

"What's going on?"

Gripping the steering wheel fiercely with one hand, upshifting with the other, Guerdo grumbled, "Ardosians."

The truck accelerated. Orian found his back pressed stiffly against the seat. As if his heart couldn't have felt heavier for Guerdo, it dawned on him then that if Ardosians really were attacking Camp Merciadel, Orian might have cost the watchman his job, or worse. There was no time to dwell.

"When we make it to the square," Guerdo began–Orian didn't think it would take more than a minute to get there, judging by the dirt flaring sideways in the mirror and the tires spinning faster than he could comprehend– "you get out when I do–immediately. You jump in the driver's seat, and you take off. Got it?"

"Where do you want me to go?"

"Anywhere. Back to Pake's farm. To your resting quarters. The dining hall. Wherever. Just go beyond the sound of bloodshed ... there will be plenty of it."

Orian gulped. The engine revved as Guerdo upshifted. The town square grew larger in the frame of the windshield as the truck barreled forward. Suddenly, they were at the edge of it.

Orian felt sick.

Flames were erupting from the hospital building. Beyond the billowing smoke, swords struck other swords. Arrows sprang through the air, sometimes through men. Blood had been spewed across sandy clay, looking like splotchy acne over the Earth's face. And the bodies. Orian could hardly stomach the sight.

Tires screeched to a stop. The tail end of the vehicle swung forward in a drifting fashion, positioning Guerdo at the edge of the fight. Gracefully, he jumped out, and Orian took his spot. The watchman had left the truck in neutral. The last Orian saw of him, Guerdo was sprinting toward the chaos.

Without thinking, Orian shifted. He gave it some gas. And he was off.

In the rearview, the battle grew smaller and smaller as he exited the town square. Side-to-side, he felt the truck drift. Orian struggled to maintain control over the vehicle. He hadn't gone this fast yet.

What have I done?

There was a pit in Orian's stomach as the night had been replaced with an orange glow in his rearview. Smoke rose above it, and he couldn't help but wonder if Guerdo was in the midst of a quick-striking battle with an Ardosian. He hoped the watchman would win.

Guerdo should have been on watch. He could have warned the camp that an attack was impending. But no. Orian had blackmailed the man, yet Guerdo was the one who had to answer for Orian's mistake, who had to risk his life to guard against the attack. It didn't seem right.

As the orange glow became an orb in the rearview, Orian's thumbs tapped the wheel. He felt an aching in his chest, tight, yet compelling. It called to him. "Keep your eyes on the road when you're behind that wheel, son," was all Pake had requested before Orian drove his precious truck. A reasonable rule, currently being violated. Behind the passenger's seat, there was an ax. In the shining blade, Orian saw an opportunity—no, a responsibility.

Whipping the truck around, Orian started for the town square of Camp Merciadel. A battle was raging, and it was one that could have been prevented, if not for him. He shifted with dispatch, the wheels turning as fast as they had under the pressure of Guerdo's boot. And just like that, the nerves, the panic, the tension, they all washed away. It always happened then, when they should have been most present. When too much was expected of him, it wasn't. Orian would rise to the occasion.

The truck whirled into the town square, where both the battle and the flames were in full heat. Orian turned the wheel, but a little too sharply, and the vehicle lost control. It slid across the red soil as though it were an ice-skating rink. Through the windshield, the world came swirling at an angle. Orian felt a bump against the rear end, but the truck was spinning too fast to see what he might have hit. It could have been nothing.

When it finally came to a halt, Orian clutched the ax firmly in one hand, and he shot out the truck, alert but dizzy. Smoke clogged his lungs, though he could still see through the foggy air. And by his judgment, he was fifty yards from the hospital, where the flames were being suppressed by nurses and doctors alike. The smoke, although faint, was cast over the battle, a still reminder to Mercians that destruction should be repaid similarly.

Men coughed as they tried yelling. There were fifty allies, at least. But something didn't seem right. There were–was he counting them right?–fifteen, maybe twenty Ardosians matching up against the wall of Mercians who pushed them back to the gate. It seemed as though he had no way to contribute.

"*Ahhhh!*"

Orian looked up just in time to see the glinting steel gliding toward his neck. He ducked and heard a *whoosh* over his head. In a somersault, Orian evaded his attacker. Rising, he held the ax before him, his only defense. He had only a moment to address the assailant: tall, hair mussed, blood streaking down his forehead, a slight hobble in his gait, and fury in his eyes. *So this is who found the path of Pake's truck,* Orian deduced. He thanked God that it had been an Ardosian he hit and not a Mercian soldier. Orian looked to the gray-white armor, stained by blood falling from the soldier's chin.

At closer glance, there seemed to be fear in the soldier's eyes, illuminated by the sparse torch flame. And why not? He'd been separated from the rest of his men, who were retreating further and further at the hands of many a

Mercian. For all the Ardosian knew, he might be left here alone. And Lord knew what the others might do to him.

"Hey." Orian took one hand off the ax, raising it in a placative gesture. "Sorry I hit you with the truck."

"*Ahhhhh!*" the Ardosian screamed again, lunging at Orian, sword pointed at his sternum. But he was ailed by a limp.

Orian skirted the attack swiftly, encumbering his retort. "Stop for just one second, we can talk this ou–Oh boy, here we go." Orian avoided the next attack. Was he skilled in his evasive technique or was the man just that slow? "I can see you don't want to do this. You don't have to fight for President Vardus! We know he's a prick."

"*President Vardus is king!*" This time the Ardosian held the sword high above his head, and Orian saw his opportunity. He held his composure, maintaining position. As the soldier brought his sword down, Orian raised his ax to parry. But that was not all. He latched the nook of the ax around the man's hilt, ripping the weapon from his grasp. It clattered on the red glowing sand. Slowly, Orian bent low to pick it up. The pointed end of the sword stared insinuatingly. Now the Ardosian had *two* reasons to hear him out.

"Listen to me. I can help you!"

A knife was procured and aimed at Orian. The persistent Ardosian could sense that only as a last resort would the young man in front of him implement deadly force. Orian was losing patience, so he allowed the soldier to work forward.

"Fine," Orian muttered. "You don't want to listen? Let's dance."

A scowl crossed his face. One leg fell back to support, and Orian's stance became athletic, prepared, anticipating the soldier's jump. Adrenaline coursed through him. Orian didn't want to hurt anyone, but he was more than capable.

Madly, the two of them circled one another, Orian with an ax and sword, the Ardosian with a knife. Blood was pooling above the man's brow, blinding one eye. Orian clearly had the advantage. What was the soldier thinking?

"Give up!" Orian called to him.

They found themselves at the center of a square of torches. Flames flicked light upon them. It was then that Orian realized how ill-prepared he was to duel against a trained soldier. His combat experience amounted to nothing. Orian hardly knew how to handle a sword, and the soldier opposing him had to be able to see it.

Thinking back to his days within the Tower, Orian recalled the times he'd return from class, having spent the duration of it on the Internet watching fencing videos from the Old Nation. He'd dart to the mirror with an invisible saber in hand, jabbing, parrying, and lunging. On several occasions, he'd performed a similar dance on his bed, with a young Ladis laughing at him. "You look like a nerd." Sweating and focused, Orian would lunge forward, the bed beneath his feet squeaking, "Yah! Hyah!" He grunted the way he imagined a man might. Orian remembered the confidence he held then, like his position atop a mattress with an invisible foe was analogous to a spot at the top of the world.

No longer were Orian's feet comforted by plush cushion. The sandy floor beneath him was compact, rough. His foe wasn't invisible, either. The man was bent low, a crutch in his step and a knife insinuating death in hand. Even with two weapons and a physical advantage, Orian suddenly recognized the disquiet he felt.

Then the Ardosian charged.

Paralyzed, Orian could not find the strength to divert the attack until it was too late. He rolled to the side, but not before the soldier sliced at his rib. Orian might not have noticed if not for the familiar warm sensation running beneath his shirt. It was only a small cut, nothing fatal. High on adrenaline, he didn't feel much. Yet the attack snapped him back into reality, just in time to diagnose the wave of confidence displayed by the soldier.

"You will go down. Every last one of you!"

Unbeknownst to Orian, a watch party had emerged from the darkness, a circle composed of Mercians standing just beyond the flaming torches that signified their dueling ring. The last remaining Ardosian in Merciadel spat angrily at all of them. Through gritted teeth, he said, "Vardus will reign. Give up now!"

Orian looked to both sides until he finally caught a glimpse of Guerdo, who stood attentively. He appeared to have been untouched. *Thank God.* The Mercian soldiers must have thwarted their attackers and sent them either to Hell or back to Ardosia in quick fashion. *What's the difference?* Orian asked himself.

Now the Mercians surrounded Orian and the wounded, dagger-wielding Ardosian. They could have ended this face-off right here. Yet for some reason, whether it be honor, tradition, or a combination of both, all fifty-or-so men were leaving the last Ardosian to Orian.

"Take him down," a bold voice commanded from the crowd. Orian recognized it as Byron's.

Though his eyes were focused on the knife and the soldier before him, Orian responded, "Just wait, I think I can get to him."

"There is no time for waiting. This Ardosian scum has outlived his time here on Earth, and with every second, his breath contaminates our sweet air. Take him down, boy."

The Ardosian must have liked the thought. He charged once more at Orian.

"Stop!" Orian tried.

The soldier kept coming.

"NO!"

The Ardosian refused his call.

Orian was left no choice. A flashing swipe came down, followed by a howl. Before Orian could process what had happened, he was standing over the fallen Ardosian, who was clutching at his right hand that was now missing, fallen somewhere on the ground. Orian saw it a few feet away. The knife was nearby.

With the Ardosian writhing before the crowd of Mercians, Orian stumbled over to the knife and the severed hand. He set the sword by them both, kicking all three items to the edge of the ring. They landed by the feet of a couple of men who eyed Orian and the ax he held with intent.

There was a shuffling in the crowd. "What's going on? Move!" General Talia's voice rose in the night. Orian looked up to see that she had shouldered her way toward the inner edge of the circle. Her eyes bounced from Orian, to the soldier, and back to him.

"Nice of you to join us, General!" Byron's voice carried over that of the howling man. "The Ardosian boy was just about to complete his first execution. Cute, huh?"

"Orian." She stared widely at him. "Don't kill this man."

"Take him, then." Orian's chest heaved. He was both frightened and exhausted. "You're the General, right? If you want him alive, take him."

To Orian's left, Byron's voice boomed again. "And violate the duel? No, no. Boy, it's up to *you* to decide."

Looking down upon the soldier who grimaced and bled into the sand, Orian couldn't imagine taking the life of another man, after he'd inadvertently done it once while in a tunnel at Ardosia. "Fine. I'm not going to kill him."

"Good. Someone, take him–" Talia began.

"Do you think that's compassionate?" Byron pressed on, stepping forward. His jaw had become even more accentuated in the midst of flaming torches. "Look! He's almost dead already. I reckon you've cut some pretty vital veins, if not an artery. And if you haven't noticed, our hospital has just taken a significant hit, thanks to *him*, no less." Byron pointed at the groaning individual in gray and white. "He's already good as dead."

"Byron, no. We can use him," Talia scolded.

Byron's stare remained fixed on Orian. "Whether you take him now, or he dies later, his fate is inevitable."

"We don't know that!" Talia screamed.

"Put him out of his misery, boy. Do the honorable thing. You've already killed him. Might as well do it with pride."

"What's the matter with you?" Talia, treating Byron as a lost cause, turned her attention to Orian. "Give us an answer, now. He won't have much time."

Orian didn't hesitate. "Take him! Save him!"

The General nodded. "Alright. Othor, grab his legs. Swede, his arms. Carry him to–"

"What a bunch of cowards! I'll do it myself."

Byron emerged from the crowd, unsheathing a fat, blood-stained blade that Orian knew to be termed a Bowie knife. He flew to the Ardosian soldier, but Orian had somehow been ready for it.

"Hey!" Intercepting the large Mercian, Orian raised his ax, knocking the knife from Byron's hands. Then, using his weight against him, Orian snuck an arm beneath Byron's shoulder and tossed him on the ground. In a split second, he was on top of the burly soldier, pressing a sharp ax blade against his neck.

The soldiers quieted.

Byron's face permeated with shock, eyes darting to his comrades. He flushed with embarrassment, then anger. "Scared little dog." Palms pressed against Orian's chest, Byron threw the young man off him.

Talia edged between them, pressing a hand against Byron once he rose to his feet. "Stand down!"

Swiping at his military jacket, the blond soldier tossed his hair to the side. "You're still every bit of Ardosian scum, boy. As inseparable from your bones as your skin, though I suppose both could be removed with a little pain. How about I do *you* a favor?"

"Enough!" Talia excoriated her soldier. "Byron, back to your quarters now." She turned to the rest of them. "Five of you, make sure Byron gets where he's going. Four more, escort Othor and Swede to a tent. Get nurses and doctors in there immediately. We have to save the Ardosian. The rest of you, designate someone to file a report. Understood?"

A chorus rang. "Yes, General."

"Wait!" she raised a hand. All men stopped. In the middle of them all, Talia laid menacing eyes upon each and every one of her men and women. "How did this happen?" There was as much silence then as there had been all night. No one moved or so much as blinked. "Surely someone has an answer, yeah? So for fuck's sake, when I ask a question, there had better be a goddamned answer! Now … How. Did. This. *Happen?*"

"It was my fault, General." One man stepped forward, and Orian's heart sank. Hiding the nerves and shame well was Guerdo. "I had fallen asleep on watch."

Talia's eyes seemed to create flames of their own. But Orian wouldn't allow anyone else to take the fall for his own mistake. That had already occurred once to a boy named Zak, and the guilt persistently ate at Orian. He didn't need another weight upon his conscience.

"Wrong, General." Orian stepped closer to her. "It was my fault. I blackmailed the watchman. If it hadn't been for me, he would have been in position to alert the camp, and the attack could have been stopped."

The General shot imposing glances at both of them. She learned quickly that Orian was telling the truth.

"General," Byron spoke up. He was lucky she didn't snap his mouth shut. Instead, she listened. "Don't you see? The boy's clearly a goddamned traitor, sent here to complete an inside job." Murmurs spread through the ranks. "It's so clear now. A squadron dropped him off outside our gate a few days ago, made him look like a helpless student, but no!" Byron's eyes needled Orian. "He was just a decoy."

"You know that isn't true–" Orian tried.

Speaking to the masses, Byron rose his tone. "I bet he's been feeding them information ever since he showed up. Are we supposed to consider it a coincidence that *he* is responsible for the absence of our watchman when we needed him most? Let's use our brains, shall we? The boy could be Vardus's golden child, for all we know!" A few men recited their agreement. "And we just let him in without vetting of any kind? Now our hospital has risen in flames, our gate has been trampled, and our pride marred. How much further should we crumble before we demand answers?"

A growing number of Mercian soldiers glared pointedly at Orian. He had no way to gain their trust, no way to compete with Byron's voice. His head drooped, but the General had come to his aid.

"That's enough!" she shouted. "The boy will remain here on my order. You're all dismissed." Stubborn, subtle protests rose, but Talia doubled down. "Dismissed, now!"

Unable to find the strength to raise his head, Orian stole only a small glance from Guerdo, who pressed his lips together painfully. Then he and his comrades vanished. In the torch-lit square, Orian found himself alone with General Talia. She stood before him, expressionless.

"I–I'm so sorry, General–"

"Stop."

Orian couldn't have appeared more crestfallen. Worse yet, his expression conveyed half the pain he felt inside. Sickness punched his gut. "I was working for Pake. I took the truck near the cliff, and I needed help. Guerdo was the only man I could find. I swear to you I'm not loyal to Ardosia."

"I know." Talia inserted both hands into her pockets, and she kept them there. The night was growing cold, fast. "Only fools listen to Byron. He's a large fool himself."

"I'm sure as a leader, you can never be too careful."

Her eyes mulled over the twisted, broken gate. "It's nothing new for Vardus to send a concentrated attack after an extraction. Each and every time we manage to storm onto his island and take his precious lab experiments, otherwise known as students, his ego takes a shot." Talia bent down to examine pools of blood left by the Ardosian, whose hand Orian had removed. "A swift counter-attack is his way of 'reminding' us that he is the one in power. It doesn't bother him to sacrifice a few good men to make a point." She looked up to Orian. "Believe me, if I thought you had anything to do with the attack, you'd have been dead already."

"That's comforting."

Disturbed by touch, the pool of blood rippled. Talia brought the finger to her nose and sniffed. "Vardus doesn't want war, not yet. Not until he knows he can win." She brushed the blood on her thigh.

Orian shifted. "Can he win?"

"Ardosia's ranks grow in number by the day. We lost one man in our last extraction, with two more injured as many as ever." A deep sigh was released. "Extraction missions have to end. We cannot go back and risk losing more men. From here on out, our best bet is to train harder, think smarter, and keep the battle on our own turf, where we have the advantage. Here, we're sure to win." The way her voice trailed off told Orian that her confidence was frayed, perhaps by the night's attack.

"Maybe your fleet could use another body."

Talia's eyes didn't leave his. She might have even considered the thought before shutting him down. "On the farm with Pake is where you belong for now."

Orian stepped over to the ax. It had been lying near a knife, sword, and a pale, dismembered hand. Wrapping his palms around the wooden handle, Orian picked up the tool. The blade held no blood. "I was able to defeat an Ardosian soldier tonight, without training of any sort."

"I know," the General said. "I saw you." Before Orian could make any case for himself, Talia turned away from him swiftly. "Goodnight, Orian."

Her boots crunched at the firm clay. Talia's stride, full of poise, carried her beyond building's edge, out of Orian's sight.

He was alone, almost. If not for the contingent of four guards who stationed themselves at the broken gate, Orian would have encountered odd serenity here. But they all stared at him, as though the mangled iron had been his doing. General Talia had assured him that he was not culpable for the attack. Orian wasn't convinced, and neither were they.

A cold chill sent goosebumps up his spine. Orian stuffed one hand into his pockets, the other bearing the ax's weight as his shaking legs took him toward old Pake's truck. Through the windshield, Orian saw the men glowering. *Hopefully the farmer is more forgiving than they are.* The key turned. The engine revved. Tires spun over sand as Orian pressed a little harder on the gas than he had intended. Speedily he drove out of the town square, toward the other end of Camp Merciadel where Pake's farm had hopefully remained untouched by Ardosian assault.

XXIII

He could not see it, but he heard it. The fan cut through air, whooshing tacitly from above, though the sound may as well have been that of a jet engine. It was all Ladis could register beneath the covers in his night-soaked room. His eyes were wide, senses alert. Ladis had been frightened many times in his life, like before his first journey to the Coliseum, or the time when he hadn't completed an exercise within the time limit, and when Orian had jumped out from behind the door after class once to scare him. Yet none of those experiences came anywhere close to the fright Ladis felt now.

"You! You! What was that?" The voice rang in his head. "You! I saw that look. How dare you give me that look?" Yjn stomped over to him, waving a baleful finger in his direction. She had been in the middle of chastising a student in the back row when she caught Ladis's horrified gaze. "Face forward *at all times*. Have you forgotten the rules?" Ladis knew them well. To his credit, he and other front-row students had been distracted by monstrous threats being issued to the back-row student. They were all watching Professor Yjn's rage as she posed an early exit from floor 102.

Ladis was hapless to be the brunt of the blame. "Uh, uh. I'm sorry, Professor."

"Apologies get you nowhere, Ladis." Her eyes scoured the room, setting everyone on edge. Faces were stuffed anxiously in their monitors. She leaned close. "What's the matter with you as of late? Your poor friend Orian leaves, and suddenly you take his place as an insubordinate fool. Is that pity I see in your eyes? Do not feel sorrow for him. He's gone. He *chose* to leave." Yjn had echoed most of his doubts. Then her tone shifted, face softening. "You're one of our best, Ladis. I can't have you faltering, too."

"Yes, ma'am."

Professor Yjn had let him alone for the rest of the day, but she may as well have been whispering cool threats in his ear all the while. Throughout the remaining exercises, Ladis was a ghost, present only in appearance until he returned to his living quarters.

And now he was bedridden by fear, feeling hollow inside. With his best friend gone and the vast majority of all his days lost to in-class exercises and anxiety, Ladis was a shell of himself. The time he had spent with Orian after class was what seemed to have given meaning to his life. The bond had fled out the window, and with it, Ladis's sense of being.

Since then, class time had been extended, twice. Demands were ramped up–failing scores rose from eighty-five to ninety percent–and Yjn's patience had left with Orian. Ladis had always taken pride as an astute student, perhaps even a brown-noser. Not one ounce of rebel had ever dared vie for the surface. And Professor Yjn used to be calm. How could it all change so rapidly?

Unsettled, Ladis understood that sleep would not find him. Under the covers, he felt too warm. Without them, he was chilled. He could lie there, subject to the mercy of the night, but he was not one to quail in the face of problems. Ladis was a man of solutions.

Blankets unfurled, and he rose. *Don't you ever want to take action?* he heard Orian's voice say. He remembered a time when his answer might have been different.

Ladis slipped into the bathroom. Not a switch was flipped, no glances were afforded to the mirror. He hoped in the darkness he might find courage. To his surprise, it came to him like sparkling dust sprinkled over his head. It wasn't much, but it was enough.

Tablet in hand, Ladis went to work. Many times Orian had taught him how to code and hack. He wished he would have paid more attention back then. As his fingers raced over the screen, it started to come back to him. Before long, there was an audible click on the other side of the door.

Ladis looked up. Go time.

Squeaking past the bathroom door, Ladis was shocked to find that the outer lock had really been overridden. His body tensed, released, focused, and relaxed all at once as the thrill of the night returned to him. Ever since he'd felt it that day when Orian had left, Ladis longed for steady doses of adrenaline, the likes of which he currently found.

What used to be sought after in comfort and safety was now discovered in the thrill–his new drug, his vice. He went out to the hallway.

What now? Orian would have known what to do. *Think like him.* So Ladis wandered aimlessly, allowing fate to take him where it must. The hall was dimly lit, scattered lights illuminating the orange doors of floor 102. Ladis followed them to the end of the hall, where he found a large steel door, one with a rectangular window looking into … a staircase?

The tablet screen lit up, but Ladis could not find anything that might hint at a staircase door. He looked and looked, scrolling through the Tower's database (covering his tracks, just as Orian had taught him–he just hoped he was doing it right) but came up with nothing. Panic would have regularly taken him here. An enhanced security presence was established after Orian left, necessitating greater efficiency on Ladis's part, lest he be caught. Yet he shrugged. Pulling at the door, a jovial wave struck as the staircase opened before him. Ladis reasoned that the door must have been unlocked in the night since students were trapped in the dim corners of their rooms. Or they were supposed to be.

Entering this new world, Ladis wondered how he could have ever underestimated the true rush Orian had explained to him. The only question or opportunity for second-guessing arose at the center of the concrete pad, where one flight of stairs went up, and the other went down. He didn't think, he just followed. Fascinated at the endless possibilities that fear had uncovered on this night, Ladis stepped forward.

Footsteps echoed along the thick walls as he ascended the Tower like a bird encountering its first flight. Ladis wondered how high he might go.

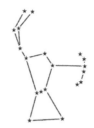

XXIV

Wide open. Prairie dancing. Wild flowers reaching for the sky. Serenity was deft to be ignored. Orian unlatched the gate. On rusty hinges, it swung open. "Come. Come on, now. Moo!" The cattle looked at Orian as if he were either a fool, a trickster, or both. They remained in a scattered herd, uninterested. It was Orian's duty to transfer the livestock from zone 6 to zone 11, and only with the help of Pake's barking dog did the empty-eyed beasts comply. Urged into motion by the nips and yips of Benjy, Pake's Australian Shepherd, one brave cow, whose dark hide shone almost blue in the sun, loped to the next zone. It began to graze, and the rest followed suit soon thereafter. Then Orian's job became simple. Don't get trampled. Close the gate when they've all transitioned.

Even with soft ground after an inch of overnight rain, hooves thundered past Orian, as loud as though they were stomping on concrete. He wondered how the one-ton animals didn't sink into the ground. Once all cattle were in zone 11, Orian closed the gate to find a tongue-out Benjy panting at his side. The Australian Shepherd lauded his own efforts by projecting a couple of approving barks into the blue sky.

"Good work, Benj." Orian patted him on the head. Benjy panted, his tongue lolling to the side. Together, they admired the herd that brayed their feasting joys at one another. Orian had learned over the past week that working on the farm could be rewarding.

"Good work to you as well, son." An old man in denim overalls shuffled through the freshly-grazed prairie of zone 6. His eyes became slits as he smiled. "Like you been doin' it since you were born."

As Pake approached from behind, Orian gave Benjy another pat. "It was all him. I'm sure if he could open and close the gate, I'd be useless."

Pake chuckled. "God gave us four-legged best friends 'cuz he knew all the two-legged ones would be as loyal as Eve in the Garden. Heck, I'll bet dogs were created on that exact day."

A red-orange stain appeared on Orian's hands, from the rusty gate, he imagined. He swiped at his pants. The fresh breeze seemed to exfoliate the pores of his soul. Flowery scents were carried to his nose, as the sun rose ever higher. It was mid-morning now after first task had been finished. Orian was starting to get the hang of his job.

"How do ya like it out here, son?" Pake placed a hand on Orian's shoulder. Beneath the cotton, scars were forming as the claw marks healed.

Benjy plodded in a circle around them.

Looking to the sky, where few clouds dotted the endless blue, Orian said, "I think I could get used to this. It'll take time, but I think I can."

"Peaceful life. That's what I tell 'em all. Those on the outside see long hours, hunched backs, and tons of crap." Orian had become overly familiar with crap. Pake cleared his throat, then continued. "Seems they're blind to the riches of nature and the providence granted through hard work. Don't know how, since they eat every day."

Silence was Orian's method of agreement. He didn't object to Pake's claims. Beneath the effervescence, Pake was full of unconventional wisdom, expressed through similes and metaphors that entertained him. Often, it was better to allow the wise to spill their knowledge, uncontested by even a nod.

Inhaling deeply, Pake closed his eyes. "This life is for me. Always has been. Just as my lady Kin was made to be my wife, pastures of prairie and fields of wheat were woven together to create my bones." With a few haggard steps, Pake found himself at the edge of the rusty gate. He placed his hands firmly on it, embracing the stains. "My age has gotten to me, Orian. I can't lie. That's truth. That's life. Can't move quite as well as before, and I can't see quite so good, either. But I can see clear 'nough to know the farmer's life ain't for you."

For a moment, Orian bit his tongue. Had Pake finally called him by the right name? His brow furrowed. "What do you mean? I told you I like it out here. I wasn't lying like I did when you asked me about Kin's pie. You've taught me so much in just one week."

The old farmer nodded slowly, with a feeble, pleasant grin. "I believe ya, son. I believe ya. Even with these old eyes, I can see you enjoy yourself out here. Like me, nature was made for you. It's where you belong." Pake scratched at his chest, turning to face Orian. "I don't mean to suggest you ain't good out here, either. But you should be livin' as no farm hand. You should be livin' as a soldier."

Orian cocked his head curiously.

"Oh, don't play dumb with me now, son. I've seen you out there, when you think no one's lookin'. Cuttin' wood, with that ax in hand. You feel powerful, right? You 'magine defending yourself, defending a people. The other day, behind the barn? I just so happened to be peekin' out my window."

Head drooping, Orian flushed with embarrassment. Toward the end of his shift a couple of days ago, Orian had found a long, thin length of scrap metal. In his hands, he had imagined it to be a sword. There in the tall grass behind the barn, he lunged, parried, and fought with an invisible foe, like he used to do on his bed in the Tower. He hadn't realized he was being watched.

"Nothin' to be ashamed of, kid. I can see you've got skill. I also saw you performin' roundhousers on my bails yesterday." Pake's cheeks crinkled. "It's a good thing straw don't feel pain!"

Casting a sidelong glance in Benjy's direction, Orian couldn't hide the red in his face. It was true. Ever since the attack one week prior, Orian hadn't been able to suppress his aspirational tendencies. He couldn't stop thinking about the way he had subdued an Ardosian soldier. An Ardosian! In that moment, he'd felt as alive as ever, which was saying quite a lot, considering the whirlwind of encounters he'd undergone in the past month. Every chance he'd been given on the farm, he'd practiced his techniques, mimicking everything he'd ever searched on the Internet. Drive, stick, lunge, *dodge*! Orian had never meant for Pake to see him. Luckily, only three instances were mentioned out of the countless. Lifting chopped wood, Orian pictured a wounded soldier in his arms, carrying him to safety. Even as Orian plucked a knife from the dinner table, he imagined bursting into action and disarming a soldier, perhaps even President Vardus himself. Feeling childish in these tendencies, he also reasoned his inner desires to protect and defend.

And what if Pake was right? What if Orian didn't just yearn to become a skilled fighter, but what if he was *meant* to be one?

"I can see it in ya, kid. You're a warrior. I don't mean to say that I don't need warriors on my farm. I do. But General Talia needs warriors like you more. You got a good heart, Ryan. Use it on the battlefield." He spoke solemnly, giving no rise to the young man's scrunched face. At Orian's confoundment, Pake wondered, "What? What's wrong?"

"Oh, no. Nothing's wrong. Truth be told, I think you're right, Pake. A soldier's heart burns inside me." Orian shook his head at the dirt. "It's just that … the night of the attack, I spoke with the General. She seemed pretty adamant that my talents were better utilized in your care, here on the farm, rather than in combat."

The farmer frowned. "You talked with Tal 'bout bein' a soldier already?"

"Mhmm."

"And she said no?"

"Mhmm."

Two fingers grazed his chin. "Tal never says no to anyone, not before figurin' out whether they're any good in training. I wonder …" He looked Orian up and down, measuring just how much of a man stood before him. "No, no." Before Orian could ask, Pake told him, "Go back to Talia. Tell her I sent ya, for all I care. But ask again, son. She'll come around. Just takes time with that one."

The way Pake's face wrinkles scrunched in confusion to obscure a few dark sunspots revealed that General Talia was never one to say no to more bodies, and Pake knew this. But she had said no to Orian.

"Where do I find her?"

On an imaginary map, Farmer Pake showed Orian just where to go. "You'll find her in her office. It's where she spends most of her days. She's a thinker."

A drumming heart found its way into Orian's chest. The thought of working at the side of men like Guerdo and Byron … it seemed surreal. Soldiers in Merciadel were more than just men. They were protectors, defenders, fountains of unbridled courage. Orian determined that he would try for the soldier's life, and this time he would convince Talia of his merit.

Orian took the old man's hand, which held a firm grip. "I appreciate everything, Pake. More than you know." Before Orian turned in the direction of the General's office, Pake's cup of wisdom had yet another drop to spill.

"One moment, Orian…"

He favored the old man with attentive regard. "Yes, sir?"

Thumbs slid beneath the straps of his overalls. "I see a man in you, but there is still a boy. At the surface, as well as below, a rebel, too. You're a man who's gotten away with much. Luck, it might be." Pake stepped closer, sighing. "I'm afraid you believe yourself to be invisible. Invincible? Ah, hell. Both of those. Ryan, you like to think nobody sees you sometimes, and I'll be damned if ignorance isn't a coat shed with age. It's fun to believe in the sanctity of one's own space. Just know this ... whether you believe it or not, someone is always watching. Know what you can get away with in life. Take nothing more."

Orian could tell Pake meant no harm, only the brightest intent, but those words ... ominous and ambiguous all at once. It's as if he had issued a dire warning. To reach this point alive, Orian had been lucky. There was zero doubt. But was the old farmer warning that his luck would eventually run out? Or, even more chilling, could he have been suggesting that Orian's luck may never have been there at all, if not for the overwatching presence of someone in the shadows?

"Thank you, Pake." Orian left him with a grateful, but curious nod as the breeze stole a handful of flower petals and scattered them.

"Oh! Just one more thing!" Pake called. Orian looked over his shoulder. "How about you stay for lunch?"

Kin's pie roiled in Orian's stomach. Per usual, the entrée had been an astute display of premium homemade cooking: soup of chicken and wild rice. No sides, since the entrée was deemed by Pake to be "more filling than the good news of the Holy Bible itself." Now, Orian cursed his upset stomach, hoping he might never again partake in Kin's pies.

By Pake's direction, Orian found himself in a room the size of a walk-in closet. An opaque window allowed only the passage of sunlight to his right. Near it was a bookshelf that stretched to the ceiling, and near that was a wooden door, leading presumably to the General's office.

Tucked in the corner was the smallest office space Orian could ever have envisioned, outfitted with a hanging shelf while a tight desk closed off the section. Behind the desk was a scrawny man with glasses and short-cropped brown hair who appeared not to notice the claustrophobic area to which he'd secluded himself. He ceased his furious bout of typing when he saw Orian.

"I-I t-told you. Talia, er, the General does not have time for v-visitors."

As he had when he arrived, Orian ignored the man's pessimism, gravitating toward the bookshelf. In the midst of flipping through "Of Mice and Men", Orian laughed at a line. "What is this?" he asked the man in glasses.

Behind the desk, he scratched at his messy hair. "W-what? Can't you r-read?"

"I can, but …" Orian flipped the book over, examining it more closely. "Doesn't this story seem a little far-fetched?"

"I-I don't read fiction. It is precisely for that reason. Risks and more r-risks that always pay off. Not reality, nope. Not reality."

"Fiction? Like … made-up?"

"Y-y-yes …" Desk man hesitated. His brows fell below his glasses, looking as confounded as Orian.

"You mean to say that someone just created a series of events? In their mind?"

The man at the desk sighed, presuming his patience was being tested, of which he had little. He scratched at his forehead this time, not his ear, and after a long pause, he said acerbically and with ample sarcasm, "Bullseye."

"Wow." The possibility hadn't occurred to Orian that a story could be written by any other medium than factual events. In Ardosia's Tower, they'd only ever been informed of history, and very little at that. Sure, there were creative liberties to be taken in their poetry sessions, but nobody had ever thought to write about something that, throughout the course of human history, had never explicitly occurred. Orian speculated that in a fictitious world, anything was possible. How brilliant! "What do you read?"

Hands clenched, fingers dancing, his head twitched. "Reports. Code. That's what I do. I c-code. I'm a coder. I'm good at coding. Y-yes, and hacking, and w-well … yes. Reports." He looked like the type who could complete a Rubik's Cube behind his back.

"Very cool." Orian was impressed and intrigued by him. "What's your name?"

Desk man's shaking hands rose to his glasses. He took them off and folded them. "L-l-look. I-I am very busy right now, a-and–"

"I'm Orian." He lent his hand as an amiable gesture. It was the type of gesture the scrawny composition of skin and bones couldn't compute at the moment. He simply stared at Orian's fingers, perhaps wondering whether they might coil into poisonous snakes.

"N-Neal. I'm Neal," he said without shaking Orian's hand. His face fell to a stack of papers. There was hardly room for the prosaic faded white paperweight and laptop on his desk.

"Pleasure to meet you, Neal. Say, is General Talia available?"

Neal glared.

With fair resignation, Orian strolled over to the bookshelf. He plucked one from the vast, dusty selection. *F. Scott Fitzgerald. Ernest Hemmingway.* Orian inferred that the names on each book were those of the writers who composed them. *Mark Twain. Jane Austen.* All these men and women had lived so long ago, many from the Old

Nation. Some were more recent than others, still at least a century old, if not two or three. *Stephen King. Dean Koontz.*

The office door opened. General Talia's head poked out. Her neck was covered by a collar of black leather.

"Neal, come in." At the General's command, Neal rose, squeaking by his desk.

A head of black hair swiveled, and her green eyes went wide at the sight of Orian. "Who gave you permission to be here? You have no clearance to be in my office! Neal, why is he in my office?"

"I-I-I, w-well, listen. I–" The poor man seemed so afraid, he couldn't speak.

"He tried to tell me to leave," Orian offered.

Neal's eyes flicked to Orian. "Yeah."

"So why are you still here?" The General leaned on the door frame.

"I have a proposition to make, General. It regards–"

"No. Neal, come in."

The General and her assistant disappeared. The door slammed behind them, right in Orian's face. Of all the obstacles he'd faced in his twenty-year life, of all the doors he'd hacked, this was far and away the simplest. He turned the knob and walked in behind them.

General Talia's office immediately struck Orian as a chamber specifically designed to instill serenity in the face of chaos. It was simple, organized, without too much clutter. Wood floors, cherry desk, and mahogany shelf. Behind the desk was a large, rectangular window guarded by–Orian could have guessed–wooden shades. By the window, antlers were mounted. It was as if every piece of the General's office had been a part of nature, now repurposed.

"Your magazine." The assistant set it gingerly before Talia. She centered it, but did not deign to flip a page.

Talia and Neal pretended not to notice Orian's presence. Or maybe they weren't pretending. The General spoke urgently as she flipped through stacks and stacks of papers.

"Four were down. How many are back up?"

"Just one, T-Tal."

She grimaced. "And what of the Ardosian?"

"He s-still breathes."

"Does he talk?"

"I'm afraid not."

Subconsciously, the General twirled a pen between her fingers while her brow crinkled in apparent concentration, cranking out the numbers in her head. "That makes six, Neal. Three from the extraction, three who have yet to return to active duty."

"Yes, General."

"Tell me, and be honest–"

"A-always."

"–is there fear in our men? Are we losing faith, hope? Or are the Ardosians finally learning how to slap an arrow onto a target? I can't ever recall a time when General Andrew was down *six* fucking men." She shook her head, distraught. "I wonder if it isn't ..." the small, circular mirror on her desk caught her eye for a split second before she shook the thought.

Neal inched closer to her, perhaps his way of providing support. Adjusting his glasses, he was frank. "It's both, Tal. I-I don't want to say it, but–"

"Say it."

"–discord r-r-rises through our ranks. It's-it's Byron." Neal went on to inform Talia of his opinions, a direct reflection of the opinions expressed to him. "He's too much t-trouble. He thinks he's w-w-weaving strength into the c-cloak, but it's really–"

"The scissors of doubt cutting its unity in half." The General finished for him, nodding sullenly. She brought the pen up to her lips, clicking it once. Then her eyes fell on Orian. "What the hell?"

Neal also turned, exasperated.

"Sounds like you could use a soldier with a little spirit." As always, Orian was brusque, but the smirk on his face seemed to incense the General.

"We also need someone willing to *take orders.* Now leave, Orian. You are not allowed in here."

"Now hear me out." He stepped forward, much to Neal's chagrin.

Perplexed, Neal asked Talia, "W-w-where did he come from?"

"Ardosia." She shrugged. "Though I've never met an Ardosian as stubborn … or as brave." Her hand moved toward a small stack of sharp objects on her desk. It was a gesture Orian deemed to be for show, effective nonetheless.

The wooden floor groaned as he backed up an inch. His hands rose to his side. "Look, all I'm asking for is a chance. I want to contribute to this battle. I feel like it's my duty."

Both Neal and Talia were intent on him. "Your duties are on the farm."

"I disagree. Even Pake said as much."

"Pake?"

"Yes. He's the one who told me to meet with you."

General Talia took a long hard look at the young man before her. Orian wondered what she saw. Was he nothing more than a foolish boy to her, one with more courage than wit? Or was there something there? Something she couldn't admit to, or that she hadn't wanted to admit yet.

Her answer finally came. "No."

Orian wasn't finished. "But General–"

"Y-your time is up." Neal approached Orian menacingly, which was kind of cute. The General's assistant was a small man, and he clearly had no intention of laying a hand on Orian.

Whether it was an act of foolhardiness or bravery, Orian skirted past the skinny man. His feet carried him swiftly to Talia's desk, where he placed both hands firmly upon its surface.

"You impetuous–" she started, her face blasting with the color of rubies.

"Hey! G-get back." Neal's hand was a feather on Orian's shoulder.

"What are you afraid of, General?"

Talia scoffed. "I fear nothing but unhealthy fear."

"Great! So you have nothing to lose by allowing me to train with your men." Orian paused. "You never gave me the chance to offer my proposition."

The General looked past Orian to consult her assistant. Her lips pouted with tension, and her hands folded together. "Alright." The front of her seat squeaked as she leaned forward. "Let's hear it."

"One week. If I'm not every bit as good as your weakest link after one week of training, I'll personally escort myself back to Pake's farm, where I'll contentedly return to twelve-hour shifts of shoveling shit onto a flatbed truck."

Biting the inside of her lip, Talia measured the young man. She looked down to his hands that were still resting on her precious wood. Slowly, Orian took them back. Once more, her hand moved to the stack of blades on the corner of her desk. Talia's knuckles went white as she grabbed them. "There are no weak links in Merciadel's military."

"Great. Then I don't see any reason to fear, unhealthy or otherwise."

"You want to prove that you're worthy?" Talia rose quickly from her chair. "Fine." There was an unseen sass to her stride as she rounded the corner of her desk. She still had all three blades in hand. Only once she was face-to-face with Orian did she pause.

Knowing it to be a sign of weakness to avert his eyes, Orian met the General's gaze with confidence.

"Grit." Talia spun around to face the wall. In a flash, one blade sunk into the circular cork board hanging five feet away. It was maybe half an inch to the right of center. "Passion." Another knife left her hand, thudding just to the left of the first. "Sacrifice." The final throwing knife implanted itself above the first two, forming an accurate triangle. The display stole an impressed grin from Orian.

Cooly, the General sauntered to the board, plucking each knife. "You'll need every ounce of these to last even an hour in my training, let alone one week."

Orian was still. He hadn't moved an inch. At last, Talia turned to him again. This time, she held out the knives for him. "You think you have what it takes? Prove it. Put any one of these three blades closer to the center than mine, and you're in."

In her eyes, Orian saw a compulsory force to decry unfairness, to demand a more equal test of grit, passion, or sacrifice. She knew the test was unfair, but Orian understood the point. Life was unfair, and you could spend all your breath detesting it or you could rise above its challenge.

He took the blades with gratitude. "Awesome."

"G-g-good luck." Neal backed away. Orian couldn't tell whether his wish of good fortune had been a taunt or genuine.

The General stood sentinel on the other side of her desk, arms crossed. She wasn't expecting much, by the look of it.

Stepping up to the line, Orian weighed the knives in his hand. He'd never done anything like this before, and the truth was that he heavily doubted his hand-eye coordination, having no experience in the athletic realm. Yet, in the presence of the General, all fear and doubt washed away. Orian's vision narrowed to the board. He stared and stared at it until the entire wall from which it hung disappeared. It was just him, three blades, and a target. Before hurling the first blade, Orian thought he felt Talia's eyes boring into his skull. Indecision rose within him then, forcing a wildly errant throw.

The General stifled a laugh as the first blade went clanking to the floor. Orian had missed the board entirely.

His resolve remained intact. "Just a little rust," he said before tossing the second blade. Orian almost leapt for joy when the knife sunk into his target, even though it landed at the bottom of the board, nowhere near the center.

No longer were there any hints of laughter. Suddenly, the room was quiet.

Orian had one throw left, one chance to earn his spot amongst Merciadel's military for a week at the very least. He would need to make it count.

Air filled Orian's lungs as he inhaled, long and steady. Impulse guided him to close his eyes, envision the shot. *Feel* the blade striking the center, he told himself. *Find* the balance. Then he felt connected to the steel in his hand.

He saw the path upon which the blade must fly to hit the center. With no more calculations to be made, he reared back and let go ...

A dull thud reverberated.

Silence was heavy. The vibrating blade seemed to wiggle back and forth for an eternity. Orian stared at it.

"I-i-impressive," Neal said.

"But not good enough." General Talia's tone was cool as ice. She patted her jacket, returning to the chair behind her desk. "Anyway, Neal, we were speaking..."

Orian couldn't summon the disappointment. A couple of inches above center was his third blade, not close enough. He had overcorrected. A gentle sigh of defeat left him. Now, the General and her assistant were consulting the state of their camp. Once again, Orian was invisible.

"C-c-cotton production is going well at the t-textile mill. Our farmer's yields are g-good, too ..."

Neal's voice disappeared behind Orian. He pulled one knife from the board. Then another. Shifting on his heels, he placed the blades carefully on Talia's desk. But there was still one more.

"...right. Have we made contact with the Yandoju tribe, regarding our impending trade?"

As they spoke of Merciadel's economy, all the while paying no mind to Orian, he bent low to snatch the first blade he had thrown. It had been lying sideways on the floor. He weighed it in both hands, marveling at how the knife glinted in what little sun funneled through the blinds. In two short steps, he found himself back at the throwing line. He looked up to the board, then down at his blade. Orian felt its weight, sensed its arc. This time, he didn't think. He just threw.

All conversation ceased at the sound of blade striking board. Orian stared for a minute before directing his attention to the General, who blinked at him.

Her mouth hung open. Astonishment quickly turned to apparent satisfaction as she favored Orian with a reluctant grin, shaking her head. Then Orian looked to Neal, who looked back at him, eyes wide behind those glasses.

"Bullseye," he said.

XXV

Each bend in the path was familiar to him. He'd followed this course with Orian to and from the Coliseum on countless occasions. On this night however, after the tangerine glow of the sun disappeared and ghostly moonlight threw spectral light at its edges, the path shone to Ladis with something before unseen. What used to be a constricting pathway disguised as a freedom tour with one destination was now a guided journey with unlimited possibilities. The adrenaline had yet to forsake him.

It was cool this night, and the starry sky had at last become apparent to Ladis. It was always *face forward, head down, do as you're told.* He hadn't accustomed himself to looking up, until now. The view he'd been missing all along was right before him. Celestial brilliance, as beautiful as Dawn's face, shone from above, as the sky was speckled with centuries-old constellations. Small as they made Ladis feel, they also pulled forth a liveliness from him, like he was seeing something new and ancient all at once.

Walking the path alone, he thought of his roommate.

Ladis had always considered Orian's luck to be hefty. He'd gotten away with much artifice and rule-breaking in Ardosia. Ladis understood now that luck had nothing to do with the being, but rather the energy springing forth from their mind, heart, and soul. This universe rewards risk-takers and punishes those who hide in shells. Ladis was tired of hiding.

Emboldened by the moonlight licking his skin, Ladis's brazen bones did not shake in the face of the guards who dotted the edges of the path. The President had placed them every so often, probably as a safety measure. Ladis could hardly believe that none had questioned him. He had no doubt it was due to the mask of confidence he now wore, hopefully convincing. It would need to be. The Schedule hadn't even called for him to leave the Tower tonight. One crack, one slip-up, and Lord only knows where the guards might dispel him. The lake lapped in tranquility at the shore. *I could end up there.* Grass stood still amidst the absent winds. *Or six feet under there.*

He felt the wave of confidence receding, so he cast out all negativity. Passing by another guard, Ladis sent forth a tight-lipped nod in the armored man's direction. *Orian was so bold, he might've raised his hand for a high five.* Audacity was like a new suit over Ladis's shoulders, and he liked how it fit. But he was just trying it on for now. Maybe someday his suit might be as striking or permanent as Orian's.

Unsure where he might find himself, Ladis rode on his heels. The nerves were striking. After the previous evening's close encounter, where Ladis had ridden the staircase to floor 127, he thought to provide himself with an extra layer of caution, though he hated to sacrifice any ounce of thrill. On that floor, he had looked past another steel door, where six guards stood sentry on the other side. Midway down a long, narrow hallway, they were facing each other with stone expressions. *Guarding something ... but what?* When one of their heads bounced to find a pair of young, trespassing eyes peaking above the sill, Ladis dashed down to 102, heart galloping along with him. He still couldn't believe he'd gotten away from them.

Ladis nonchalantly flipped his wrist to check the time. *7:40. Just under an hour until curfew.* If he wasn't tucked within the walls of his dorm by eight-thirty, they would know. The guards would quickly discover that Ladis wasn't abiding by the Schedule, and who knows what might happen next? Once more, his eyes flicked to the lake, then the ground. He didn't want to end up beneath the surface of either.

Ladis nearly jumped. The rustling leaves of a newly-planted tree drew his eye, though he never felt the breeze razzle the hairs on his arm. *Hmm.* It appeared as though fate was speaking yet again, this time through nature. The tree stood tall to his left, hinting not at the scratches of its baseball-bat sized trunk, nor the intertwining twigs that were in desperate need of pruning. The tree hadn't wanted Ladis's attention at all, except to show him where he must go. A few strides ahead was a guard who stood nearly as tall as the tree. Nothing of him was precarious at first glance, save the tremendous size of his biceps. Apparently, he hadn't skipped arm day in years.

Ladis's eye latched onto the grass beneath the guard's feet. Was it ... lying sideways? His eyes followed the trampled grass that might have been hard to spot, if he hadn't then been searching for something out of the ordinary. Nevertheless, it was undeniable, and it stretched much further than the guard's feet, out into the darkness beyond, climbing toward a subtle crest. *Almost like another, secret path.* The concrete bent closer to the lake there, further from the island's center. Was it a coincidence that at that exact location, the student pathway diverted to the shoreline while a covert path wended through the grass? Ladis used to believe in coincidences, not anymore.

Slowing his pace, chest thumping faster, Ladis knew how to unearth more thrill than he had yet felt. Quick thinking, fast acting. This lifestyle was an adjustment, one that Ladis embraced. He had to divert the guard's attention, but how?

Swiftly, he procured the tablet from his pants pocket. He tapped a few times on the screen and stowed it away. Then he approached the guard.

"Excuse me?"

Big bicep guy was rattled, like he hadn't been spoken to since beginning his fitness journey. "What! What! Hey–" The guard fumbled for something at his belt.

Placatively, Ladis raised one hand. "I need your help."

"Huh?"

"Back there, a couple of guys were walking toward the Tower. I'd guess they were at the Coliseum tonight, as our Schedules dictated. In passing, I thought I heard one of them say something like 'we're gonna storm the Suite and hurt the President.' Of course, they didn't really say hurt. They used another word." Ladis hadn't been to the Coliseum since his own Schedule had demanded it of him a week ago, but he sold the lie to Bicep Guy like it was a brand-new creatine supplement. "You know, ever since that tragedy happened with those intruders..." Ladis's eyes drooped. He acted as though it required all his strength to summon the words. "My guard is up. I-I just thought you should know. If we see something, say something. That's what President Vardus told us."

The man in Ardosian armor was appalled, looking left, then right. Immediately, he went to his radio. "Unit 1743, do you copy?" He waited, then, "UNIT 1743 DO YOU COPY ... golly, comms are down again."

Ladis stifled a laugh. *Did he just say golly?*

Shifting his weight nervously, the soldier stared with massive intent upon Ladis. "Where'd they go? Where!"

"That way." Ladis pointed behind him.

Bicep Guy took a few deep breaths, jumped up and down as if he were preparing for a race, and took off. Ladis watched the big man barrel down the winding path until he disappeared behind the closest building.

Now Ladis was alone with a couple of options. One was green and soft, enticing. The other was hard as rock, boring and lacking innovation.

Stealing down the trampled grass, Ladis pulled out his tablet. Chuckling to himself, he said, "Comms are down, huh?" He clicked once. "Not anymore." The tablet was stowed securely in his back pocket as he strode into darkness, on a path that he posited had never before been used by an Ardosian student. Somehow, he knew himself to be the first, and that knowledge made him chuckle happily. Ladis held his chin high and shook his shoulder-length hair back. In stepping off the concrete path, Ladis had officially entered a new stage in life. For better or worse, he would never turn back.

A church and a house. Two structures Ladis had never expected to visit on the island of Ardosia. Despite all odds, he found them, following the slim folding grass. Without the persistent moonlight, he may not have known where to go, but the path gleamed brightly at night where the blades had lain sideways. It took him here.

Past a thicket of trees and bushes, Ladis weaved, crawled, and cursed as a few pines pricked at him. He did it all tacitly. To his surprise, he encountered no guards after Bicep Guy, but he wasn't taking any chances, striding furtively through the property.

He consulted his watch. *7:55.* Here in the clearing amongst the trees, the moon and stars emitted an enhanced radiance, like a spotlight over the house on the hill and the church in the valley below. Ladis's heart was more inclined toward the house, but the humming, bumping, and clamor escaping the cathedral drew him there first. He remembered Orian mentioning something about the absence of churches on the island. Well, here was one, and it piqued Ladis's curiosity.

In this foreign area of the island, Ladis was enshrouded in song. Cicadas buzzed vociferously, as if they were hovering beside his ears. The crickets trilled with tranquility. Even now, as night fell, birds chirped, though not as persistently as they may at the sight of a new sun. And then there was the church. As Ladis ambled carefully toward the cathedral, the dramatic booms became more and more apparent to him. He stuck to the grove edge, blending with the twigs.

Deep vibrations crawled out the church, snaking through the grass and up hardwood trunks. Ladis felt the tremors in his toes, his legs, his chest, his fingers.

Whatever the method of worship behind those hallowed walls, Ladis was impressed by their resounding faith. He could never have anticipated that the Lord might call him to a service on this night.

Keeping low and to the trees, Ladis crept until he could come no closer. *Could it be possible?* There were no guards surrounding the premises. Ladis had spent ten minutes in the outer woods to be sure, anticipating that someone was waiting for him to emerge from the grove and reveal his guilt. *8:05.*

Blackout excitement preempted Ladis's entry. His nerves pulsed in unison with the faithful rumblings now, quick and steady. When he felt the shaking in his hands, he knew the thrill was upon him. But more could always be obtained.

He started forward.

One singular LED light shone above the dense wooden doorframe. A firm fist latched around the handle. Ladis swung it open cautiously and entered the church.

No bodies, friend or foe, stood beyond the first door. It was a bland room Ladis found himself in, square with no lighting. Cobwebs littered the high corners. The dark, rotting wood was caked in dust. Spirit hung in the air, eerie and disquieting. It was unseemly for a church entrance, whether due to the doll-sized marble statue perched on a table in the center of the space–with its head missing, no less–or the nauseating lights flashing at its back from the congregational entrance, Ladis wasn't sure. A sign might as well have hung before the next set of double doors, saying, "PROCEED WITH CAUTION."

Ladis stood on his toes to peer through the glass panes looking into the church. There, the source of commotion was displayed. At least a hundred men and women, middle-aged and over, moved decorously about the cathedral. Champagne glasses in hand, they placed select hors d'oeuvres on skinny plates to delight their pallets. Professional garb wrapped them. Men in suits and ties and variations thereof, women also in suits and ties, but some opted for knee-length dresses. If not for the disco lights swirling and the metronomic beat emanating from massive speakers near the altar, Ladis might have assumed this to be a formal gathering of sorts. But they seemed so misplaced, and the beat was so low and ominous, all adding to his unease. *What's going on in there?*

Ladis hadn't recognized anyone beyond the second set of double doors. The impulse within him begged that he prod forward for closer inspection. What harm could it do if they were all but strangers to each other? Yet Ladis was severely underdressed for such an occasion, in a white T and gray dress pants. His attire alone might have outed him.

Then his heart skipped a beat, grateful he had bucked the enticing thrill-ride this once. From a jumbled rush at a snack table emerged none other than Professor Yjn, short, her hair tied back by a sword-like pin, and eyes endlessly scouring for trouble. Ladis ducked, lest those eyes find him.

Why is Professor Yjn here?

Just then, a strong, familiar voice boomed over the loud speakers, answering his query.

"Alright, alright! Professors, stuff your plates, fill your glasses! I believe we have garlic-salted sprouts, rice balls, and more than enough champagne to have us all merry by night's end. Sit, sit!"

Huddled beside the entrance doors, Ladis listened to the clambering beyond ... but he wasn't satisfied. He wanted to *see* it.

Built into the side wall, there was another door. Leading to where? Then Ladis recalled where he was. *Churches have balconies.* He turned the knob and slipped through to a set of creaking stairs. Luckily, there was a profusion of shuffling within the church to mask the fluttering of a fly on the wall, a fly like Ladis.

"Settle down, friends."

Ladis recognized the voice from morning prayer. Echoing off the ceiling arch, the President's low, commanding tones traveled to the balcony with ease, lightly thrumming against the out-of-tune organ. Each ring hummed beneath the strength of his words so that they sounded otherworldly. Ladis was convinced he couldn't have felt more unsettled ...

Then he reached the final step, where the balcony proved his theory woefully incorrect. Never before had he seen floors rotting so badly, nails strewn across the ground like someone had chosen to play a game of 52-screw pick up. Pews, or that's what Ladis assumed them to be, were half-broken, toppled-over nests to thousands of spiders. He wasn't sure whether the arachnids were already crawling on his skin or his mind was playing with him.

At the front end of the balcony, there was no rail to prevent children–or anyone, really–from jumping off the edge and into the congregation below. In the absence of a rail, here at the back of the church, Ladis could see the altar just fine. Even so, he inched forward, and the wood creaked ever so slightly.

"I know, I know. St. James Cathedral hasn't hosted us in quite some time. Years maybe?" Vardus waltzed casually before the altar, microphone in hand. An effective entertainer he was, smiling, engaging the crowd. "Stefany, you look nervous, I can see it in your face! All of you are so antsy. Calm yourselves, folks. I know you're wondering why you're here, and I'll get to it, I promise."

Ladis's shoes and hands collected dust as the wood creaked beneath him. He inched himself forward on all fours and was shocked to see a full congregation. Albeit, the church was small, but Ladis's initial estimation of a hundred might have been low. There may have been double that present, including himself. Except he was only a shadow, and shadows didn't count.

He stationed himself beside a leaning pew, kneeling low, an invisible genuflector.

"What?" The man in black addressed his peers. "Is that grumbling I hear? Oh, come on. I see that patience may have to be an exercise I assign to my teachers, huh?" His jest elicited a sniggering wave. "Fine, fine. I'll spill it." Vardus spun. As he did, a large, pale fabric of sorts rose from the altar's center, stretched and rectangular. A projector screen. It flashed to life, as colorful as the disco lights. "Ta-da! It's Professor Appreciation Day!"

Another bout of laughter traveled through the congregation, this one coming much more easily, followed by civil applause.

"Your work has not gone unnoticed, ladies, gentlemen, and others! I see you! I see *all* of you. Now," he paused, sincere. "We've had our fair share of bumps in the road. Eh, Cedric?" He glared. "I kid, I kid. Cedric, you've been great."

Ladis crawled forward again to enhance his view just slightly, sticking to the shadows. Up here it was dark, the disco lights below illuminating only the front half of the balcony. As long as he held back, Ladis would not be seen, or so he hoped. In moving forward, his attention diverted momentarily to the sacristy. *That's odd ... no cross. No Lord.* He wondered how old the church must have been.

"As learning hours have increased, all floors have risen to the challenge, exerting the necessary energy to transform our children into the next effective generation. With your help, we can–" the altar screen changed to that of a bowling lane, "–keep the ball Role-ing!" The pun stole a few laughs. "And you know what? While we're at it, how about we serve out a few special mentions, shall we?"

Applause lifted, as well as a few screeching whistles.

Once more, Ladis crawled closer to the balcony edge, dwelling in the blackness untouched by swinging colored sabers. "Ouch!" he stifled the scream beneath his breath, bringing a pricked finger to his mouth as he sucked the crimson from it. Ladis must have caught a stray nail, yet the pain only lasted a moment. He supposed pain deferred to adrenaline, particularly now.

Recently, Ladis had felt many rushes, but he was certain that none would compare to this. He was in the middle of some secret meeting, ostensibly between Ardosia's staff and Vardus himself. The President had visited floor 102 not long ago, yet Ladis found himself just as starstruck now as he was then. Yeah, the President appeared on screen every morning for prayer, but it wasn't the same. To be in the presence of someone who would undeniably go down in history, seeing his face ... it was surreal.

President Vardus rattled off names, and they stood at his beckoning. Each one was treated with heavy cheers before they settled down again. "Professor Raun, for improving O-rates by five percent! ... Felipe, for putting the hammer down and sending a disobedient off." There were other names mentioned as well. "Giun! ... Wencel!" The President went on and on, and the cheers grew louder as the energy within the cathedral burgeoned. "Cedric, you get a shoutout, too!" Laughter and applause. "And last, but not least ... how about we give it up for our very own Professor Yjn!"

Ladis's heart jumped. *Professor Yjn! But ... why were they so quiet?* All jubilation was suddenly hushed. The beat subsided. If a mouse stirred, the whole congregation would have known. Ladis slowed his breathing. Why did they stop cheering?

At last, Vardus came over the mic. "Ms. Yjn, come on up. Go ahead. Come on! Where are her cheers?" He leaned forward, looking expectantly on them all. His head swiveled back and forth. Not a peep was uttered. "Hmm, yes. I suppose word travels quickly on such a small island, where rumors and whisperings are trapped at the edges of my Wall. They bounce around and around, until all ears are found." He nodded solemnly.

At this, Ladis frowned. What was he talking about?

"Six," Vardus said finally. "That's as many as we've ever lost on a single floor. I'm sure you've all heard of Professor Yjn's debacle, yes? Mhmm. I thought so." He turned his attention to the left side. "It's okay, Ms. Yjn. What's gone is gone."

All those present remained still as the statues lining the outer walls. It didn't make sense to Ladis. Were they *scared* of Vardus? How could it be? He'd always been most felicitous and welcoming. Ardosia's President was a good man, Ladis believed. Yet a good man can be feared, not for his nature, but for the power he wields. However, Ladis was being exposed to a side of Vardus he'd never seen before. The President's face had grown dark as his garb. Ladis didn't like it.

"Professor Appreciation Day … do you know what that means?" Vardus strolled ponderously at the front. At this point, his questions were understood as rhetorical. He had a point to make. "No one? Alright, let's break it down, shall we? Someone give me the definition for the word appreciation–actually, how about its base? *Appreciate.*" Before anyone was given the opportunity to answer, he went on. "To increase in value or merit, right? Yeah? I see a few heads nodding, so I must be right. Let's begin."

The images on the screen flipped. The disco lights faded and fell, enshrouding everyone in darkness. Ladis saw his opportunity to lurch even further forward, so he did.

"Since Ardosia's institution, I've selected only the best to lead future generations of students forward. Pat yourselves on the back," he said somewhat genuinely, "because you have all been chosen. You teach, you lead, you watch. You are my eyes and ears. Through each and every one of you, I've studied the behavioral analytics of our student population over the years–O-rates, role placements, and otherwise." A graph popped up on the screen. "Without fail, year after year, these have fallen. Some years dramatically, others even more so. It begs the question … how have we failed our students? How have *I* failed you?"

Curiosity and speculation raged through the ranks, professors looking on one another, a cacophony of whispers rising to the Lord.

President Vardus wiped agony from his brow, and brimming confidence crossed him. "These questions led me invariably to answers, as I'm sure you've guessed by now. Many years of toil, sleepless nights, and ample anguish brought me solutions in the face of obstacles. I pondered many solutions, but one has surpassed all others." He turned behind him as the screen flipped. "Ladies, gentlemen, and others ..." his arms went out at his sides. "I present to you the Twister Program."

At his cue, the projector screen illustrated something that Ladis could not decipher from this distance, but it elicited decorous applause. He moved closer yet.

"You see!" Vardus declared, his baritone voice ringing throughout. "After so long, our failures could no longer be considered our own. We have all fought sedulously for our cause, for our people! For our way of living. Here on the island of Ardosia, we have the best of the best in all of history. But a virus has arisen in our students, one that *must* be quelled. Thus, I bring you the institution of Twister."

From there on, the President rolled through his slides, one-by-one. With each turn, Ladis crept ever slowly toward the edge of the balcony. He did it all subconsciously, enamored horrifically by this ... this Twister. The President explained it all in great detail, laying out each step of his deliberate plan. No stone was left unturned, no questions remained unanswered, and by the end, Ladis's mouth hung agape.

My God ... the matador at the Coliseum. The Exercises. It all made awful, terrible sense. *Oh, my God ... help us.* Ladis should have listened to Orian. He should have escaped when he had the chance. A glance at his watch revealed the time of 8:20. Hell, he should go *now.* But Vardus's presentation was far from over.

With each new slide, cheers rose, escalating into chants. There was hesitation amongst the masses at first, but the cogent speech had wooed them.

"Once Twister has been completely implemented, our work is over!" More cheers. "We will have won the war by obtaining peace! We will have defeated our foes, and Ardosia will be a bastion of supreme education, with no need for a military for the rest of time! With the help of all of you, my esteemed colleagues, eminent in my eyes, from this day forward, and with the help of Twister … you, me, and all the valuable souls of Ardosia *will* appreciate." A crooked smile fell from President Vardus's lips, as all professors rose in unison to laud their leader. All hooted and screamed the President's name. All but one.

Ladis had an aerial view of it all. Toward the back of the right section, one professor was seated tightly. He appeared to be younger, but Ladis couldn't tell for sure. It was the man's voice, after all cheers subsided, that confirmed Ladis's suspicions.

The lone professor stood. "You've all gone mad!" His accusations were met with a few jeers, but he overpowered them all, decrying their insanity. Ladis prayed from above that he might be heard. "This … all of this. Have you all but lost your morals?"

Vardus raised the mic to his tranquil lips. "All of you, be seated. All but …" the congregation heeded his command, save for the remonstrator. "… you." Vardus descended the stairs, coolly striding toward his only protestor. "Professor Ivan? Is that you? My, my. Wherever did you find the courage?"

Ivan did not quail when the President met him at the aisle, though he appeared to consider it. After all, he hadn't just the need to explain himself to Vardus, but to his colleagues as well. "Mr. President, you cannot be serious with this. I ... I mean, to say the least, this Twister plot of yours is duplicitous, founded in deceit that I'd have thought only Satan to approve." Professor Ivan stood straight.

Above, Ladis crept even more forward to see. The wood offered a subtle creak. It was dark below, but the voices were strong.

Ivan continued. "What if the students are not our problem to fix? What if they're our solution?"

Vardus put forth a steely gaze. His wrath seemed to be lying directly beneath it. His long, drawn-out pause unnerved Ladis. Tension rose within the cathedral then as all awaited the President's passionate reprisal.

But Vardus offered a calm response, much to the surprise of both Professor Ivan and the shadow in the balcony. "I'll take your criticism into consideration," he said flatly. Then, into the mic, "Thank you."

It was everyone's cue to leave.

Ladis checked his watch. *Shit. 8:25.* There was no way for him to make it back in time. And now, with all professors preparing for the exit, Ladis's escape was more than simply improbable, though among them, there was a hesitation to leave. If they waited long enough, he might have a chance to escape.

Shooting upright, Ladis rose to his feet. He propelled himself forward, when *CRACK* followed by *BANG* sucked Ladis beneath the balcony floor. It happened in a blur. He found himself in a cascading flurry of splinters, nails, cobwebs and dust. Crashing downward, Ladis was suddenly at the back of the cathedral. On hands and knees in a guilty circle of splintered and rotting wood, nails, and dust, Ladis felt hundreds of eyes on him. Most of all, he felt the stare of President Vardus.

"What the–? Is that a–"

Ladis defied the pain, though he felt it, and he rose, shooting out the double doors before Vardus could project his inquiry over the speakers.

Sprinting through the grass, toward the meadow, Ladis castigated himself. "You idiot, you dumb son of a ..." He'd been so foolish, chasing the rush, prying for knowledge. Ignorance was bliss. He, of all people, should've known not to challenge it. He'd become obsessed with the thrill, blind to reason. What had he been thinking?

Right now, there was no time for second-guessing. He had to leave. He had to get out of Ardosia, *immediately.*

Through the woods, exactly from where he had come, Ladis ducked rolled, and emerged out the other side, untouched by pine, but more importantly, untouched by Ardosians.

Frantically, he searched for the path that had taken him here. Now the moon had lost its dazzling brilliance, no longer illuminating the grass in any particular fashion. The path was gone.

Ladis wasn't good with directions, but he had to act. As fast as his legs would go, Ladis ran and ran and ran. He kept on until he found himself near a small square building, overrun with vine and weeds. It appeared that mud had been caked on its outer walls, thrown there by nature.

Fifty yards from it, he halted. There were guards surrounding its perimeter.

"*Shit.*" He bent low.

Luckily, there was a tree nearby, the base of its trunk wide enough to seclude him. He shuffled behind it, breath heaving.

He learned the hard way that there were repercussions to be had by both risk-takers and cowards alike. Life administered their punishments all the same. It was up to the selector to decide which poison would be worth the effort. Even now, Ladis was unsure whether he'd chosen right or wrong. Pursuit of thrill was the most daring venture he'd yet undertaken, but it had taken him somewhere he was never meant to be. Ladis didn't yet know if regret latched onto his soul.

Ladis would have to formulate an escape plan, though he feared it was too late and that his fate had already been sealed. He thought of the lake, of the ground. *Don't send me six feet below,* he prayed.

Hearing no response from God, Ladis determined that he would have to get himself out of this predicament on his own. So he thought.

Taking the concrete path back to the Tower simply would not do. Any soldier who encountered a student after curfew would know to apprehend him. Besides, the Tower was no longer his destination. Anywhere but the island, that was where he needed to go.

There, beside the tree, Ladis mapped out his escape, all while keeping a keen eye on the square building ahead, in case guards should wander. It seemed that they hadn't heard him … not yet.

No longer was he concerned with reaching the Tower. Ladis cared not at all for the possessions he held in his dorm room. Those could burn, for all he cared. After witnessing first-hand the intentions President Vardus had for Ardosia's student population, Ladis felt a rippling urgency to put as much distance between himself and the island as possible.

He could pass by the Tower, climb one of the many bridges that hovered over the lake, connecting the Wall to the island, and leap over the outer perimeter. There in the jungle, he would doubtless be forced to confront predators of all shapes and sizes. Truth be told, he felt his odds were better against a set of razor teeth than against this *Twister* thing.

Ladis pondered another escape route. *I could run through the center of the island, sneak past a few guards, and swim out, just as Orian had done.* He shook his head. *No ... maybe I should–*

The strongest hand in the world gripped him then. Ladis's heart stopped, and he tried to reel away from his captor. The man was simply too strong.

"Tricky boy." Bicep Guy stood over him.

Attempting to wrench free, Ladis pulled and pulled, but the grip was too strong. "Let me go, please!" Ladis begged for his life. He knew it would prove ineffective, but it was all he could do.

The soldier's laugh rose high into the night sky. "No. I don't think so." He favored Ladis with a look that he might offer a protein shake–thirsty for retribution. He dragged Ladis along despite his efforts and said, "I'm going to enjoy throwing you into a cell, where you can rot beside all the other traitors."

XXVI

It was a scalp detox day, so the bun was undone. Amidst the cloud of steam, Vardus was still, his hair soaked and falling to shoulder. He remained there, amongst the gray tile walls of the shower, for an hour at least, abolishing the tension of proper guidance that gripped his soul in clenching fists. His meeting at the cathedral the previous evening couldn't have gone more smoothly, apart from the anomaly holing a crater through his balcony. But that was later resolved. The boy had been dealt with.

Twister had been met with more enthusiasm and support than Vardus could have ever anticipated. It corroborated his judgment. *My professors were wisely chosen.* All but one, it seemed.

The taut, mud-colored curtain was folded, brought back to *just* the right angle. Seven inches from the right, always. The streaming shower ended. James couldn't say he felt totally relieved, but his shoulders were tight no longer.

In all black he dressed. The top three buttons of his collared shirt undone, to breathe, to usher the world close to him. He combed his straggly beard, then poked a thick nail through his hair to hold the bun.

Vardus padded barefoot to his desk. Slides found his toes, a seat formed at his back, and a mighty inhale filled his nose. He forded Woody a sidelong glance. Behind the glass, the tiger snoozed in his den, but he was nearly too big for it. Woody had grown immensely in a matter of weeks. Soon, he would be too large for the cage and would need a new home. Vardus was prepared for the incvitability and had made arrangements long ago

"Come in, Matthew!" he yelled at the large double door.

Promptly, the bald man stumbled in, a worrisome look on his face. Vardus didn't ponder how long he'd kept his Right Hand waiting. Ardosia's men abided by his Schedule.

"Sir." Matthew adjusted his tie with one hand, a tablet in the other. He placed little distance between the desk and himself.

"Tea?" Vardus asked as he poured, knowing his assistant would decline. There was one mug, and warmth was already swirling out of it for the President.

"No, Vardus. Thank you."

"Very well." James brought the cup to his nose and sniffed. It was too hot to sip. "Do you know your namesake, Matthew?"

"Of course I do."

Vardus told him anyway. "It comes from the Bible, as most worthy names do. Matthew wrote one of the four gospels. You were named appropriately, my friend. I trust, like Matthew of old, you've brought me good news."

"Some of it is good." As always, Matthew shot straight arrows. It appeared that there would be some grievances to discuss.

A callused hand rubbed over swirling rivers engrained in the desk. "Any further improvements since our previous discussion on yield?"

"No, sir."

"Then we will not discuss it again."

"Indeed." Matthew scrolled through his tablet, as though the first bullet points he wished to review had suddenly been immaterial. Then he nodded. "Our O-rates–"

"Truly, you haven't come to lecture me on O-rates, either." Vardus had heard enough of them as of late. "What else?"

Matthew swallowed. He paused, scrolling further down. "Class time has been increased, by your request, in addition to security presence. Due to these increases, we've seen a practical disappearance of student incidents. Despite … other numbers," he avoided the topic of O-rates, "students seem to be in line. Your methods have been successful."

After the Savages had taken many of his students, who left on their own accord, Vardus took it upon himself to ensure it wouldn't happen again. After all, problems and solutions always began at the top.

Matthew went on. "I do, however, caution you. I've taken closer looks, both in person and on camera. I'm afraid our students are scared, Mr. President.

Furthermore, I worry that their fear may be only masking their growing resistance. Raising testing standards, placing more soldiers in visible areas … there's a waxing anxiety among them."

At that, Vardus closed his eyes and smiled.

Matthew frowned. "Have you misheard me, Vardus?"

"No, no. Wonderful news. It's all wonderful." His dark eyes flew open. "I've been too soft for too long, my friend. Before, I fought not to expose my children to fear, but I've learned now the foolishness of hiding from our solution. Studies have shown time and again that fear compels. Fear drives progress. And so it has. From here on out, it will mark the tips of our arrows and be driven through our enemies as well. I appreciate your concern, Matthew, but our methods have been diligently coordinated." He took a relaxed slurp of tea. To Matthew, he said, "Continue."

Matthew's eyebrows rose, and the worry adorning his brow vanished. "It looks to me as though I have no more bad news." Perhaps unknowingly, he'd had none to offer in the first place. "Of our resurgence mission, I have jovial report, of course. The Mercians were caught unawares when we attacked. Our men drove deep into their camp and set fires. Only one made traction, but it was their hospital that went up, no less. As for our men, one fell to their three. It was the best of our resurgent operations yet." Scrolling through his tablet, Matthew displayed a graph for Vardus. "Our success suggests the improvement of our ranks and the decline of theirs. I'm pleased, Mr. President, and you should be, too. I might even propose," he looked wary to utter it, "an advancement on Camp Merciadel."

The President's smile couldn't have gone any wider. "Aggression suits you well, Matthew."

"Now, now." He held up both hands. "I may propose a tactical entry, not unlike our previous resurgence, before we attempt anything further … but if you wish to attack, I've no more dissenting opinions."

As leader of Ardosia, Vardus held many ambitions. Among them was the eradication of the Savages. Well, no. Perhaps it would be more accurate to say he wished to decimate their hope, their cause, their poisonous ideology. If not for a Right Hand like Matthew who kept his aggressive tendencies at bay, he may have sent all his men in a full-frontal attack at first opportunity. Luckily, his Right Hand had prohibited such rash action, and Vardus now understood Matthew's wisdom in such counsel. "Build your army. Gain skill, continue to study," Matthew would say. Then he'd hold his index fingers up. "I know as well as you that we are already suited to wipe the Mercians out. We are. Of course, we are. It might, however, be more satisfactory if the boot that crushes the ant gains some width first."

Now the boot was massive, and Matthew could see it, too. It pleased Vardus that they were now on the same page.

"And what of our recruiting efforts?"

Matthew seemed to stand straighter. He was enjoying the conversation. "I thought you'd never ask." Again, he scrolled. "Twenty percent of Ardosian students have seen re-assignment, geared toward our military, of course. Professors have heeded your command in that regard, suggesting that roles may be better found in our brave and mighty ranks. It's been met with success, and … oh," a frown returned, as well as the worry marks at his forehead.

"What's the matter?" Vardus slurped. The tea was getting colder.

"Nothing. A misreport, clearly."

"Speak it."

"As you wish. It says here that we're recruiting even below the graduation age of twenty. Many at nineteen and others at eighteen or below … they're already being sent to train? Of course, this is false, of course it is." The Right Hand sent a wary eye toward the President. "It is false, correct?"

Soft cotton slides cushioned Vardus's feet as he stood and stretched. His yawn frightened Woody, who had suddenly woken. The tiger stuck to his den.

Multi-colored light warmed the President's back and shone against his Right Hand's bald head. James towered over most everyone, Matthew especially. Matthew was a short man, but even as he stood below the President, he neither groveled nor flinched. Like Vardus, he was intrepid, though he never hesitated to worry.

"My professors have done exactly as I've asked." James rode to Woody's enclosure, where a crack persisted in the glass. He hadn't gotten to fixing it yet. "You said it yourself, my friend. A larger boot squashes insignificant pests more efficiently."

Matthew wasn't sure. "I-I did say that, but … do you not see this measure as overkill, let alone an unnecessary risk? Students who haven't undergone the full extent of our education cannot guarantee their loyalty. You know this, Vardus. Of course, you know this."

A weak reflection shone in the glass. Vardus spoke to it equally as much as he did Matthew. "One can never go too far to ensure victory."

In the glass, James saw not only his current form, but also his previous self. In particular, he saw the man who sparked a revolution, the man who defeated the Old

332 | TWISTER: REBELLION

Nation, ripping it in two. A bloodbath though it was, he had overcome the oppressive forces guiding the Nation, to form his own perfect union in Ardosia. Looking back, there were many lives that could have been spared, but James didn't dwell on them. Blood was the price paid for greatness. It always had been. At some point, whether the spills amounted to a single drop or a lake of sorrowful cries and dying breaths, scarlet rain merged with the endless sea all the same.

Easing toward the President, Matthew seemed to understand. As a result, his confidence faded. He hardly held the courage to make the accusation, but he did it anyway. "You're afraid of the Mercians."

Vardus addressed his Right Hand's insanity with a mordant scoff, nothing more. He thought of all those who had resisted him before, not least of all Professor Ivan. *And look where it got them.* Ardosia was all but inexorable now. *Nobody will have the strength to defy me. The Savages are but ants in the looming shadow of my boot.*

Matthew could have pressed on, and in his head he might have, spewing thoughts like, *That's it. The military, the Wall, the desperation … he fears Ardosia's fall, most of all at the hands of Merciadel.* Instead, he wisely nodded. "That's all I have, Mr. President."

James turned to him. "Dismissed."

The Right Hand's choice to discuss nothing further was prudent. As the double door latched shut, it echoed lightly off the walls, isolating President Vardus. *The bald man cares too much for them,* he thought in regard to his students. It was no matter. James had always sworn that he would see peace in his day, and he was closer now than ever to ensuring its perpetual existence in the world.

While his blood boiled at Matthew's resistance, Vardus had no time to sulk in his frustration. The Coliseum was calling to him. Truth be told, he'd never anticipated an evening in that Golden Suite more than he did now. As James rolled out the door in a suit of black, he could see it all, the blood, the screams, all preempted by that vacant, robotic stare. To this point, Vardus had been vexed by his program's failure, but nothing would delight him more than relishing in the sight of a helpless, defiant Professor Ivan, whose fate would be decided by a dysfunctional Twister Program. James couldn't wait to watch him fall.

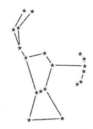

XXVII

"Get up!" Commander Cael shouted. "Your feet must never fall out, or you're nothing but a fawn in a maddened panther's clutches."

The admonishment seemed rather targeted to Orian, but he supposed that was the point. Guerdo offered his hand. Orian took him by the forearm, and he was hoisted off the dirt.

"Again," Cael said sternly, his tight, pointed jaw stabbing anxiety through Orian. Then the Commander discovered another duo worth reproaching. "Oh my God, who just exposed their backside? Kaija? Is that you?" Cael's navy-blue apparel floated amongst the sandy ranks.

The training grounds had been stationed near the front of Camp Merciadel, where an obstacle course rose beside a wide-open expanse of gravel, sand, and clay. Conveniently located cattie-corner to the hospital, soldier training had become an increasingly passionate matter. One quick glance at the charred outer walls of the medical building led to a newfound passion for the soldier's life in almost all cases. There was also the shattered gate, which had since been replaced, but a new shiny metal was a solemn reminder that the old barrier had fallen, and that this one was equally as susceptible to failure.

Orian wiped the dirt off his cargo pants, readjusting his grip on the wooden practice blade. Internally, he scolded himself.

"Focus." Guerdo's eyes were a captivating tube that connected the dueling partners and demanded Orian's attention. "Frustration sparks imbalance of the mind and body. Stay level, stay cool in your head, and your body follows suit."

Orian nodded coolly, breathing like a meditating monk. *In ... out.* Although the breathing exercises he'd been taught had to this point been unfruitful, he did them anyway. Much like the rest of his military training, it would take time to become a consummate soldier.

"Let's go again." Orian shook the inexperience from his shoulders. *I am a soldier, a Mercian soldier now. The best of the best.*

A chain clinked low at Guerdo's side as he stepped back. With every movement, thrust, parry, and jolt, the golden links clanged bell-like tones as they dangled from his pocket. They were distracting, but Orian knew better than to complain. Excuses were sour attempts to justify premeditated failures.

Wood clacked as their blades met. Orian's arms, back, and shoulders were screaming at him, sore from the previous day's training, and the day before that, and the day before that. If not for his time working on Pake's farm, he might have already given up. Long hours of exacting exercise had been an arduous adjustment, considering the lack of physical movement he experienced on the island. In the Tower, he sat at a podium, did mental exercises, went back to his room, rinse, wash, repeat. But Orian didn't miss the lifestyle one bit, even though it had been easier on his joints and muscles.

"*Gahh!*" he groaned as Guerdo's blade smacked his knee. Orian's dueling partner had gone easy on him, he knew, but the pain shot through his leg nonetheless. Even more challenging to deflect than Guerdo's blade was the rising fury. Orian was supposed to suppress it, but it gave him energy. What if he were to embrace the frustration instead?

Orian had nearly fallen to one knee, which would have conceded the fight, but he rose. He allowed the anger to course through him. Tingling adrenaline flowed. Gripping the wooden pommel, Orian lunged forward with blinding speed.

"Whoah." Guerdo stumbled backward unexpectantly. Suddenly, the inexperienced soldier's attacks came quicker and with more strength behind each blow. Guerdo deflected them all the same, but sweat was finally forming at his brow, granting Orian a satisfactory grin.

Before the next move came, Orian had anticipated its arrival. He'd paid close attention to Guerdo's tendencies, the way one foot retreated as he turned his hips, how the blade swirled in toward his side. Orian's ribs stung from the same move having been successfully completed before. This time he was ready.

Orian parried, but in a way that used Guerdo's momentum against him, his wooden blade clattering against the sandy clay as it tumbled from his hand. Orian whirled about until he was at his dueling partner's back. Guerdo was equally awestruck, flabbergasted, and hurt as the wooden blade smashed against his lower back, bringing him to knee. In a flash, Orian had managed to escape his foe's vision and rise victorious for the first time, a move he was proud of … until a low voice rebuked his efforts.

"That stunt'll get you killed in battle, Ardosia." A head of golden hair strode arrogantly toward him.

Chest heaving, Orian subtly rolled his eyes at the familiar tone. "Byron," was all he said as he turned.

The large, broad-shouldered soldier wore the same colors as Orian now. They were equals, or they were supposed to be, anyways. Still, the fact hadn't squashed Byron's condescension. Since Orian's first day in the military, he'd been dubbed by the dubious douchebag as *Ardosia*, a nickname he could admit was enormously insulting and infuriating. Nevertheless, Orian kept his cool. "I apologize. Maybe you could show me its ineffectiveness."

"Against a competent opponent, you'll find their blade in your head." It was a jab at Guerdo, who was still on a knee, breathing heavily to subdue his pain.

"I'd be interested to see how you'd fare," Orian said plainly.

"What?" Byron sneered. "You mean to take me in a duel? I knew you were reckless and impudent, but my, oh my…"

"Of course not. I could never wish to overcome someone so esteemed, private." Orian had no need to leer at the man. He knew he was already in Byron's head.

Many of the surrounding duos paused. They drew their attention toward an impending duel, one fought with quips rather than swords. Orian tended to win these battles. To his surprise, Commander Cael stood idly by, unamused.

"Can you believe this guy?" Byron tapped his partner's chest with the back of his hand. "Boy, Ardosia ... you're ballsy, I'll give you that."

Chains clinked as Guerdo had risen to his feet at Orian's side. "It was a good move, Byron. He outmaneuvered me as well as any have."

"Seems twice he's done it now, sleepy."

Guerdo stroked his auburn beard. "Kid's smart. Smarter than me. Smarter than many of us." He kept his gaze lasered on Byron, who evidently didn't believe in the possibility of intelligence stemming from a product of the island.

"Smart doesn't leave his side exposed to attack the flank."

"Then perhaps you could call it wit or courage, hence why it appeared so foreign to you."

The large man stepped forward. As he did, a strange noise from above stopped him. Byron looked up, as did the rest.

What Orian saw in the sky was hard to describe, knowing only that it was falling toward him at the speed of gravity.

"Step back!" a woman called.

Guerdo grabbed Orian's arm and slung him out of the way, just as a large metal object crashed in his place.

Orian brushed the sand off his pants, again. Then he rose to get a closer look at what had almost taken his head off. The men gathered around the object that had fallen from the sky, toppled sideways on the red sandy clay.

"What is that?" Orian asked.

It was white and rounded, metallic as well, with propellers attached at the top. And through its belly was an arrow.

"It was a fucking drone." General Talia pushed her way through, standing over the object disdainfully. The golden scarf flowed seamlessly at her neck, a recently-fired crossbow at her side. No one was forded exoneration as she laid a scowl on each of her men, not least of all Cael. "Commander, explain."

Hands behind his back, Cael held his chin high. "I take full responsibility, General. It appears our men have lost focus, engaging in childly brawls, rather than useful combat." He shot imposing glances at both Byron and Orian. "We did not hear the drone overhead."

Talia worried her temple. Her jaw was tight with silence, a tension hanging in the air that could have been cut with a wooden blade. She spoke to everyone at once. "You know the thing about men with egos much bigger than their worth?" She looked mostly to Byron when she said, "They partake in insecure squabbles and argue vociferously over whose cock is smaller. All of you are meant to be close like brothers, not fighting like them. In your boorish behavior, you've let down your guard, abandoned your sense of alertness. Our entire complex could have been compromised." She cast a pointed glance to the drone that she had taken down. It was impossible to tell whether it had just arrived or if it had already captured a complete reconnaissance of the camp. "How the fuck did it slip beneath our radar?"

Neal appeared out of nowhere. His glasses were pressed tight to his face, making his eyes look bigger than usual. His salmon-colored shirt showed egregious sweat stains beneath his arms, as if he had run directly from the office. "It-it looks like Ardosia has uncovered a few tech secrets. I-I was l-lucky to have intercepted it myself."

"I'm glad you warned me right away. I figured one of these fools would have had it on the ground by the time we arrived, Neal." Talia's face was red with rage. "Don't blame yourself."

"I d-don't."

Each and every Mercian soldier wore regret on their face and in their body language. As a warrior, you were required to hold your head high, show no signs of weakness, because more than anything–physical adaptability or strength with weapons like swords or bows–being a soldier was about the mental battles. Yet many held drooping eyes, or clenched fists, or gritted teeth–all signs of failure and defeat.

Talia's scowl washed away, but not completely. Slowly and intentionally, she rounded the drone, over and over. "Let's not pretend that all failures are your own, gentlemen. Like General Andrew used to say, 'Successes and failures alike begin as raindrops above a mount. They trickle from top to bottom, either in droplets or tsunamis.' I aim to be half the leader Andrew was, so I'll offer up an opportunity for criticism. I promise no backlash, no bullshit. Where could I have gone better, men?" Still circling the drone, Talia peered through her ranks. Her men and women were quiet. She looked them over, once, twice. "No one? Nobody has an ounce of constructive advice for Commander Cael or myself? Drones surpassing radar, attacks breaching our front gate, and internal battles are all terms of success to you all … interesting. Well, we must be doing alright if *no one*–"

"I have something to say, General." Only one soul was brave enough to speak.

No man stirred nor moved an inch. A collective flinch wound its way through them.

A dissenting breath slithered its way through Byron's disbelieving smile. "You can't be serious. General, are we really going to take advice from–"

"Byron!" the General snapped. "For once, would you SHUT THE FUCK UP?" It appeared as though her nails might draw blood from her palms any moment. Then she relaxed. "Now," she looked toward the one man who had enough audacity to offer Merciadel's greatest militaristic mind a handful of advice. "Go ahead, Orian."

While the welcome invitation was forded to him, the General's eyes shone with a fire that said, *This had better be good.*

For a week, Orian had undergone Talia's military training. It was arduous, in terms of both mind and body. Yet, through all the exercises and practiced scenarios, Orian noticed immediately a handful of issues that might pass easily by the gaze of someone with a less keen eye for tactics. Years spent scouring the Internet for new ways to improve a military had sharpened Orian's sense of efficiency. In those days at the Tower, he had simply inclined himself to the information because it greatly intrigued him. If he'd have known that he would assume a militaristic position someday, he would have spent even more time evading Professor Yjn's in-class exercises in pursuit of all the knowledge his brain could muster.

Orian stepped forward and raised his voice so that everyone might see and hear what he had to say. Ever since he'd begun training, these words had been waiting to spring forth like an erupting volcano. It would take a conscious effort to present the matter as respectfully as possible.

Orian's heart was racing, and it clogged his throat at first, but he calmed himself and spoke confidently, like he belonged there. "If I may, General, I've joined your ranks for seven days now. These have been some of the most humbling and eye-opening days I've yet seen. With regard to your men, I'm madly impressed with the knowledge and skill on display. You teach man-to-man combat very well."

Talia blinked.

A handful of Mercian soldiers were already flinching.

"But," Orian continued, "when it comes to working as a team … well, for lack of a better term, the training sucks."

Many Mercians reeled back in suppressed laughter, not wasting their time in sending up a prayer for the poor dumb boy who couldn't keep his mouth shut.

General Talia hushed them. "Alright, alright." A thin, amused smile crept over her face. "And what is it that you might suggest?"

Orian was not nervous. He'd seen the issues plain as day from the moment he began his training. It was almost as if he had spent the entire week preparing for this.

"An individualistic, scramble-to-the-top ideology is currently wreaking havoc in this camp. I've heard rumors of a Colonel opening? Anyway, I understand the necessity for personal ambition completely. Without individual competence, the collective may never be achieved." Orian looked back to Guerdo, who urged him on. "Here, though, it has been taken to an extreme. Just yesterday, beneath the barbed wire, Joseph was caught and sliced. A real brotherhood, you described us as such, would not have passed by him without a second thought. But we did. Two days prior, Private Fennor left training with a face as bloody as the day he was born. Not one soldier dared to help him once we were dismissed."

Talia's smile was washed away, replaced, however, not by anger but by intrigue. "Go on."

Orian effectively had all attention. "If a unit does not work as one, if it leaves the weakest link on the ground, if it forgoes innovation, the entire unit fails. Right now, I believe we're guilty of just that. We are taught to care, train, and fight for ourselves, and ourselves only. It's a tactic that will not take us far."

Commander Cael and General Talia exchanged glances. "We'll take your words into consideration, Orian. Thank you."

"Well," Orian tried. "If I may, I'm not finished."

The General could hardly believe his gall, but she'd dealt with the new recruit enough since his arrival to know that rebellion was instilled deep within him. "Commander Cael?" she looked to him for a second opinion.

"I see no issues with letting the boy speak."

"Very well." Talia turned expectantly toward Orian.

I am no boy. Orian wondered how long it would take to prove himself a man. "Okay. Okay…" Orian was fumbling for the words all of the sudden. He was abruptly riddled with anxiety, and he didn't understand why … until, upon glancing about the soldiers, he realized his point might be better made without words. "Let me show you," he said.

Orian dispersed the crowd, waving them back and back until he was alone in the middle of them. Regaining his wooden sword, Orian traced a large rectangle in the sandy clay. All watched closely from outside the visible barrier.

"This," Orian said as he finished drawing in the sand, "is Merciadel." He thought it best to add a few details, to give a better visual representation. Then he thought a few men and one woman might help make his point. He grabbed Guerdo, Private Kaija, Frank, and two other men, pulling them to the center of his rectangle. Every one of them was then positioned either in a corner or in the center of Orian's miniature map. "And *this* is our current defense plan, the one that you teach, General. Kaija, she's at front. Guerdo at side. Frank at flank. All others placed variably within the camp's limits."

Standing nearest to the visual map, General Talia looked over it with pride. "Correct. You've caught on well. This protects us from an Ardosian attack at all angles– front, back, side-to-side, up, and down. With approximately twenty to thirty men in each position, we are unassailable." She looked to Orian, curious. "You're going to have to speak well if you're to tell me this isn't working, Orian. You'd be brave to issue an argument against a plan that most would consider foolproof."

"… have to be downright dumb," Byron quipped, just loud enough for most to hear.

Orian did not waver. "This is a defensive strategy, one that has proven successful, no doubt. Yet to deny innovation is to deny progress. What I'm suggesting, General, is an offensive strategy."

"Our current strategy is one that has and will thwart all future attacks."

"Right, and the Ardosians have come to expect that."

Talia crossed her arms. "Until they stormed us unawares by our very front gate entrance. We weren't in position then."

Many had thought Orian's argument to be lost. He could see it in their faces. What they hadn't realized was that the General had just made his point for him.

"Bingo," he said satisfactorily. Orian began to thread his way through the men he had placed in his miniature map of Merciadel. Then, one-by-one he rearranged them. "To be successful, we have to think not only as our most effective selves, but also as our enemy." First, Orian moved Kaija, then Frank. As he did so, they were stubborn and incredulous to find themselves elsewhere on the map.

Talia focused unbelieving eyes on Orian's proposed strategy. She even intermingled with it, moving within the sand-written boundaries. "I … so let me get this straight, just so I understand. You want to leave not only our front uncovered, with no defense, but our flank as well? Which would leave us completely and utterly vulnerable to attacks from either end."

Many jeers rose from the Mercian soldiers, not least of all Byron. "Is there any further proof that the boy is a traitor? The plan is suicidal, reckless, implausible at best. Send him back to Ardosia!"

It seemed half the ranks were on Byron's side.

Guerdo leaned in close, whispering, "Orian, what are you doing?"

"I've got this," Orian kept under his breath. "Trust me."

Orian waited patiently for all the commotion to subside. He appreciated those who had yet to throw judgment his way. Even with most men leering conspicuously at Orian, they remained outside the rectangle, save for General Talia.

"I suspect you have more to say, Orian, so you'd better make it quick." Her eyes were sharp, but Orian could see that she had not lost interest.

Think like your enemy. "Look, everyone here knows Vardus, who he is, what he's capable of, and that his military personnel rises in number daily. We also know that he's an overconfident, arrogant prick. What happened last week …" Orian was referring to the front-entrance attack, where the gate had been toppled over by Ardosians. "It may have provided us with just the opportunity we were looking for. I'm sure you can all see it. Right now, Vardus is on his high horse, thinking that with one battle, he's won the war. He may even go so far as to expect Merciadel to leave its front entrance unattended again, should he wait for the right time to strike … and he'll be even more delighted to view the flank similarly."

Men were beginning to stir, and General Talia was loath to stop them. Orian had little time to sell his case, or he'd surely end up in the middle of an angry brawl.

"We are not abandoning our front and rear defenses entirely. I'm suggesting, rather, that we make it *look* as such." Again, Orian demonstrated with the men and woman at hand. Guiding Kaija into one of the squares within the larger rectangle, and later doing the same with Frank on the back end, Orian offered his opinion succinctly. "By luring the Ardosians into our camp, we'll accomplish three feats at once: securing their overconfidence, proscribing any possibility of a hit-and-run, and catching them off guard when, from the bushes, we leap at them and make our soil fertile with Ardosian blood." He looked to everyone when he said, "We'll be hidden within buildings near the center of our camp, the heart of Merciadel attended to. Then, once they're in, *we* come out. It's risky, I know. But the reward here is so much greater. Herein lies the possibility of ending the war altogether."

The silence was loud. Suddenly, all heretics were hushed, even Byron. Rather than issuing threats or critiques or praise, they all simply stared at the model before them. Orian had no idea whether it had meant his success or if he'd just dug his own grave. Then the General consulted her Commander aloud.

"Cael?"

He put his hands on hips, sucking in a deep breath. Getting closer, Commander Cael worked for a more intimate look at Orian's blueprint for a new offensive strategy. He looked to Orian and said, "Where did you learn this?"

"As I've said before," Orian was placid. "I've read a lot on the Internet." *And it's easier to generate a new perspective from the outside, when complacency isn't an option.*

Cael bit the inside of his lip. "General, I'll be honest. I can't tell if it's brilliant … or the dumbest thing I've ever laid eyes on."

"Perhaps it's both," she said as she wove through the center of it. From all angles, she investigated. The indecision was leaving a pit in Orian's stomach. For a minute or two, General Talia said nothing, instead circling the rectangle drawn in the sand, when at last words left her. "Dismissed."

Her men were wary to move. Even Orian was shocked. There was so much tension in the air, so much left to be resolved.

"Did you not hear her?" Commander Cael's voice rose high in the daytime air, though even he couldn't hide the same lingering thoughts that crossed his face. Still, he shouted, "Dismissed!"

"Wait!" The General had apparently changed her mind. Every Mercian froze. Wandering over to the drone she shot down, Talia squatted beside it, tugging the arrow from its belly and notching it into her crossbow. At first, Orian was worrisome that she might fire the arrow straight into his heart, but she had no intention of doing anything like it. Not yet, at least. "I'll need someone to take this drone to IT. See if they can't get it back online and hack its code, find everything we can on the island."

No one volunteered, for which Orian was grateful. "I'll do it," he said. "The IT building is just beside my living quarters. It'll be on my way."

A piercing gaze flew to Orian. Talia searched him. "Very well," she said. And again, "Dismissed."

This time, the Mercian unit left with more dispatch. Orian stayed where he was, listening to the whisperings and speculations until they were inaudible. Commander Cael had left with his men as well.

"Guerdo," the General said before he could depart.

Guerdo turned. "Yes, ma'am."

"Escort Orian back to IT. Be sure he doesn't get lost."

He nodded. Chains clinked quietly at his side.

As Talia rose with Neal at her hip, she ambled in the direction of her office, but Orian stopped them both.

"General," he said firmly. Her head pivoted slowly to him. Neal's eyes were wide. Orian gulped. "What can I— we expect? Uh, in terms of strategy moving forward."

"I don't know." Talia's head turned to the sky at an angle. "I'll think about it."

About to press his luck further, Orian was silenced when his arm was gripped with enough strength to warrant a flinch. Talia and Neal left then.

"That's as far as you'll get with her," Guerdo said lowly. "Now stop."

"How am I supposed to sleep tonight, not knowing?" Orian couldn't help but quail at the thought of being on the wrong side of General Talia. He wondered if he had pressed his luck by speaking up.

"Tonight, sleep like you always do," Guerdo said. "Maybe better. Although it doesn't seem like it, the General keeps her word when she says that no suggestions will be met with reprisal. Not from her, anyway." Guerdo's chains hummed as he bent low to pick up the massive drone. He grunted but soon had it comfortably within his grasp. "I've never heard that woman say anything other than 'no' when it comes to ideas that contradict her own. I'd say you're doing fine, better than the rest."

Together they made for the IT building. Most of their trek was made tacitly. Orian hadn't felt the need to speak, and neither had Guerdo, not until they were close.

"Watch your anger," Guerdo said, out of the blue.

My anger? Right now, Orian was anything but angry. Nervous? Sure. Anxious? Yup. But he wasn't angry.

"The move you made on me earlier … I'm impressed, genuinely. Backside attacks are something I don't often give up. Yet I could see the move wasn't made with anything but the fury in your heart. If you continue to follow your heart's impulses and ignore that of the mind, you'll end up just as Byron said: with a blade in your skull. Do not let matters of the heart cloud your judgment, ever."

Oddly, Orian thought Guerdo and Pake's warnings to be comparable. Pake had told him to embrace love, but be wary of it. Love was another matter of the heart. Were they afraid he was too emotional and that he might get caught in a web of carnage? Maybe they were right. Finding that balance was key, he knew, something in need of his attention. "Alright," Orian said solemnly.

At the sound of Guerdo's dangling golden loops, Orian couldn't help but wonder aloud, "What are those? Why do you wear them?"

Looking down around the drone in hand, Guerdo saw his chains, as if for the first time. "Been wearing 'em for so long, I forgot they were there."

"A military thing?" Orian guessed.

"Of sorts."

On the Internet, Orian had read about military men tattooing marks or sigils on their chests, backs, arms, or wherever. Some even kept mementos or pins as an homage to their time served. He wondered if each of the four links hanging from Guerdo's pocket represented a year in the military. Orian had spent ample time with Guerdo in the past week, never once asking how long he'd served for Merciadel.

"Four years," Orian ventured. "That's how long you've been a soldier."

"Good guess, but not quite."

Their boots bounded over the stone path that led toward IT. With the day well upon them, Orian could see large beads of sweat running down Guerdo's face. His shaggy auburn hair was an insulator, and he'd been straining with the drone.

"Here, let me take it the rest of the way."

Guerdo shook his head, but he passed it off, nonetheless. He wiped his brow, then his scalp, and lastly his beard.

The drone nearly fell out of Orian's hands immediately, as it threatened to topple over and damage itself further. Guerdo had made the object appear so light, and it was anything but.

"Each loop represents a man who has fallen at my side, four chains as a constant reminder."

Orian suddenly felt contrite that he had asked. "I'm sorry."

"Gives me a reason to train and fight harder. If I'd have been a more competent partner, they might still be here."

They are here, Orian thought every time the golden chains clinked.

"Here we are," Orian said at the front entrance of the spotless steel walls comprising the tech building. He balanced the drone on his leg for a second to readjust his grip. Nodding to the door, he said, "I think I can take it the rest of the way."

"You sure?" Guerdo's eyes were red and swollen. A half-day's rest would suit him well.

"Positive. Find a bed to curl up on, soldier."

Guerdo saluted him with a smile and turned back the way they came.

As Guerdo marched down the path, Orian wanted to exhort him with a reminder that fate had been a part of this world for much longer than their existence. It was no use to take the blame for what its seemingly chaotic impulses had in mind.

"You're a good soldier, Guerdo. A good man, too."

Another salute emanated from Guerdo. Then he disappeared beyond the bend.

Grunting at the weight of the chunk of metal in hand, Orian examined the IT entrance with as much intent as he had when Talia gave her order, which is to say none. He turned away from it, aiming directly for his little shack. *There might be just enough room for you on my desk,* Orian thought, holding the drone. He would have some fun tinkering.

XXVIII

In nature, there were no unwelcome noises. Birdsongs were joyous in the morning, afternoon, and evening alike. Whistling winds and quaking leaves instilled comfort. For the heart and mind, nature was practically silence, although some have been said to succumb to their own insanity in such silence. The voices, the tremors, the turbulent thoughts crept out of their corners in the absence of sound. For Hudson, those were no more than rumors. For almost two decades now, he'd obtained his peace in nature. It was shameful of those who would come to ruin it.

The noises of nature swirled through cracks of open windows, meeting Hudson's large, old ears at the dining table. Wispy steam rose from his tea, as he was in the middle of inscribing a message via pen and paper. Hudson had just read the excerpt in the magazine. He was sorry to hear about a recent mishap, but would offer only his condolences, for his assistance he had retired long ago.

Outside, the winds picked up. They must've been low, sweeping more through the bushes than the branches above. It was a persistent breeze that had picked up … perhaps too persistent. The pen dropped. Hudson froze. He listened closely …

Wind could rustle bushes, but it could not trample them.

Quick as a lightning strike, Hudson shot from his seat. He reached for the bow … no, the crossbow would do this time. The old man had lived in nature long enough to know the difference between the winds and the footfalls of bears, tigers, or panthers. This was none of those. The sound Hudson heard was one that hadn't reached his drums in years. It was the sound of man. Many men, actually.

Through the peephole in his arching wooden door, Hudson saw ten, twenty, maybe thirty in armor. Donning the colors of gray and white, Hudson had no need to wonder from where they had come.

We had a deal, Hudson thought acerbically.

Yet from the way they approached Hudson's residence, it appeared as though the deal had been off. Shamelessly, the contingent flocked from the trees, all the way up to Hudson's door. Before they could knock, Hudson twisted the handle, opening just a crack.

"You shouldn't be here." It felt strange, unnatural to speak with anything but an animal, or at least a four-legged one.

"Good day, sir!" a smug, pale, and rose-colored face greeted him. The man stood ahead of his fellow soldiers, arms at his back. None were hesitant to brandish the crossbows they held, all of which were much, much newer–and probably quicker–than the old man's. "My name is Lieutenant Luke."

Stoic, Hudson said nothing. His stare was cold as a winter freeze. Hiding half his body behind the door, he clung to the shadows.

Luke leaned to the side, lifting his chin to get a better look at Hudson's outdoor garden. "I see you've had much success growing vegetables! My, I can smell the onions from here."

No you can't.

"Say, sir. We're here from the great island of Ardosia, men of the Pres–"

"I know who you are."

Hudson remembered the gray and white distinctly. They were the colors that killed his wife, daughter, and son.

His stark reply wasn't a compliment, but Luke seemed to have taken it as so. "Amazing." From behind his back, he procured a water-stained length of parchment, where a message was once present. He held it before Hudson, as if he wished for the old man to take it, which Hudson did not do. Luke didn't waver. "By decree of President Vardus …"

Hudson gritted his teeth.

"… at least fifty percent of all yields will be collected for the benefit of the island. And in return, we offer our protection."

"You must leave." Hudson spoke quietly, but he was by no means timid.

"I'm sorry, sir. We–"

The wooden door creaked open further, and as Hudson filled the frame, Lieutenant Luke bit his tongue. He must have lost his courage. So did his men, it seemed. There were thirty of them, sure. Even so, none appeared willing nor ready to take their chances.

This time, Hudson told them, "You will leave."

"Sir, it is not my order, but–"

"And never come back." The step Hudson took was miniscule, but menacing enough to make his point.

Luke reeled back just enough. Every bit of smug had floated away with the breeze. The self-proclaimed lieutenant fought to bring it back with a sorry grin. His eyes flicked to the garden and rested there for a long moment. "Our apologies. From the island of Ardosia, we wish you a good day."

With that, Hudson went slowly backward.

"Oh," Luke stopped, a finger on his chin. "Perhaps you could help us?"

Hudson growled quietly.

"Maybe you've seen other residences, or ..." Luke measured Hudson's home, "...huts around that you could lead us to?"

Pressing a massive fist against his thigh, Hudson forced sharp cracks to rise from his fingers, like tiny pops that suggested the breaking of other, much larger bones.

Lieutenant Luke, stubborn though he was, appeared to have received the message. "Very well." He gathered his men, and they departed, many with mortified faces. The Lieutenant gave one last desirable glance at Hudson's garden. Defeat somehow hadn't crossed him yet.

Hudson's door shut only when the Ardosian soldiers vanished over the hill.

The entrance became dark where Hudson stood. Incensed by the intrusive presence of unwelcome men, he fought to dispel the rage. In truth, all men were unwelcome, Ardosians more than others. There was only one man whom Hudson permitted on his property, but their interactions were few.

Hudson couldn't recall the last time he'd felt so angry. It was an emotion he'd proscribed long ago. Even in the presence of his troubled mind, where his wife's voice echoed, the laughter of his children persistently rang, where their last moments were seared at the forefront of them all … Hudson was not enraged. If anything, he felt helpless to them, although he'd be loath to admit it.

Now, like a roaring red sea, the huge man was overwhelmed by his anger, struggling to ward off the urge to track down those men as if they were deer. He'd hunt them as such, too. It'd be so simple. Hudson could see it already.

He'd follow their scent, the smell of cowardice and egoism. It wouldn't take him long to track them to a valley, where he'd wait high upon a precipice with longbow in hand. One-by-one, he would send arrows into their weak hearts, reserving two for Lieutenant Luke.

And remove them from their families, just as James had done to you?

Hudson whispered to himself the words he'd been taught long ago by his own father: "Retribution is an act for those unwilling to accept."

Suddenly the flaming hatred burned no more. In his life, Hudson had vowed to be many things: a great father, a noble warrior, a forgiving man. He would never allow himself to become his enemy.

Brooding, the old man was sourly abashed that he'd succumbed to his emotion even for a moment, though he understood why. For an instant, he was impressed with himself. It had truly been something to *feel* again.

He returned to his desk, where a half-written message was waiting to be finished. The pen flowed freely in his hand, albeit with an added pressure. Once finished, Hudson read his message once over, then twice. It suited his liking, so he folded it.

His hands weren't proportionate to the rest of his body ... they were even larger. Blue snakes curled atop his hairy white hand, returning superfluous ounces of blood to his heart. Despite their size, his palms were caressing pillows, when he wanted them to be. On several occasions, they had held sick rabbits, chipmunks or squirrels, sometimes birds. And now he held a bird of his own, in the form of a message.

Lightly, Hudson carried the small paper out his door. Mounted at his front entrance was a box, its cap made of metal. It clinked after Hudson dropped the note inside.

At some point overnight, the only man allowed on Hudson's property would find the note, whereupon the words would be printed in a magazine excerpt and sent off. This man did not work for Hudson. Rather, he was employed by someone else, someone far away. He was a message carrier and deliverer, nothing more.

The rest of Hudson's evening flowed smoothly. For dinner, he prepared his sides–peppers, onions, and mushrooms–tossing them in a mixed jumble at the bottom of his cooler. Next went the entrée, which tonight would be ribs. It would take Hudson many more moons to work through what remained of his frozen meats.

He carried the cooler to his firepit, prepared his meal, and carried it back. When he returned, he ate, he cleaned, he sat in his rocking chair, and he thought.

"You did this on your own, Hud." The screams of *Esmer, Adger, and Loren Steehl. Lastly, "And for the record, I am sorry." Bullets shattering the stillness of sky.*

Over and over, the traumatic video feed played through his mind. He never did see the rounds that flew through his family, and Hudson often wondered if this act–what had been referred to as a gesture of empathy by Vardus– was worse than the sight itself. Since the video went black as the guns fired, there was no closure, and there never would be. Only in the next life when he saw the faces of his wife and his children would Hudson's soul unclench itself from the bonds of aching loss.

When at last Hud surpassed the cries, his mind would often steal further into the past, precisely to a time when the Old Nation was one.

A black, starless sky had draped its thin coat over the buzzing, whirring, and archaic carnival sounds. Hud could almost hear the thrill-ride screams, dinging winners, and three-tone bells, even today.

Under the florescent bulbs of a game stand did the golden streaks in her flowing brunette locks illuminate. Her young voice spoke to him. "Take your shot, cowboy."

His spine tingled when she touched his arm. Hud pulled the miniature firearm close, aiming down the crooked sights. So primed in his element, not even the rampant heartbeat that accompanied her touch could sway him.

Ding. Ding. Ding.

Three thin aluminum ducks folded backwards, and with seven shots remaining, Hudson won the prize. He did it for her.

When the striped shirt handed her a plush reward, Esmer stroked its soft, round edges. "I got a bear to protect me now." She looked at Hudson, not the toy, when she said this.

"He'll be there forever," Hud said to those rich blue eyes.

Perhaps they'd only been seeing one another for weeks at this point. The lapses in time were fuzzy after so many years. Hudson knew only that days, not weeks, confirmed his unending unity with Esmer. Souls meet their worldly counterpart and burst with exploding enthusiasm.

He could have opened the gateway to his soul to her then, if he hadn't been interrupted by the abrupt clearing of a young man's throat.

"Hudson?"

Retrospect shed light upon the moments where raucous anxiety was held back by the ignorant walls of serenity, the same moments where joy was at its precipice, soon to descend maddeningly over a roller-coaster cliff. Sometimes Hud wished a clairvoyant whisper could have warned him.

"Mr. Vardus?"

It hadn't made sense, seeing him here. His suit of black seemed to absorb the carnival lights, stealing the luminescence from his face. Hudson guessed Mr. James Vardus to have been rallying elsewhere on the property. But he was there amongst the games, and somehow he'd known Hudson's name.

"Please, call me James."

He stuck out his hand, and Hudson shook it.

Vardus's pulsating touch could still be felt to this day. It was always at this moment that Hud awoke from his trance, though his mind continued to stir.

That day close to four decades ago altered Hudson's life to an unimaginable degree. It was as if by shaking the hand of James Vardus for the first time, he'd been stolen into a realm of darkness from which he'd never return.

He remembered how Vardus asked to speak with him alone, how he agreed, and the look of concern beneath Esmer's farewell smile.

"I'll find you," Hud said to her.

"I know." Esmer looked to him, then to Vardus before leaving. It ached to remember how beautiful she'd been, how beautiful she always was.

"Walk with me," Vardus commanded.

Through crowds of cotton-candy carriers, stuffed animal toters, and fried-corn-dog holders, Hud walked at his side. Hudson had trouble recalling what they talked about while escaping the massive crowds, only having vivid memory of the knowledge Vardus somehow had of him. Hud wasn't sure how he'd managed to obtain a lifetime of information on a guy who stuck to the shadows of his community.

"Popular guy, you are," James had said.

"Me?"

"Lots of people smiling and waving at you back there."

They'd passed the games and blinking lights to find a darker corner of trampled grass. It was quieter there.

"I think they were smiling at you," said Hud.

"Perhaps." Vardus adjusted his tie. "But the ones who called you by name surely weren't talking to me."

Hudson was friendly to those humble folks of his community. When he passed them, he said hello. Nothing more than proper manners.

"Such manners earn favor. People see a right and just man like you, Mr. Steehl, and they latch onto the nobility you present. Makes them feel better about themselves."

"The people I surround myself with are much better folk than I."

Vardus smiled widely. "No doubt they're no match for your humility."

That night, Hudson allowed Vardus to talk. And talk he did. James was good at it. Obviously, to move the masses in the way that he did, it was a necessity. James didn't have a party back then. He hated the nature of party politics. He didn't even consider himself a politician. It's what made him a revolutionary. He differed from the line of postage-stamp clowns who preceded him.

In the course of one night, Vardus had been able to recruit Hudson to his cause, although he was hesitant at first.

"I like to keep in the middle, stay out of the pie-throwing contests."

"Of course you do. So do I!"

Vardus smiled that smile and went on to remind Hudson that everyone had to make a choice when faced with one. Saying no to James then was practically support of the opposition.

"Genocide, inequality, unfair treatment of those less privileged. I stand against this, and I know that you do too Mr. Steehl. The good fight needs more good men on its side."

In those days, the darkness swirling behind Vardus's eyes was not so evident. Hudson used to think it was never there at all, that James had been a true pursuer of justice, but the years had changed him. It seemed to happen all at once after the war. If there were a clever scheme behind those eyes, Hudson fell for it. And if there had never been a scheme at all, Hud attributed Vardus's collapse into mendacity to the corrosive allure of power.

It began with a handshake, escalated into back-row rally appearances, then into behind-the-scenes assistance, and finally into a position as Right Hand in their newly-founded society of Ardosia. Esmer warned him all along that the business he was entering was dangerous. Never had Hud cowered before danger. If anything, he was called to it.

Now, sitting in his recliner, hearing those screams in the far reaches of his head, he wished he'd have listened to his wife. He wished he'd have never met Vardus, that he would have said no to him, just once. Then he'd never have been ripped from his family. The Steehl family could have ended up on the wrong side of the nuclear war, but at least their souls would have all escaped this treacherous world together. And Hudson wouldn't have to be alone, listening to their faraway cries.

In the night while he slept, Hudson woke only once, at the sound of what he presumed to be the messenger. The mailbox tinkered open and shut. He fell asleep.

Then old Hud woke again to subtle stirrings. He listened closely for a while but did not hear anything after a few minor shifts of the wind.

At last, he fell to dreariness.

When Hudson woke in the morning, he did as always, beginning with a pleasant greeting to the chilled morning fog in naught but his bedclothes–which is to say the hair on his chest.

He stumbled beyond the door. The sun hadn't quite risen. Either that, or its rays hadn't been laced with enough heat to cast the cloudy air aside. Hudson itched himself as he looked left, then right. *Hmm.* He frowned. Something in the air wasn't right, and it wasn't just the fog. He went to the messenger's portal. With a massive thumb, he flipped the cap off the mounted box. *The messenger has been here.* A sniff, intuition, and a tingle inside told Hudson, *So has someone else.*

This morning, the birdsongs hit Hudson's ear not in wonderful notes, but in nightmarish tunes. They were screaming at him. *Run! Run! Stay cool, cool, cool.* Could he have been dreaming still?

When Hudson Steehl re-entered through the front door, he strode calmly to his kitchen, looked out the window and saw it. There was always merit to his anxiety, and this time, it swelled madly into ferocious enmity.

Not bothering to cover himself, nor lace boots to his ankles, Hudson exited through the side door, emerging barefoot at the head of his garden, although it could no longer be considered as such.

It was now a warzone.

Where tomato plants once flowered and bore fruit, where peppers had soaked up sun, where onions had been planted firmly in the soil to absorb nature's rain, all had been pillaged, desecrated, and destroyed. *My home is not a warzone.*

Hudson imprinted large feet into the rich dark ground as he floated like a ghost in a graveyard past his destroyed plants. Thorns from rose bushes lay about and occasionally stabbed at his heels, but Hudson felt little anymore, anyway. *As if the man hadn't taken enough of me ...*

He double-checked all his plants: onions, peppers, tomatoes, cucumbers, carrots, and all. "They've taken everything," he said to himself, incredulous. Not one morsel of sustenance remained. They hadn't bothered to leave Hudson with even another meal's worth of vegetables, *his* vegetables.

Standing over his fallen companions, Hudson felt a blaze go up within him, one that wouldn't smolder so easy as the rest. His eyebrows turned down into a pointed scowl as he recalled Lieutenant Luke's smug face and the way he'd have loved to turn it inside out.

XXIX

At the end of her morning rounds, Talia edged past the charred corner of the hospital building. Inside, repairs had been made to the emergency room so that it was functional and nothing more. Aesthetic repairs would come later.

"Doctor Shelly."

The tall blond in glasses came at once. Her suitcoat was unnaturally white, which was a good sign. It meant that no blood had been shed recently. "General."

"How have our men progressed?" asked Talia, though she could see behind Shelly that they were positively recovering, just slower than she wished. The three soldiers were sentient enough to eavesdrop on their conversation, but they were too immobile to look her way. One was sipping on something through a straw, his neck straining to reach that far. Another pretended to rest but was alert at the presence of the General. The last simply stared at the ceiling.

"Their release can be anticipated soon. As I've stated before, it's going to take–"

"Time. Yes, I know." Talia looked off to the side. She became caustic with impatience. "Good thing we have plenty of it."

Shelly said nothing, blinking lightly behind those glasses.

"Thanks for your help." Talia left then with a courteous nod. She was genuine in her appreciation for the medical staff at Camp Merciadel. They were a remarkably well-trained team. Still, she hated the sight of wounded soldiers.

Her next stop was the training grounds just outside. From afar, beneath the shadow of a large oak, Talia, in a camo long-sleeve and trim black pants, was invisible to her men and women. She watched as they trained, somewhat dissatisfied. Or maybe it was the discomfort associated with change that she found so unnerving. *Orian.* His name seemed to sum up her thoughts of him. A rule-breaker, a natural rebel, a maverick in his own right. Talia didn't know how, but he'd managed to convince her that changing strategy was appropriate.

"It's such a r-r-risk," Neal had warned her as they conversed in her office.

"Stupid, I know. I'm not even considering it."

"Is that why we're t-talking about it?"

She had been standing at the throw line, knives in hand. One sunk into the center of her target. "Our scheme has worked so well for so long. The balls on that boy to challenge … everything. It drives me mad."

"Must be l-like looking in a m-mirror, huh?"

Talia turned to him, eyes narrowed. Her mouth hung open, ready to retort, but she couldn't deny the validity of his claim. She'd always been a rule-breaker herself. *And now as General, I'm creating rules on behalf of a people. How ironic.*

After a few more detailed conversations with Neal and Commander Cael, they could no longer refute Orian's suggestions.

"We'll begin training this week," Cael said in front of her desk. Before leaving, he wondered, "Do we consult Orian throughout? This is all new to me, and he seems to understand it better than I could."

"No." Talia shot him down aggressively. Then, "Maybe."

And now she saw that training in progress, and she couldn't avoid the truth that Orian's scheme was brilliant. It was a risk, as Neal had stated. But Neal always calculated risks, even if they were negligible. It was his nature.

There, beside her commander, was Orian. He directed Talia's men and women to their stations as if he'd been a leader his whole life. It came so naturally to him, to the point that Talia begrudged his ability. At times, she felt her position as General to be so rigid, confining her creativities. It hadn't felt natural to her, not at first. If only the boy wasn't so inclined to conflict …

Her eyes drifted cooly to Byron. Often, she contemplated his status as a Mercian. Sometimes, Talia wished to banish, castrate, and shave the hair off his head, all at once. Other times, she could admire him quietly. Byron was a great soldier who had saved many men. In life, it seemed that those who made the largest marks were destined to drive conflict as well.

Training would end soon, and Talia had a few points of discussion to review, both with Cael and Orian. She left the shade, and her boots crunched over a few acorns as she approached her men. They were leaning over, hands on knees, sucking in precious air when a few sets of eyes wandered to find her. One soldier straightened and slapped his partner's side so that he might do the same. Soon, they were all straight as planks.

"Dismissed." Cael saluted. The Mercian unit responded as one with salutes of their own. At his side, Talia stood tall, and her men left the grounds, sweaty and bruised.

"Orian," she called. The young man looked curiously to her, his dark skin reflecting shiny sweat. Instantly, he wound up beside them. "Tell me, do my men seem ready?"

"No," Orian and Cael said together. They shared wary glances, wondering who should continue.

Orian was brave, as always. "But they will be. A little more time, and–"

"What if we don't have time?"

"I don't need much."

"*We*," Cael corrected. He addressed the General. "The switch has many of them ... baffled, I guess you could say."

"Is this our best option, then? Or are we wasting our time?"

Orian appeared ready for her imposing stare. "No, General Talia. They're going to get it. We're so close, I can feel it. But one more thing ..."

"Yes?"

"If I'm going to be handing out instructions, no matter how subtle, shouldn't I receive a promotion of sorts? You know, that way your men feel a bit more compelled to listen?"

Cael looked to be just as amused as herself. Talia couldn't decide whether to laugh or berate Orian. To Cael, she said, "Dismissed, Commander."

He couldn't stifle the chuckle as he left. Cael was several feet away when, between his laughter, he mumbled, "Good luck, kid."

"So?" Orian asked the General.

"Walk with me," Talia instructed.

Orian did.

Day turned to evening as blinding brightness gave way to brilliant sky, where the sun was an orb shedding its redness over the clouds. Winds grew still and so did the camp.

Their boots thudded on stone as Talia led the young man. In her chest, she felt something foreign, almost like she could sense the beat of her heart yet again. It had been ages since she'd felt such a sensation, probably since … *Ardosia.* But that was before the island had curdled in her mind like old milk. She once looked favorably upon that place. No longer.

And yet, beside Orian, she swore herself human. What was this boy doing to her? Had she come to enjoy his presence? In her mind and heart, she knew they were kindred spirits, seeking justice in the world. Daily, Talia shook, worried, and scratched. It was the anxiety within her that commanded leadership. She wondered if Orian felt it, too.

"You're a troublemaker, Orian. I can tell your nature is that of an earthquake. You shake the ground and create unimaginable waves. I'm scared that you may be too reckless for your own good."

Unfazed, the boy looked at her. "But?"

"What do you mean, *but*?"

"I can tell there's a but, because if there wasn't a but, you wouldn't still have me guiding your men in this new effort of ours, would you? Speaking of ... how about that promotion?"

Talia was almost stunned, but her intrigue was made even more evident through her toothy grin. "Did I mention your avarice? Greed only serves to hurt, young man."

"Quit that!" he shot back, offended.

"Quit what?"

"Calling me boy, young man, squire, all that bull–"

"What would you have me call you?"

Orian stammered. "Uh, well ... not that."

Talia nodded. She was taking him to her office where they would sit and talk business, just the two of them. If she felt like it, she might even pour herself a drink. Orian too, if he asked. But she need not get ahead of herself.

"You're right," she said.

"About?"

"The *but*. There is a but."

"Mhm."

By now, they had concluded their walk. Side-by-side, they stood in the building's shadow, where an elevated landscape of daylilies, petunias, and shrubs edged the siding. The bed ended beside the door that led to her office.

"The words do escape me when it comes to you." At his excitement, her eyes grew cold. "Don't get ahead of yourself, boy ... I mean, Orian. No, I'm not giving you a promotion, even if your wish is to receive it only in title, *but* I will say I've seen you in action, I've watched the way in which you conduct yourself and the men who serve me and Camp Merciadel ... you remind me almost of General Andrew."

His brow crowned. "You've talked about Andrew before. Who was he?"

Talia told him. Everything from the mentor to the father to the martyr he was ... she laid it out before him. Her intent was not to flatter, though it may have come off as such.

"Must've been a cool guy," Orian said.

"He was a true man, but as with everyone, he had a fatal flaw."

"Which was?"

Suddenly, the door to the building swung open, revealing Neal in a turquoise shirt, glasses invariably pressed tightly to his face. He walked in on the conversation late, but he seemed to pay it no mind.

Talia was sure to catch Orian's eye. "His desire to lead brought him to the front of the pack, where he lost his life."

Orian's chin rocked slowly in understanding. "Ah."

They shared a solemn glance. Talia understood that General Andrew had never hoped to guide men just to be seen as greater than. It was forever his goal to show those at his back a face of courage in times where seemingly none could be found. He wanted to prove to them that he would never ask something of his men that he wouldn't do himself. And if any should fall, he wished that he would be the first of them. Eventually, General Andrew had received his wish. It took Talia many years to understand that whether dying in battle with greatest honor or dying in the corner shaking with tears, both outcomes saw that you would never be with your family again, even if the only family you had was a band of fighting brothers. While the General respected Orian's desire to lead, as if he were called to it, she didn't want to see the boy die trying to prove his worth as a man.

"G-general. I hope I-I'm not imposing."

"No," she said, offering a squinty grin while maintaining her visual embrace with Orian. Kindly anticipating a one-on-one debriefing, Talia hadn't counted on Neal still being in the office. "We were just finishing up. Orian, dismissed."

The young man saluted. "Ma'am." Instead of walking directly to his living quarters, Orian bounced up onto the sliding block wall that contained the flowerbed. His arms became wings that balanced as he teetered left and right.

Neal couldn't help but be distracted by the reckless behavior. "W-w-whoah! Hey, th-that's not a g-g-good idea! Get d-down!" Frantically, he went over to offer his hand, but Orian didn't take it, instead tip-toeing along the blocks. Orian had to have been wary of panic settling in Neal's stomach, which is probably why he went all the way to the end, where he launched himself high and came down in a somersault, nearly stopping the poor assistant's heart in that instant.

Neal gasped in horror. "Y-y-y-you don't even k-know the r-r-risks associated with a j-jump from th-that height."

Laying a comforting hand over Neal's shoulder, Talia couldn't help but chuckle as he flinched and stifled a scream. "It's alright, Neal. Orian, tell Neal you're sorry for worrying him."

With a final salute, Orian smiled. "Sincere apologies, Neal. I'll see you tomorrow, eh?"

"N-n-not if the L-Lord is good."

At that, Orian hustled contentedly to his quarters.

Talia ushered a petrified Neal through the office door and into her own space, where she sat at her desk, thinking.

"W-w-what is it?" Neal could sense a disturbance in her.

"Nothing," she lied. *It's that boy ... man, whatever he is.* She'd spent many years knowing that the sputtery assistant before her was the only man she could trust. Even Cael struggled to secure her confidence. And then there was Orian. It would take years before Talia could even begin to consider the word trust. He was a stranger, but that didn't change her instinct, which when it came to him, was different than most.

No one had ever risen to rank so quickly. And this boy had only been here for a short time. Talia would never give Orian any kind of promotion. There were soldiers much more tenured, much stronger, who deserved the position of Colonel. Morale would only be decimated if she were to offer the promotion to a complete stranger, although Orian couldn't much be labeled as such.

Loath to admit it, Talia didn't consider Orian a stranger because she and him were nearly one and the same. He was just not quite as mature, not so familiar with the word *consequence.*

Neal adjusted his glasses like they hadn't already been snug. He was intuitive. "He is a s-scrambler."

Pressing her lips together, Talia understood what he meant. Orian was a twisting tornado, tearing roofs off houses, lifting foundations, and whirling those who should cross his path. There was no doubt he caused mayhem, but Talia wondered if he was the type of twister not yet discovered. Maybe people, places, or things weren't left destroyed and destitute in his wake. What if, instead, he made them better? Talia feared the possibility that she was just beginning to be swept up by his torrent. Would he spit her out and leave her bruised and torn, or would he raise her and Camp Merciadel to new heights?

"That he is."

"Y-y-you still believe in th-this plan?"

"I do."

"Okay. Just be c-careful. He's b-b-bullheaded. I have inferred that much."

Dim beams slid through wooden shades, lighting the space well enough. They warmed Talia's back, seemingly offering her more support.

"That's just it," she said. "Maybe it's time we messed with a bull."

His tiny hut hadn't grown at all, and he hadn't placed anything inside. A bed and a desk had already been arranged within when he arrived at Camp Merciadel, and they were all that adorned his quarters still. Despite that, he found the claustrophobia-inducing rectangle to feel more like home each day.

Orian sauntered to the desk, where a tablet and some tools rested face-down. He'd convinced IT to loan him the tablet screen a few days ago. Inside the building, it was dark, hues of purple and blue cast on the walls and several rows of monitors. Orian couldn't believe his eyes when he had run into none other than …

"Trixie!"

"Orian? That you? Well, I'll be … I di'n't think you made it off that damn island, boy. Never saw you when they brought us here! Heard them talkin' 'bout some dumb young Ardosian with an O-name. Should've known it was you."

"Yeah," Orian had shrugged. "I took the scenic route."

For half an hour, the two of them caught up. Most of Orian's time was spent listening to Trixie explain how she got assigned to IT. "I think that main girl, the General they call her, she liked me enough to give me a good spot, you know? So here I am, tappin' keys all day in the 'good fight'."

Orian later explained that her conspiracy about the dolphins in Ardosia's lake had been true. "Of course it's true," she said. Orian asked, "How did you know?" Trixie just grinned. "I have my sources." Trixie seemed to ponder her dolphin conspiracy, and if Orian wasn't mistaken, he'd given her an idea. The light popped in her head and came shining through her face. But nothing more was said.

After Trixie found a tablet for him to borrow, she asked when it might be returned. "Eventually," he said. Orian would keep his word, but at the moment, he had too much use for technology. As for the tools, he slipped a few of them in his pocket when he was sure no one was looking.

Beat and worn from another day's training, Orian should have gone to rest. From the chair at his desk, he considered the folds of the comforter, the plumpness of the pillow. The mattress was firm, but he didn't mind it. Yet all that interested him was not atop the bed, but rather what was below.

He bent low, grunting. It required much effort to haul the lump of metal out from underneath, even with Orian's increased strength. Training had pasted muscle to his body like a baker slaps frosting onto cake. When he succeeded at last and hoisted the drone onto his desk, Orian took a moment to look down at his chest, arms, and shoulders. No doubt they were larger than ever before and even more toned. Not only was he beginning to look like a soldier, but he was starting to feel like one, too.

The tablet came to life. For an hour, the tools worked their magic, occasional sparks flying from the machine. Orian nearly lit his shirt on fire once, and it made him laugh. He fiddled and tinkered until the buzzing of the wings came at last. Orian backed up an inch. "Good," he smiled at the repair. With more work and lost sleep, Orian would have the drone up and running … and then he'd really be losing sleep.

Twenty-five feet tall was the carbon-fiber barrier, now complete. When the sun gleamed off its edge, rainbow pixels of purple, blue, and sometimes orange were brought to life. Vardus had felt secure within the Wall, knowing the ample protection it provided. Now atop its edge, he felt tall as the Tower in the background. Professor Yjn was there, too. Together, they stood solemnly at the edge of the jungle, past the lake. Far below them, free from the cage he'd grown in, was Woody.

"You are free now!" Vardus called down to the tiger that was now almost full-grown.

Although the cat didn't understand, it prowled at the edge of the Wall, aiming gratitude toward its master. It was either that or malice. To Vardus, it made no difference.

"Where will he go?" Yjn wondered.

"Wherever he wishes." The President watched as the Bengal tiger plodded over the sand. It must have felt strange against his paws. All Woody had ever known was the hardwood beneath his cage and the grass he pissed on. "He won't make it far."

Professor Yjn laid confusion on him. "What do you mean?"

"In the wild," Vardus said placidly. "He was raised like a housecat and will act like one for the rest of his life. Housecats can hardly support themselves, even when humans are around."

"You didn't train him?"

The President guffawed. "Only the wild can offer a cat the proper training, just as only a professor can teach children to read, write, and speak."

"He's just going to die, then?" Yjn was peering down at the tiger as it lost focus on them and began flinging sand around with its curious paws. "Maybe it will learn to live on its own."

"Perhaps he could, but he'll have no way to hunt, no way to gather food, and he'll be eaten by the others eventually. The jungle is no place for the weak."

Yjn didn't understand. "Why can't he hunt? Isn't that an instinct?"

"Perhaps," he said again. "But without claws, he'll have to batter his prey to death."

"Without claws? Wh-what …" she trailed off.

Now Woody was sniffing at the foliage, marveling at its allure. The massive orange cat pounced against a tree, jumped into vine, and rolled over the ground. Then, as if he'd forgotten the island and Vardus entirely, the tiger scampered into the jungle and melded into the brush. James's pet was gone.

"You've got to save him, Vardus," Yjn's shaky voice urged. "Leaving an animal helpless may as well be murder. It's-it's, I don't know … it's inhumane."

James rested both hands behind his back, regarding the merciless jungle with unaffectionate eyes. The President of Ardosia had done many things in his life that none could come to understand, not until the fruits of his action were gleaned. That was the burden of visionaries. Many struggled to see the world in the same light, and few were humble enough to swallow their doubts. "He still has a chance, though slim." He turned to his esteemed professor. "They call lions 'King of the Jungle", but it was a fool who coined them as such. It is tigers who reign supreme in the wild. Tigers are the true kings."

Yjn said nothing, her eyes swelling red. Maybe she'd lost sleep as of late.

"Our friend Woody, however, is a message. To the jungle, to the people, to the world. To all who should find him, whether he be dead or alive, they'll know him as proof that someone has conquered the true kings. Someone has risen above them. And they'll know something else, too."

Professor Yjn drooped slightly in defeat and asked, as though it was her duty, "Which is?"

"All weaponless beings cannot attack. Whether we arm ourselves with knowledge or arrows or claws, we should not forget their inclination to war." Vardus looked out over the vast jungle as he said this.

The younger professor shook her head erratically, in short, subtle bursts. "I … I don't understand."

Vardus placed a gentle palm against Yjn's backside. A gentle squeeze might comfort her, he thought. He could reason with her confoundment, as the line between peace and perpetual bloodshed was incredibly thin, and it was often blurry. "Someday, you will." *The fate of all societies rests in the ambition of visionaries and in the resignation of all others.*

After Woody's release, Professor Yjn was sent back to her floor while James returned to his office, or room, or study, however he wished to use it. Woody's glass enclosure had been removed, so there was now more space than ever–space enough for him to think, breathe, and decompress. But his meditation would have to wait.

"Matthew, come in."

The bald assistant waltzed through the double doors in a gray suit, per usual. "Sir," he said on the opposite end of his desk.

Vardus whirled a finger about, since he had no time to waste. "Full debriefing on reconnaissance, yield … you know the drill. All territories taken and discovered, I need to know of them."

Matthew had been ready. His pudgy hands scrolled confidently until he pulled a page up for Vardus to see. "Your tactic to deploy recon teams saw tremendous success, Mr. President. Not only did yields sky-rocket for present farms and villages, but we were also able to ascertain new assets from subsequent tribes we encountered on our way."

"They submitted easily, then?"

"Easily enough."

Vardus knew what that meant. A bruise or two had been inflicted for the acquisition of loyalty. After viewing the yield report, he almost couldn't believe their success.

Leaning closer, James did a double take. The enthusiasm threatened to spring forth from him in a bout of celebration. "List all our territories. This is ... absurd." He smiled.

Matthew scratched at his cheek before sliding through the list. He began with those who had provided for Ardosia for years: "The Tojika, Urelia, and Zombiki tribes were first to submit their crops. Tribes Shomwe and Leistor were discovered as well." Matthew listed farms like Smith, Hart, Wenitz, and more, who were also mightily generous with their crop. Even with their increased contributions, there was still much unaccounted for, which Matthew told derived from "... a small village across a pond in the jungle. They called themselves Bothrania." Both Matthew and Vardus chuckled at that. "And then it says here that a contingent stumbled upon a hut with a large garden outside of it. Lieutenant Luke reported there, indicating that 'all produce was graciously donated.'"

Vardus had been listening closely before, but something alerted him here, drawing his attention even closer. Lieutenant Luke had a reputation. "A hut? In which village?"

"Um," Matthew scrolled further, tapping occasionally on the screen. "Says here that the hut was by itself."

Vardus leaned forward in his chair. "By itself? As in ... no civilization nearby?" James fought to think. He knew all territories within fifty miles of his island ... or so he thought. Was there one he was forgetting? *A single hut ... who has the knowledge and ability to support themselves, to survive out there alone?* A mighty pang melted Vardus's insides with anxiety. "Look further in the notes. Do we have a description?"

The assistant stammered. "Uh … all I have is a hut, garden–"

"Not a description of the location," Vardus spat. "I need a description of the man."

Fumbling with the tablet, Matthew finally came up with an answer. "They say he was old, white hair, kind of quiet, and … really large?"

James rose from his desk, slowly. He was pensive, deep in thought. Then in one swift motion, he gathered the chair he'd been sitting on and threw it headlong into the stained-glass window. "*FUCK!*" Glass shattered and fell to the floor in sharp, tiny pieces. The chair clattered against the hardwood, its arm malformed. "*FUCK, FUCK, FUCK!*" It was seemingly the only word he knew.

"Mr. President, what's the matter?" Matthew looked alarmed.

Slamming his palms down on the desk, Vardus gave his Right Hand a crazed look. It took him a long while to speak, so Matthew sat uncomfortably in his rage, waiting. Finally, James managed, "It's goddamn the man himself. Who else?"

Matthew reviewed the description, reading it several times over before it clicked in his head. How hadn't he understood earlier? When it came to him, he grew quiet. "Oh, my…"

Without his consent, Vardus's men had stolen from the man whom Matthew had replaced as Vardus's Right Hand, the one who no sane brigade of men would be so brave or rash to challenge, and the only man who Vardus truly feared. "Hudson Steehl."

Working madly to redress the issue, Matthew brainstormed myriad solutions to their problem, but he would not find one.

"We had a deal, God damnit!" Vardus couldn't contain himself. Hudson had been the size of a bear back then, and by the sound of it, he was even larger now. *Lord knows what'll happen when you poke him.* "Nobody was supposed to even set foot within a hundred yards of that man's property. I gave the direct order to *everyone*, did I not? Have I lost the ability to elucidate my speech in my years? Tell me, Matthew."

"I share your frustration, Mr. President." Adjusting his tie, Matthew calmed himself, effectively doing the same for James. "The order had always been clear. Obviously, this occurred by no fault of your own."

James slammed a fist on his desk once more. He was growing tired of disobedience. It had always been the bane to his existence. "Someone must pay."

It was not a question. "Lieutenant Luke," Matthew knew. James nodded, so his assistant asked, pointlessly, "The Coliseum?"

Ardosia's President had no need to nod. "Hell, give that son of a bitch Twister 1.0. His arrantly reckless head ought to melt immediately." James made sure Matthew understood his assignment before waving him out the door.

But before Matthew made it, Vardus stopped him. "Wait!"

Matthew blinked.

"No." James took a deep breath, swallowing. Shutting his eyes, he thought deeply. How could Lieutenant Luke be punished for greed? Vardus, while upset that orders had been directly disobeyed, could admire an ambitious man. He'd told his high-ranking officers to *take command* and *return with what is ours.* This held true in both war and conquest. Besides, James was a forgiving leader. "Tell

Luke he's under surveillance, and his name will surely be called next. I'm feeling extra gracious today."

Matthew nodded, slightly confused. "So ... no Coliseum?"

"That is correct."

His eyes flitted to the ground and back up. "Yes, sir."

"Dismissed."

Vardus needed to be alone.

Shaking with rage, he inhaled deeply to alleviate his stresses, but they would not go easily. A tinge of remorse bit at him as he observed the colorful broken shards strewn about the floor. *Jolly*, he thought. It would take his people at least two days to fix and replace the stained-glass window. That's how long it took the last time.

Bitterly he rode to his bed, where he did not contemplate rest for a moment. He simply stood there, overlooking the crinkled sheets. They were dark and gray, a void in which he could momentarily lose himself.

Disorder, Vardus scoffed internally. It was eating at his island like an airborne venom, infecting all who should breathe. Ivan, Lieutenant Luke, and many before them. Who would be next? Yjn? Matthew? James could hardly bear to wonder at who might fall ill to the virus of defiance. It was a problem with people, and it had been since the dawn of time. Only he could resolve it. *Twister has to come soon*, Vardus thought scornfully. *Before it's too late.*

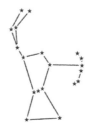

S cars, bruises, shooting pains, and all travail. They were meant to engender growth and resolve, designed specifically for discomfort. Without them, the gift of healing would have no use.

Orian told himself all of this as he rose groggily from the cot that must have been designed for an infant. He'd been resting on it for the duration of his stay at Camp Merciadel, which had risen to ... five weeks? Six? He could not tell. Orian had discovered that, when given a purpose, time worked more swiftly, to warn that there may not be much of it left. He studied the firm mattress with contempt for a moment but immediately reminded himself, *You have a bed to sleep on now. It's better than dirt.*

Training was doing a number on him. At first, he expected to harbor the physical pains and work through them with grit and sheer toughness, but those had slowly begun to give way to anger and impatience. Someday, his body would adjust, right? Rearing his shoulders back and moving his arms in a ponderous circular motion, Orian was able to work some of the stiffness out. He was grateful, too, that although the soreness was ever-present, it didn't seem quite so bad as it had when he first trained with swords.

Persistence and optimism. They had gotten Orian off the pitiful island of Ardosia, through the jungle, past a bear, a boar, and a panther, and all the way to Camp Merciadel–a place he could call home. Yet even here, the two tenets of tenacity had their uses.

The sand-colored shirt worked slowly over his chest. He latched the button of his pants. Then a yawn escaped him, high and exaggerated. Waking before or alongside the sun had been the most difficult adjustment of all. It may not have been so arduous for Orian if he'd allot himself the proper time for rest, instead of working on…

Shoot!

Before Orian left his quarters, he double-checked his desk, where he had accidentally left the drone out in the open. The white paint on its metal body was still scratched, but all other parts were in working order after he spent most of the previous night tinkering. Gently, he stowed it beneath the cot before rushing out the door.

Rusty hinges rode alongside the doorframe, and they squealed when Orian went to shut it behind him. No matter how carefully he tried to suppress the annoying sound, the hinges did not seem to care. They yelled at him, regardless. Sometimes, depending on Orian's early-morning mood, he might yell back. "*Shhhh!* I have neighbors who are trying to sleep."

And he did. Orian had yet to meet his neighbors, however, as their schedules did not align with his. They were more of the common folk, likely working in the textile mill. Orian knew their jobs were equally as important as his, if not more so, but they rose later than him and, consequently, returned later as well. Since their schedules were opposing, there was no time to bump into them, not even to talk about the weather, or politics. After his promotion from farm hand to soldier, Orian could have been stationed near the other soldiers, where he *would* frequently interact with neighbors, but he had taken a liking to his shack, for no knowing of his own, and requested to stay there. Maybe he enjoyed being different than most. Sticking out, to him, wasn't always so bad.

As the hard soles of his boots collided with the stone path, the *tha-thump* of Orian's steady pace hadn't even been audible to him. His eyes were puffy still, he could feel them. His head was seemingly filled with a sleeping liquid that both aggravated his skull and begged him for rest. The dreariness would not leave him until the sun rose, which, as he looked past architecture and spotty trees toward the horizon, would be relatively soon.

On a regular day, Orian might have been forded another half-hour of dreams. Rather than dwelling on the thought of lost sleep, he wondered at the topic of his meeting. Two evenings prior, Talia had requested that she and him meet alone before training. "Don't be late," she had sternly warned him. Then she sent him off without clarifying the issue at hand.

Ever since, Orian had pondered whether they would discuss the new strategy. So far, its implementation had been a success in Orian's eyes, albeit a slow one. As with all good things, it would take time.

Orian liked to think of the execution of his defense plan like an airplane. He used to watch those take off on the Internet on occasion. At the start of the runway, they were still, revving the engines, preparing for takeoff. Even as airplanes began to move, they were bound to the ground for quite some time. It wasn't until the front tire left the pad that an aircraft could even think about flight, and when the nose aimed for the sky, nothing could keep it down, not even gravity. Much like a successful takeoff, Orian's defense strategy began with the slow turn of a wheel before it could take flight. *And we're right there. I know it.*

In the still darkness of the morning, not even the birds had risen to sing their songs. The stars had receded to shine on the other half of the Earth, but the sun had yet to take its place.

At last, Orian acquired energy from an unknown source, and the *tha-thump* of his boots grew even steadier, his pace accelerating. *What if she wants to send me back to the farm?* Orian thought, perhaps unreasonably. It would not be the worst fate to befall him, should he have to return to Pake and his wife Kin, though the thought of the old woman's pies instilled a gagging dread in him.

Or maybe she was finally considering his promotion. Orian's face lit up at the possibility, but he knew it might never happen, surely not so soon. General Talia was a woman who worked slowly, to be safe, certain, and secure in her choices. Her decisions were never rash, not usually anyway.

Then what? He began to move with even greater dispatch. *Tha-thump, tha-thump, tha-thump,* his boots went. Her office was no more than another minute's walk away. *Tha-thump, tha-thump, WHOOSH.*

Orian yelped, startled by the sudden noise that brushed past his ear. The stone path had led him to the edge of a building constructed of concrete and clay, near the training grounds. Here, he paused. At his back, a rickety noise had interrupted the uniformity of his two-step. It was a familiar noise, almost like an ...

"Arrow." Orian calmly identified the weapon impaled between two stones, stones he had just traversed. Its wooden shaft was still rattling, the fletching at its end shaking violently. In the dark of the morn, Orian was forced to lean closer. *Byron?* was his first inclination. Perhaps the jock was playing a foul trick on him. Orian rolled his eyes, but another tip came slashing down from the air, missing him narrowly. It clattered against the concrete and clay structure.

"Byron, quit that!" he yelled into the darkness. "You're getting a little too close for–"

The sun had just then peeked lightly over the horizon, giving the sky enough guidance for Orian to see them. *Oh. My. God.* Subconsciously, he had seen them before, but they had been shielded from view by the black sky. There were so many of them, too many to think they could be real. Ranks so deep and numerous, they twisted and turned and carved the valley, melting peripherally into the mountain. Orian thought they *were* a part of the mountainous hills at first, discovering now that they were a separate entity of their own. His stomach curdled at the awful realization–Ardosia had sent them ... and they had sent them all.

Near the outer edge of camp, Orian was stunned. *They were never supposed to approach from this angle.*

NEVER. Then he wondered why in the flying fuck his tendency to freeze in the face of immediate danger had suddenly returned to him. They would not need to send another arrow over the fence for him to start scrambling. Orian slapped the inertia from his body. He was an object in need of some serious motion.

Orian darted.

Just then, another barrage of arrows came raining from the sky. Orian stumbled around the building, and it shielded him as his boots sent sand, gravel, and dust flying. Almost losing his balance from sprinting so quickly, Orian skirted and weaved through the camp's interior, where scattered trees and one-story buildings might provide him with cover.

In no time, Camp Merciadel's gates would be inundated by a sea of gray and white, doubling, maybe tripling Merciadel's entire population. It was an all-out Ardosian attack.

Orian thought naught of his meeting with Talia then. He had to raise an alarm. He had to alert the General's men that doomsday was suddenly upon them, whether they were ready for it or not.

Rushing madly toward the center of camp, where a lone guard would stand watch over the gate, Orian started to yell. It was his only hope.

"ATTACK! ARDOSIANS!"

To his luck, with no prevailing winds nor birdsong, sound carried over the camp effortlessly. Quickly, his warning must have reached the ears of the overnight guard, for a moment later, the horn bellowed its frightening tune.

Frantic, Orian yelled one more time, in hopes that he might awaken the soldiers. *"ARDOSIANS! THEY'RE ABOUT TO ATTA-"*

An explosion echoed over the grounds, drowning out his cries. It came from behind. Orian turned to see the most horrific mushroom cloud of smoke and fire emanating from the Eastern half of the camp. Orange craters glowed beneath the black. By his extrapolation, the destruction appeared awfully close to his living quarters. But there was no time to dwell on whether or not he might have a place to sleep at day's end. He would have to make it there first.

Orian didn't know how or when, but he managed to come across an alert, stout man in navy blue.

"Commander!" Orian yelled for his attention. Cael had been still as a gravestone as his eyes watched the plume rise in the distance. "Commander Cael! Over here!"

He was held captive by the sight of it, though it appeared that the experienced officer's eyes offered no more interest than they might at the sun of a new day. Orian was nearly perturbed at the Commander's ease. Then he remembered Cael's constant reminder. *If the war ain't tomorrow, you'll lose it.* What he meant was that a soldier was to prepare like the next day could be his last. Evidently, Commander Cael lived by that because he seemed unfazed, even now.

"Orian." The commanding officer spoke in a low tone. "Status report."

It was impossible for Orian to believe he could calm himself in such an instant. Tugging at every inner fiber was the desire to run and cry, to flee for his life, to wrap the nearest man in a desperate hug, even if it were Commander Cael. But his training had taught him to be better than that, and to let go of the fear that tied his legs, his arms, and his tongue. "If it isn't their entire unit, it's close. We won't have much time. In fact, I'd be willing to bet they've already breached our outer gate and will be coming this way. We can only hope they leave the common men and women alone."

Cael gave a skeptic glance. "Have you met Vardus?"

It took much of Orian's strength not to allow his head to droop. Ardosia's President was relentless and would attack likewise.

The officer was undeterred. "One unit must be sent to the neighborhoods, another to IT, and a final to the textile building. If those fail, so do we. Vardus isn't compassionate to begin with, so we can't expect him to be in war."

"So our defense …" Orian wondered. "What will we do?"

"What have we trained to do?"

"A defense plan that attacks, but I don't know if it'll work. I mean, none of our men were in position to start."

Cael's pointed chin rose as he smirked. "Good thing there's plenty of time for luring before we set the hook."

Orian nodded, understanding his assignment. The two men saluted one another and were off.

He felt so unprepared, so underqualified to organize an entire unit of men. In truth, Orian had no clue how the responsibility had fallen on his shoulders. When offered the chance to give his opinion, he had. Somehow, that had gotten him here.

Sprinting to the soldiers' quarters, Orian found them all moving frantically, entering and exiting the armory. There, some grabbed crossbows, others drew wooden bows. The rest found swords in their grasp. Seeing them, it occurred to Orian that he was without armor. He would need to don some, but the armor he owned was all the way on the other side of the property, in a shack that he wasn't sure existed any longer. He knew there was some to be found in the armory, but it was hopeless at best. *Better than nothing,* he conceded.

Before he could attempt to arm and defend himself, Orian had orders, a duty to fulfill. Now many Mercian soldiers, strong men with great will, seemed lost despite their training. Indecision had bitten and rendered them immobile, embroiled in brotherly feuds.

"We go here!" Private Kaija, the round-faced stout woman pointed South.

"No, no. You're to go this way. Trust me."

Who else might sew the stitching of doubt but Byron?

Orian called, "Byron! Enough. Kaija, proceed as normal. We move forth as we have trained."

Adjusting the pack slung over his shoulder that presumably held medical supplies, grenades, and a few other weapons, Byron held his head high in protest. "It'll never work. We don't have the time to find our positions. You've yet to experience the chaos of war, boy. It's something no one can train you for. Now is not the time for rookies to lead veterans."

Orian offered his hands. "I couldn't agree more. The order has come directly from Commander Cael."

That seemed to shut him up.

"Guerdo, Kaija, Simmons, and Tom." Orian pointed to each of them. They all responded promptly by lengthening their stature, placing either one or both hands behind them, depending on whether they brandished sword or crossbow. Guerdo's chains clinked at his side. Orian nodded to him last. "You know your assignments."

"Yes, sir!" they said in unison, each collecting and galvanizing their respective contingents. Then they were off, leaving a group of twenty or so behind.

"Byron," Orian called next. "I don't care how you do it, but you're to lead the rest to IT, the mill, and our neighborhoods. You'll have to split up, quickly."

"It may already be too late," Byron protested.

"It may." Orian's skin was warmed then as the sun flourished at the horizon. He stood still and soaked it in, knowing that their efforts may or may not prove to prevail. It didn't matter. They had to try.

Byron fell default to Orian, who was unmoving. "Alright," he said at last, not before an aggressive eye roll. Then, just like that, he was in leadership mode. "Charlie, to IT. You know it better than I do. Xavier, to textiles. Take your closest troops with you. If we're to die today, we'll want our brothers near us. The rest, you're with me."

Admittedly, Orian was floored by the broad man's sudden shift in demeanor. Byron was like that, able to flip the switch and turn into the perfect soldier. If only the switch got stuck in the "on" position …

Shadowed by the brilliance of the Eastern sky, the soldiers departed, their weapons clanking and swaying as they ran. Orian saw how bizarre it was to go off to war when the sun had just risen. There was never a good time for battle, not day, nor afternoon or night. Dawn was above all the most inappropriate time, but it was a matter he'd have to take up with an Ardosian soldier or two before he aimed to take their heads off.

Byron was last to leave. "Where will you go?"

"Wherever I am needed."

He nodded, respectfully and not. "Good luck."

Orian wasn't sure where he'd go. In training, he'd mostly been conductor and had overseen the task of giving himself an assignment. Yet he knew where he'd be. Byron had even said it himself. *If we're to die today, we'll want our brothers near us.* Orian would ambush those who entered by gate, alongside his partner Guerdo.

"We're early," Guerdo said when Orian reached him.

"Inscrutably."

Orian had found Guerdo and his contingent of men precisely where they were supposed to be. Stowed well within the property in an abandoned, cobwebbed building, they waited. It used to serve as a place to train in the winter before General Talia decided that enduring the cold would be more beneficial to her men. It smelled like old dust, dry and eerie. Every subtle movement echoed off the high arched ceiling that was barely visible in the unlit space. Orian couldn't believe they had made it here before the Ardosians arrived … surely they wouldn't be far off.

As Orian greeted his fellow Mercians with confidence, Guerdo studied him curiously. "Where'd you get the bib?"

"Hmm?" Orian wasn't sure what he'd meant until he looked down and saw the feeble leather covering his chest. "Oh … yeah. Kinda left my armor at home. Wasn't expecting …" he looked around at the dark, shallow room in which he and thirty others were huddled, waiting to spring an attack. "…this to happen."

Once more, Guerdo surveyed the leather over Orian's shoulders. "Training armor?"

"What gave it away?"

Chains rung as he shifted slightly. The thought that a single arrow could take Orian down must have distressed Guerdo, but he acted calm nonetheless. "You'll stay with me then."

"As if I had any other options."

Then they were quiet and motionless. Knowing what was to come, the screaming and crying, the fires and the blood … the death, it made Orian stir inside. He'd seen death once, and he may have caused it then, too. He thought back to the man he kicked into Ardosia's lake and how in his last breaths, the man had no words, only screams as porpoises ripped him apart.

Somehow, Orian had overlooked the fact that he may have to kill again as a soldier. *Soldiers don't kill*, he corrected himself. *They defend.* Still, he hoped his hand wouldn't be forced to *defend* too much, either.

"*Shh, shh, shh!*" someone from the darkness whispered. They paused to listen closer. "What is that?"

Together, the unit grew more still. Orian focused on the noise beyond the door but couldn't discern what it was. It sounded to him like the wind had picked up, maybe enough to cast branches through the air. How could it escalate so rapidly? Orian thought the morning air had been still as ever. He listened closer yet.

"Madre de Dios," Guerdo muttered. "They're burning it all."

Now he could hear it, too. Crackling embers, it could be no other sound, coming closer, swelling in strength, no doubt destroying the camp as it spread building by building.

A man became restless behind them. "Fuck this. We can't just let them burn our home to the ground! You're an idiot for this one, boy. General Talia, too, for putting *you* in charge. I knew this would be useless." He worked to spur others into action, standing and working toward the door. Luckily, there were enough to subdue him, though not without defensive retorts. "We're hiding like a bunch of women and children right now, not defending them."

Internally, Orian dealt with the quandary. His face might've shown it too if not for his training. For the sake of himself and the men he was with, he was stern, convictive. "We will stay. We have to. It pleases me no more than it does you to hear them pillage this place, but they outnumber us two-to-one, if not more. If we do not wait for the right time to strike, it will be more than architecture that burns to the ground. It'll be you and me, too." He could tell they were listening, but he also saw an opportunity to light a match of his own within the hearts of General Talia's best. "Right now, they think they have us cornered, halfway destroyed. Let's show them what Merciadel is, *who* Merciadel is, and how a real God-damned army wins."

Met with silence and many blank faces, Orian felt a nervous pang strike at his gut. Then one nod turned into two, and three. Soon, even the protestor himself huddled contentedly beside the other men, patiently awaiting his time.

Guerdo gently knocked Orian's shoulder with a closed fist. "Well said."

It wasn't long before hundreds of footfalls thundered about the area just outside. They came quickly, stopped for a moment, and then continued.

The Mercian unit were all waiting for their cue, staring their bloodthirsty desires into Orian, who would unleash them upon Ardosia's men eventually, not yet.

"Steady," Orian whispered.

Suddenly, the old structure seemed to get cloudy. One soldier coughed, and soon many had fists clenched at their mouths. *They're setting our site ablaze*, Orian panicked momentarily. He could tell the Mercians wanted to leave and that they were beginning to question if he was suicidal by the wide-eyed glares he received.

"Steady," he repeated, breathing in deeply before the smoke could fill his lungs. Many others followed suit.

Orian knew he must wait for the exact right time. It was the only way it would work perfectly according to plan. Boots were still bounding outside, and he would wait until their sounds ceased. Catching Ardosia in the back was how they would win.

Shutting his eyes, Orian went deep into concentration. He heard Pake's voice then. *Don't 'magine you've been in love?* To this day, Orian couldn't say whether he had. Being here with these men, soon battling to the death with them, Orian felt differently. Pake had told him that you can fall in love with someone or some*thing*. Although Orian had yet to discover truly what love was, he knew he thrived off adversity, craved the fight for justice and freedom, and would rather be nowhere else in the world than here, within the walls of a burning building, nevertheless. Perhaps it was love of struggle. Perhaps not. Pake had assured him of love's power. He would soon discover for himself how powerful it could be.

Smoke was beginning to fill his lungs, but the Ardosians had passed. It was time.

"Now!" Orian called.

Funneling into the light aided by both the fires of the sun and the fires of hell, the Mercian attack was strong. Like minnows in a stream, the Ardosian unit had been led precisely to the cage, where an open field in the middle of camp caught them in between Mercian ranks from all sides. The collective look on their faces was one of utter shock, and it stayed that way as arrows struck their chests, necks, and stomachs. Dandelions and tall grasses laid idly and drank their blood as their bodies fell like sacks.

Ardosians toppled, much like Orian envisioned the Tower might someday, and they had not a clue where the attack was from, perhaps because it came from everywhere. The Mercian archers had climbed rooftops of the few unlit buildings to fire the second round of arrows. There was panic within the Ardosian cause then. Countless opposing orders left them in a state of confoundment and uncertainty while numbers perished at an alarming rate. Just as Orian had planned, they were sitting ducks.

He saw across the field, atop the roofs that had not been set aflame. From left to right, the Mercian archers in their black and gold armor remained untouched as they launched arrow after arrow. Even from such a great distance, General Talia stood out amongst the ranks, with her golden headscarf concealing everything but her eyes. Arrows left her crossbow with dispatch. She was aiding her men, but their efforts proved fruitful for only so long.

Finally, the Ardosian military began to disperse. Their massive cloud of gray and white had fallen apart as they rushed for the outer edges of the field.

Orian had seen this all and had expected as much. Guerdo was beside him then, chains dangling at his side. They looked at one another as Guerdo said, "For Merciadel."

"FOR MERCIADEL!" they shouted in unison as the camp burned brightly at their backs.

Then the field became a storm of swords as all those with a blade sprinted toward the fleeing Ardosians. It was up to them to extinguish what remained of Vardus's men, which was many still. Even considering those who had already fallen, Orian estimated that they were yet outnumbered.

Swordsmen from all angles rushed the field, where the tall grass was ignorant with morning dew, as if nature had not a clue that many men would die today. Maybe nature didn't care.

Orian and the soldiers who accompanied him trampled a bright green path as their passion and soul stood behind every roar, barreling toward the enemy. The black and gold steel mesh adorning the chests of the Mercian unit made little sound. Even as they ran, it did not clink nor clang like armor of old. It was advanced and silent, making the first sword strike a stark cry that cracked the air like lightning. And the storm followed.

An inseparable duo, Orian and Guerdo moved, whirled about, and cornered many men. The first fell at Guerdo's hand, and so did the second. Orian hoped the entire battle might continue likewise, but his hand was forced quickly.

Suddenly, he found himself pitted against a short, broad man, whose cheeks were dotted with wrinkly age. The Ardosian had looked him in the face with little emotion, no cries, roars or screams. Offering a simple assessment, as though he were aiming to stick a sword through a straw man, his movements at Orian were robotic. They were effective, Orian could see, and he grunted fiercely to deflect the first several blows, but even an inexperienced soldier knew that all weapons were twice as deadly when a heart was attached at the helm—swords, spears, arrows, and pens alike. Performing the same move he had on Guerdo in training many weeks ago, Orian flustered the man in pale armor by setting up a flank. His sword drove through flesh like an ax through wood. It was tough at first, but Orian knew he had many more splinters to create. The body slumped to the ground like a pillow with blank, lifeless eyes.

With no time to dwell on his status as a murderer or a defender, or whatever he was, Orian forged on. The second man fell, his white armor turning red. Then the next, and the one after that, too. Orian's shoulders, back, sides, and all were screaming loudly as ever. Adrenaline kept him going.

It seemed victory would be achieved rather easily as Orian and his dueling partner trumped every challenger. And then a tall soldier stood high over Orian. Outmatched in both height and reach, Orian knew he would need his partner to best this man. But Guerdo was in a battle of his own. Forded no time to think or plan, Orian was caught off guard as the sword came spiraling toward his face. It was all he could do to parry. Stumbling backward, he deflected the next set of blows. Orian was on the defensive, with no way to attack. The Ardosian was too swift.

Backing away to create space, Orian's boot was caught on a small hump in the field, and his body lurched sideways. He'd always been upset when he was referred to as "boy". Splayed on the ground, even further below his colossal attacker, Orian never felt so helpless, so much like a boy. The Ardosian wasted no time, raising his sword in the air, and as the glimmering steel tip drove down, it stopped suddenly.

Orian had shut his eyes, expecting to open them to the underworld. At the sound of a blade slicing through flesh and bone, Orian opened them. The Ardosian had been stabbed through the heart, and standing behind him was none other than Guerdo.

"Call for me when you need help next time, okay?" Guerdo tossed the Ardosian aside, his auburn hair and beard a swampy mess of sweat and blood.

"Yes, sir." Orian was helped up, but he was given no opportunity to thank his savior. They were bombarded at once.

As if falling into a dream, Orian lost himself and became oblivious to all those around, besides the men he encountered. He'd come so close to death that the world hardly felt real anymore. Suddenly, taking the lives of men had become simpler, less emotional. The seconds felt like minutes, and somehow the hours did too. Time had become immaterial.

In the heat of battle–which was a literal scorching heat with the ongoing blaze at the field's perimeter–Orian and Guerdo had been separated. After besting one more man, Orian scanned the field frantically for his partner, until he was caught in another battle. Orian would have to hold his own.

This Ardosian was younger and seemed to operate with a tad more emotion than the one before him, because he laughed heartily when he saw Orian and the cowhide on his chest. Glaring, Orian thought, *My armor may be weak, but my sword is not.* He lashed out at the islander and fought valiantly in a duel with him before emerging victorious once more.

Then, as quick as a switch, the dark cloud that had passed over the field was gone, and it was over.

Orian's chest was heaving dramatically, spattered blood dripping down the leather pressed tight against him. It took a moment for the blur in his vision to recede. When it did, Orian wished desperately for its return. His mouth gaped as he scanned the remnants of his first battle.

Lost to the profusion of fallen bodies, Ardosian and Mercian alike, the field was no longer dominantly green. To Orian, it was gray and white and red and black and gold and awful. As far he was concerned, the scarce patches of green were invisible.

Succumbing to the immense array of immutable destruction, Orian couldn't help but come to his knees. He ached worse than he ever had before. If not for the Mercians who remained standing, Orian might've lashed out his eyes or fallen upon his own sword to avoid the flurry of despair that dragged him down. Orian saw many of his comrades, living but haggard, and many more who laid in the grass. Camp Merciadel had won, but at what cost?

Fires burned still, though some were weak. Turning, Orian looked to see what remained of the men in Guerdo's contingent. *One, two, three, four, five …* he counted. *Six?* He couldn't have counted right, but with such a small number, it was impossible to get it wrong. Discouraged, he counted again anyway, coming up with the same number three times in a row. There had to have been thirty men with him before the battle began. How had so many fallen? And where was Guerdo?

The moment Orian asked himself, he saw six men who came together, forming a half-circle at a nearby point in the field. Their eyes were cast down as they sheathed their swords in solidarity. When one of them saluted, Orian feared the worst. There was no more room for despair in his soul, no remaining corners in his body for sorrow. Yet a jarring rage had wiggled its way in. Like a disease, it spread throughout him, transforming the heavy blue and gray misery into a searing red fire.

He didn't jump or run or cry out. Instead, Orian lifted himself and ambled ponderously to the body. It was as slow as he'd ever walked. Inside, he thought if he could delay the inevitable for long enough, it may never come true.

Upon reaching the half-moon of men, Orian found the sight to be more than disturbing. Guerdo's mutilated face could hardly be recognized as his own. It made Orian hope despicably that it was someone else. It was a fragile hope that was shattered immediately at the sight of four golden chains.

Waving grass reached up around Guerdo's body. Perhaps it was calling him to a better life. Orian knelt at his side, grasping the chains with one hand. They were cold, like Guerdo's corpse. Gazing upon the face that had seemingly collapsed upon itself and the bloody singed beard on his chin, Orian couldn't find it within himself to shed an honorary tear for his fallen comrade. That made him angry, too. Had Merciadel's training turned him into a monster, incapable of demonstrating any emotion?

"Good man. Guerdo was a good man."

Orian looked up to a dark fellow, whose eyes were welling with tears, but he never allowed one to fall. Longing to say something on Guerdo's behalf, Orian opened his mouth, but nothing came out. He was mute, silenced by grief.

In decorous accord with their training, each of the six men quickly paid their dues with a word or two or a nod. Then they marched toward the field's center, where all Mercians who remained were gathering.

Knelt at Guerdo's side, Orian knew his training. He wasn't to hang around long. But in his mind, he knew he would never be able to escape this moment. As his eyes shut painfully, he ripped the chains from Guerdo's pants. He clenched them tightly. *Your burdens are now mine, my friend,* he thought, knowing he would need to add one more link to the golden loops. Orian stowed them in his own pocket, leaving his fallen partner on the cold wet ground.

At the center of the field was a congregation of beaten and bloodied men. In between them all was Commander Cael, donning armor as royal blue as his usual garb. General Talia was there too, seemingly unscathed. There was a reason she was a leader of soldiers. She was an elite one herself.

Low mumblings of the crestfallen hung in the air. Byron and two others had rejoined the group as well, and they were conversing with the General. Orian didn't need to be an expert in body language to decipher the sort of news they brought.

"There were too many, General." Byron wiped at his brow, later placing his hand defeatedly on hip. For the first time since Orian had known him, his chin had fallen, and his low voice had grown raspy and choked. "IT and the textile buildings … we managed to salvage them."

"And the houses? Our women and children? *Your* women and children?" General Talia had undone her golden scarf. It was now curled up in a ball, crushed by the force of her shaking hand. She wasn't angry. She was scared. "Now is not the time for you to finally shut your mouth, Byron. Speak to me."

"We lost many of them. The Ardosians were overwhelming us, flooding our ranks with numbers no amount of talent could match. We told them not to, but the women and children began to fight, too. We were overrun, and if not for them, none of us would be standing."

"How many?"

"We stopped counting after fifteen and came here to provide backup."

Did that mean fifteen women and children dead? Gone?

"And what of our infrastructure? Our gate, fence, buildings ..."

Byron's sky-blue eyes focused on the General. He said nothing, only shaking his head.

The corset of armor she wore constricted Talia so that her frame could not be reduced to bent-over sobs. It held her straight. Her voice began to shake as much as the rest of her body, despite her obvious efforts to maintain composure. "Charlie? Xavier?"

The two men who accompanied Byron shook their heads slowly.

All of them were huddled in a tight circle, except for one. Outside of it was Orian, a lone wolf, separate from the pack. He couldn't help but feel like the weight of the losses was on his shoulders. *It was my plan that got them all killed.* If he'd have shut his mouth, maybe none of this would've happened. *Or the outcome would have been worse. We could have all died.* Orian wasn't sure what to believe.

Just then, Byron saw him standing a few feet from their circle. The scowl that crossed his face was malignant, maybe even murderous. Approximately fifty soldiers still stood, and all their eyes were now on him. They were an imposing sea of black and gold. Having already shed his armor, Orian felt even more defenseless to their stares. His sword was on the ground somewhere behind him. It didn't matter. Even if every one of them came at him now with the intent to kill, he wasn't sure he'd argue with death anyway.

"This is what happens when rookies lead veterans," Byron said loud enough for all to hear. "Men die. Women and children, too. How does that settle, boy?"

Orian retreated within himself. He had nothing.

"*HOW DOES THAT SETTLE!*"

"Enough, Byron," said Talia, feebly. "We do not point fingers after bloodshed, neither at those alive nor dead. If you felt compelled to do so anyway, you ought to be aiming all accusations toward me. The General gives orders, and I gave them, did I not?"

"I share as much of the blame." Orian had never heard Commander Cael's voice shake before. Looking around, he said, "But what reason is there for blame? Unless my eyes deceive me, we've won. Catch a glimpse o' the fallen Ardosians. Every last one of them came here with the intent to wipe out our cause, the Mercian cause, and none will return."

"Not none."

"Hmm?" Cael and Talia questioned Byron.

"A few did return, with some of our own, no less. Look at our northeastern corner. It's where most of our blood was shed, and it's where fifty or more of the Ardosian scum escaped. They took at least two Mercians with them, if not three. One was a soldier."

"How do you know this?" General Talia was utterly confused. "I never saw any Ardosians flee."

Byron motioned to the two men at his side. "When we started this way to provide backup, we came across their group. Luckily, they never saw the three of us, or we'd have been taken as well."

"I saw them, General," said someone in the back. There were a few more hums and nods of agreement.

Orian's eyes scoured the field once more despite himself. One of the few guarantees in life was death, but why was it so painful to accept? The sight fueled tremendous hatred and anger, at Vardus, at that damned island, at God. And the Ardosians had left with some of their own. Easily, without dispute, this was the worst day of his life.

Within the circle of remaining Mercians, reports were taken by General and Commander, but Orian wanted nothing to do with it. He had to get away. So he turned, marching purposefully toward the Eastern end of the field. The movement must have caught Talia's eye.

She stopped everything at once. "Private Orian!"

Head down, Orian did not slow his pace. "Yes, ma'am."

"Private, pause!"

Fighting the urge to heed her command, Orian slowed slightly but did not stop.

"Private!" she said again, forcefully. At this, Orian did stop, but he did not turn until he was commanded by Talia. "Face me."

She had emerged from the circle of men. Weariness was worn wet on her face. Orian gave no thought to how she must feel. Currently, he was far too racked with detrimental emotion to consider sympathy. He was glowering when their eyes met.

"Where are you going?" she asked the question more like a concerned friend than a General.

Byron spat, "Probably back to Ardosia, where he belongs."

Jaw clenched tight as a strung crossbow, Orian shook his head. Words were of no use anymore. It was time for action. No response was uttered. He simply left. Byron's jabs, Talia's commands, and all other jeers were drowned by the echo chamber of Orian's brain. *It is no longer enough to be away from the island. My problem was never that I was on it. It's that it exists.*

To his surprise, no one followed Orian past the field. He was given a path of solitude to his living quarters. He just hoped the shack was still standing, because he needed what was inside. The drone would prove to be useful.

On the way, Orian passed hundreds of smoldering piles of wood, places that had once been homes. Civilians cried and hugged one another beside every other pile. But Orian saw them as much as he saw the wind.

When at last he found his living quarters, Orian was reminded of his luck. Somehow, the houses to either side had gone up in flames, reduced completely to ashes, yet there alone was his shack, unharmed. Standing there, he almost wished that it had fallen, that *he* had fallen. Nothing could assuage his guilt as he remained standing, breathing, while so many others had lost that privilege.

Stiffly, Orian climbed the steps. The door opened and slammed shut as he disappeared beyond the frame.

XXXII

Wendl had never bothered to notice the way the horizon kissed the sky in the evening, how the sun seemed to dwell amongst the forest and brush the tree heads before it went to bed. He was focused, like the scope on a sniper. *Bang, bang.* He envisioned what it would be like to hold one, but alas, the guns were expunged long ago and had been replaced with crossbows like the one he held now.

The cage-like surface upon which he stood rattled with each step. It annoyed the shit out of him, but he was a patrolman, and patrolmen paced. Back and forth, back and forth. He looked over the edge, down to the calm waters of Ardosia's lake far below. Wendl wondered curiously if he might catch a glimpse of a dolphin's fin. None showed, however. If they had, it was too late. He didn't care to watch for them, anyway.

Strolling the Wall for the evening watch was such a bore. *My services could be so much better used out* there, *out past the trees, in the jungle, fighting wolves, and bears, and shit.* Sure, he may have been too plump for an adventurous lifestyle as such, but he would lose the weight if he had to. He knew he would. Some of his friends had been fortunate enough to receive promotions–many of them, actually. Wendl knew why. They were being sent on a very important mission in the jungle, but Wendl wasn't chosen by the President.

"God," he cursed to himself. "I could be in Vardus's spot, that big tall man."

Sometimes, Wendl second-guessed his life as a watchman, working for such a tyrant. If Wendl was a leader, he'd be nice to his people, especially his workers and soldiers and watchmen who watched for him. Wendl was a watchman, not yet a leader. He was familiar with the struggles. Hell, he didn't even have a friend to talk to out here. The nearest guards were on steel bridges of their own that connected the Wall to the island, and those were *so far away.* Wendl could yell to one of them, but that was against the rules. He'd tried it once. And he wasn't to call via the radio unless there was an emergency. Often, he just pretended to speak to someone over the walkie-talkie, as though he were a part of some covert operation.

Rattle, rattle, rattle went the bridge beneath his shoelace boots that fit too snugly around the ankle. Wendl wasn't sure what he was supposed to be watching for–pigeons, cranes, eagles? Those were the only creatures that could ever hope to rise past the insurmountable Wall. Even black bears and leopards, with their incredible tree-climbing skills, had no chance of scaling the greased carbon-fiber pad that composed the outer edge. Nevertheless, Wendl would have loved to see them try. At least then his shift wouldn't be so damn *boring*.

Little did the watchman know, he would soon get his wish. Not long after his internal tirade of peevish moaning, an invasive buzz rang through his ear, even more exasperating than the rattling bridge. It went on and on for what felt like forever. Wendl heard it; he just couldn't see it. The buzzing became so damn pervasive, so *annoying*, that he prayed, *Dear Lord, please make it stop, and I swear I'll never again complain about the bridge, or my life as a watchman, or my crappy genetics that made me short and somewhat pudgy. I swear it.*

The buzzing noise seemed to come from all around. Standing more defensively now, with his finger resting lightly on the trigger of his crossbow, Wendl crouched, alert. He was beginning to regret his querulous tendencies. Maybe boring wasn't so bad, after all. When things became *not* boring is when his heart began to race so violently that he thought he might collapse.

As always, Wendl feared the worst. He thought the buzzing must have been a swarm of invisible insects that were coming to bite the flesh off his face and then fly into his ears. The thought made him shake profusely. *No, that's not possible,* he reminded himself. Year after year, Ardosia released enough insecticides at the edge of the island to fend off the next plague of locusts, should God be so inclined to rehash some old memories.

Wendl cleaned out his ear, but the buzzing persisted. He'd been a moment away from calling for backup when he pointed his attention skyward … and there it was, coming toward him. His index finger twitched, firing an erratic shot through the sky, nowhere near the source of the sound. Notching another arrow, Wendl aimed high once more. Upon a closer look, however, he slumped discontentedly. *Oh, I should have known.* Lowering the crossbow, the watchman stamped his boot firmly against the bridge. It rattled beneath his anger. This happened every time a drone flew overhead. It always scared the shit out of him.

Like all drones, this one had originated near the Tower. Usually, they were sent out past the Wall, overtop the trees, and deep into the dense jungle. However, this large white drone seemed to be flying a lot higher than the others, and after drifting long in Wendl's direction, it halted directly above him. For a long while, it stayed there with the watchman gazing up toward it as though it were a UFO sending an extraction beam upon him.

Then, in an instant, the buzzing sound stopped.

Oh, shit! With barely enough time or sense to react, Wendl leapt for safety as the drone plummeted straight for him. The crash rattled the bridge more intensely than Wendl had ever heard. He knew himself to be athletic, but what he had done … to evade certain death so quickly and gracefully, Wendl sat in awe of himself. Planking on his elbows for a few seconds, the watchman did a little shimmy before he climbed to his feet. Then he went to inspect the drone.

Lying in a crumpled mess of worn and scratched metal, the drone laid sideways with one propeller missing and another hanging by a wire. Wendl chuckled when he saw the beaten machine. It looked like a rock, one that had been slung directly at him. With a wry smile he regarded the darkening sky. *Not this time David. You'll only ever defeat one Goliath.*

On the drone, there was a small screen. Flashing red were the words: LOW BATTERY. It made Wendl's brow furrow. How could a drone have low battery if it was just leaving the Tower? Giving it some thought, Wendl's eyebrows rose. What if it hadn't left the Tower at all? What if it was a spy drone?

Wendl's head shot in all directions. The watchmen to his left and right were oscillating specks on their respective bridges, and more importantly, they were oblivious. Somehow, they hadn't heard the drone fall, or they didn't bother to examine the situation. For once, Wendl was grateful they were so far away.

Repeatedly questioning himself as to how he should properly handle the situation, Wendl ran through several scenarios. *I should pick this up and take it straight to Vardus. Then I might get that promotion!* But no ... Wendl had heard one too many fluttering rumors of Vardus's unbridled rage as of late. The watchman had no inkling of desire to end up on the wrong side of the President. After pondering his radio for a moment, Wendl wondered if his manager could aptly resolve the situation. *But that shit requires paperwork. Ugh, I* hate *paperwork.* Finally, Wendl settled on hoisting the fat chunk of metal over the railing so that he could watch it–and all his problems–disappear into Ardosia's lake far below.

It fell and fell forever. Bent over the railing, Wendl simply hoped and prayed that the watchmen to either side wouldn't hear or see the splash. Even if they did, Wendl reasoned they would never accurately estimate what had caused the sudden explosion at the lake's surface. Likely, they'd misattribute it to a dolphin surfacing.

When at last the drone vanished in a swirling watery tornado, Wendl projected a massive sigh of relief. He picked up his crossbow, shook the stress from his body, and returned contentedly to his boring shift as a watchman. Laying the crossbow cooly against his shoulder, Wendl grinned. He'd never been so happy to hear the bridge *rattle, rattle, rattle.*

XXXIII

Weeping shadows swayed remotely upon their faces. The central fire flicked sideways, daring to escape. Meanwhile, Talia's men hummed their tune.

Triumph down in falling plains
Calls for horns and merry things
'Til one should pass beyond the gate
That bars a good man's diamond rings

Ooooo
Mmmm
Dooooooomm

There were more verses. Talia's ears simply blocked them out. So did her mind. In one trembling hand, she unscrewed the top of the jar. There was a fine powder kept inside.

"To Sunnie." She poured out the ashes, directly over the outdoor furnace. Graciously the flames accepted their tribute, and the one after that, and the one after that.

By the time that Talia made it through to the last of the jars, it had to have been well past midnight. The parting ceremony had begun at sunset. She told her men that they were free to leave whenever, but their responses were the same.

"We won't get any sleep tonight. We may as well stay."

She knew she'd chosen honorable men to serve in her ranks, but their persistence brought a tear to her eye.

Small wooden logs served as their seats, arranged delicately around the fire. Talia ran a finger in a thin line over the bark. *So dry.* It felt as though with one stray ember, her seat would erupt in flames.

It was long ago when the logs had been placed here, not far from the center field, oddly enough. She remembered asking General Andrew about his choices of oak and birch–both types of wood that catch fire easily–before he threw in the first soldier's ashes. Sitting beside her, he replied, "We're all to be consumed by fire eventually. It's best we don't forget it." She remembered being frightened by that, but she had yet to see someone's seat go up in flames. Still, that didn't mean it was impossible.

Now Neal was sitting idly at her side, just as she had been at Andrew's. She could sense his fear of the flames and the endless list of risks his beautiful mind could never ignore. But he was silent as the moon, as his eyes bouncing from the fire to the dirt by his feet.

At long last, General Talia poured the last bit of ashes into the fire, where a pile of them had nearly put it out. She stood tall, saluting. "May God look upon your service to Merciadel as a service to humanity, worthy of reward in Heaven."

When she sat, the parting ceremony officially concluded. Solemnly, her eyes drank in the fire that was so dense and heavy. Talia didn't move. Neither did anyone else. Together, she and her men sat in silence.

The battle. It had come out of nowhere. Sure, Talia had preached that she and her men should always be at the ready, to be prepared for tomorrow's war, as each day presented its own obstacles. But she never believed that Vardus would be so rash as to attack so quickly.

Standing atop a building at the grass field's perimeter, she launched arrows into the hearts of Ardosians, alongside many of her men. Although they had succeeded, the perils of that battle were great. It had been the largest, most fatal war she'd witnessed, and it all happened so fast. Talia felt as though she had no more than blinked, and half of Merciadel's population vanished in that instant. Right now, she wanted them back. She mourned their loss.

It wasn't until the fire was almost out that anyone dared to speak. To Talia's surprise, it wasn't Orian, though her eyes went to him as Private Kaija wondered, "What now?"

Talia kept her gaze on Orian, whose staring, intense eyes reflected the fire. Elbows on his knees, he did not waver. She'd never seen his face so dark.

Finally, she thought it best to respond to Kaija, but Talia had no clue what to say. *What now?* Somehow, she hadn't put any thought to it. *A good leader is always to be prepared,* she could hear General Andrew's reproach in her mind. Gently, she pondered if it was okay to mourn.

Andrew would have scolded her for that, too. *The time for mourning ends the moment our last jar of ashes empties.*

"We wait," she said after a pause. "We rebuild."

"Yes, Gener–" Private Kaija's soft tone was interrupted.

"Great plan." The remark was riddled with sarcasm.

Without the energy for a scowl of contempt, Talia simply faced Byron. He was in the second row, leaning at the edge of his log.

"What do you suggest, Byron? That we attack? That we abandon Merciadel and its people for revenge? Enlighten me, as you so often do."

He stomped his foot in the sandy clay, springing up dust. "I'm tired of waiting. I'm God damn tired of rebuilding. How many times do we have to watch them burn our home to the ground, just to set the stack of teetering blocks upon one another and wait for them to knock 'em all over again?"

"You're right," said Talia tacitly. Her response hushed them all, even Byron. "In one day, the strength of our nation has gone from a strong, burning fire to a quivering candle flame that Vardus may well blow out soon. I'd imagine he'll be sending a tactical unit to take care of the rest of us within the coming days." She looked them all in the eye when she said this, but discouragement was not what they needed now. "Maybe he will, maybe he won't. It depends on his numbers, of which I know we've made a great reduction."

The night was still. Even the crickets hadn't bothered to sing their songs because they didn't know the lamenting kind. Talia felt as though she hardly had to raise her voice to be heard. Maybe it was because her army had been cut in half, twice over.

Again, she looked to Orian in the third and final row. He was seated just as he was before, and his eyes had grown even more ominous, burning with fires of their own. The way he kept his stare on the flames told her that he was both lost and determined, like his mind had stolen him from the presence of his comrades, both fallen and not.

"I know right now it's easy to point fingers and to blame. I'll remind you of two things: you're all free men, always. Although you've pledged your service to Merciadel, the verbal contract is not binding. You won't be pursued or murdered, should you choose to abandon your role in my army so that you might follow your own intuition. Secondly, the only person here worthy of blame is myself. Point fingers at me and no one else, if you must."

Good and bad leaders alike are always culpable. Talia's statement had reflected that belief, but she struggled not to fall into the trap of uncertainty. Once more, she stole a glance at the dark young man in the back row, wondering why she had changed course. Talia wasn't swayed by anyone, but since the day Orian showed up at Merciadel, it felt as though she had endured nothing but constant change.

Talia flinched suddenly at an intrusive memory. She'd been fighting amongst her soldiers in the field, watching Mercian and Ardosian fall one-by-one. No matter how familiar she made herself with war, its sting would never attenuate. While she watched her men die, she remembered thinking, *The old ways would have worked. They would have saved us, right?* But even though large numbers had been decimated on that tragic day, Talia could not ignore the unbelievable feat that she and her nation had accomplished. She knew that had it not been for Orian's intervention, not only would more men have perished, but surely their entire estate would have fallen along with them. The damages were tragic, but Orian's plan had worked flawlessly, and it had been executed even better.

Despite such success and a so-called "victory", Talia could hardly stomach the losses. So many men and women gone. Merciadel was now but a wounded buck, waiting for mercy in the form of one final cut to its throat. She wasn't sure what she could do to save her nation, to rebuild her people. But she would find a way.

Other than Byron, there were no bitter suggestions sent forth. It appeared that no one had the courage nor pride to say any more. Eventually, giving into exhaustion was all that was left to do.

Collectively, the Mercians who'd outlived their partners stood. They saluted the fire, many with tears still streaming. Talia would not remind them that there was no more time to mourn. She hadn't finished yet herself.

First among them to leave was Orian, and he stormed off in the direction of his quarters, opposite the soldier cabins. Talia peered above and beyond her shuffling ranks, who were offering one another comforting embraces. She found his silhouette melding with the night. It wasn't like the young man to simply disappear.

Standing beside her was Neal, who offered a gentle, trembling hand that he placed on her shoulder. It was oddly comforting, but her mind was elsewhere. So were her eyes.

"It's funny," Neal said once they were close by the smoldering pile of brothers gone.

"What?"

"How m-much he reminds me of y-y-you. Sometimes, that is. But I-I'd never tell you to run with s-s-scissors, like I would him."

If Orian was the young man she knew him to be, and if he truly was so similar in spirit to herself, he'd already traveled through the long and bitter land of self-accosting and internal berating. Something *had* been brewing beneath his charcoal skin. Burning, burning, burning. As her men departed from the ceremony, Talia was left to wonder only at how large the flames of Orian's impending fire might be.

She narrowed her eyes. Merciadel's General had spent enough time around impulsive mavericks like him. It didn't take a psychic's intuition to estimate the depths of his vindication.

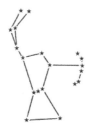

XXXIV

Waiting was unbearable. It was a waste of time, and there was already little enough of that left. Orian had no choice in the matter. He had to be sure everyone was asleep before he left Camp Merciadel.

Before he could even contemplate parting with his new home, Orian had laid in stillness within the confines of his living quarters, reviewing the risks. *I'll be outnumbered a thousand to one. The odds are unfathomable.* But since when had that ever stopped him?

During his wait, Orian laced a tight leather vest over his shoulders, black as night. His cargo pants were just as dark, and they had many pockets. Once he gathered what he needed, they would be full.

He had the tablet in hand, ready to go. There was a slot in his vest where the tablet could be stowed away when he didn't need it. That way, his hands could be occupied by a more lethal weapon. Orian wasn't sure what kind he'd fashion, but he would have an abundance of options.

Restless, Orian paced in his tiny shack. It had been so hospitable to him over the past weeks. The space had truly felt like his own. Now it was dark, and his boots echoed off the thin walls as he *thump, thump, thump*'ed from side to side. At least his only goodbye would be offered to this little building. Nobody would have the chance to see him off.

At last, when the time was right, Orian paused, taking a deep breath. Dangling from one belt loop were five golden chains. Even in absolute stillness, they found a way to ring. His eyes shut. Through the darkness beyond them, he saw a man with shaggy auburn hair and a scraggly beard, hiding a pale, spotted face. *I'll make things right, Guerdo,* Orian promised as he held the cold chains in his hand.

Watching Guerdo's ashes spill into the draught of fire, Orian had burned so deeply, so uncontrollably. *Learn to control your anger,* Guerdo used to instruct him. How could he do that now? The closest friend Orian had acquired within Merciadel was gone. So many others had been killed.

His eyes opened rapidly. Determination filled him, piling onto a plethora of residual rage. Orian needed no more reason to begin his journey.

With a hint of sadness in his eyes, Orian nodded his farewells to the shack. Then, tablet in hand, pack over his shoulders, Orian delved into the night like an angel of dark vengeance.

While returning to the island instilled mountains of hot dread in him, Orian couldn't wait to sneak past Ardosia's Wall like a virus, invisible yet deadly. He was going to hit Vardus where it hurt. The awful excuse for a President horded power like a fat man did Twinkies. Ultimately, people were his power, and Orian couldn't wait to steal it away. General Talia had said it herself. They were done with extraction missions. Orian would have to do it on his own. *Ladis, I'm coming for you.*

Even though he was certain that every Mercian would be fast asleep by now, Orian crept between buildings furtively, crouched and low. A crescent moon shone timidly in the sky. Its brightness would not reach the ground tonight, making Orian nothing more than a shadow.

He'd gotten no rest since the parting ceremony by the fire, but he was not tired. The adrenaline wouldn't wear off until his mission was complete, that much he knew. Hell, it hadn't left him since that bloody battle at the field. Orian had never witnessed anything so tragic. The enormity of the day haunted him unyieldingly, which was why he had to move. It was unlike him to stand idly by and do nothing … so he wouldn't.

His first stop of the night was a building known as the ATE (Advanced Technical Equipment) storage facility. Attached to the IT building, whose bright reflective panels shone with a million sparkling eyes, was a much smaller, much less flattering square, packed with hundreds of various gadgets. Orian had learned about it when visiting Trixie one day after training.

"Check this out." The effervescent woman had led him through a locked door, accessible only by key. " *Voila.*"

Inside, there were shelves and drawers filled with trinkets and gadgets that IT designers had perfected. Each of the shelves was organized to stringent specification, in alphabetical order. "Wow," was all he'd said to Trixie.

"Damn right, it's a wow. Here, come look at this one. Made it myself." She picked up a circular object with four straps attached to it in an "X" pattern. "Sonar camouflage. Sends reverse signals that make you invisible. Does some other stuff too."

"Incredible."

Now, after hacking into IT, Orian had found himself stranded in darkness beside the very door that would grant him access to all those useful tools. If only he could remember which drawer had contained the set of keys …

Orian searched and searched, fruitlessly. He was beginning to waste too much time. While shuffling madly through a random drawer amidst the darkness, Orian's eyes bounced back to the ATE door. *What if it's already unlocked?*

His hand found the cool knob, and he twisted. The sigh that left him was one of relief and exasperation. Smooth as a violin, the door squeaked opened, and Orian found himself inside.

He'd planned meticulously. Orian knew what he needed. First, he went for the "Sonar Camo" device that Trixie had created herself. Then he stole a few small but heavy metal circles, carefully stowing them in his pack. Spending no more than a couple of minutes filling his pack with more gadgets, he receded from the ATE and left IT without a trace.

Orian's first half of the escape complete, his hand itched for something with a steel tip. The armory was next.

Back out into the night he went, aiming for the arched tent that contained spears, bows, knives, and all. Orian had no more nerves to feel. Butterflies had been expelled long ago, and as a newly-trained warrior, Orian found himself to be an instrument of both peace and demolition.

Several torches guided him on either side of a stone path, their flames erupting with feeble strength. It was as if even the fires knew what had taken place beyond this gravelly earthen floor. They demanded reprisal from Orian. He was eagerly willing to issue it.

Creeping low to the ground, Orian came upon a high-arched tent adjacent to the soldiers' cabins. Not even the slightest hint of noise escaped the log-built structures nearby. Each of the inhabited cabins held a burning torch beyond their steps, while the previously occupied units shone no light. Orian could hardly stand the sight of so many lightless candles.

He whipped the tablet out purposefully. It took him ample time to hack past the multi-layered security codes entrenched in Merciadel's system. Orian was impressed, but he was not bested.

There was a deep click, followed by another, and Orian swung the vault door open and crept forward. As he latched the heavy steel door shut, he was encamped in blackness, the only illumination to be found was on his tablet screen.

He scrolled furiously beyond the archival codes and found nothing about lights. Orian had been in here before, several times, but he had never bothered to look too closely at the LED's that would shine above. He couldn't figure out how to turn them on. Without light, he'd struggle to find the right weapon to wield.

Orian scrolled and scrolled and typed, until ...

The blinding blue-white lights flooded the armory, catching Orian off guard. He shielded his eyes, utterly confused. There had been nothing in the code to alert him to a successful hack. Orian jumped when he heard another voice.

"Light switch." A powerful and commanding tone echoed about the arched walls. "Building's so old, the lights are still controlled by a switch, Orian."

It took him several moments to blink the brightness away. Orian struggled to focus, but he didn't have to. He knew General Talia's voice well.

He addressed her simply, as though he had nothing to hide. "General."

Finally she came into view, donning the pitch-black armor corset that made even her olive skin look pale. A golden scarf wrapped firmly around her neck, her night-brown hair tied back. The crossbow in her hand was pointed casually at Orian. "I knew you'd be here."

Somehow, he did not fear her threatening manner, or death for that matter, and his expressionless face indicated as much. "Oh, yeah? How's that?"

"I saw you tonight. Many times, actually. Each time I saw your face, it grew darker and darker. I've seen that look before, but only in the mirror. Too much hate not to be spurred into action."

"Ah." There was a flicker in one of the LED's above. It prompted Orian to scour the room with his eyes. It was just he and Talia alone. He wondered what she would have of him. "So you know why I'm here, then."

"For the same reason that anyone has ever walked beyond that door: they've got someone that they think needs dead or saving." An arrow tip glimmered in the light as Talia moved forward, her weapon aimed straight at his chest. "I'd be interested to hear your plea, Orian. I could arrest you now for treason ... or I could handle this myself."

"You could." Orian's eyes fluttered innocuously about the room. There were bows hanging from one wall, swords mounted on the other, and spears suspended from the ceiling. On the long, tarp-covered island in the center, there were crossbows. Orian could make a sudden movement for any of them, but there was no need. Besides, he didn't underestimate the General's ability one bit. She'd have him skewered like a cabob if he were to try anything rash. "But I don't think you will."

"Mmm, why's that?"

"You understand who I am, what I am. We're cut from a similar cloth. You can tell a rodent not to burrow, the wind not to bluster, or people not to war with each other, but some things are incorrigible. It isn't simply my choice to return to that island. I have to."

"And you think I would do the same?"

"You have, on several occasions. If not for your fear of bloodshed, though a healthy fear, you'd go back again, wouldn't you? It's always been your mission to save innocent people from being turned into mindless, numb corpses."

She appeared to contemplate him. "Got a plan?"

"Of course I have a plan. You taught me never to approach anything or anyone without one."

"You saw what they did to us ... on *our* home soil. We led them to an ambush, and yet we perished. If Ardosia or anyone else were to mount an attack on us right now, they'd wipe the rest of us out like we were nothing more than ants."

Orian had reminded himself of just that hundreds, if not thousands of times in the past two days. At the moment, they were sitting ducks, and he wasn't going to watch any more men die. He knew what he had planned could work. It *would* work.

"How do you think you can overcome them by yourself?"

"What we're doing now is exactly what Vardus expects of us. We may have damaged his fleet extensively, but his numbers will return. Ours won't, unless we do something about it."

"Well spoken," Talia smirked. "But that doesn't explain why you were prepared to leave on your own."

Loping around the center island, Orian rubbed a hand over a crossbow stock, prompting Talia to adjust her grip. He backed away. "I could never ask someone to follow me into this battle. The Wall, the carnivorous animals at guard, the Ardosians at watch … there are too many variables to surpass noisily. As it has always been for me, I'll be more equipped to succeed alone."

The General lowered her bow, as if to say, *That much we can agree upon.* "Sometimes it's nice to have someone watching your back."

Orian snorted. "You think anyone here would have my back? Sure, some would gladly watch it … just so they could wait for the right time to stab. Your men believe me to blame for all of this, and who am I to say they're wrong?"

Hundreds dead, unrecoverable. No amount of action could redress the issue, but Orian had never been one to accept defeat.

"They hold me equally as liable, if not more so, so don't be too conceited to believe that this issue pertains only to you, Orian." At last the crossbow was lowered. "And for the record, I'd have your back."

Narrow eyes studied the General. Straight as the Tower she stood, always. For a moment, Orian wondered what it would be like to have the best warrior alive at his side. He favored the thought of solidarity. *But it couldn't hurt to have her help.*

"Tell me about your plan, Orian. I'm curious."

So he did, from start to finish. It was well thought-out, as Orian had known it would need to be. And after speaking it aloud, he felt even surer. "Vardus believes he has struck his final blow in the battle against counterinsurgency. I'll be sure he has."

"How long have you planned this?" She frowned, stepping closer to the island to set the bow down, but she did not take her hand off.

He tried to recall, but even he wasn't positive. Shrugging, Orian placed his hands flat on the island. "I began preparing it after what happened at the field. Otherwise, I guess it's been brewing in the subconscious for a while." Her shadowy eyes met his, and Orian could sense something in them, opportunity knocking. "Come with me," he said.

After a long, considerable pause, Talia responded simply. "Alright."

Orian's face might as well have been smacked by the backside of a spade for how flat it went with shock. "Huh?"

"I'm going with you," she said sternly. "What? Was it an impulsive question you asked? Did you not mean for my help? I know there's a shortage of readily-available meals in the jungle, but the eye candy I provide won't be anything to feast on."

Having never before struggled for words so pathetically, Orian stammered. "Uh …" He had no idea where that last part had come from.

"Relax, Orian. I'm messing."

About coming with me or the eye candy part? He hoped it was the latter. Not to say that Talia wasn't visually appealing; she was. But intimacy was a realm which Orian had not yet dared to travel. Her jest had been uncharacteristic, eliciting much discomfort. "Oh, so …"

Hoisting her crossbow off the wooden island, she held it firmly in her hands once again. "You're wasting time. We should go now. Plus, I'll have to make a pit stop at IT, it sounds like." She began walking.

"Wait, wait." Talia paused at Orian's order. "You're joking, right? This is some kind of catch. Byron is waiting for me just outside, isn't he?"

"Do I look like I'm joking?"

After consideration, Orian determined that she was keen to join him on his trek back to the island of Ardosia. Still, he hadn't expected her aid. "Won't you tell someone? It'd be discouraging betrayal at least if you were to leave without notice."

The General went to the vault door, rolling her eyes. "Already got it covered. Tonight after the ceremony, I promoted Commander Cael to General in my absence. Neal was there to hear it as well."

It took him a moment to understand her meaning, but when he did, Orian marveled at the woman before him. "So … you were already going to leave for Ardosia? And you knew I would, too? You placed a hefty bet on me, General."

"I place no bets," she said firmly, a grin tempting to crack. "Gambling is for men." Swiftly, she opened the vault door, leaving Orian scrambling behind her.

"Hold up, I–" but she'd already fled into the night. *Shit.* Frantically, Orian considered the bows. *I'm an awful shot, longbow or cross.* That eliminated those, proposing either a sword or spear. All his time in training had been spent with swords, so it only made sense to stick to his strengths.

Orain darted out the door a second later with a sword in hand, not forgetting to flip the light switch on his way out.

He'd expected to be leagues behind Talia already, as she'd gotten a head start on him, but when he left the armory, she was just outside. Orian's brow furrowed when he saw her next to Neal.

"It's too *damn* r-r-risky."

"Neal," she placed a comforting hand on his shoulder. "We'll be alright."

Typically, Orian would have foreseen pajama pants with stripes on Talia's assistant, or something that would fit him more comfortably in the dead of night. But Neal was cloaked in Merciadel's malleable black armor instead. It suited him as well as menacing reptilian scales would suit a kitten. The sight was intriguing.

"You remember what I told you?"

"If you're n-not back in f-f-fourteen days ..." Neal couldn't manage the words. Orian suspected it had nothing to do with his speech impediment.

"Gather and pray," Talia finished for him, which Orian took as code for: *The battle, along with everything and everyone we know, has been lost.*

Orian knew that he and Talia were likely freedom's last hope for Merciadel. The weight should have been too much to shoulder. Not for Orian. He embraced life's toughest challenges. This would be the toughest of them all, he knew, but it did not scare him.

"But that's n-n-not why I'm here."

"What is it then, Neal?" she asked, but then she hugged him. "I'll miss you, too."

"N-n-no!" he shoved her back. "L-listen to me." His aggression caught everyone off guard, particularly himself. "Sorry," he said before making his plea. "I'm coming w-with you."

"Neal ..." Talia was touched.

She spent the next five minutes coaxing him to alter his train of thought. She needed him here, at Merciadel. Talia told him over and over, but he wouldn't have it.

Both the moon and downright stubbornness were reflected in his glasses. The torches flickered then. "You're not l-listening!" He shifted subtly. "I heard your p-plan. You need someone else who can h-h-hack. That's me."

Orian thought back to the first day he'd ever met Neal. He was in the waiting room adjacent to Talia's office, tight and compact. The assistant had been squished into a small corner space, rapping at a keyboard like a maniac. It made sense to him then that Neal must have been a technological whiz.

"No, Neal. For the last time, I need you here. That's an order."

"Tal." Neal was insistent. "R-r-remember? Strength in n-numbers."

Pensive, Orian stepped forward. "He's right, General." There were several steps in his plan that he hadn't overlooked entirely, but they would certainly have better odds of success with a second hacker in the fleet. Preferring solo missions, Orian could hardly believe what he was about to say. He looked the skinny man in the eye. "Neal, we'll take you."

There was more than apprehension in the General's demeanor. It was clear by the fear in her eyes that she dreaded the thought of losing anyone else. Flickering torchlight cast shadows over her face that was replete with reluctance. The General shook her head, "I ... I just don't know."

Taking Talia's hand gently, Neal said, "I s-swore an oath to protect Merciadel, same as you." He turned to expose the pack on his shoulder. "Y-you wouldn't make me unload after I packed all this, w-would you?"

There had been more compelling arguments made in history, Orian was aware, but he saw Neal's resolve and needed no more convincing. In spite of the obvious persistent fear that laid beneath his skin, Neal was committed to his word. There was something to be said for his courage.

Looking between the two men, Talia eventually conceded. "Fine."

Orian's eyes swept over the shadowy structures of Merciadel. He'd come to love this place, and after two cycles of the moon spent here, Orian considered it more of a home than the Tower had ever been to him. He reasoned with his emotions here, particularly the ones that begged him to stay. Thus far, Orian's life had been a journey. Though most of it had been spent in practical solitary confinement in a skyscraper on an island, he'd always felt as though he was working toward something. The day Orian arrived at Merciadel, his journey was finally over. He'd at last found his resting place.

Yet now, as he, Neal, and Talia gathered in preparation for yet another, more dangerous journey than they'd ever encountered, Orian realized that life itself was one long path, filled with chapters that amalgamated to form one, solid journey. Trials ended only after a final breath. So Orian's journey would continue, as he unveiled a new chapter along the way.

Jubilation was undeniable in Orian's chest. Another adventure, another chance to encounter the same emotions he always had in the face of adversity, and this time he'd have a squad with which to experience it all. Perhaps challenges were Orian's love. By Pake's order, he would pursue that love relentlessly.

It was near impossible to shed his smile. "Wonderful." He shook Neal's hand, which felt as firm as a tissue, but Orian could see by the redness of his face that he was gripping hard as he could. Orian looked to him and General Talia, determined. The three of them together hung closely in the torchlight, dark figures of justice. "If anyone can do this, it's us. I wanted to go alone ... but we'll be stronger with three."

The General laid her crossbow casually against her shoulder, the arrow pointed high at the bright star in the North. "Four," she corrected. At Neal and Orian's critical faces, she explained, "Someone owes me a favor, and I've got a feeling this is the type of mission he's been dying to go on."

Made in the USA
Monee, IL
15 January 2024

50740281R00243